THE DIVERGENT FATES ANTHOLOGY

MATTHEW S. COX   ROBERT J DEFENDI   J S HUGHES

MARK W. WOODRING   J. P. SLOAN   JAMES WYMORE

WILBERT STANTON   PATRICK BURDINE

BENJAMIN SPERDUTO

DIVISION ZERO PRESS

Editor's Note: Some stories make use of communication via implanted cybernetics. These conversations are not audible to the outside world and occur only within the head of the character. Conversation using these implants is denoted by Asian bracket quotes: ⌈This is an example of communication via an implanted device.⌋

Ebook ISBN: 978-1-949174-02-1

Paperback ISBN: 978-1-949174-03-8

Edited by Matthew S. Cox and Mark W. Woodring

CONTENTS

FOREWORD

Around 1995, I started on the groundwork for a science-fiction RPG setting. I remember going through a handful of names for this project, but ultimately, Divergent Fates is the one that stuck. The name originated from the story arc of Mars' citizens seeking independence from control by Earth government, and also the conflict between the United Coalition Front (a stratocracy consisting of the remainder of the US and Canada having merged after the Corporate War) and the Allied Corporate Council (Most of Europe as well as Mexico, a satirical corpocracy.)

This setting (and the resulting RPG ruleset) grew and evolved over the next twenty years or so. Eventually, around 2012 when I finally got it in my head to "get serious" about the whole writing thing, I spent quite some time debating between science fiction or fantasy. I wound up going Sci Fi (at least at first), and choosing to write in the DF (Divergent Fates) setting since I already had tons of groundwork laid and background material ready to go. The first manuscript I finished was Virtual Immortality, but due to its length, I wrote Division Zero #1 as a smaller, less intricate story that would be easier to shop around to agents/publishers.

Fast forward a couple years and thirty something novels later (no, they're not *all* set in the Divergent Fates universe). I had a couple novels out via Curiosity Quills, and another author who publishes with them contacted me (Jason King). He asked if I had any interest in writing a short story set in his Valcoria world. I accepted, and wrote *A Dream of*

Clouds for that anthology. That, of course, got me wondering about a similar project.

To that end, I contacted a number of authors I'd met along my writing journey who I knew wrote in cyberpunk-esque settings and pitched the idea of an anthology of stories set in the DF universe. What you are about to read is the result.

Each of these authors adds their own unique flavor to the DF world, and I hope that you enjoy their stories as much as I did.

Happy reading!

-Matt

LOOSE ENDS

MATTHEW S. COX

Haunted by a repeating nightmare, Kirsten watched helpless as Marisa screamed, sliding down the angled roof of the Intera tower. Kirsten shot upright as the little girl vanished over the edge to a hundred-story fall. The child's scream echoed in her mind, invading her darkened bedroom.

Sweat trails raced each other in a trickle down her back. She shuddered, trying to get the image of the girl's desperate eyes out of her mind. A moment later, she remembered to breathe. Her thrashing had pulled the sheets from the Comforgel pad, exposing her sweaty skin to the dense plastic. The dull, orange glow from the viscous slab made the heat seem even worse. She cringed from the sensation of her skin peeling away from the gel-filled mattress as she sat up and swung her legs over the side.

Cool air washed over her. She slouched forward, elbows on her knees, head down. Even in her underwear, the malfunctioning unit threw off too much warmth for sleep. Kirsten pulled open the nightstand and frowned at the bottle of SynVod inside. *Couple swigs and I can pass out.* She pushed herself to her feet and paced around the bedroom, waving a hand at her face to cool off. It didn't take long for her underwear to become clammy and damp. The idea of flinging her top and panties off formed and died within two seconds. Comfort took a back seat to embarrassment—a ghost could walk in at any time. She plucked at her tank top, cringing at the sopping-wet fabric.

The damn bed is too hot. Sleeping naked wouldn't help. Her cheeks warmed with blush. *Never mind the chance of Theodore catching me.*

She grumbled at the silver bar atop the nightstand. It sensed her eyes pointed at it and displayed the time: 3:27 a.m. *What is wrong with me? I just got rid of one nightmare and now I have another.* "Argh! It's not fair." *That's not even what happened. Marisa didn't fall.*

With a sigh, Kirsten trudged to the bathroom. "Ugh. Why is my brain doing this to me?"

A few minutes later, bladder empty, she returned to the nightstand, grabbed the bottle, and took three healthy gulps. Cheap, synthetic alcohol flowed like lava down her throat; the fumes scorched her nostrils like a fire-breathing dragon. Eyes watering, she gasped for air and gagged. She screwed the top back on, coughed twice more, and put the booze back in the nightstand. *Damn that's nasty. Not like I get this crap for the taste.* She faced the kitchenette and fell backwards into the hot, squishy pad with a slap like dropping a steak on a marble counter top.

Come on. Kick in. She stared at the pattern of dots on the drop ceiling overhead. *Three sips won't ruin me in the morning. Just enough to take the edge off.* Her mind leapt to the image of the bottle that had always been in Mother's hand. Kirsten rolled on her side and curled up with fear in her eyes, not of her mother, but of what she might become. She swallowed the bile creeping into the back of her throat and closed her eyes as the first wave of lightheadedness came on, making gravity swirl.

Beep beep beep beep.

Kirsten moaned. One instant, she gazed over the soft orange light below her at a dark, grey wall at 3:34 in the morning. The next thing she knew, the clock read 6:30 a.m. The pulsing alarm smashed into her brain. By 6:37, the cruel, monotonous tone became more intolerable than the concept of moving. She tried to swallow, but her throat felt as if packed with cotton.

"Mnnn... At least the headache took the day off." She slid off the bed to the floor, sitting with her legs apart and hands on the carpet between her thighs until the world stopped spinning. Eventually, she pushed herself upright and trudged to the alarm clock, placed with strategic intent twenty feet from the bed, and clawed her fingers at the air over the clock.

Blessed silence.

She slipped out of her still-damp underwear on the way to the bathroom and apologized to the white box as she stuck the sweaty things in the top hatch. The machine thrummed to life, leaking the scent of lavender as it cleaned them. Soon, they'd be wrapped them in plastic and added to the top of the stack inside. After a brief cycle in the autoshower, she took a fresh set from the bottom of the same device and tore open the thin plastic wrapper. By 6:52, she clipped her metallic silver uniform belt in place and shot a forlorn look at her fridge.

I'll eat at my desk.

"Lock," said Kirsten on the way out of her apartment.

The door chirped after it closed. She took the elevator to the ground floor, waved at a pair of elderly spirits holding hands in the lobby, and headed for the main entrance. Inspiration flooded her mind as her hand hit the push-bar on the exit. She spun on her heel and marched past the empty reception desk to a silver door much newer than the way out to the street. As expected, it didn't open for her as she walked up. *Cheap bastard puts a manual door on the building but has a normal one for himself.*

Kirsten pushed the button above the access panel. After a minute of silence, she hit it again.

"What?" The voice of the building manager creaked like an old floorboard.

"Sorry to wake you up Kyle, but I need to talk to you about some repairs in my apartment."

His groan sounded through the door as well as from the speaker. "Who and what?"

She shook a fist at the wall. "Kirsten Wren, nineteenth floor, apartment twelve. The Comforgel pad's thermal regulator is stuck on 'small dying star.'"

"You're already on the list." He yawned. "Parts take a while ya know. Try sleeping naked."

"I've been on 'the list' for six months. I'd like it fixed by the end of the week."

He mumbled something incoherent, already sounding close to asleep.

Kirsten growled. She held up the armored guard on her left forearm. "Override."

The police code caused the door to chime and slide open. She jogged down three steps into a pale blue corridor reeking of sweat socks and bleach. Mops, buckets, tools, and spare parts for various appliances and furniture stacked up against both walls. Fifteen meters in, the door to Kyle's apartment stood opposite the access to the building's storage room. A little farther beyond that, a red door led to the emergency stairwell. She doubted the 'do not open – alarm will sound' sign, its threat likely as empty as Kyle's promise to fix things.

Kirsten barged into the super's apartment, halting with her hands on her hips two steps past the door. Kyle lay sprawled on a queen sized Comforgel slab—his glowing faint violet—in a pair of tight, white briefs. A twig-thin woman with a fuchsia bob and matching panties had wrapped herself around his left arm. Kirsten raised an eyebrow at the cluster of Flowerbasket inhalers on the pillow behind him.

She swatted at the panel to turn on the room lights. "Kyle."

He moaned, moving only his right arm, which he draped over his eyes. "How'd you get in here? Go away, kid. Trespassing's illegal."

"Technically, so is Flowerbasket." Kirsten folded her arms. "Six months, Kyle. I want my damn bed fixed."

"Dammit, kid—" Kyle sat up and froze with his mouth open, staring at her clingy, black uniform, silver belt, and the conspicuous E-90 laser pistol on her hip.

Kirsten flashed a saccharin smile. "Little less cute than a Hello Kitty tee shirt, right? Yes, the uniform is quite real."

"Y-you're a cop?" He blinked.

At the word cop, his 'girlfriend' leapt from the bed in a flailing mass of bony limbs, and ran into the closed bathroom door—knocking herself senseless. She fell to a heap, still and silent.

"If I run her ID, I'm going to find at least an eighteen year old, right?" Kirsten took a step closer.

"Shit. Uhh. Yeah." Kyle shifted to sit cross-legged and rubbed his face. "She's like thirty. I don't go for the young ones, or I'd have hit on you."

Kirsten glared. "I am not a kid. I'm twenty-two."

He blinked. "Horseshit. I pegged you for some fourteen-year-old runaway."

"A runaway who can pay for an apartment?" Heat flooded her cheeks.

He opened his mouth to say something, but changed his mind. "Uhh, yeah. About that bed. Fine... fine... I'll look at it today. Probably a blown voltage regulator or temp sensor."

Her anger faded some. She kept a glower on him as she walked over to the unconscious woman, squatted, and patted her on the cheek until she stirred. "You okay?"

The woman stared with unfocused eyes at her for a few seconds. Once they both aimed in the same direction, the color drained from her cheeks. "Y-yeah. I didn't do anything."

"What are you running for then?" Kirsten offered her a hand.

"Umm, wasn't awake. Bad dream." She grabbed a shirt from the floor and covered her breasts, cowering from Kirsten.

"If someone associated with the police did something to you, I'd like to know about it." Kirsten's anger with Kyle evaporated.

"No." The woman stood long enough to sit on the side of the bed. Kyle put an arm around her. "Couple years ago, I was with this guy... he got shot by cops. His brains hit me in the face."

Kirsten cringed. "Sorry."

The woman shrugged. "It's okay. The bastard deserved it. Prolly woulda been my ass dead if the police didn't find me."

"Sorry." Kirsten gave her the contact info for victim services. "If you need someone to talk to... Dr. Loring's great." She headed for the door, but paused. "Sorry for letting myself in, but six months?"

"Yeah, yeah." Kyle scratched at his head fast enough to frizz his hair, and got up. "I'll go do it now." He squinted at her. "If you're a cop, why are you living *here?*"

Kirsten held her hands out in a weak shrug. "I was young, didn't really understand money. Wanted out of the dorms as fast as possible and this was the cheapest place I could find on short notice." *Now I know why.*

Kyle chuckled.

THE INCOMPLETE REPORT POPPED UP IN HER FACE AS SOON AS KIRSTEN'S terminal powered up. She scowled at the nagging machine. Another panel with a message from Captain Eze scrolled open, asking her if she planned on sending in the reports regarding the Intera Tower incident any time soon. She set the clear plastic carton with her jalapeño omelet sandwich on the desk next to her coffee and spent a few minutes trying to complete the report by sheer force of will.

Staring at it didn't help much.

Officer Morelli glided by, giving her the usual wary look he always did. It didn't matter if she responded with a pleading 'I'm not going to melt your brain, don't look at me like that' face or an angry scowl. Every time he saw her, he'd scurry away. Today, she tried something different.

"Hey, Tom?"

He froze like a kid getting caught sneaking out of class early. "Yeah?"

"Is it—and please be honest—that I'm surrounded by ghosts that freaks you out, or my dinky rating in mind blast?"

"Yeah," said Nicole. The redhead spun around in her chair to look at him. "You know she's real sensitive. It bugs her when people don't like her."

Kirsten bit her lip. *Projecting much?* "I'm just curious. We're all on the same side here."

Morelli's glance darted back and forth between the two women. The scolded-dog posture left him, and he approached with an almost-confident look in his eye. "It's not the mind blast. You ever hear about that guy Hawthorne from East City?"

"Yeah." Kirsten's gaze dropped to his chest. "Another astral sensitive. Went crazy and killed himself. There wasn't much in the report."

"Oooo." Nicole's chair rolled over as if motorized, under her telekinetic power. "Crazy?"

"They wouldn't tell you the unofficial story." Morelli lowered his voice and leaned closer. "He tangled with a demon. Word is, it got into his head and possessed him."

Kirsten frowned. "You believe that? There's no such thing as demons. Wraiths, sure. Demons? It's all part of the BS."

"What do you call Harbingers?" asked Dorian, from his desk.

"I have no idea what they are." Kirsten grabbed her coffee. "But they're not demons. A demon is something from religious mythology."

"Common among several disparate belief systems." Dorian winked. "Not to mention, depending on who you ask... ghosts are a figure of religious mythology too."

Kirsten sighed at Dorian. "You're not baiting me now. I've got too much work to do."

Morelli and Nicole exchanged looks.

"Yeah, so..." Morelli backed away, headed for his workstation. "One of these days, you're going to have a demon latched on to you, and I don't want to be anywhere near it."

"Guess he doesn't think that little crucifix he wears will help him," said Dorian in a deadpan voice.

Kirsten's giggle rattled Morelli, who averted his gaze as he fell into his seat.

Nicole draped herself over Kirsten's desk, eyeing the egg-on-a-roll. "Looks like I left a mental scar."

"Hardly. These are good." Kirsten swiped it before Nicole could ask for it. "Want half?"

"Naah, I'm too hungry. Half 'a one would tease. I'll order one for myself." The redhead pulled out her NetMini. "So you're still doing the reports on the Intera thing?"

"Yeah, I never should have—"

"Eze wanted to talk to you about that boy." Nicole thumb-typed on the small holo-screen.

"—complained about those two idiots talking about Lucian in front of his daughter—"

"Oh, I got a 288 outta 300 on my re-qual. You think I should upgrade to a '90, or is the E-88 enough?"

Kirsten leaned on her desk, cheek on fist. "—Now the reports gotta go over to Div 1 and everything's gotta be—"

"The E-90's got a blue beam, which goes with my eyes, but the green is pretty too." Nicole put her NetMini back in her pocket.

"—perfect, in place, and complete." Kirsten grumbled. "Congrats on the score. Wonder when they'll make me go to the range again. Seriously, you're choosing weapons based on if it goes with your eyes?"

Nicole shrugged. "You're I-Ops. It's more important for us tactical peons, and the '88 gets more shots on an e-mag, but doesn't pack as much punch. Seems like it's more of a choice of style so, yeah, color becomes a factor."

Kirsten rushed a mouthful of spicy eggs. "You're not a peon."

"I'm still enlisted, not like *some* people with special rare powers." Nicole gave her a playful raspberry.

"Wren," yelled Eze, from his office.

"Uh, oh." Nicole winked, and scooted back to her desk.

"I deserve whatever he's gonna throw at me." Kirsten lolled her head to the side and rolled her eyes. "I've been putting this report off for two weeks."

She swiped her hand at the terminal to lock it, and trudged to the Captain's office. He smiled as she entered. Kirsten halted at attention before his desk, staring at the wall above his head.

"First, relax." Captain Eze gestured at the chair next to her. "Second, this isn't about the Intera Tower report, although I would appreciate you sending that in before my retirement dinner."

"Retirement?" Kirsten blinked as she sat. "But you're not even fifty—"
Smooth. He's being funny.

Captain Eze let his smile speak for a few seconds. "I received your psych report."

Oh, crap. Her knees clamped together as she stiffened in the chair. She couldn't bring herself to ask how she did, managing a nervous, mangled smile.

"The report says you're no longer having that nightmare. I'm glad to hear you're making progress." He poked a finger at a few brighter green spots on his holo-terminal. "In regards to your request to adopt the boy you recovered a few weeks ago... Evan Dawson."

Please... Her brows tilted up in the middle as her eyes widened. "He was so frail when I found him."

"Medically cleared, but he's on supplemental nutrition. He's having some difficulty sleeping in his own room."

Kirsten slid forward in her chair. "I'll go talk to him."

Captain Eze held up a hand. "Let me finish. They've agreed to let you take the boy in on a trial basis, pending further psychological review—for both of you."

She leapt to her feet. "When can I bring him home?"

"He's not a stray dog." Captain Eze chuckled. "Considering he's already seemed to attach himself to you and is having nightmares, they were considering as soon as tonight. A week or two to see how it goes. Astral Sensitives are so rare, they think the advantage you'd have helping him understand his gift outweighs the worry of a possible... bad situation." He paused for a moment. "Unless you think it's too much responsibility."

"I..." She pictured Evan's pleading face in that awful apartment, the way he cowered in a ball at the sight of a stimpak. "I'm terrified I won't be good enough for him."

"They—and I—think it would do the both of you a lot of good." Captain Eze stood and rounded his desk.

Kirsten felt more like a teenage daughter about to be given a new car than a cop facing her superior.

He offered a hand. "It's a big responsibility, but I think you are quite capable of it."

She accepted his handshake. "Thank you, sir. I don't know what to say. I... I'll do everything I can to make this work."

"I'm sure you will." He grinned. "Now... about that report."

"Right away, sir." She snapped off a salute and rushed out of his office.

KIRSTEN SLUMPED OVER HER DESK, CHIN ON HER SOFT RIGHT FOREARM, poking her left index finger through immaterial buttons on her terminal, answering *yes* to questions like 'have you completed this report to the fullest extent of your ability to recall all pertinent facts as they occurred.'

Beep.

'Do you certify all information entered in the report as truthful and accurate.'

"Yes," droned Kirsten, clicking again.

"Hmm?" asked Dorian from behind.

Beep.

'You submit the preceding report pursuant to the laws of the United Coalition Front, National Police Force. You acknowledge that you are required to present any testimony necessitated during judicial proceedings that may result from this Inquest.'

"Yes." Kirsten sighed with relief as the screen collapsed back to a blank desktop. "Finished this damn report."

She brought her left hand down on top of her head and tried to rub the eyestrain out of her skull. *I hate reports.* Her massaging hand migrated to the bridge of her nose as she sat up straight and let her weight go back in the chair.

"Agent Wren?" asked a small voice.

Kirsten jumped. "Gah!"

A tween girl in a clingy, black Division o admin uniform clamped both hands over her mouth in an effort not to yelp. Straight, dark hair hung down her back to her belt line. Her almond-shaped eyes vibrated with trepidation. She looked like a tiny version of a Division o investigator, except for the lack of a sidearm.

Dorian walked over. "She's adorable. Those boots are like little copies of your duty-issue ones. They're cute in an 'I could stomp your head in' sort of way."

Kirsten spared a second to smirk at him before she abandoned decorum and grasped the child's hand while eyeing the nameplate on her chest.

"Sorry. You snuck up on me, Samantha."

"Cadet Peña, Ma'am." The girl saluted with her left.

"Oh, this one's into it." Dorian chuckled.

Kirsten frowned at the slender hand in her own. *What awful thing happened to you to wind up here?* "Are you even twelve yet? You don't have to salute me."

The girl seemed thrown off balance, hesitating for a few seconds before shaking her head. "I'll be twelve in eight months." She stood taller. "You don't have to feel sorry for me. I'm only going to school here. My parents aren't asshats."

Kirsten thought of Nicole's habit of telepathic eavesdropping. "Did you peek at my thoughts?"

"No, Ma'am. Telempathy is my most developed talent. I can't help but feel emotion and I recognized that pity spike." She smiled. "I'm not a dormer. I was about to go home, but Sergeant Reed sent me up here to find you. There's someone downstairs asking to see you by name."

"Who?"

The girl raised her arm, revealing a datapad she'd had hidden at her side. She projected a holo-panel image of an older teenage girl, as pale as a porcelain doll with black hair and blue eyes. The only color on her face came from a touch of red at the corners of her eyes.

There is *something familiar about that girl, but I can't remember ever meeting her.* "Did you speak to her?"

"You attract the tragic ones." Dorian offered a sympathetic look.

"No, Ma'am. I'm only a cadet. I'm not allowed into potentially dangerous situations." She lowered the datapad and clasped her hands behind her back in an 'at-ease' pose.

Oh, sure. They send me out there at sixteen. Kirsten rubbed her forehead. "Thanks, Samantha."

"Cadet Peña?" The girl fidgeted.

Kirsten grumbled. "You're not enlisted yet, sweetie. Don't grow up too fast." She rendered a reluctant salute. "Dismissed."

"Ma'am." The girl saluted, turned, and ran off like a child.

"She's playing. It's fun for her." Dorian stood next to Kirsten. "There's something familiar about your visitor."

"Yeah." Kirsten locked her terminal and glanced at him.

He winked. "You've recovered a few children in your illustrious career. Maybe she's one of the early ones."

I was only a kid myself when I started. Kirsten headed out of the squad room, jogging towards the elevator at the end of a blinding white corridor. "Who sets a sixteen-year-old loose with an E-90?"

Dorian raised both eyebrows. "People with no other way to stop a pissed off wraith."

She stopped in the small capsule and spun to face the door. "Yeah..."

The walk to the interview offices took three minutes. Kirsten swiped her forearm guard past a scanner to open a set of sliding doors leading to a hexagonal room where a dark-skinned man occupied the only desk. His wide jaw and large frame gave him the silhouette of a combat cyborg, though he had no implants. Sergeant Reed's skin-tight Division 0 blacks seemed about to split open at any of six different places.

"Agent Wren." He offered a quick salute, though the look on his face said he regarded her as little more than a kid.

"Sergeant Reed." She saluted him back. "You sent for me?"

"Room three." He pointed.

"Thank you, Sergeant." Kirsten went left, down the first of five hallways leading out.

"You're one of the few officers he doesn't glare at." Dorian walked at her side. "I bet it's because you always act like he's the one with seniority."

"Well, he is," she whispered. "I'm only an Agent because I'm an Astral Sensate. He's got experience."

Dorian feigned putting a hand on her forehead. "I don't feel a fever. You don't talk like a low-ranking officer."

She stifled the urge to chuckle as she waved at the silver square on the wall, opening the door.

The teen stood, hands clasped in front of her with a hopeful, sad smile on her face. Her sheer indigo bodysuit had a series of slits baring skin on the outside of her legs and arms; a few patches of dirt hinted that she'd been staying in a grungier part of town. A dingy jacket draped over the back of a chair carried the unmistakable cloying chemical/sour fruit odor of The Beneath.

"She's somewhere between exotic dancer and street waif," said Dorian.

"Kirsten!" The woman ran over and hugged her. "Thanks for seeing me."

"Go ahead," said Dorian, grinning. "You know you're going to stumble over remembering her. Read her surface thoughts."

Kirsten furrowed her eyebrows. "No, that's rude."

"Sorry," said the girl. "I... Uhh—"

"Not you." Kirsten smiled and took a seat. "I'm really sorry, but I feel like I've met you before, but I can't remember you."

The girl cried despite smiling. "I'm Adrienne Lewis."

"I'm leaving," said Dorian.

"Oh, knock it off." Kirsten glowered at him for a second before looking back at the girl. "Adrian? Wow, you look amazing."

Adrienne bit her lip and melted into the chair she'd been in. "Thanks... I..."

"Please tell me Daniel is okay?"

Dorian edged backward.

"He's great actually. We talked and talked... He kept telling me it's who I am and I needed to be happy. On some level, he was disappointed, but he'll find another guy. The way he is with me now feels like I've become the kid sister of his last boyfriend. He treats me kinda like a big protective brother." Adrienne smiled.

"That's awkward with a capital A." Dorian cringed.

Kirsten blinked. "I really can't get over how... total it is. If I didn't know you before, I'd never believe." *Wow, we're even the same height now...* *guess she likes short.* "You'll get sick of being short sooner or later."

Adrienne took a few calming breaths. "Genetically, I'm a hundred percent female. No different from if I'd been born this way. I... had them shave a few years off too. Biologically, I'm sixteen again."

"You realize he had to steal probably twenty million credits to do that right?" Dorian folded his arms.

"Something's really bothering you." Kirsten leaned close. "What can I help you with?"

Dorian shook his head. "Allowing him to steal a small fortune isn't enough help? You should've charged him for psionic tampering with credsticks. Do you have any idea what the media would do if it got out that a technokinetic can manufacture money?"

Kirsten gave him the side-eye.

"Someone's been following me. Last night, he—" Adrienne broke down in sobs.

Dorian's expression became a mixture of unease and sympathy.

Kirsten's heartbeat quickened. "He can't hurt you anymore. You're safe here."

"No..." Adrienne fumbled to open a small, shiny violet purse shaped like a square. She retrieved a tissue and held it to her nose. "I don't think that's what he wanted."

Kirsten hit a button on the table to begin recording. "Tell me what happened."

Adrienne laced her fingers together in her lap. "I've been trying to convince my parents to come topside. They're considering it." She smiled despite a case of sniffles. "I'd just climbed up from the Beneath into an alley at the edge of Sector 5128. My apartment's a little bit north in 5180. Anyway, every time I'd gone through there for the past couple of days, it felt like someone was watching me. Like some hungry *thing* stared at me."

"Welcome to being a woman," said Dorian, shaking his head.

A twinge of guilt struck Kirsten. The uniform shielded her from similar attention, and she didn't much go outside except for work. "Go on."

"Last night, this guy grabs me. My first instinct was to throw him off and punch him in the head, but he was too strong. I couldn't get away. He dragged me to the ground, pinned my wrists together in one hand and pulled out this massive knife. I couldn't get away..." Adrienne shook, fumbling the tissue to the floor.

"He threatened you with the knife?" asked Kirsten.

"The man didn't threaten anything. He just smiled at me with this terrifying look on his face. His eyes were completely black."

Dorian tapped his chin. "Okay, that's strange... but not beyond the possibility of cybernetics."

"He hissed something strange. I... couldn't make out what he said. He never once tried to rip my clothes off, just kept whispering to himself. When he stopped, he raised the knife and I knew he was gonna kill me. He wasn't a rapist; he wanted to kill me."

Kirsten reached across the table to hold her hand. "You got away. That's what counts."

Adrienne offered a sheepish smile. "I... uhh... zapped him." She cringed. "I'm sorry for shocking you. I'm... Wow, I can't believe you're actually willing to help me after I did that to you."

"She's a saint." Dorian smirked.

"I was a little upset with you." Kirsten's cheeks warmed with embarrassment. "For leaving me like that. I'm over it. So, what happened?"

"That's when it got scary." What little color existed in Adrienne's cheeks faded. "The bastard hit the ground twitching and dropped the knife. I shoved him off and got up to run, but couldn't help but look at him once more." Her voice fell to an emotionless half-whisper. "Black smoke came out of him, and it sounded like a dozen people stood around whispering at me."

Aw damn, that sounds like Harbingers. She probably killed the bastard. "I need you to focus. Think about what he said to you. I know it's scary, but try to remember it. I'd like to look for myself, okay?"

Adrienne nodded.

Kirsten locked eyes with her, focusing in on current thoughts. A blur of walls, trash compressors, and rain-slicked metal alley surface flashed by. The interview room faded away as Kirsten's reality became Adrienne's memory of that night. A sharp pain at the back of her head made a voice cry out in her mind; a hand seized her by the hair from behind and pulled her into a painful one-armed crush. A tall man scooped her off her feet. She struggled, too weak to get away. The ground and sky smeared into a blur seconds before a sharp impact to her back. Wet grittiness seeped into her clothes. A face hovered over her, blocky of feature with prominent brow ridges and a long chin.

Eyes of solid black stared into her soul. His breath reeked of rotten eggs. Kirsten's heart pounded in her head as one huge hand clamped her wrists together. The man slid a fourteen-inch combat knife from his belt, covered in a pattern of thin, red lines. She concentrated on that instant, pausing the memory in time. The markings on the blade appeared to be some manner of ancient writing, a mixture of complex pictograms and small runes.

Adrienne's internal voice pleaded for her life, though she couldn't force words past her fear.

The figure loomed down; blood leaked between his teeth as he grinned. After flashing a look of patronizing sympathy, he raised the knife and whispered, "*In abyssum irent.*"

An upwelling of terror shattered Adrienne's paralysis. The unfamiliar sensation of an electrokinetic releasing their power followed. Her skin tingled everywhere, followed by a numbing sensation where his hand touched her arms. The man flew ten feet up in a smoking arc and bounced off the side of a dull green trash crusher with a *boom* that echoed off down the alley. Adrienne crawled backwards for a few seconds before attempting to stand, unable to look away from the convulsing body.

Thick, black vapor exuded from the attacker at several points, coalescing into a mass which—despite being a cloud—felt as if it watched her. A hint of a humanoid face and fangs manifested, but from there, the memory contained only scenes of panicked running and screaming.

Kirsten released the telepathic link to find Adrienne curled up in the chair, crying. Kirsten comforted her for a few minutes with hand squeezes and reassuring pats while Dorian paced around the back of the room, looking uncomfortable and guilty.

"I killed him, didn't I?" whispered Adrienne.

"I don't want to say anything until I have a look. Did you notify Division 1?"

Adrienne shook her head, flaring her jet-black hair. "No. I hid in bed for hours until I remembered you. I came right here. I think it followed me home." Adrienne shifted and looked down. "I feel uneasy there... kind of like I do right now."

"Many psionics can sense the presence of paranormal energy, even non-astrals. My partner is a spirit and he's close by. You're feeling him right now." Kirsten tried to sound comforting. "I need to go to your apartment. Soon."

Adrienne nodded. "Okay."

Kirsten pursed her lips and tried to ignore the grumbling emanating from the back seat of the patrol craft. They cruised a hair over two hundred miles per hour at the level of the fifty-second story, about twenty feet above civilian hovercar traffic. She followed the Navcon route to an apartment building in Sector 5182, right in the heart of 'averageville.' Ten five-mile grid squares in every direction filled with the same hundred-story residence towers, as if some lazy game designer had copied and pasted reality over and over.

Adrienne curled up in the passenger seat, leaning against the door and sniffling. A few minutes into their flight, she looked up. "I didn't mean to kill him. He was going to kill me and I freaked out. I don't want to get arrested. I can't believe this is happening."

Dorian muttered, "I can't believe you gave him my seat."

Kirsten bit back the urge to scream 'her' at Dorian, and pulled up to avoid a lumbering advert bot. She rolled the car into a right turn around a silvery office building in the shape of an obelisk, the video display in the armor-plated windscreen editing out the late-afternoon sun glare on the mirrored surface. "From what I saw, it looked like an em-surge." She tapped her fingers on the sticks. "Oh, sorry. That's short for emotional psionic surge. Most psionic abilities are affected by the user's emotional state. Periods of extreme emotion, good or bad, can amplify the output. Usually it hurts afterward, like pulling a muscle."

Adrienne bit her lip. "Is that like a crime of passion or something?"

"Not exactly, but I can tell from reading your memory that you didn't intend to kill. You wanted him off you. I can't think of a clearer instance of self-defense." *Something's definitely strange here.* "You did see something unusual."

"Am I gonna have to find a new place? Is my apartment haunted now? My parents were going to move in."

Kirsten looked at her for a few seconds before nosing the patrol craft into a diving left turn. "How'd it go with them?"

"Better than I thought. When I found them, they didn't even recognize me." Adrienne blushed and laughed. "First thing Dad said was 'nice tits.' He about dropped dead when I told him who I was."

"I bet," said Dorian.

Kirsten sighed at him.

"Once the initial surprise wore off, they told me they suspected for a long time I wanted to be a girl. I don't think they really understand... inside, I've always *been* a girl. It took them awhile to believe I was me. My genetics are fully modded. I can even get pregnant."

A chill swam over the cabin. Dorian shivered.

"That's amazing." Kirsten smiled.

"We talked over their... uhh, extreme views on government and they agreed that maybe they had taken it too far. I got an apartment, and since I look like a teenager, they insisted I needed parents again." Adrienne swirled a strand of hair around her finger. "It's kinda nice. I was tempted to go to school, but I'm still legally nineteen so... I wasn't sure if that was like wrong or something."

Dorian shook his head. "I'm surprised he didn't go all the way back to five."

Kirsten kept silent and forced away a memory of sitting in her father's lap.

"Okay..." He let off a resigned sigh. "I'm surprised *she* didn't go back to five."

"You had them make you younger?" Kirsten pulled up, heading for the top of the building.

Adrienne shrugged. "My life really sucked from like sixteen to nineteen. I wanted a do-over. I would've gone even younger, but it was so damn expensive." She chuckled. "Would you believe to go under sixteen requires consent from a parent or would-be guardian?"

"There's so much wrong with that I'm not even going to say anything." Dorian shook his head.

Kirsten set down in a parking space on the hundredth story roof. "How far can they go?"

"Six or seven if you have two hundred million to burn, are willing to spend six months unconscious in a tank, don't mind a ten percent chance of death, and can talk someone into accepting legal guardianship for you." Adrienne frowned. "My parents are a little too old for that. Not to mention I got kinda worried about the amount of credits I was pumping. Figured I'd use it and disappear before the ICFC came looking for me." She reached for the door handle. "Besides, I didn't want to be a little kid again. I like my freedom."

Kirsten zoned out, lost for a moment in a daydream of another chance at a normal life. *Mother didn't get really bad until I was six...*

Dorian leaned up behind her, whispering, "Don't feel ashamed of the beautiful person your experiences have made you. You are strong, tough, and the kindest woman I've ever met."

Kirsten tried to swallow the lump in her throat.

"K?" Dorian smiled. "Evan needs a mother, not a little sister."

"Yeah." Kirsten's sorrow faded to a sense of diligent purpose. She squeezed the exit release, causing the door to rise out of her way.

Dorian flashed a crooked grin. "Besides, where would you get that much money?"

Kirsten swallowed the urge to laugh as she got out. Adrienne led the way across the parking deck to the elevator bank and down to the thirty-ninth floor. Air blowing in through the seam in the doors carried the scent of exotic spices dueling with the stink of wet carpeting. The elevator stopped; a half-second before she wondered if it had malfunctioned, the doors slid open with an electronic *ping*. Kirsten whistled at the lifeless pea green walls and dingy carpet the same brown as cattail reeds. Yellowing light fixtures seemed to suck life from the world.

"Wow." Kirsten whistled. "This place looks exactly like Albert's building."

"I think all these residence towers were built by the same company," said Dorian.

Adrienne fumbled to pull her NetMini out of her tiny purse. "Who's Albert?"

Kirsten rubbed her throat at the memory of icy fingers squeezing around her neck. "He's the suspect I was really chasing when I arrested you. He was a ghost."

"Oh." Adrienne trembled.

She waved the little device at the wall, causing the door to open with a weak pneumatic squeak. Kirsten followed her in and walked an orbit around the living room. Nothing leapt out as unusual, though the air held a weak taint of foreboding. Dorian headed into the back while Kirsten made her way into the dining area and kitchenette.

"Not a bad little place you got, except for the uninvited guest." Kirsten traced a finger along the counter top. "Something's been here, but it feels like residual energy."

"Is that good or bad?" Adrienne crossed to a silver fridge. "Water?"

"Sure. Probably bad. Its presence was strong enough to 'stain' the apartment from being here."

Dorian returned. "Nothing in the bedrooms but a strange feeling."

Kirsten accepted a narrow cylinder-shaped bottle and twisted the end cap to make a small straw pop up. She walked in a slow circle around the apartment, sipping water while searching for paranormal energy.

Adrienne leaned against the kitchen counter. "Is it because it's not dark yet?"

"Nah." Kirsten smiled. "Spirits don't go into hiding in the daytime."

Dorian chuckled. "If something did follow hi—her here, maybe it gave up."

"Did anything else happen after you got home?" Kirsten still sensed only the same pervasive eeriness in the surroundings.

"Well..." Adrienne sported a light blush. "Since you are a cop, I suppose I can show you. One sec." She set her water on the counter and walked into the back.

"You should follow her," said Dorian. "She could be going to get a weapon. You have no idea what she's capable of."

"Suspicious," whispered Kirsten. *He's right. I don't really know her.* She put a hand on her E-90 and edged down the hall.

After a few minutes of doors and drawers clattering about, Adrienne emerged from the bedroom in a lavender satin robe, barefoot, and devoid of weapons. Kirsten relaxed and let her hand off her sidearm.

"My breast and back," said Adrienne, still blushing. "Scratches."

She opened the robe enough to show off three red lines, which started at her left collarbone and ran down over her breast. Adrienne faced away, and let the garment fall off her shoulders, catching it at her elbows. Angry red marks crisscrossed her back, six groups of three in varying lengths.

"I tried to use a stimpak." Adrienne shivered. "All it did was burn so bad I passed out."

Kirsten took a step closer. "May I?"

Adrienne nodded.

Cool skin met Kirsten's fingertips, though within a quarter-inch of any line, Adrienne's back felt fever-hot. At a touch, Kirsten sensed the presence of paranormal energy. She raised her forearm guard, capturing several still images of the scratches, including a thermal scan showing 96.4 degree skin marked by red lines reading as 106.66 degrees.

Kirsten frowned. "Oh, this one's got a sense of humor."

Dorian leaned into examine the holographic screen floating over her arm. "Or there's something significant to the number."

"Nice try." Kirsten let her arm fall. "Humans made that up, and the spirits know that so they're messing with us."

"Huh?" Adrienne shifted to look over her shoulder at Kirsten. "Nice try?"

"There's a weak presence attached to you." Kirsten saved the images into a new Inquest Report. "I'm going to get rid of it. This is going to look scary, but I promise it can't hurt you."

A sudden peal of techno-trance music rang out, making Adrienne yelp. She pulled her robe up and closed it, grabbing the counter to keep from falling over.

"What the?" Kirsten looked at the ceiling.

"Doorbell," said Adrienne, shivering. "It's been going off on its own."

"I got it." Kirsten held a hand up. "Stay here."

Adrienne backed into the counter, fear plain in her eyes.

Kirsten trotted to the door and waved a hand over the silver panel on the wall. The nondescript grey panel slid sideways, revealing a stooped man in a clear vest and Mars-red fatigue pants, riddled with stains and rips. His bare chest bore such a number of purple autoinjector bruises he looked like a 'connect the dots' art project. He slouched forward; hair like an enormous azure flamingo had died on his head obscured his face.

"Who the hell are you?" Kirsten put a hand on her sidearm, but decided to reach across to her stunrod instead.

The man swayed as if intoxicated while emitting a menacing chuckle.

"Is someone there?" Adrienne peeked around the archway from the kitchen.

"The marked one." A hiss of a voice escaped the figure in the door. His head snapped up, wild eyes trained on Adrienne. His hair flew back, baring a tattoo of a carved stone O at the front of his throat.

Adrienne's water bottle slipped from her fingers as she screamed. At first, the shriek formed from terror, but the tone changed to one of pain as she sank to her knees, arms twitching.

A wave of paranormal energy burst forth from the man. He surged into the apartment, swatting Kirsten aside like the ninety-pound sprite she was. She twisted to catch her fall, landing on her hands into a sideways roll. Dorian rushed in front of the charging maniac, though his fingers found no purchase, passing clear through him.

Kirsten leapt to her feet and swung her right arm to the side, calling the lash. A tendril of scintillating blue-white energy unfurled to a ten-foot length. The man seized Adrienne by her arms, lifting and slamming her down on her back atop the kitchen's island counter. He tore her robe open, exposing her breasts, and reached for a knife handle at his belt.

Adrienne gurgled, seeming in too much pain to move or scream.

"Hey!" Kirsten shouted as she ran at him, rounding the lash into a strike.

The thug arched his back as the energy whip hit him, loosing a scream mixed of human and something... else. A voice far deeper than any mortal could produce howled at a deafening volume. Lights faltered. Car alarms out in the street sang.

Head tilted back, the gang thug moved in a slow, menacing turn. The hate in his all-black eyes gave way to worry at the sight of the lash coiling around Kirsten's legs. He seemed to forget Adrienne existed, staring with fixation at Kirsten. Simmering hatred bloomed to an angry roar as he stomped at her. Decorative glass sculptures on shelves rattled and windows shook. Kirsten braced against the onslaught of paranormal fear, resisting the terror he tried to force into her mind. She pushed back at the spiritual presence inside him with her psionic energy. *He's not as strong as he looks.* She shoved with a surge of mental force, cutting off his bellow and knocking him to the floor.

Adrienne rolled on her side, whimpering. Blood seeped from the claw marks on her chest and back as if the wounds had been inflicted only seconds ago. Her expression, red and contorted from pain, begged for help. Kirsten raised the lash as the man ambled to his feet.

Dorian stuck a hand into the thug's chest, straining and pulling on something inside. "He's... possessed."

Kirsten snapped the lash around, but the maniac dove to the side with surprising agility considering his size. Confident the energy whip could cause no harm to the living, Kirsten let it hit Adrienne to complete the swing, planning to spin into another strike. The shimmering cord made contact with something, snagging on Adrienne for a second before pulling away—as if she'd struck a weak spirit.

Adrienne went limp with relief, gasping for breath, no longer screaming.

"You..." The man pointed at Kirsten, all trace of malevolence fading to worry. He ambled for the door and broke into a run. "*Claustritumus.*"

Kirsten looked back and forth from the girl to the fleeing man. Sensing no immediate threat to Adrienne, she bolted after him. He ran down the corridor, heading straight at a window, arms crossed in front of his face.

"This death is on your soul," he shouted.

No! Kirsten pushed herself forward with all the desperation she could find, leaping into a tackle at the jumping man. She wrapped her arms around his thighs as his upper body smashed the reinforced glass. Kirsten spread her legs to the side, grunting. Her boots slapped into the wall and all the man's weight tugged at her grip. She leaned back, trying to keep her ass on the floor so he didn't drag her along with him.

He howled with rage, scrabbling at the window frame. Shards of broken glass clanked around as he strained to pull himself forward. Kirsten roared past gritted teeth and hauled back with as much strength as she could summon. His legs slipped an inch in her grasp, and another. Her butt left the carpet; her boots acted as a pivot point. The man's legs slid up around her body and her hips crashed into the wall. He dangled, only her failing grip between him and a fatal drop.

"*Stop.*" She growled, a brief reflection of glowing light in her eyes appeared on the wall.

Cold slithered over her and down her back. The struggling man went still for a second, and screamed. Stench watered Kirsten's eyes; her face hovered inches away from soiled pants. She choked back the urge to vomit, straining to look over her shoulder at another presence without losing her hold on him.

Behind her in the hall floated a wispy shadow of darkness in the vague shape of a human silhouette. It waved at her, an over-polite finger curling gesture with long, smoky talons.

A voice like scraping glass sent tremors down her spine. "Do not fret if your strength proves too weak to hold him. His soul is tainted." The shadow drifted down the hall. "Farewell."

Kirsten let off an angry scream of determination as the man slipped another inch. Her arms shook from fatigue. *It's getting away.* She glanced at her boots, spread as wide as the corridor would allow, wedged in the corners. Her thighs shuddered; she couldn't move her legs. *I... can't let him die. Dammit!*

She squeezed her arms tight, fingers aching where she clasped her wrist at his gut, straining to hold on. "Command, b-backup call."

Her armband beeped.

"Shit!" screamed the man. "Help!"

Dorian raced out of Adrienne's apartment, chasing the fleeing specter.

I'm not gonna be able to hold this lunk long enough for backup to get here. "Dorian!"

Her partner glanced over his shoulder. "He's Oblivion. Let him go."

Kirsten braced her knees against the wall as the man flailed. "I don't care what gang he's in. I can't let him die."

The thug screamed again, flailing his arms in a futile effort to grab something.

She closed her eyes, tightening her grip on his shins as much as her protesting muscles would allow. *Please don't slip. Please don't slip.*

"Fine," said Dorian, sounding close.

Kirsten concentrated on her astral power, allowing it to permeate her body and render her tangible to spirits. Dorian wrapped his arms around her from behind and pulled. Inch by excruciating inch, their combined strength dragged the panic-stricken man back. As soon as he could reach, he clamped his hands on the window frame, crunching jagged glass, and pushed. Kirsten fell on her back and turned her head to the side at the last second before he fell sitting on her; loaded pants pressed warmth into her cheek.

"Get off me." She almost vomited.

The man wheezed and collapsed to the side, staring at bloody handfuls of glass. "Sixty... stories..."

Kirsten sat up, watery-eyed and gagging.

"Whatever that was, it got away," said Dorian. "Hope this guy was worth saving."

"He's alive, Dorian. He's worth saving." She moved to her knees and held her left forearm up to grab an image of the ganger's face.

"At best, he's a chem dealer. At worst, a murderer or rapist. Oblivion is a pack of nihilists. They want the world to end and don't care what happens." Dorian shook his head. "Who knows what that entity is going to do? I hope we didn't just kill someone else."

"When was the last time a true nihilist begged for his life?" Kirsten frowned at the holo-panel floating over her left arm. Johnathan Breem, twenty-six years old, six active warrants for sexual assault, two for strong-arm robbery, three for assault with a deadly weapon, and two for 'non-complaining rape.' She frowned. "Dorian, what the hell is 'non-complaining rape?'"

"Citycams recorded the assault, but the victim never came forward. It means there's no complaining witness, but we can charge him based on the video."

Kirsten sighed.

"Thinking you should've let him go?" Dorian raised an eyebrow.

"No. That entity wasn't that strong. I'm sure another decent hit would have destroyed it. It will be licking its wounds for a while. Maybe I can find it before it does something." She grumbled. "It shouldn't have left such an imprint on her apartment, not as weak as it was."

"Maybe it's a demon?" Dorian grinned.

Kirsten rolled her eyes. "Don't start. Not now."

The man clutched his hands to his chest, still breathing hard.

"Johnathan Breem," said Kirsten. "I hate to be the bearer of bad news after you almost died, but you're under arrest for"—she pointed at the little holo-terminal—"reasons."

"You're supposed to read the list of charges," said Dorian, also smiling.

"I'm too exhausted. Besides, I'm sure he knows." She shut off the panel. "Div 1 will give him the drill. Now that he's spirit-free, he's not my jurisdiction."

Johnathan sat up and looked at her with a 'you're a tiny little woman, what are you gonna do about it' face.

Her eyebrows flattened into an unimpressed line as her eyes glowed for an instant. "*Stay put.*"

"Okay." He laid down. "Do I have to sit in shit?"

"You shouldn't have crapped your pants." Kirsten gagged.

Johnathan gestured at the broken window. "Sixty stories."

"*Roll over.*" Her eyes flickered again.

He did.

She collected his arms behind him and cuffed him. Adrienne poked her head out of her door.

"Wait inside," yelled Kirsten. "I'll be back in a few minutes."

She knelt beside Johnathan for two minutes and forty-nine seconds, eager to be able to get away from the stink. Four figures in gloss black Division o tactical armor rushed from the elevator and headed towards her. One look at their height said Nicole wasn't one of them. *A story for later.* She forced herself to stand; every sore muscle made itself known.

Kirsten pointed at Breem. "Warrant hold. Div 1 wants him."

Squad Corporal Forrester raised his visor. "How'd you wind up stepping in it?"

Ugh, the smell. Did he have to use that phrase? "Wraith possessed him, tried to kill the girl in 60-10"

The one woman among the tactical squad glanced back. "Guess that's where the crying is coming from."

"Yeah." Kirsten edged past them. "Johnathan should behave himself for at least another three minutes. Can you babysit while I deal with her?"

"Sure thing, Ma'am." Forrester nodded.

"Suggest?" asked Cortez.

"Yeah." Kirsten muttered. "Too tired to fight, and he's three times my size."

"Stunrod?" asked the woman.

"Diaz... Check his pants. I did *not* want to smell that." Kirsten cringed at the mere thought of what a stunrod would've 'cooked up.' She headed for Adrienne's apartment. "Oh, I need my binders back whenever they collect him."

"You got it," said Forrester.

Kirsten jogged back to the still-open door and ducked inside. Adrienne sat in a ball on the floor in front of the couch, still in her bloody robe. She looked up as Kirsten approached and sat beside her on the cushions.

"You're bleeding."

"Yeah, I noticed." Adrienne sniffled. "I'm not used to crying this much. I mean, I always was kinda emotional, but it's gotten worse."

"Gotta love hormones." Kirsten opened a belt case and pulled out a four-inch red autoinjector with a yellow safety cap over the tip. "I hit something when the lash caught you."

"I don't remember." Adrienne sniffled. "It felt like I was wrapped up in red-hot barbed wire. When it stopped, I was in pure euphoria."

"The last time you tried a stimpak, it didn't work, right? Maybe whatever spirit was lingering inside you did that?"

"Sounds like a demon," said Dorian. "Three scratches... the sign of the Devil."

Kirsten glared at him. The word 'Devil' would be forever associated with Mother. "Mythology. This was a wraith."

Dorian folded his arms. "The last time you messed with a wraith, its claws were icy, right?"

"So? Maybe there's different kinds. I'm no expert on this stuff, just kinda winging it."

Adrienne looked at her. "Are you okay?"

"Yeah, just tired and a little sore." She handed over the stimpak. "You're still bleeding."

"Okay." Adrienne flicked the plastic cap from the tip and pressed the air hypo into her shoulder. The autoinjector emitted a faint hiss.

"Judging by her lack of screaming," said Dorian, "I think it worked."

Adrienne stood. "I want to get out of this bloody thing and clean up. I- is it gone?"

"It ran." Kirsten leaned forward and rubbed her face. "I don't think it'll come back for you. I got the feeling the energy in those scratches drew it like a beacon."

"I'm scared." Adrienne shivered. "Please tell me it's not coming back."

"I got a piece of it." Kirsten stood. "Even if it does remember you, which I doubt, it'll probably be a few weeks before it's got the balls to show itself. I'll hunt it down. You have my PID. Vid me if you see or feel anything unusual."

"Okay." Adrienne wrapped her arms around herself, shivering.

"Hey." Kirsten put a hand on Adrienne's shoulder. "Whatever it was, it targeted you at random. I really doubt it'll come back."

Division 1 officers in blue armor tromped past the door. A few seconds later, Johnathan shouted angry threats until the electronic *bwong* of a stunrod silenced him. Despite being at a safe distance in Adrienne's apartment, Kirsten covered her nose.

I have to believe I did the right thing.

"Thank you." Adrienne hugged her, careful not to make contact with blood-soaked cloth.

Kirsten smiled. "If you'd feel better having someone along when you go to drag your parents back to civilization, let me know."

Adrienne reached up and held her hand. "I never thought getting arrested would be a way to make friends."

Kirsten laughed. "I don't advise making a habit of it. Have you considered signing on?"

"Nah. I'm not cut out for it. I'm a big ol' chicken." Adrienne summoned a weak smile. "I'm still trying to get used to my emotions going all over the place."

"People with your mechanical talents tend to work in Admin, not front line." Kirsten glanced at the time on her arm. "Ack! I need to go. Crap. I just got done with reports."

"You should know better." A whimsical grin formed on Dorian's face. "This job is ten hours of reports for every five minutes of action."

Adrienne walked her to the door. "If I can't find a decent job in a couple weeks, I guess I'll look into it."

A man in blue armor waited outside.

"Great. Guess the paperwork starts now." Kirsten nodded at him and smiled back at Adrienne. "You look great. Try to get some sleep."

"Bye. Thanks, and sorry again about the…" She wiggled her fingers as if throwing lightning.

"Don't mention it." Kirsten stepped into the hall.

"That the vic?" asked the cop.

"Yeah, but not Johnathan's. He was just a vessel for a spirit."

"Demon," said Dorian.

Kirsten picked at her eye with her middle finger.

"Uhh, okay." The officer raised his arm, dangling her binders from two fingers. "Thanks for the assist. Mr. Breem's been staying off the grid. So what filled his pants?"

Kirsten swallowed bile. "The spirit tried to throw him out a window. Guess he's afraid of heights."

After giving a statement of events, she made her way back to the roof where she'd parked. Dorian took the passenger seat with the smug grin of a usurped king once more on his throne. The console lit up at her touch. Kirsten clutched the sticks and eased the patrol craft into the air.

Dorian glanced over. "What's got you so nervous? Your hands are shaking."

"I'm taking Evan home tonight, assuming he wants to go." She almost mistimed her entry to a traffic lane, causing an alarm inside as well as a horn outside. "Really? You just did that? What kind of idiot beeps at a police vehicle?"

"They can't hear you shouting." Dorian tapped on the 'window.' "Inch thick armor."

She leveled off in the lane, glaring at the silver Halcyon-Ormyr that just *had* to get in front of her. "So tempted to flick the lights."

Dorian waved her down. "You did mistime it. Don't turn into a Div 1 jackass who thinks traffic rules don't apply to cops." He paused a moment. "Relax. I'm sure Evan will jump at the chance to get out of the dorm."

Kirsten clenched and released the sticks, battling the knot of worry growing inside her belly. "What if seeing me makes him think about being locked in his bedroom and beaten? What if he panics as soon as I walk in?"

"He won't." Dorian pointed at the windscreen. "Mind that ad-bot."

She dove two meters to avoid a damaged floating billboard straying into the traffic stream. A few angry pokes at the console sent a feeler over to Div 1 to deal with it.

"I hope you're right, Dorian..."

THE ANTISEPTIC WHITE CORRIDORS OF THE DIVISION ZERO DORMITORY shaved eight years from Kirsten's mind, bringing her back to feeling lost and alone. She walked past small bedrooms; children glanced up from datapads, games, or toys, their faces filled with every emotion ranging from joy at being safe to abject terror. She locked stares with a pale black-haired girl of about five cowering under her bed with her thumb in her mouth.

That was me my first night here, only I was twelve. Kirsten smiled and waved, though the girl didn't react. Before Kirsten could surrender to her heavy heart and go talk to her, one of the nannies darted into the room with a large stuffed rabbit and an armload of pink datapads. Kirsten stared at the floor and moved on. Four rooms later, she edged up to a door marked 23.

Evan lay on the bed in blue pajama pants and no shirt with an expression somewhere between bored disinterest and a sullen frown. Light from a video game holo-panel flashed, tinting his skin blue while painting an enlarged silhouette of him on the wall. His disheveled mop of hair looked like a puffball in shadow.

He still looks so scrawny.

Kirsten knocked. "Hey."

"Kirsten!" His eyes lit up; he tossed the datapad to the side and scrambled off the bed. "You came!"

She caught him out of a sprint, scooping him into a hug. He clamped his arms around her for a long moment before leaning back to look at her. The gleam in his green eyes destroyed any fear he'd be afraid of her.

Dorian smiled without a word, and wandered off down the hall.

"I keep hearing people tell me you're not happy here." Kirsten smiled.

He looked worried. "How long are they gonna let you stay?"

"Oh, not too long. I'll probably leave in less than an hour."

Tears collected at the corner of his eyes. His gaze started to fall to the floor.

"Do you want to come with me?"

His head snapped up, mouth agape.

Kirsten sat in an orange cube-shaped chair near the door, setting him on his feet in front of her. "I used to live in here when I was little too, and I know how lonely it can be... especially for astrals. People tend to be creeped out by us."

Evan stood mute, tears running down his cheeks.

"Since we, uhh, have the same sort of power, they said yes when I asked if I could foster you... if you want." She bit her lip. "I mean, you don't *have* to."

"I wanna stay with you." He jumped on her, sniffling. "Please."

"Okay. Get dressed. We'll stop for dinner on the way."

"Yay!" He bounced around the room cheering for a full two minutes before flinging off his pajamas and beginning a search for underpants.

Kirsten laughed at the sudden shift from sorrow to uncontained happiness. Evan jumped into his clothes, the plain black tee shirt and pants given to every dormer, and stuffed a bunch of datapads, gadgets, and more clothing into a backpack before running back to her.

"Am I gonna stay with you?" He couldn't stand still.

What am I doing? Am I ready for this responsibility? She clasped his hand. "I'm not sure. I want you to, but *they* want to make sure it's in your best interest."

He looked crestfallen. "How long?"

It's up to me. I can't mess this up. "At least two weeks. I hope longer if things work out."

Evan's emerald eyes sparkled as he stared at her. His open mouth stretched to a smile. He nodded in a matter-of-fact way, grabbed her hand, and pulled her to her feet.

"Can we go home now?"

"Okay." Kirsten led him out to the admin station, where she waved to get the attention of one of the MedTechs. *At least he's optimistic.* "Hi. I'm Agent Wren... signing out Evan Dawson."

He grumbled. "Just Evan."

"Got it. Looks like a two week pass. We'll need him back in three days for about a half hour. Routine medical check." The nurse held up a data-pad. "Wave, please."

"Oh, he's still going to school here. Thanks." Kirsten swiped her armband over the device, making it beep. She faced away from the counter and took a knee. "You ready, Ev?"

"Uh huh!" His sneakers squeaked on the over-polished tiles as he failed to drag her faster than a walk.

Kirsten held his hand and walked with him toward motor pool. *I hope I am.*

MATTHEW S. COX

Originally from South Amboy NJ, Matthew has been creating science fiction and fantasy worlds for most of his reasoning life. Since 1996, he has developed the "Divergent Fates" world, in which *Division Zero, Virtual Immortality, The Awakened Series, The Harmony Paradox, and the Daughter of Mars series* take place. Along with being an editor at Curiosity Quills press, he has worked in IT and technical support.

Matthew is an avid gamer, a recovered WoW addict, Gamemaster for two custom RPG systems, and a fan of anime, British humour, and intellectual science fiction that questions the nature of reality, life, and what happens after it.

He is also fond of cats.

Published Novels:

Divergent Fates setting: Virtual Immortality; The Division Zero Series (Division Zero, Lex De Mortuis, Thrall, and Guardian); The Awakened Series (Prophet of the Badlands, Archon's Queen, Grey Ronin, and Daughter of Ash); The Daughter of Mars Series (The Hand of Raziel).

The Roadhouse Chronicles Series (One More Run); The Tales of Widowswood Series (Emma and the Banderwigh, Emma and the Silk Thieves); Chiaroscuro - The Mouse and the Candle; The Far Side of Promise anthology

Young Adult novels: Caller 107, The Summer the World Ended, and Nine Candles of Deepest Black

Operation Chimera (Co-written with Tony Healey)

Short Stories: (Innocent Deception - Curiosity Quills Chronology), (Out of Sight - Curiosity Quills Darkscapes), (Stolen Orchid - Actuator Borderlands Anthology), (The Ruin of Man - Actuator Chaos Chronicles)

Links:

Website: http://www.matthewcoxbooks.com/wordpress/

Facebook: https://www.facebook.com/MatthewSCoxAuthor

Amazon: https://www.amazon.com/author/mscox

Pinterest: https://www.pinterest.com/matthewcox10420/

2

LAST FLIGHT

J.S. HUGHES

Daylight still dances across the peaks of the Rocky Mountains, but the desert below us is already dark blue and hazy. Serene, in fact. Nothing to suggest a war raging below. At least, not from this height. The bastards hide, and we search.

"Mockingbird, this is India base. We've got you seventy clicks south of the safety line."

The base radio crackles through my headset. I don't respond.

"What's the point of a scouting mission if you're not allowed to learn anything about your enemy?" I ask my co-pilot via the intercom.

"A fat paycheck," Carson says. An obvious answer to a rhetorical question. "One I'd rather survive to spend. Listen to your orders and turn this damn thing around."

Carson's a genius when it comes to instrumentation and the guts of this scout plane. He does a job few others can. So, he's got to work for the government or the corporations. Since he's in the plane with me, there's some part of him that still wants to do the right thing. If he was in it for the money... well, I'll just say the enemy pays better. I can't blame him for wanting to turn back though. He's got something to return to.

"Come on, Carson. You're worth more dead, I'm sure. Besides, no one *told* us to turn around."

He huffs, the breath crackles in the cockpit's intercom. "You know what they mean."

He's right. I smile, flip the switch, and respond to base. "Roger, turning her 'round."

As I tilt the wings toward our port side, something in the distance catches my eye. A glimmer at a ridge on the horizon—the one-in-a-million kind of thing sensors can miss. A sliver of a sunbeam hitting a windshield, bouncing into space at just the right angle to hit my eye as we fly through it. Before I can register it, the light twinkles out, but it's enough for us to pinpoint them. "Got a visual. Might be a convoy. You seein' it?"

We got lucky, and it's about time.

"Yup, lots of heat down there. If we see them, they see us." Carson says.

The voice from the radio snaps back. *"Might be an anti-air battery. Return to base. That's an order."*

"You got radar?" I ask Carson.

He groans.

I pause for a second, inching far enough to get that ridge in range of the underside radar—Carson might want to get home, but if he's too scared to do what he's paid for, he might not have a home to get back to. He'll do the job if I give him the chance.

"Roger." I ease the stick to the left, exposing the underbelly and an array of sensors to the southern front. "Well, you got a good view of that camp. At least scan that shit while we boogie out of here."

He clicks off his radio, cussing me. I smile.

"Don't worry, Carson, looks like we're cl—shit." Warning lights flash on the terrain radar. Holy shit! Seventeen signals—ground to air missiles. We must have seen something important. "India base, we're under fire. I'm readying chaff."

"Fukkingoddamitt, Raleigh!"

He doesn't need a radio. His voice penetrates the glass and metal. I want to smile; maybe later. For now, it's game face.

"India base, are you getting this data?" Carson says.

"Roger, Mockingbird. Keep it coming."

"Okay, Raleigh, keep us in the air for another twenty-six seconds... thirty-two... what the hell? It's lagging. Okay... stable. Forty seconds more."

"Roger!"

I dive to get close to the treetops, hoping to trip up the missiles' tracking before they reach effective chaff range. Check fuel gauge. Engage afterburners.

"Eighteen more. Almost."

My eyes bounce from one readout to another, always returning to the radar. Seventeen little dots begin to converge, three clusters... two... one.

"Three! Fuck, Rah, I can see 'em behind us." His voice is shrill.

I pull a hard turn, eight Gs. My vision greys out on the edges.

Carson groans. "Done!"

"Releasing chaff." I ready the stick—this is going to be rough.

"*Data transfer confir—*"

KraaaThoom!

The instruments blink out. At least one missile didn't get confused by the chaff. Black smoke wraps around the wings and cockpit. When the instruments kick back on, the horizon is spinning. I've done this a million times—in a simulator. It's mostly the same, except we're a brick in the sky, beholden to the laws of physics.

Carson's yelling, but his voice is miles away, a high-pitched squeal.

"Hold tight. Gonna try something!"

Surfaces on the port wing don't respond.

"Okay, not that."

I try the starboard flaps out of desperation—it works, the horizon stabilizes, but the hydraulics can't hold the pressure—the aileron snaps off. Now we're in a flat spin, and I'm out of working levers.

My vision greys out again. The static haze creeps closer to my center of vision. The sounds of air rushing over us fade into a metallic ringing. I can't speak, and I can't hear Carson. He can't take these kind of Gs, probably out cold.

We have one engine working. I punch the throttle, hoping to turn this spin into an S-glide. It's working, sort of. We're flattening out, but rolling. The G forces shoot over eleven.

Nothing left now but to pray the auto ejection seats survived the blast.

I COME TO, STARING DOWN FROM A REDWOOD ON THE SIDE OF A mountain. It's hard to tell how far we drifted or in which direction. The sun's below the mountain ridge, but the clouds still reflect enough light to see. I recognize the sprawling desert at the base of this mountain as the one we'd been sailing over minutes before. A dozen klicks off, there's a plume of smoke. So much for the fastest ship in the fleet.

The ground is too far for me to drop and not break a leg or two, but that smoke's a homing beacon. The parachute might be camo—but not too many trees have a five-hundred-square-foot sheet draped over them.

Taking advantage of the height, I yank the cords to spin a little and scan for a matching chute. Carson's more exposed. His chute is lying in a white stretch of stones in a flat spot a few hundred yards down the mountainside. And he's still in the ejection seat, not moving.

Three black specks appear on the eastern horizon, heading right this way. I've got to move fast.

Using the knife from my front pocket, I saw at the chute cords.

The first snaps and the seat swings. To land on the uphill slope, I need enough momentum before I cut the rest of the cords. It might not be much difference—maybe five feet—but that might be the difference between a broken leg and inevitable capture, or running out of here free and clear.

I pump my legs back and forth like a kid on a swing set, the hillside approaches, and the knife slices through the nylon.

What's about to happen isn't something I care to think about.

Once, I was flirting with this girl in a bar back home. Daisy dukes, white tee shirt cut off at the midriff. Damn, she was hot. Never looked at me really, but smiled as she peeked through the side of her glasses when she took a sip of her drink. She must have liked the uniform—a lot of girls do. Right when I thought I was going home with her...

Crunch.

Hitting the ground from twenty feet up feels a lot like twenty jealous boyfriends sucker punching you everywhere at once.

Acutely aware of every organ in my body, I wonder if I'm paralyzed or even alive, but my toes crinkle in my boots. First my legs lift. Feet are on the ground, and knees in the air. After twisting the harness, I'm free.

Tall trees spotting the mountainside provide the illusion of cover. From overhead, this spot is as exposed as the desert below. I need to get unseen, but staying alive is the first priority. After pulling the survival gear from the underside of the seat, I run to Carson.

"Buddy," I say. "Are you all right?"

He groans. Blood covers his suit. A mangled shard of metal protrudes from his gut. It's two inches wide, flat with a slight twist where the metal cleaved from the chassis in the explosion, and there's no way to know how deep it goes. Globs of blood flow out in dark, thick pulses.

Finally, he coughs, and blood trails down his cheek. "Tell Nadine... I'm sorry."

If I leave the shrapnel in, the enemy could save him. Best case, he'll wind up a P.O.W. but alive. Then again, he knows things. He knows codes and locations. Even if he didn't, they'd torture him anyway, just in case.

He's a risk if they catch him, and he's a liability if I try to take him with me. My heart and my options let my brain and my training take over.

"I will, Carson. I promise. I am too."

I close my hand around the metal protruding from Carson's stomach. It's warm. Metal should never be warm. It should be cold and rigid, but it's not. It's slick from blood, so I hold tight and pull. It slides out with no resistance and falls away into the grass. I wipe the blood from my hands. Carson's face goes pale.

I should have waited. Maybe a minute longer. He could have said something else. Maybe some line that means the world to his nascent widow. What solace is *I'm sorry* anyway? I'll let her know he died a hero—I hope that's true.

I kneel by his side for a few more seconds before I push his eyelids down and snatch the dog tags from his neck.

They're heavy. Not from the aluminum wafers, nor the rubber rings around them, keeping them from jingling in my hand. The chain doesn't provide any heft. I know dog tags, and these are too heavy. There's still a smear of blood on them. Maybe that's why.

His dog tags are stamped *CATHOLIC*. Should I pray? To whom? The Father, the Son, or the Holy Spirit? I was never good with religion.

Something howls deep in the woods—like a wolf, but heavier. I look back at the thudding enemy machines gaining more of the sky with each second. Impending capture reignites my priorities. I stuff Carson's dog tags in my pocket—all I can do now is get these to Nadine, and that means keeping myself alive.

Carson's survival pack is lodged in the seat—damaged from the crash. No time to pry it out, so I slash the sides and take what falls out. My best chance is to keep moving, so I head into the thicker woods to the north.

I glance back one more time at Carson.

I'm sorry.

I WAKE UP CURLED INSIDE A HOLLOWED LOG. I'VE LOST COUNT OF THE days. The water in the emergency canteen is long gone, and I haven't found another source, only dried out creek beds. I know this can't go on for much longer. A few days of no water is more than anyone can take. I shouldn't be alive.

The socks I left hanging to catch the morning dew are as bone dry as the air. It hasn't rained here for weeks—or months, it seems. Not even sure where here is. Oregon, maybe? Tall trees line the mountain ridge and white sands spread out to the horizon below me.

After collecting what little I have, I put my shoes on and head north.

The trees and rocks wind a labyrinth along the mountainside. No matter how many steps I take, the scene never changes. Fallen tree trunks litter the slopes, most too brittle or dry to serve as anything but a bench to rest on while I nibble on the flavorless crackers I found hidden in the survival pack—lucky, I thought I had run out. At night, the wind is biting, but with the ground as dry as it is, starting a fire might kill everything for miles. My skin is numb at this point anyway. I don't feel the cold so much.

The sun rises over the desert plain below. All it shines on is a wasteland, more rocks and a smattering of scrub bushes. The light doesn't bring any warmth with it, but it's welcome anyway. The forest responds more to the light than I can. A bird hops from a tree and soars away, mocking me with a caw. Even the trees are livelier in the daylight. Their constant susurrus drones on to fill in the void.

I would talk to myself, but I've got nothing to say. My thoughts dwell on Carson. He would have never let me live it down, crashing a plane, getting him killed. He'd have ragged me about it forever. His voice in the back of my mind is a depressing companion, but better than the loneliness of the endless woods. I should have let them take him. Sure, he might have lost us the war, but he'd be alive. When I get bored, I talk to his dog tags. The blood remains bright red, highlighting the 'a' and 'r' in his name. It weighs me down, but also keeps me moving. The thought of Nadine's face as she takes those metal chips terrifies me, but might be the only thing keeping me moving. I owe it to him.

Not far ahead, a motor thumps. It's the first sign of civilization I've run into since after the crash. But is it the enemy? Surely they would have given up searching for me by now. Maybe it's a patrol. It's not as if there's any fence or sign reading, "Bad guys here! Inquire within."

My feet take me toward the sound, as if they know better than I do.

It's not the enemy—at least not the one I expected—but they don't look friendly. Without knowing, I choose safety and crouch behind a tree amid the scrub.

Six men occupy a vehicle resembling a Jeep, but someone welded metal plates to the side, painted it red and blue, and attached something the size of a fifty-cal machine gun to the roll bar. Two men are hanging off the sides. They're all dressed in worn clothes and armed with rifles, some of which look handmade. I've never seen any of this before. It's like a post-apocalyptic movie—maybe I made it to California.

As the Jeep comes to a stop, a tall man with an eye patch and a few missing teeth yells, "Cammawn little scrap! We knows you out 'ere. We don't wan' hurt ya."

The wink at his companions makes me think he's lying. I'm glad they aren't looking in my direction, but I feel sorry for whatever they're hunting.

There are a lot of them, but the Jeep might have a radio. If I can get them away, I might be able to call in a rescue.

I grab a fist-sized rock and hurl it into the woods in the direction they're facing.

"Ahhh, ya ain't gon hide fer too long."

Four of them follow my ruse. They leave the Jeep running.

I ready my pistol at the fat man behind the gun mounted atop the vehicle—hell, the idiot has a bull's eye painted on his face. He's asking to get shot.

I may not have been trained for this, but survival means doing what you have to and improvising. Once I take Bull's Eye down, the guy wearing all the football pads will take a second to react, one more shot and he'll be out of commission. I'll drive off before these rednecks know what happened.

As I wait for the others to get far enough away, I watch the remaining two. The Jeep guard, Mr. Quarterback, looks through a pair of binoculars, then slaps the gunner on the leg. "Out dere! Skeer him out the woods."

In response, Bull's Eye swivels the gun around and starts firing into the trees south of me. The weapon makes quick work of trees along the edge of the road. The ancient limbs of a three hundred foot redwood crash into the roadway, snapping into pieces. I can't tell if he hit what he was aiming at, but the debris blocks the passage to the South.

I take aim at the gunner.

"Dere he goes! Get 'im." QB squeals and jumps in place, and this time I see what he's shouting about.

A boy is crouched behind one of the felled trunks. He can't be more than twelve. His hair is long and wild, and his face is dirty. Are they hunting a kid? I knew this place was rough, but this is insane.

The gunner is going to fire, and I doubt trees are going to stop those rounds, so I take a shot at him before he gets the chance.

The crack of my weapon echoes between the mountain and a large hill on the other side of the Jeep. The big man slumps as he pulls the trigger. The tip of his weapon swivels toward Mr. Quarterback—and me.

I fire at QB as I run toward the Jeep.

He's too preoccupied avoiding friendly fire to notice me. He goes down with two shots to the back. Tougher than I expected.

I climb into the Jeep and try to dislodge the heavy man from the gun, but he doesn't budge. He's an immovable heap of flesh, rank and slippery. For my effort, I only help him along as his heft pivots the machine gun to the opposite wood line. Not the plan, but it'll work.

The kid flees down the hill. A mistake. These barbarians can pick him off from the ridge. I need to get to him before they do, but after I slide down into the driver's seat and slam on the gas, nothing happens. The damn car won't go. I fiddle with the gear shift, but nothing.

This gun won't keep going forever, and even if it could, those men in the woods can walk around the line of fire. I'm going to have to run for the kid. I might technically be a paid killer, but I draw a line at hunting kids in the woods, and these guys are on the wrong side of it.

I run down the hill, screaming for this kid to stop, but it makes him run faster. He must think I'm one of them. Hurdling tree trunks, I follow, gaining on him, but he doesn't give up.

I'm almost in arm's length, and he turns around. His eyes are as wide as the setting moon on the horizon—and glowing white.

"Kyreeeeeeeee!" The kid squeals like nothing I've ever heard.

I stumble. "What the shit?"

He doesn't answer, but stops behind a tree.

"Let me help you. Those guys are going to kill you. I have a weapon."

The glow in his eyes fades. He looks confused. "You aren't... I thought."

I scramble over debris, take cover behind a squat tree trunk, and turn to him. "No, I'm not with them. I'm a soldier, a pilot. I crashed, and I just need to get to a radio, and... water." I pat my throat. "You help me, and I'll help you."

He nods and motions for me to follow.

THE KID NAVIGATES THE SPARSE WOODS LIKE IT'S HIS PERSONAL JUNGLE gym. He skips from tree to tree, slinging himself into turns by holding on to the trunks of smaller ones, letting go when he likes the new trajectory. He bounds over rocks formations without looking down or studying it for hand holds. He jumps up like a goat and springs to the next one, breaking only to look back when I lag behind.

Keeping up with this little ball of energy takes all of mine.

Numbness from days in the elements allows me to follow along for hours as we press deeper into the thick trees at the base of a much taller mountain. As I struggle to lift myself over the boulder he slid down from, the sound of water energizes me. I top the rock to see a crystal-clear stream.

I fall into the water and drink without a thought of the filth, contaminants, or microbes I'm gulping along the way.

The boy laughs at my splashing.

After getting my fill, I stand on my knees. "What's your name, kid?"

"Jayan," he says.

Until now, his clothes had been some beige blur I could track and follow. Now I see them as they are—rags and leather shaped into a tunic, with a fur-covered loin cloth pinning the fabric and a four-inch knife to his hips. He fills a leather canteen, which had been strapped over his shoulder, and drinks from a cupped hand. He is at least ten years old, having not yet hit puberty, but not childlike. As he stands, the effort reveals muscle and sinew along his hairless legs, too toned and wiry for his age. The darkness of his skin matches his light, dirty hair, making it hard to know where his face ends and the matted mop on his head begins. The dirt and tan skin give him the illusion of a flat and featureless face, but those eyes shine with years of experience. This child owns the strength of a soldier, or more accurately, a warrior.

I had known things were bad since the war started, but how could kids this young be living on their own? Unlike Carson, I really had joined the military for the paycheck, so maybe I was channeling my dead co-pilot, but I needed to help this kid. He saved me, so I'd be returning the favor, and I had a feeling he knew the territory.

"Who were the men chasing you?"

"Rawders." His expression remains fixed, as if he's appraising me. "Dey wanna sell me, maybe eat me—didn't ask."

I stand up fully and approach him.

He reacts by stepping backward and glaring. His hand hovers at the knife on his waist.

I laugh. "I don't want to eat you."

He's not reassured.

"How about this? I want to give you something. Look." I pull Carson's dog tags from my pocket. "These belonged to my friend. He died, and I'm taking them back to his wife. Will you help me with that?"

He narrows his eyes. "I must get back. My village needs me."

"Then take me with you. It's one step closer to me getting home too. I can help."

I let the tags drop while I hold the chain, and his hand relaxes, falling away from the knife.

"Take 'em. If you have them, then you're my mission. I get you back to wherever you're from, and you can give 'em back."

His lips, white from being pulled too tight, loosen and the color flows back into them. He inches forward with one leg and snatches the dog tags from my hand. We both step back as if each of us had expected the other to pounce.

He examines the metal chips with suspicion, like they are going to fly away. He cuts his eyes toward me, then the tags.

"You can wear them around your neck." I mime draping the chain around my neck.

"Kay." He put the tags on. "Swear you'll help."

I placed my hand over my heart. "And hope to die."

He grimaces. "Kay, den we need to run. Rawder's gon be back." He wades across the stream.

"I don't know; I shot two of them. Do you think they'll stay on you after that?" A Jeep engine starts again. "Guess so."

I follow again, into the woods.

WE DASH PAST TREES AT THE CHILD'S ENERGETIC PACE UNTIL THE JEEP engine no longer echoes behind our footsteps.

"Can we slow down?"

He shakes his head, and points toward the moon.

It hangs bright, ascending into the dark sky with no clouds to conceal it or the stars behind it. I guess he means we keep going while there's enough light out. Since he is the best and only guide I'd found, I keep at it.

For most of the day, the trek has been downhill, but as the shadows fall over the mountains, the grade flattens and suggests it might begin to climb. I welcome the change of pace, but I can't be happy for the uphill battle. I'm tired, but feel compelled to follow.

Jayan doesn't say a word for another hour. As we approach a hill, he points. "There, the cave-ins, many cave-ins. We can sleep in the cave-ins."

"Good, I'm exhausted." I don't see any caves, all I see is darkness and the silhouette of tall trees on an indigo sky. I'm lucky his tanned hides are bright enough that he stands out from the dirt. Otherwise, I would have been lost as soon as the sun set.

It doesn't take long for him to scurry up the hill, and I see what he's been so excited about: a row of cabins.

"Cabins," I say. "They are cabins, not cave-ins."

In disgust, he points at a sign carved into the building. "Cay-bins. Can't you read?"

I chuckle and push open a door to be greeted with a moldy, musty odor. "Well, I guess it's better than nothing."

The amenities aren't much different than the woods. Glass is missing from the windows, and there isn't a clear divide between the plants growing outside and the ones which have taken root along the dirt floor. At least, I think it's a dirt floor. This place is so long forgotten, it could be rotten wood or the dirt blown in through the lack of windows.

Inside, the lone door opens into a room with a pair of collapsed bunk beds. A skeleton of rusted springs are all that remain of the mattress's carcass.

"No better in here," I say.

As I walk in to the main room again, Jayan has a pile of sticks gathered in the floor and is rubbing another back and forth between the palms of his hands.

"Wow, you're quite the boy scout aren't you?" I check my pockets for the book of matches from the emergency kit I pulled from my ejection seat, but they are all gone. I throw the useless cardboard wrapping down.

I expect him to take the paper for tinder, but Jayan remains focused on his project. He spins the little stick, his hands sliding down to the bottom. He doesn't give up, each time reaching back to the top and spinning it again. As I'm about to ask him if he needs help, a tendril of smoke rises from the plank at his feet. He cradles his little ember, pulls in the dry leaves, and catches one leaf aflame. The fire wraps around the pile of twigs, and soon we have a modest fire burning.

"How long have you been out here?" I ask once he's finished encircling his fire with rocks and rusted shards of the bed frame from the other room.

"Two full moons since I set out from my village."

"Why'd you leave?"

"Before I can return as a shaman, I had to complete the vision quest."

"You're shitting me? People still do that?"

His eyes narrow and his tiny nostrils flare. The light and shadow bounce over his face, giving his already serious look more gravity than a ten-year-old ought to conjure.

"No... sorry. That's cool. I don't mean to belittle your beliefs. I didn't realize there were still natives out here. I figured they'd been driven out already."

"I'm the shaman for my village." His chest heaves and his chin juts up to me, revealing his pride. "Or I will be when I make it home with this."

He lays his knife before the fire, blade shimmering. "It was lost. My vision led me to it."

I reach down and grab the knife. Jayan looks worried as I inspect it. A bone handle bound by leather holds the blade in place. It's heavy, the metal is smooth but uneven—hand made. I place it back where it came from.

"Well, I'll help you get home little shaman Jayan. I have to thank you for bringing me to that stream."

He tucks the knife back into his belt and looks away, so I stare through the hole in the wall at wispy grey clouds passing between me and the moon. For the first time since the crash, I feel like I might get a good night's sleep.

MY DREAMS ARE FORGOTTEN WITHIN MOMENTS OF WAKING. THE ground is cold. It's still dark.

Jayan, nestled in a bundle of leaves, is placid and dreaming. His youth apparent in the still state, I observe for a moment. The war must have slid these people back centuries if a child his age can roam the wilds on some religious quest.

A shaman? He's too old to believe in that mumbo-jumbo—I assume no one taught him anything else. He should be playing video games or baseball. The war alone can't be to blame for this. The government should have stepped in to protect these people. Maybe they tried and some fast talking corporate goon convinced them they were being oppressed. Fear the government? Pft, fear the man who defiles the water, then has the gall to charge you for a bottle of it.

Jayan shifts in his sleep and Carson's dog tags slip onto the ground. I tuck them back into a pocket on the boy's furs. They seem more real to me than the rest of the world, more solid and believable than the war zone or the cabins. Their weight binds me to earth, and keeps my thoughts from dissipating. They attach my feet to the ground, and keep them stepping. Even if I don't hold them, those metal wafers and this boy anchor my mind in the moment. Tiring of introspection, I lift myself from the decrepit floors and take a walk to see the sun crest on the horizon.

I pace circles, not venturing far enough to let the cabin slip from my sight. A flat stone atop a ridge becomes my vantage point for nature's daily spectacle.

At first, the dawn is suspicious in its silence. Birdsongs smatter it like speckles of paint on clear glass. The sky opens in shells of blue, pink and gold, pulsing to life as the clouds rush to greet the sun. Beams of light reach up from the horizon gabbing at the darkness and pulling the sun closer to breaching the night. I crave the day's warmth, but hazy morning light is cold still, and I sigh.

A clamoring ruckus below me breaks the serenity. Wood cracks, a boy screams and is quickly muffled. A large, leather clad man drags Jayan from the Cabin.

I know the kidnapper, the man with the bull's-eye tattoo. It can't be him! I shot him in the face. I must have missed before, but I can't see how —I saw him slump over.

It doesn't matter for now. I stumble down the ridge and follow them while firing shots, but none connect. Bull's-Eye doesn't react to the chase. He bounds through the trees, cackling like a buffoon.

"Jayan!" I yell out of desperation.

My feet become heavy, and breath won't come. No matter how hard I try, I can't press on. Soon they're out of sight. Something is wrong with me —I was rested, I should have been able to keep going, but everything feels like an eight G turn. My vision blurs, and all the sounds around me, even my own pleas for the man to stop, fall away like echoes in a ravine.

I'm filled with the desire to return to the campsite. I don't want to—I want with all my will to continue this pursuit, but I don't. I crawl back until I see Carson's dog tags on the ground along with Jayan's knife. He must have dropped them when he was taken. I grab them both—two promises to keep.

Maybe the fat man poisoned me or something. I check, but there's no sign of it. My sight and hearing return, and I'm re-energized. It makes no sense—how could I have failed so completely right when he needed me.

I try not to focus on what went wrong, but on what to do next. A massive man clomping through the woods can't be hard to follow.

THE LARGE MAN'S FOOTPRINTS ENDED WHERE JEEP TRACKS BEGAN, AND I follow those all day. The night is at its darkest when I reach a ridge overlooking a ramshackle campsite. The marauder base is set between a cluster of rocks and a wall of tree limbs. Both barriers seem placed intentionally for protection. A black and smoldering fire sits at the center of six pieced-together leather tents. It provides some light, but the moon provides more. And at the far side, the marauder's jeep blocks the single ground path into the area.

Two Y-shaped sticks are set at opposite sides of the fire—the supports of a spit.

There are no signs of Jayan or any signs they have eaten him. Strangely, I hope they wanted to sell him instead.

I climb down the ridge a few hundred feet away to avoid being seen. The climb is slow, enough that the sun is peeking over the horizon when I reach the bottom and sneak back toward the Jeep. It may block the entrance, but it doesn't stop me from crawling through. Without a guard at the entrance or anyone patrolling the camp, I sneak in without notice.

Marauding cannibals don't seem like morning people, but I still try to keep as quiet as I can, both to avoid detection, and to listen for any cries Jayan might be making—not that I could hear him over the loud snoring from the tent.

As I peel back the makeshift leather door, a stench of layered human filth, decay and carrion greets me. I cover my mouth and scan what's inside.

Skulls of different animals, including a human's, hang from a string draped across the interior. Mud and blood encrusted knives and guns lay about without any attempt at order. A set of football pads lies to the right of the entrance, and there's a living, breathing body half-covered beneath a hoard of furs. That's the second man I thought I killed back from the grave. He's lying on his stomach, so I can see where I shot him—or where I thought I shot him. Two bruises, that's it—large bruises, but no open wounds. What the hell is going on?

I check my gun. The magazine is full. I fired enough shots at Bull's Eye to empty it. I don't remember reloading, or even having another clip. Maybe my mind is playing tricks on me. I could be hallucinating from something. Did I dream it all? I couldn't have. I look at Jayan's knife in my left hand. No, I was there. I helped him, and he saved me by leading me to the stream. I know I shot them. They must be using some kind of advanced technology—or maybe these are corporate mutants I keep hearing rumors about. Whatever they are, I know they have the boy and I have promises to keep.

Quarterback groans and rolls over.

I step over him and drop to my knees, pressing the knife against his throat.

"Scream, and I end you."

His eyes open wide, and he squeals with both the volume and quality of a wild boar—my hand does little to muffle him. His windpipe buckles as I pull the knife blade across his neck. His noises falter.

Shit!

I cut open the back of the tent, crawling out and scurrying into the pile of limbs and leaves for cover.

In seconds, the camp is alive. Two marauders with axes begin to patrol the perimeter of the camp when the other three investigate my victim.

"E's dead, boss. Someone cut 'is throat!" Bull's Eye reports to the large man with the most tattoos and the largest weapon—a modified sledge hammer with welded-on spikes, bound in razor wire.

"Find the murderin' weasel!" The boss roars, revealing a mouth full of black, menacing, metal teeth.

I weave through the trees at the back of the camp, navigating toward the largest tent. They don't see me in the brush, so I wait until I have an opportunity to scurry into the large tent.

Amid the weapons, carcasses, and a headless plastic doll, I find Jayan with cloth stuffed in his mouth. His hands and feet are bound to the remnant of a narrow tree trunk which serves as the main support for the tent. His leg is bleeding.

I cut his bindings, and he looks at me with worry.

I whisper. "I took one out, but I can't take them all. Can you run?"

He nods and reaches for the knife in my belt, and I pass it back to its rightful owner.

I peer across the campsite, looking for an opening to run, but there's not a chance. If I shoot any of them, I risk giving our position away. For now, concealment is all that's sparing us. Even if my aim was dead-on, I don't know if bullets will keep them down for long enough to get away. I feel the world closing in on me like I'm in a flat spin. I'm trapped. I have no control. There's nothing to do but sit and wait. The crash replays in my mind in a split second. Finally, the obvious solution kicks me in my big dumb brain. I point at the jeep keys dangling from the tusk of a half rotten boar's head.

"Grab those."

He snatches them and grins.

"Run for it. I'll cover you." Still kneeling, I throw open the front flap of the tent and raise my weapon.

Jayan slips between my legs and dashes across the camp, but he's slowed by the leg wound.

Bull's Eye points and grunts in our direction, and Bossman raises his weapon. I fire a round as soon as the weight is at the apex of his swing. The weapon slips as he falls backwards.

Bull's Eye screams. "The tent! Someone's in da tent."

An ax crashes through the boar's head, splitting it in twain. The blade embeds itself into dirt floor inches from my foot. I lunge away from it and through the wall of the tent, landing with furs over me.

The ax wielder pulls his weapon out of the ground, taking the tent, including my cover, with it. Exposed, I scramble to my feet and follow Jayan.

He slashes at Bull's Eye. They are in close combat, so to not risk hitting the boy, I hold my fire.

"Get clear!" I shout to Jayan. "I can take him out. Just run."

Before that can happen, a shirtless axeman bears down on me. Pivot and fire. I hit him center mass, but see no sign of injury. He falls, and a dark ring grows away from the spot in the chest where I hit him—no other wound. His chest heaves. I have no time to think any more about this now. I turn again to Bull's Eye as Jayan leaps back using the y-shaped posts of the fire pit for cover.

Bull's Eye staggers back, falling after three shots.

I catch up to Jayan, urging him forward with my hand in his back.

As he starts the Jeep, I fire twice more—one for each standing Marauder.

Jayan struggles with the Keys.

"Do you know how to start it?"

He grunts.

"Let me do it."

His eyes widen and his mouth opens as if I had cursed his mother. He's not staring at me—through me.

I turn to see Bossman's metallic grin and a spiked hammer in a trajectory to land on my face.

"Kyreeeee..."

Bossman staggers, dropping the mace. His pupils dilate, and blood trickles from his nose, eyes, and ears. He falls to his knees, and topples face first into the dirt.

"... eeee." Jayan's arm slumps over the steering wheel.

"Holy shit, kid. What is that?" I ask.

"Pain," he says. "Let's go."

I try to push him into the passenger's seat to drive, but he slaps my hand from the wheel.

"No you can't. Let me do it."

"Fine, but don't blame me if someone pulls us over."

He pushes the seat back so he can stand and operate the pedals—a task he accomplishes with surprising skill for a feral child.

Jayan navigates down the mountain and into the desert where we hit something resembling a road. The terrain is flat, but rough. To either side of us is white rock and desert fauna, plants wily enough to survive. A mountain rises from the northern horizon and by the time the sun reaches is apogee, fear subsides enough I can stop looking back for mutants chasing us.

Before arriving at the base of the mountain, we pass landmarks I find more familiar. The occasional utility pole—stripped of cables but still standing. Mangled steel spikes might have belonged to road signs. No doubt marauders took those to make weapons or armor. Nearly flattened buildings, much in the same condition as the cabins we slept in the night before, but less upright. The road even resembles blacktop here, patches of asphalt and stone cobbled into an almost-smooth ride.

This place is desolate and abandoned, but there aren't any signs of war here. I expected to see smoldering tanks or bodies propped against buildings. Desolate, but serene. Still, I sense malevolence here. I'm happy when the trees once again outnumber remnants of what man put into the land.

A few miles in, Jayan pulls the Jeep over.

"I need water." He points into the trees to the right side of the road and climbs down.

I follow. "So, how much longer do we have?"

Jayan fills a water skin from the stream. "Not long. My village is at the top of the mountain."

"Are your people friendly to the corporations?"

He stares at me like I'm speaking Japanese.

"Am I safe there?" I point to the U.S. Air Force emblems on my uniform. "They're not going to shoot me?"

"They won't hurt you." He drinks from the waterskin and closes the cap.

"Well, I guess I trust you. Do they have electricity? Phones?"

Again, I get a blank stare before he heads back to the Jeep.

"I need to call my people. Remember this?" I pull out the dog tags. "I need to get these back to someone."

He shakes his head. I sigh.

"We drive again. Come on."

As we start driving again, I notice we're starting to climb. It feels good, like some kind of release.

"Why is your village in a mountain? Why not by the water?"

He laughs at me. "We have water. The mountain is safer, quieter. The madness doesn't reach us there."

"And neither side knows you're up there, huh? Well, I guess I owe it to you to keep your secret. But I have to say, you should move somewhere safer. It's dangerous here. There are all kinds of bad things out there worse than the marauders."

He nods.

"You sure you don't want me to drive for you?"

He laughs at me again. "Yes, very sure."

"Well if there is anything I can do, just ask."

The blacktop wears away, and Jayan makes a sharp turn up a hill, off what I presume to be road. This continues for half an hour before the trees become sparse.

Finally, we come to a long wooden wall. Two towers flank a twenty-foot door.

Jayan shifts the car into park and yells, "I have returned!! Jayan has returned!"

I spot movement in the towers, and the door swings open.

Hundreds of people flow out of huts alongside a winding dirt road as we enter this village—as I see more of it, I correct myself. This is a city, somehow hidden in the mountainside from corporations and the government alike. I see no emblems from either side. It's like their own private Switzerland.

We round a corner and I understand why Jayan laughed at my suggestion of moving toward the water.

An enormous lake spreads miles across at the top of the mountain. At once, I know where I am. Crater Lake—the remains of a ten-thousand-year-old volcano. I'd seen it as a child, and from the sky. But as to how a city could spring up in the middle of a war, and no one notice, I can wager no guess.

The Jeep stops in the middle of the street. Too many people surround us for it to matter now. Villagers grab Jayan, carrying him on their shoulders. They chant his name and cheer. The crowd drifts along around him, leaving me alone in the back.

"Umm, you're welcome?"

I walk with them, trying to get the attention of a man and woman traveling together. They're bickering about whether they'll be able to see the coronation. One of them stares at me for a second, but they don't respond.

"No, that's okay. Don't need anything. Just the guy who saved your savior, that's all."

Most of the population is on the street, and no one gives a damn I'm here. I follow along, waiting for everything to die down so someone will help me or I can catch up to Jayan.

At the crater's rim, I stare across to the smaller island in the center of the lake. I can spot my little friend across the way, but the horde is blocking the bridge, so I scale down to the water's edge, and sit.

The crowd doesn't dissipate until nightfall—after a huge celebration. I take what food I can, and mingle among the party-goers. All the while, looking for someone important, or anyone at all who will talk to me.

Finally, someone approaches as I attempt to cross the bridge and find Jayan, an old man with wispy white hair wearing furs and skins carrying twisted staff.

"You did them a great service, and they don't even acknowledge you are here, right?" His yellow teeth click together from his body shaking as he smiles.

"Pretty much. What is going on here?"

"It's not their fault. So few can see the truth. This is why it is so important that Jayan has returned. He is the protector. He is the shaman now." He motions for me to step on the rope bridge.

I follow, assuming the child is in the fancy building at the other end. "All I want is a phone or a radio. Some way to get in touch with my people."

"My name is Hoyada. I think I can help you. Let's find Jayan and get you what you need."

Hoyada sidesteps two guards at the entrance of the building. They pay neither him nor me any mind. A fire is burning in the center of the circular room. Wolf, bear, and mountain lion pelts line the inside walls along with tapestries and ornamental statues. The young boy sits on a large chair covered in pelts and cloth. Two men are guarding him.

I chuckle as we approach. "Are you some kind of prince? Why didn't you say so?"

"Please leave me," Jayan says. Two men standing at the side entrances step out.

I start to turn, but Hoyada grabs my hand. "Not you."

Jayan runs to the old man, wrapping his arms around him. "Gran'pa!"

Hoyada smiles and strokes the furs on the boy's shoulders. "We must help him, Jayan. If all you say is true, we owe him that."

The boy nods. "Come. It's time to show you."

We walk back out the way we came, and the guards attempt to follow when Jayan leaves, but he orders them to stay.

"We go alone." He says to me as we cross the bridge. "You have done much for our village, and I owe you my life. I wish I didn't have to repay you this way."

"He'll understand." Hoyada puts his hand on Jayan's shoulder. "Soldier, when I was young, my grandmother was the Shaman of this village, and she would tell stories of things her grandmother had seen and of what those who came before her had seen.

"Every shaman of this village must take a spirit quest. It is on that quest he or she learns what they will face, to understand what it is that surrounds us, and why we have to protect this sacred place. On my great, great, grandmother's spirit quest, she encountered a particularly forlorn entity. A soldier like you, dying of thirst. Though his uniform was that of many years past, he still held fast to his mission. She tried to help him, tried to lead him to water, but when she turned to assist him over the rocks, he vanished. She was far too late. The man had been dead for centuries. Many had seen him before, and many since."

"What does this have to do with me?"

"Unnumbered souls are lost in the Badlands, most are trapped, but some roam free, searching for things which drove them in life."

As we reach the top of the ridge, a sea of lights unfolds along the horizon. In the south, they merge into single strip of light that fades into nothing behind the curve of the earth and the same to the north.

"For hundreds of years, you've been trying to return those things you gave me," Jayan says.

"Your war is over, Soldier," Hoyada adds.

"No, I'm alive. I've only been out..." I check my gun. The magazine is still full. "... for days."

I reach for Jayan, but my hands pass through him. The Jeep, I couldn't make it move, and the marauder boss's hammer, no way I could have dodged it. "What is happening? This isn't real. I'm not... dead."

Jayan steps back and lowers his head.

Hoyada grabs my wrist. "Trust me; I know what I'm talking about."

Jayan speaks in a weak voice, "I became Shaman when grandfather passed, but..."

"He shouldn't have been thrust into this so young, but I couldn't hold on and his mother never had the gift." Jayan's grandfather looks into my eyes; his skin is pale, and he moves without disturbing the ground beneath him.

"I don't remember—"

"Because it's hard to accept. It's easier to believe the lie."

"I took Jayan's knife when the man kidnapped him. How could I do that if I'm a ghost?"

Hoyada smiles and reaches for the boy's weapon. "All things have two sides. A physical and a spiritual, but for most things, the spiritual side is weak. But with knowledge of the spirits, I made this weapon's two sides strong enough to defend myself against the spirits. It's the weapon of a shaman. It can hurt you, but it also means you can wield it. I lost it years ago, and Jayan saw it in a dream. That became his quest."

Recent memories replay with a new truth. My hand passed though the gear shift of the jeep when I first encountered the marauders. A haze lifts, and I can see. I couldn't move Bull's Eye for the same reason. Jayan laughed as I feigned splashing in the creek. I felt the cold water in my throat, but it was my mind. A deep denial escapes my mind. The gun, it never fired. There is no gun.

"I shot those men. I mean, I didn't kill them, but something happened when I shot them."

Jayan nods. "You have great strength. Old spirits have power. You hurt them because you believed."

The grandfather beams with pride at the boy.

"Was I part of your quest?"

The old man grins. "I suppose, in a way. Jayan was lucky to have crossed your path. Something out there must have been looking out for both of you."

I fall to my knees. At least I think they are my knees. The dirt isn't displaced by them at all. "This isn't helping me! You said you were going to help me."

"You did to your emblems what grandfather did to the knife," Jayan says. "I felt it when you handed them to me. You are bound to them."

"Most souls bind themselves to their bodies, trying to hold on, but you chose something else," Hoyada says.

"My promise... my mission."

"They are more real to you, aren't they?" The old man stares at the metal tags in my hands. "Now it's time to finish it. Return them to their rightful owner."

"How?"

"Look closely, there is a light on the horizon separate from the city. Focus and let it take you," Hoyada says.

I stare into the distance. I think I am crying, but my tears don't moisten the earth.

Jayan's face fades as he says, "Thank you."

I feel my heart pounding, but nothing is there. The light brightens, and I see a silhouette.

"Carson? Please, forgive me. I thought it was the right thing."

"Of course." The voice echoes around me. "I think it's been long enough."

Another figure approaches his, feminine. Two more follow her—I don't recognize them, but I never met his children, yet I know that's who they are. An uncountable mass fills in behind. My mother and father to the left.

I reach into my pockets for the dog tags.

I extend my arm and let them dangle.

They are as light as air.

J.S. HUGHES

J.S. Hughes is a professional nerd (from back before it was cool). From designing board games, firing lasers into vacuum chambers, or working as a Space Camp Counselor, if it's geeky and fun, he is on top of it. He received a Ph.D. in Applied Mathematics in 2010. As a mathematician, he's researched scary sounding subjects like numerical bifurcation analysis and simulations of metamaterial cloaking.

When he's not teaching computers to do math he enjoys music, woodworking, playing video games, (he met his wife in Sethikk Halls) and of course writing. Storytelling has been a constant in his life from a young age. On his bookshelf, you'll find hard science fiction, high fantasy, and paranormal horror.

He almost certainly believes in bigfoot.

Connect with Jeremy on twitter @JeremySHughes

Visit him on Facebook: https://www.facebook.com/J-S-Hughes-237730336271609/

3

SNAKE OIL: A TALE OF THE BADLANDS

J.P. SLOAN

John Bell ducked under one of the jute hammocks swinging below Jericho's northern rampart as a dusty wind rolled off the Rockies. He peered up at the corrugated aluminum canopy jutting into the hazy autumn sky and a silhouette of a young man with a rifle slung over his shoulder halfway across the rampart by the north gate.

He cupped his hands to his mouth and called, "Billy Dan!"

The man stood motionless, peering over the edge of the city wall.

"Ey. Billy Dan!" he repeated.

No response.

John Bell turned a half-circle, scanning the ground for something useful to throw at Billy Dan, and found a round stone with a good weight to it lying against one of the foundation boards of the nearest building. He wound back his arm and let the stone fly.

When the stone struck Billy Dan between his shoulder blades, the youth released a squawk and turned to face the city.

John Bell shouted, "Ya deaf?"

Billy Dan scowled. "Hey, John Bell. You, uh... you should come look at this."

"Look at what?"

"Just, you better come look."

With a sigh, John Bell trotted past the ramshackle lean-to strung with hammocks and over to the aluminum ladder lashed to the outer wall with faded bights of rope. When his boots hit the steel grating of the perimeter scaffold, a light clatter echoed over the town of Jericho.

Billy Dan swiveled at the hips, nodding down below at the stretch of open road leading out of Jericho's northern gate.

John Bell squinted through the dust blowing off the mountains at two figures standing on the road. One a stranger, a man with a neat beard sporting a waist-coat and a wide-brimmed hat, hunkered over a steamer trunk stowed in child's wagon.

The other figure, John Bell knew all too well.

He scowled at Billy Dan. "What'n hell is she doing outside the gate?"

Billy Dan shrugged uncomfortably.

"Damn it," John Bell grumbled, moving back for the ladder, "you gotta tell me these things."

Billy Dan called down after John Bell, "She said not to bug you."

"Yeah, I bet she did," John Bell groused as his boots hit the ground again.

He rushed past the hammocks and out into one of the main avenues between a clutch of original buildings. A ribbon of open sky lanced down the north-south axis of misshapen structures huddled one on top of the other, filling the oval walls. He tucked his head and stepped through the solid wood-paneled door to the sheriff's office, one of the original buildings that hadn't been dismantled for firewood or building materials. It housed the mayor's office, the sheriff's office, and the jail.

John Bell rarely ever used the jail. Most crimes in Jericho merited little more than a wrist slap and an apology. The last person to inhabit that tiny cage of iron bars was long dead, a victim of one of the lean winters... his name still scrawled onto the surface of a pre-war flat screen TV in grease pencil.

He reached for his keys, opened up the gun cabinet behind his desk, snatched his rifle and a pocketful of rounds, then locked it behind him. He only paused by the mayor's office door to shake his head. He wouldn't let her do this to him again.

By the time he'd unbolted the gate and trotted out to the middle of the road where Adeline and the stranger held their parlay, his patience had withered from next-to-nothing down to exactly-nothing.

Brandishing his rifle over his shoulder, John Bell stepped up next to Adeline. "What's going on, here?"

The stranger pulled his hat off, grinning with impossibly white teeth and extending a filthy hand. "You must be Sheriff Bell? An honor and a pleasure to meet you, sir. My name's Willis Ragmund."

John Bell stared at the hand.

Adeline pivoted slightly. "Mister Ragmund is an itinerant merchant, Johnny."

Ragmund added, "Old world medicines and treatments, chemicals of succor and salvation."

John Bell scowled. "Ain't interested."

Adeline sighed and turned to face John Bell directly. "As it turns out, he has something of specific interest to Jericho."

"Nothin' he's selling is anything we need."

She lifted a brow, her face flushing, her "one more word and I'll verbally gut you in front of this stranger" face.

Ragmund said, "A simple powder, really." He reached back to unsnap his steamer trunk, revealing a series of glass jars. The glass itself was probably worth more than the contents, glass being in short supply as of late.

Ragmund lifted a fat mason jar to the sunlight, considering the yellowish powder inside, and gave it a couple shakes.

"What's this supposed to be?" John Bell grunted.

"Fertilizer," Ragmund replied. "Rich in nitrogen. Easy to spread."

Adeline cocked her hip and waited for John Bell to respond.

He gave her a measured nod. "Can I speak with you?"

Ragmund lifted his hands as Adeline withdrew with John Bell.

"What?" she huffed.

He looked over his shoulder, then whispered, "You can't keep walking out the gate like this, Addie."

"I have Billy Dan covering me. It's just one man, and he's clearly dust-wearied."

"Doesn't mean much if he pulls a knife on you, demands he be let into the gate. Does it? Or... worse?"

She scowled. "I'm a better judge of character than that." She added with a mumble, "We both know I won't let anything like... well, I won't let *that* happen ever, ever again."

John Bell winced and stepped away a pace.

"Look," he said once he'd composed himself, "we don't know what's in those jars. Could be poison. Could be toxic, or radioactive. Could be sand, for all we know. I don't see no point in risking the town to any stranger, much less some dog-eared hawker with a wagon."

Adeline ran her fingers through the hair at her temples. She used to do that at night when they'd lie together in a hammock at the top of the old bank building, watching the sun set over the mountains. Back when they'd gotten the town walls built. When they could finally breathe easy. John

Bell lost himself in a brief instant of nostalgia, before she cleared her throat.

"The crop is weak," she stated. "Ever since we had to dump the old cistern."

"What's he asking for?"

"Food and water."

"And that's it?"

She nodded.

John Bell peered over his shoulder once again at Ragmund. "He's not looking to stay?"

"Says he has more settlements over east he wants to try."

"I don't like that he knows about other settlements."

"He's obviously been in the Badlands long enough to know how not to get killed. I say we need him more than he needs us."

John Bell gripped the stock of his rifle and chewed his tongue a second. She wasn't wrong.

He turned back to Ragmund with a quick kick, and approached.

"That's fertilizer, huh?" he called.

"Yes, sir. Fresh. Made it just last week."

"Made it?"

He nodded. "Indeed."

"How ya manage that, might I ask?"

Ragmund cocked his head, and gave his jar another shake. "Sorry, my good man. Trade secret. If I go around spreading my recipes, I'll put myself—"

"Fine. You're good for two nights. Then you're on your way."

Ragmund squinted. "Five nights."

John Bell pursed his lips. "Three and breakfast, then I want you the hell out of here."

A CLUTCH OF JERICHO TOWNSFOLK GATHERED AROUND THE quadrangle as Miss Suzette trod carefully over rows of potato vines. She paused by a trellis of tomatoes, pulling off a half-rotted, half-ripe fruit and slipping it into her composting bag.

John Bell dusted off the solar panel atop of the bank building at the south end of the quad, and turned his attention to the scene below, a knot twisting in his gut. The soil in the square had been used and re-used, tortured to death and reanimated with night soil. It was enough to squeeze out a crop to feed the town most years. Sometimes more than enough. But the dysentery hit the town last spring, and they'd lost two children and one of the elders. John Bell was forced to dump the cistern where they kept the night soil. He never trusted it again, despite urgings from one or two of the old farmers including Miss Suzette.

Ragmund reached out to take her hand, guiding her over the last row until she settled onto the flagstone sidewalk next to the remains of the old post office.

"Now," he announced as he cradled his jar of yellow powder in the crook of his arm, "this is concentrated. Doesn't look like much, but a fine sprinkling along the top soil will energize your crops within a week. Assuming you have access to clean water."

Miss Suzette nodded. "We fill up the rain tanks about every two weeks."

He smiled and handed over the jar.

Suzette unclasped the lid and looked inside, pulling her face away from the jar immediately.

John Bell tightened his grip on his rifle, keeping it angled low toward the roof of the bank.

"I told you, ma'am, it was concentrated!" Ragmund chuckled.

Suzette coughed, then smiled. "Yessir. That's a powerful aroma!"

He guided Miss Suzette along the first row of potatoes, advising on dosage as she sprinkled a nearly invisible coverage of the sandy yellow fertilizer over the top of the soil.

The townsfolk lost interest quickly, and soon Suzette was busy dosing every row as Ragmund watched with crossed arms and an air of haughty contentment.

John Bell marched down the inside stairs of the bank and back out into the quadrangle, sizing up Ragmund with a squint.

"Ya hit many settlements from the north? It's where ya came from."

Ragmund turned his head slow, then nodded. "One or two."

John Bell prodded, "Not many that Red Mesa ain't thumbed under."

The barest of shadows crossed over Ragmund's eyes, though his face betrayed no emotion.

"True enough," he whispered.

"They give you grief, Red Mesa?"

Ragmund turned back to the crops. "I avoid them at all costs. As should everyone."

"Well. You're a smart man, then. Didn't have you squared as one of them. Just surprised they ain't put their hooks in you."

"They have plenty of hooks, Sheriff. Some dig deeper and harder than anyone could imagine. As for me"—Ragmund flashed a quick grin—"I keep my feet in a wandering way, and I wander far away from Red Mesa."

John Bell stood next to the man for several minutes as Miss Suzette wrapped up her work. Once she'd handed back the jar and dusted her hands, Ragmund applauded her and turned for the candles, clamor, and scents of cooking meat in the dining hall.

John Bell lingered for a while, casting a glance up to the rampart across the way from the quadrangle.

Adeline stood on the platform, arms crossed against the cold breeze washing from the mountains as the sun began to set.

He nodded to her and moved to join the rest of the town for dinner.

THE DINING HALL FILLED WITH HUBBUB AND FURY OF AN ENTIRE TOWN eating at the same time. It was a rare occasion, one reserved for the three big holidays, a wedding or a funeral, and of course, harvest. The long table by the stage held Ragmund, Adeline, and the two students of the month who enjoyed a special place in front of the assembly. The fifth chair remained empty. John Bell eyed the empty chair from his seat far in the back. That was his seat, and he hadn't taken it since...

Well, since.

Billy Dan hunkered down across from John Bell, leaning over his platter to whisper, "It's some shit, ain't it John?"

"Yep."

"We gonna get some crop by frosts, ya think?"

"Maybe."

Billy Dan tucked into his food and watched John Bell with spritely eyes. "Ya think it's crap, don't ya?"

"I don't know what I think, Billy."

"Don't sound like you."

"Okay," John Bell replied with a sigh as he set down his fork. "I think we're wasting food on this dust-foot. That fertilizer's probably just a lot of sand."

"Then why're we feastin' for this guy?"

"Because people need it, Billy. They need something to not be complete-ass horrible for a hot second. You get that?"

Billy Dan mulled it over as he chewed a gristly piece of dog meat. "I suppose."

"No one survives if they assume they won't. So we let this Ragmund fellow spread his dust and we send him on his merry way. And in a week, we'll take another look at the harvest."

"What's the worst that can happen, right?"

John Bell winced. "You cross yourself right now!"

Once the children had been sent to bed after dinner, some of Joe Crispin's white lightning got passed around, and an afterglow settled over the town. John Bell hunkered away in his office, listening as folk wandered to bed. Adeline had set Ragmund up in one of the empty beds left after the dysentery hit the previous spring, so John Bell haunted his jailhouse dutifully, trusting no one would bother him.

He drifted to sleep well after the sun had set and the last of the guitar pickers had hung up their instruments. Memories of raiders disturbed his sleep. Of violence. Of Adeline.

His eyes snapped open as the rusty whine of the front gate jerked him awake. Someone was at the gate. No one was permitted to touch the gate except for himself and whoever he'd posted on the wall.

John Bell reached for the gun cabinet to snatch his rifle, then crouched down to slip out into the dark alley. Two doors down, he spotted the space around the front gate. The metal whine had ceased, so he waited with his breath held and ears sharp, spying into the darkness.

After a few minutes, another scrape of metal pierced the night air.

He straightened up against the side of the old postal building as a silhouette worried at the bolt to the front gate. He padded forward with the rifle held high as the figure finally managed the bolt open. The figure turned to check behind him.

Ragmund.

John Bell waited to be spotted, but Ragmund simply turned back for the opening and slipped outside, guiding his little red wagon behind him. John Bell considered the moment, questioning which response would be the wisest. He could call him out now, and possibly stop him before he got too far along the old dirt road leading around the hill. Or, he could simply bar the gate, let Ragmund make his discreet exit, and forget he ever existed.

As John Bell eased the rifle back down, a notion stirred in his brain. He trotted over to the ladder for the parapet. At the top, he found Old Hoke slumped into one of the captain's chairs they'd salvaged from a pre-war vehicle, snoring into his soup-catcher. A bottle of Crispin's Lightning rested in the crook of his arm.

He kicked the sole of Hoke's boot. The old man snorted, then flailed as he awoke, nearly rolling off the parapet.

John Bell lifted a hand.

"Uh, oh. Uh, sorry John!" Hoke blubbered.

"I set a guard for a damn reason, Hoke."

"I know..."

"Next time I catch you three sheets whilst on guard, I'll put a bat to the back of your head."

"Sorry, John."

John Bell squinted into the distance, and Hoke labored his way to his feet to join him. The tiny dark figure of Ragmund had nearly rounded the far hill.

"Who's that?" Hoke whispered.

"The person you let slip out the front gate."

"Huh?"

"It's Ragmund."

"The hell's he—?"

"Don't matter, do it? He's leaving. Knew he'd go sooner than later. Sooner was just sooner than I'd figured on."

John Bell leaned against the outer wall to watch Ragmund's progress. He didn't appear to be in any specific hurry, as if out on some evening stroll with his wagon. Nor did he ever really look back to see if anyone followed. That alone put a burr under John Bell's saddle, and he frowned as Ragmund disappeared into the distance.

"Shit," he mumbled as he moved for the ladder.

"Whatcha doing?" Hoke asked.

"I'm going to have a last word with our esteemed guest. Come lock the gate behind me."

John Bell hit the ground, and moved for the old oak plank shed built off the outer wall. He unlatched the doors and stepped inside, squinting into the absolute darkness. He reached out for the familiar shape before him, and flipped on the main switch on the handlebars of his bike. The instrument panel hummed to life, flooding the room with a modest glow. The battery was flush enough to make two hours out. That'd be all he needed.

THE BIKE WHISPERED ITS WAY ALONG THE DIRT ROAD, AND IT WASN'T long until John Bell spotted Ragmund plodding along before him. He kicked the bike to a coast, then held himself up by a foot, giving the man more lead. He continued like this for the better part of an hour until Ragmund finally left the road. The eastern sky blossomed into a deep cobalt as stars began to flicker away. Morning was coming.

He switched to performance suspension mode, and steered off the road, rounding hills and navigating brush while circling his quarry. The first rays of genuine sunlight spilled across the plain as Ragmund finally halted by a clutch of granite boulders. The man pulled aside a sheet of dusty muslin to reveal a contraption of wire racks and glass, from which he lifted a fat bell jar to the sky to examine its contents.

John dangled his rifle over the handlebars of his bike and observed with amusement as Ragmund poured the yellow powder into another mason jar, stopping finally to wipe his forehead.

Without turning to John Bell, or in any way otherwise recognizing his existence, Ragmund declared, "You keeping an eye on me, then?"

John Bell snickered. "Well, leaving the way you did, figured you were either on the run or up to something dastard-like."

Ragmund peered over at him. "I'm at my work, Sheriff. But I appreciate your concern."

"You left my gate open. That's bad news for me."

"Figured you was watching me." Ragmund gathered his materials to lock them securely in the steamer trunk on his wagon. "If you wasn't, then that's worse news for you."

"Yeah, I had words with my guard."

Ragmund dusted off his coat before finally turning to face him.

"So, are you sore about me leaving? We both knew this was short-term."

"I honestly have no problem with you disappearing and staying disappear'd. Just want to be sure there ain't no surprises that come with this neat little arrangement."

Ragmund lifted open hands to his side. "Nothing here." He squinted. "You have a nice city, Sheriff. People are... positive."

"As best as can be, I suppose. Those that don't choose this life find a way to make it theirs nonetheless."

Ragmund lowered his hands, nodded, then turned to take the handle of his wagon. "I'll be off."

"Where to?"

"East."

John Bell looked down to his rifle, then stowed it behind him on the side bag of his bike. "Shoot straight with me. Is that shit of any use? Your piss powder. That's what it is, right? Piss and sand?"

Ragmund nodded. "It's an old technique. A bit crude, perhaps. But I don't take people's food without a purpose."

"So you say."

"So I say," Ragmund repeated. "Tell me, are you a believer, Sheriff?"

"Believer? In what?"

"Well, I suppose that depends."

John Bell leaned back on his bike and ran a finger underneath his nose. "If there's a God, however you size him up to be, I figure he's got a lot of apologizing to do."

"And what of the Sentience?"

John Bell eased forward, his jaw tight. "Hadn't... hadn't figured you for one of those."

Ragmund chuckled. "I was just asking. You don't strike me as the Gore 'Em and Bore 'Em type. But your surviving the way you do? It's a curiosity."

"Well, I don't place much stock in superstition. Or in needless violence. People are people, and by and large, they just want to be left alone."

Ragmund's eyes took a sharp cast. "How long you think Jericho will be left alone, Sheriff?"

John Bell sucked in a long breath. "Long enough, with any luck at all."

Ragmund nodded and tugged on his wagon. "Luck has very little to do with it. We all embrace the Beast at some point."

John Bell asked, "You, uhh... you need a hand or anything?"

"Oh, please. I've been on foot for three years, now. I have my way. I'll see myself along, but thank you all the same."

John Bell sat on his bike, watching Ragmund lumber along the open plain, his trunk-laden wagon wobbling over the uneven terrain. He plodded on, relentless, tireless. The man was pure frontier gristle, and John Bell found himself grinning as Ragmund finally disappeared to the east.

IT TOOK TWO DAYS FOR MISS SUZETTE TO MENTION THE WITHER TO John Bell. She confessed out from underneath her tucked chin that she'd noticed some brown curl in the potato leaves that same night she'd spread Ragmund's fertilizer. The next day more of the crop had shown signs of dehydration. It was the needless use of water that put the shame into Miss Suzette's confession. Water she'd wasted trying to save a poisoned crop when it could have gone to the people of Jericho.

John Bell stared down at the fields from atop the post office as Miss Suzette sniffled beside him.

"Poison?" he grumbled.

"Best... I can tell," she gasped, "it's salted. Something like it. Seems like the soil's been salted pretty good."

John Bell turned to Suzette and lifted her chin with a steady finger, staring into her face with open, unguarded eyes.

"Is it likely this was a mistake? I mean, pissing into a jar and letting the sun dry it out. That's like to leave some salt."

She shrugged. "I've never seen that done before. I don't know."

John Bell lifted his face to the sky, then shook his head. "The sand."

"Hmm?"

"He mixed sand into the jar to knock his dried urine loose. The soil in these parts lends to salt."

Suzette frowned. "He put the salt sands into his..."

John Bell scowled, and gave her a squeeze of the arm. "This ain't your fault. You need to know that."

"I spread that horrible poison all over—"

"It ain't your fault. You hear?"

She nodded miserably.

John Bell saw her down to the ground.

Adeline, who'd been watching from the side of the growing beds mustered her dress and trod up to him. "The entire crop."

"So I hear."

She lifted a hand. "Please, for the love of all that is holy, do not say you told me so."

"Addie, this is our food. We're a month away from the first frosts. I'm not going to waste time with recriminatin'."

Her face soured.

"I want him," she rasped. "I want that man here. I want him behind bars. I want..."

She didn't complete the dark thought.

John Bell sighed. "Truth be told, Adeline, I don't think he meant this to happen. Probably kept wanderin', didn't realize he was in salt sands."

She sneered up at John Bell. "You're apologizing for him? I... I let him in. I made this happen!"

"And we'll figure something out."

"Johnny!" she shouted. "We're going to gather up some volunteers. Shouldn't be hard, since we're looking at another starving winter. We'll get the old barrels out, and hike up the mountain to just underneath the frost line. There's soil up there. We'll start new beds."

"It's too late for that."

"I know. For this winter, it's too late. But come spring, we'll need unsalted soil. Right? And best to get that soil while we still have some strength left. Still have... people. Come May, we'll maybe have six good backs left."

Adeline shivered, then leaned into John Bell.

He cautiously wrapped one arm around her shoulders.

Adeline moaned, "I don't want another starve, Johnny."

"I know."

"I can't... I just, I can't." She sniffled, and a tremor took her entire frame. "I can still taste it. The taste... it doesn't leave you."

"Stop."

"I can't forget it."

John Bell squeezed her hard, tears welling in his eyes. "You stop this."

"It'll have to be the children this time. There's just too many under twelve."

"We're not there, yet."

Adeline dropped to her knees.

John Bell followed her to the ground and comforted her as best he could.

THE FIRST CREW LEFT JERICHO WITH A FLEET OF TWELVE BLUE PLASTIC fifty-gallon barrels mounted onto wooden wheels. They'd take a good three days up the mountain, and depending on how cold it was up there, they'd be two days digging up fresh, arable soil. Then two days back.

The better part of a week, by John Bell's figuring.

He wanted to join them, but Adeline noted that word had gotten out regarding the failed crop. The growing fields were in the direct center of town, and it was hard to miss the fact that the annual harvest had suddenly been canceled on account of trusting a stranger.

Murmurs in town had spread quicker than John Bell had wanted. Blame spread between John Bell and Adeline. Seemed no one had much confidence in the current leadership in town. They were, technically, outsiders. The latest to find Jericho. They'd come together, and within a year they'd rallied the original townsfolk into building the walls, planning for agriculture, even got the school running. They'd put a nice shine to this diamond in the rough of the Badlands, but now they were looking at yet another starving winter.

There might have even been enough acrimony to spur a coup of sorts, only everyone knew whoever was in charge come three months' time would have to decide who got brained, butchered, and passed around to keep the rest of town alive. And the children were always the first to be served in such times.

Leaving that decision to John Bell and Adeline would be vengeance enough. What worse fate could one arrange?

John Bell considered the coming months as he held his head in his hands at his desk in the jailhouse. Dirt would be incoming. They'd need a new location for it. The old gardens were salted, now. Not much use in trying to re-use that real estate.

A notion to attempt a winter-months greenhouse flitted through his brain, but he swatted it away. The weather in the Badlands didn't suit greenhouses. Not enough sunlight. Not enough life.

Perhaps Ragmund was onto something. The Sentience, whatever that nasty old bugbear was, may have kept the light to a minimum specifically for that purpose.

He should have been a man, damn it. John Bell should have said "No" to Adeline when she brought Ragmund in. He knew it... he knew the man was trouble. But Adeline had made up her mind, and she'd always been his weakness.

He had so much to make up for. Anything he said to her aside from complete acquiescence...

No.

This wasn't his fault. It wasn't Adeline's.

It wasn't really even Ragmund's.

It was a sour hand dealt by the Badlands, and he'd have to figure a way to get his bearings before anyone suffered.

Surely, the greenhouse idea had some feet under it.

John Bell stood, scratching his arm, running a quick mental inventory of the Jericho talent pool. Old man Sullivan had experience in one of the East Coast cities. Was it engineering? Or did he drive trains? Someone had to have a sense of purpose in this damned town. Enough sense to grow crops indoors, with some kind of light source. Enough to keep everyone alive

He stepped outside the jailhouse, and some kind of bellowing call resounded over the plain.

What was that, a horn?

He stood still, ears perked.

Footsteps bounded around the catwalks near the outer wall. He peered up to find Billy Dan sprinting along the parapet, his face filled with intent.

John Bell rushed up the nearest ladder to join him as well as Old Hoke, who had a rifle trained on three figures in the road, lined up in front of a truck. Their hair was greased back, dark and slick. Motor oil, probably, with some glint of red mixed in, offering an illusion of a bloody halo over their faces.

Red Mesa.

John Bell swore under his breath as Old Hoke shivered.

Hoke rasped, "What... what'll we do?"

John Bell stared at the men as they stood still and silent, a line of statues gazing upon the town of Jericho.

"Let them make the first move. There's just three of them."

Billy Dan grunted, "That we can see, anyhow."

John Bell reached over to pull down Hoke's old service rifle, then crossed his arms as he took position directly over the gate.

At length, the center of the Red Mesa men stepped forward, long strides toward the gate, pausing as soon as he was in easy earshot.

"Good morning," the man called with a polished, genial tone.

John Bell nodded once.

The man continued, "You must forgive our sudden intrusion on this fine morning. And if I might prevail upon your courtesy, may I ask what is the name of this settlement?"

John Bell looked over at Billy Dan and Old Hoke. Their mouths were set, though their eyes were wide and anxious.

"Jericho," John Bell replied. "Like from the Bible."

"I know the Scriptures, if not your settlement. How long have you been here?"

"Since before the war. Old times. We just built it out and in a touch."

The Red Mesa emissary stared down at the ground, then nodded to himself.

"Well, we come not with trumpets, but with empty hands, my friend. I think you recognize our affiliation, if you've been long in this corner of the Badlands."

"I do," John Bell ventured. "Red Mesa?"

"You know who we are, then?"

With less verve, he replied, "I do."

"Fear not," the man declared with outstretched arms. "We are not here to... acquire you. We have no designs on your town at present. Nor your food or water. But as our reputation may precede us, and as too many independent settlements in these hills lean toward preemptive violence, I feel compelled to warn you that we have, at present, a sniper stationed in the hills just east of us." He lifted a lazy finger in a roughly eastward direction. "He is a shockingly accurate man. And I dare say he has a line of sight even to the top of your wall."

The emissary removed a glove, held it at arm's length, then tossed it into the air.

The glove slanted sideways with unnatural speed. A second later, the hills to the west resounded with the flickering echo of a gunshot.

John Bell reflexively crouched.

The man continued once the echoes had subsided, "Mind you, this is for my protection alone. In case your compatriots decide that our conversation is taking a turn for the discourteous."

John Bell glared up to the distant hills to the west, then to his men.

"Well," he grumbled in response, "I suppose we should keep things courteous."

"Excellent. And so, I should come to the point of our intrusion."

"Please do."

He motioned for one of his compatriots to join him. As the second man took position, he stared with wide, wild eyes all along the walls.

"We were sent by our Holy Father to find a man. A villain, really. He travels with a wagon filled with jars. Ragmund was the name he gave us, though he may have a new name for every settlement he violates."

John Bell puckered his lips, then sighed. "Ain't no one here by that name."

The spokesman turned to his compatriot, whose eyes continued to sweep back and forth.

"Is that so? I should warn you, my friend here"—he slapped his compatriot on the back—"has talents both uncanny and useful for emissaries such as myself. He has a way of tasting the truth of words, if you will. This is a courtesy I extend. Too many are not offered such forthrightness, and find they pay too heavy a price for dishonesty."

Billy Dan whispered, "Sumbitch likes to use his mouth, don't he?"

John Bell shot him a hard glare, and turned back to the Red Mesa men. "Well, that's alright, 'cause I'm speaking true. No Ragmund here, nor men with wagons."

The emissary pulled his hand up to his truth sniffer's shoulder, and waited. The truth sniffer offered no response.

The emissary nodded.

"Very well. Another question, though... if you would indulge. Have you been visited by such a man? You see, this is a matter of great importance to our Holy Father. This man must be found and brought back to face our justice."

"Why?" John Bell prodded. "What's he done to Red Mesa?"

The emissary's face hardened. "He's killed. Poisoned one of the Holy Father's favorite concubines."

"I'm sorry to hear that. Truly."

The emissary ran a hand underneath his nose as his eyes adopted a savage caste. "The Holy Father is neither patient nor forgiving. And anyone who offers this creature up for judgment would be held in Red Mesa's... regard." He shook out his arms and gave the third man lingering by the truck a look. "I think you recognize how valuable can be our regard."

John Bell took a step away from the wall and peered again to the west as he took a deep breath. How would Red Mesa react to this? If Ragmund had managed to kill the Red Mesa warlord's woman with whatever snake oil he'd peddled, would Red Mesa decide to eliminate anyone who'd come in contact? They'd been known to raze entire settlements. And much, much worse.

He looked down to the men in front of the gate. The truth sniffer locked eyes with him, his face drawn into an expectant sneer.

He knew. He already knew.

"Yeah," John Bell muttered. "A few days ago. Traded us some fertilizer for food. Ruined our entire crop. So, you can say we're of the same mind regarding this Ragmund."

The truth sniffer blinked furiously, then lowered his chin.

The emissary grinned.

"Then, if you would be so kind, in what direction did he take his leave?"

"East," John Bell muttered.

"Sorry?" the emissary prodded with a hand held to his ear.

John Bell repeated, "East! Two days on foot."

The truth sniffer remained unfazed, and the emissary gathered himself with great deliberation.

"Well, then," the emissary announced. "We have a new direction.

Allow me to extend the Holy Father's gratitude for your assistance, such as it was."

The Red Mesa men returned to their truck and piled in. The driver made a U-turn, and they departed.

To the north.

John Bell gripped the side of the parapet with white knuckles as Billy Dan released a sigh of relief. "Woo. Thought they'd have us, for sure."

Old Hoke glared at John Bell. "You know you set them on that man, right?"

John Bell turned to Hoke. "What?"

"You know what Red Mesa do. You know how they are. They'll be on him in a day, and then they'll..." Hoke took a breath and shuddered.

John Bell scowled. "Yeah. I know. And you think he don't deserve it?"

"Deserve a gallows? A bullet to the head? Sure! He done us wrong, and we're gonna starve this winter. And he went and did the Red Mesa a stupid damn service. But..."

"But what, Hoke?"

"They'll take their time. They'll skin him, maybe. Put him on a post. Maybe even cut him to pieces bit by bit and eat him while he watches. I'm sayin' they'll do evil."

John Bell crossed his arms. "They had a telepath, you ass! You think all that's a fate you won't wish on a dust-caked charlatan? That's what they'd do to every last one of us, if we'd hedged. So, stuff your high horse."

He descended the ladder, lips tight, and when his boots hit dirt, he turned to find Adeline staring at him.

Her face was drawn. Sad. She took in a slow breath. "Are they gone?"

"Yes."

"Did they follow Ragmund?"

John Bell shook his head.

Adeline blanched. "Then"—she sighed—"we have to find him."

"Excuse me?"

"They're going back to Red Mesa. They're gathering an army. They'll be back."

"They believed me, Adeline. They had a telepath, so I shot straight with them."

She crossed her arms. "And why would they leave us untouched, Johnny? They know we're here. The Holy Father. In his diseased brain, he has a reason to come for us now."

"Then we have to move," John Bell whispered.

"No. They have ethanol engines. And most of our stronger people are still on the mountain. They'd come back with soldiers. No, the only way to avoid being taken by Red Mesa is to find Ragmund, and offer him as tribute."

"Tribute?"

"Yes!" she shouted, reaching out to clutch John Bell's shirt. "We haven't done anything yet to earn our independence from Red Mesa. But we give Ragmund over, and we can negotiate."

"You really think they'll negotiate?"

"You heard that man," she replied, releasing his shirt. "This is personal to the Holy Father. And they care what the independents think. We'll have a shot, Johnny. And really, it's our only shot. So we have to take it." She added with a dip of her head. "I know how that man operates."

He took a half-step away and ran a hand over his jaw.

She was right.

There were no options.

"I'll get my bike."

THE SUN HAD SET FOR AN HOUR, AND THE BIKE WAS WELL INTO ITS solar-charged batteries before John Bell found the flicker of a distant campfire warming a clutch of boulders. He eased the bike forward, steering clear of gravel. As he approached yet closer, John Bell keyed off the bike, snatched his rifle, and crept up on the campfire with a cartridge ready to fly.

He spotted Ragmund sitting on his steamer trunk, nursing a mug of something.

John Bell lifted his rifle and prepared to bellow a call for him to hold his hands up, when Ragmund tossed a lazy hand toward a rock across the campfire.

"Care to join me, Sheriff? Saved you some tea."

John Bell stiffened, then marched forward with rifle trained on Ragmund.

"You're coming back with me," he declared.

"So, no tea then?"

"Heard me coming, huh?"

Ragmund finally turned to face John Bell. "I was expecting you."

"You have to come back with me."

"Food situation worse than I figured, eh?"

John Bell scowled. "Worse than food, Ragmund. Red Mesa paid us a visit."

Ragmund's face pinched ever so slightly. "Ah. Them."

"They say you killed their leader's woman."

Ragmund sighed. "That was unfortunate."

"Unfortunate? These people turn folk inside-out. They level settlements just for giving them the stink-eye. You played with fire, is what you done."

"It was a water treatment. Meant to clear toxins and such."

"Don't tell me you pissed in their water," John Bell grumbled.

"No. That would have been kinder. I'm not entirely sure what it was, to be perfectly honest. Some white powder. Smelt of almonds."

"You put some random crap in their water, then strolled away? You are a son of a bitch, you know that? And a stupid one, at that."

"I truly had no choice," Ragmund groaned as he straightened his spine.

John Bell lifted his rifle to his shoulder.

"Please, Sheriff. I mean you no distress. I will come with you. Clearly."

John Bell sniffled. "They... they mean you harm. You understand that?"

Ragmund nodded miserably.

"If I were in your shoes," John Bell added, "I'd be thinking about any way to escape this situation."

"There is no escape from my situation," Ragmund whispered.

John Bell screwed his eyes into a wince as he considered the old, balding man. "I'll, uhh... I'll have to tie you up."

"Is it truly necessary?"

"You doomed my people to a cannibal winter, Ragmund. If you're looking for sympathy, you're drawin' your bucket out the wrong well."

JOHN BELL STOOD BESIDE ADELINE IN THE JAILHOUSE, BOTH WATCHING Ragmund as he pulled off his boots with great labor.

"Just like that?" she whispered.

"Just like that. I get the sense this man's ready to own up to his sins."

Ragmund snickered from inside his cell. "If I had sins to repay, my good Sheriff, they'd be in too far an arrears to ever see myself squared."

"Hell you say," John Bell groused.

"I've killed, Sheriff. I've killed more than I know. It's not the ones I've seen die," Ragmund added as he leaned back on his cot, "it's the ones I imagine when I try to sleep. The ones I've never seen."

Adeline asked, "Why do you do it? Why not try to find some place in the Badlands? This... this is too much effort for a rational man. Pulling poison from one town to another. It's... insane."

Ragmund snickered, then laughed aloud.

As he composed himself, he replied, "It is, at that."

John Bell prodded, "So, answer the woman. Why do it?"

"I told you, Sheriff. I have no choice."

"That's a lot of shit," John Bell barked. "You had a choice. Once, maybe. You made this happen to yourself. I'm not shedding the first tear for you—"

Adeline pulled him aside.

John Bell succumbed to her touch, his head spinning as he caught his breath.

Adeline muttered, "He's not worth getting upset over."

"I disagree," he whispered. "He's put us into a situation."

"A situation which we'll navigate on our own. I haven't forgotten, Johnny. I haven't forgotten how reluctant you were to let him in. I was the one who went out to greet him. I just..." Her eyes darkened. "I needed to know someone could be trusted."

John Bell winced. "You had no way of knowing."

"I should have been more like you."

"No. Don't do this."

She held up a hand and pushed him away, though her touch remained as he took a half-step backward.

"When... when we have to make the hard decisions. Come January. I'll be the first to make things... well, to save as many as I can."

"No!" he grunted. "You're the mayor of this town. You don't just lie down and get butchered."

"It's my fault, Johnny. Entirely. If I'd trusted you. Your sense of people. We'd have food. We wouldn't have Red Mesa bearing down on us."

"You don't know that. They were looking for this sorry toad. They'd have found us anyway. And then we'd have nothing to offer them. So, maybe you're gonna save us. Ever think of that?"

Ragmund snickered, but didn't add anything.

Adeline moved for the door. She exchanged a long glance with John Bell, jaw tense, but smile tender as a spring shoot. She pulled open the jail-house door, its planks scraping a clear swatch of wood from the floor dust, and took her leave.

John Bell turned to the cell to find Ragmund staring at the door. John

Bell's gut twisted, and he lifted a finger at the man behind the bars with a tremble.

"Best keep your eyes on the ground, mister."

Ragmund glanced back to John Bell with a smirk and leaned back on his bench.

"The two of you were together once. No?"

John Bell didn't respond.

Ragmund pressed, "What happened?"

"Shut up."

"She's not strange to you. That must be nice."

"Do I have to tape your mouth shut? 'Cause I got plenty of tape."

Ragmund chuckled.

John Bell added, "You are very damn chipper for a man about to be handed over to Red Mesa."

Ragmund's smile faded.

John Bell continued with a nod to the door, "She's a friend, is all. All it is." He snatched his rifle from the cabinet and laid it on his desk. He pulled his cleaning kit from a drawer and began to lay the bits and pieces out on the desktop.

"Oh," Ragmund stated.

John Bell tried to ignore him, but after a moment looked up from his desk. "Oh, what? What's the 'Oh?'"

"You're a terrible liar, is all." Ragmund swung his feet up onto the bench. "A virtue I suspect your townsfolk take advantage of to their great relief."

John Bell sighed. "Please do shut up."

"She seems sad. Every time she looks at you, the shadow of grief crosses her eyes."

John Bell paused, gripping the arms of his chair tight.

Ragmund sighed. "Oh, my. Yes. That is much worse. To have loved her, and lost her?"

John Bell swiveled toward the cell. He glared at the man with impatience.

"What did you do?" Ragmund pressed. "Say something wrong? Do something wrong?"

"There ain't a shred of this that's any of your business," John Bell replied.

"Was it... were you unfaithful?"

John Bell jumped up from his seat and marched toward the door, reaching into his pocket for the keys. "You son of a whore..."

Ragmund swung around on his bench, holding up his hands.

"Wait now. Hold up. Don't... let's not do anything ungentlemanly. I apologize. You hear? I'm sorry."

John Bell had the key in the lock and half-turned before he stopped to take a breath. The blood drained back out of his face and he exhaled.

The prisoner's expression drew long, and he shook his lifted hands. "Didn't mean to strike a nerve quite that deep. Was just making conversation."

John Bell pulled the key back out of the lock and returned it to his pocket. "Please stop."

"I can't help it."

"Why can't you just sit still and quiet?"

The man huffed and swung his arms out to the sides. "Not much else to do in this cell."

"Yeah. That's kind of how jail works."

"Is this your plan? Hold me until Red Mesa shows up again?"

"That's about the long and short of it. Least until I'm convinced they won't ever come back."

Ragmund nudged, "You suspect that's likely?"

"Not especially." John Bell shook his head and returned to his desk to clean his rifle.

Ragmund tried various positions in and around the bench, raising a quietly histrionic series of huffs.

John Bell asked, "You ever lost someone?"

The man's face pulled back into a thin, tight mask of measured emotion. "Yes."

"Know what's worse? Losing someone, then having them walk right back into your life."

"Is that what happened? Was it Red Mesa?"

He folded his hands beneath his chin. "She was out, back when we used to scavenge. We'd trade with others when we'd find 'em. Make deals. Addie was visiting some scrap hill northeast of Jericho when..."

"How long was she gone?"

"About a year," he grumbled, "before she escaped. Came home. Never the same, since. Not sure if that's my fault or hers."

"You have my pity."

John Bell slammed his fist against the desk. "I don't need your damn pity!" He looked up through the bars, considering the man as he stared at the floor. "You do recognize what you've done. Right?" He stood and approached the cell, leaning against it as Ragmund watched from his bench. "You've ruined our entire crop with that powder piss of yours. What's more, the salt sands you just scattered over our crops done rendered it useless for growing. That's years of food we can't go without. Do you have any idea what we'll have to do this winter?"

John Bell's voice cracked, and he turned away.

Ragmund's eyes reddened and he glanced at his shoes with a quick nod.

John Bell gathered himself and added, "And you haven't killed any of mine, yet. I can't imagine what's boiling in that skull of that Red Mesa maniac. So maybe you can sit there and ruminate on that while I enjoy a moment's peace?"

"It won't matter," Ragmund replied in a flat, dry tone bereft of all mirth. "Until you're ready to embrace the Beast, the Beast will devour you."

John Bell stared through the bars for a long moment before returning to clean his rifle in peace.

THE GROUND BEGAN TREMBLING A FULL HALF-HOUR BEFORE THE FIRST of the Red Mesa convoy appeared around the far bend along the northern road.

"More 'n last time," Old Hoke groaned as he stood watch with John Bell from the parapet. A line of vehicles crept into view, and John Bell double-checked their progress with his binoculars. Three long-beds pulled by diesel-belching pups rounded the far hill, flanked by twelve smaller vehicles all ranging from pre-war era motorcycles to one or two newer models John Bell had never seen before. Those might have been poached from interlopers from the civilized world. Poor bastards. The convoy settled ranks at the first bend of the mountain road, right by the bare granite outcroppings rising up to the ridge line.

John Bell squinted at the horizon after passing back the binoculars. His stomach twisted tight. This was the moment. He had an asset in Ragmund... his only asset at the moment. But Red Mesa was large, well-oiled and well-manned. Tales of their ravaging settlements in order to poach resources and women had spread even as far south as Jericho.

And they may yet possess some secret asset more valuable than Ragmund. A variable worth more than the value of that man's life, and the continuing existence of Jericho. It could be the simple whim of a madman. It could be a trigger-happy sniper stationed, no doubt, in the hills once again. It could even be one of the truth-sniffing telepaths Red Mesa had apparently cultivated. And as John Bell turned to climb back down to the ground, the most likely variable gnawed at his gut.

It had been fourteen days since the volunteers had left the town gates to harvest clean soil, and hadn't been heard from since.

Adeline stood at the front of the jailhouse, arms stiff at her sides.

John Bell gave her a questioning look, and she nodded once.

He double-checked then triple-checked his rifle, and decided he needed more cartridges. He rushed past Adeline into the jailhouse, and plunged his hand into the top drawer of his desk for ammo.

Ragmund stood in the center of his cell, eyes low.

"They're here," he stated, not in a question.

"Yep," John Bell grunted.

"Don't try to win. You can't."

John Bell glared at Ragmund for a moment. "I'm just trying to survive."

"Remember," Ragmund shouted as John Bell swept back toward the door, "they're beasts. They speak a language of suffering."

John Bell paused, then continued back out onto the street, where Adeline kneaded her hands.

"Everyone secure?" he asked.

"I assume. Billy Dan was tucking them into the cellars, last I saw"

John Bell nodded. "Then it's time you get yourself below."

She scowled. "I'm not hiding. I must be strong. I am the mayor, after all."

"They don't care if you're mayor," he snapped, waving his rifle toward the front gate. "And what they do to women..." John Bell choked on his words.

Her eyes took a hard edge. "I know. All too well."

He grimaced and swallowed against a sob.

She continued, "If they brought telepaths, they'll know I'm here. They may even recognize me."

"Which is why I want you underground," he whispered.

"If they find me here, they're going to level everything until they pull me out. If I'm on the wall with you—"

"—I won't let them take you again."

She blinked away his words and ran a hand over his jaw. "That was another life."

"I... I'm not ready to let go."

Tears welled in her eyes. "We found this town. Together. We made this town something to be proud of. This is our new life. And we have to protect it." She tilted his chin to face her. "And we're going to do that together."

He breathed, "I miss you, Addie."

Tears flowed over her cheeks, and she nodded.

He escorted her to the rope ladder, and she climbed up before him. Old Hoke stared back at John Bell with wide eyes.

"What's she doin'—?"

"She's the mayor," he replied.

The three stood shoulder-to-shoulder, watching as the convoy of vehicles lifted the last hill along the road, approaching at a casual, inexorable speed.

John Bell turned toward a bustle of noise behind him, Billy Dan climbing the ladder.

"Everyone secured?" John Bell asked.

Billy Dan nodded, and pulled a rifle.

A phalanx of motorcycles swept in front of the north gates, its riders scanning the wall with long glances before returning to the main convoy. Three of them joined a long sedan as it moved to pass the first of the long bed trucks.

Old Hoke whispered, "What was that all about?"

John Bell replied, "Sizing up the gates and the walls, is my guess. How thick it is. How easy it'll be to tear down."

"Aw, hell," Hoke grumbled.

Adeline nodded to the long sedan. "That's Holy Father's car. He came personally."

"Is that a good thing or a bad thing?" John Bell asked.

She muttered, "He always comes when they take a settlement."

John Bell gripped his rifle tight.

The three motorcycles formed an arrow as they preceded the Holy Father's car up to the gates. They each killed their engines and dismounted as the first of the flatbed trucks eased itself sideways in the clearing before the northern wall of Jericho. John Bell gripped his jaw tight as the bed of the truck swung into full view. A line of figures stood along the bed of the truck, each bloodied and beaten either unconscious or dead, tied to blue barrels filled with soil.

Adeline sucked in a breath, and Old Hoke released a spate of profanity just loud enough for John Bell to hear.

John Bell reached over and stifled Hoke's gun arm as it began to rise. He stared Old Hoke in the eye and slowly shook his head.

The truck came to a stop, displaying the beaten townspeople like figures on crosses before its engine cranked to silence.

The sedan remained still, its engine still running.

John Bell stared up past his captured people to the remainder of the convoy. The other two trucks remained by the granite slope. Red Mesa thugs scurried over the containers as long metal struts extended via hydraulics along the sides of the beds.

"Siege engines," John Bell grunted.

Hoke shook his head. "The what?"

"They brought catapults, Hoke. They came to take us down."

"Then we fight!" he growled, pulling his arm up against John Bell's grip.

"No. We talk."

Adeline leaned over and gave Hoke a long glance, pleading with her eyes.

He eased his gun arm and hung his head. "What'll become of us?"

"Well, we won't be taken," John Bell replied. "We have what they want. And if that's not enough, then..."

Adeline sighed and straightened up. "One of them's coming up."

The lead motorcycle rider removed his helmet to reveal a motor-oil-slicked mane. John Bell recognized him as the emissary from before.

The emissary raised his arms out to his sides, dangling his helmet in a loose grip. "Good afternoon!" he shouted.

John Bell didn't reply.

"Well," the emissary continued, "I must confess I honestly hadn't expected we'd return to your charming little burg. But, things being what they are, and you keeping who you've been keeping, I feel it was inevitable."

John Bell cleared his throat and answered, "We weren't hiding the man you was looking for. But we have him now. We went out and found him, and we're ready to hand him over."

The emissary grinned, then lowered his arms. "Oh, that. Yes. Outstanding news, my friend. News, frankly, I feel you should deliver to the Holy Father personally."

"Alright, then."

The emissary stood still, staring up at John Bell.

John Bell shouted, "I'm ready when he is."

The emissary laughed. "Oh, dear Lord son. The Holy Father does not stand at the bottom of walls, shouting up at lesser beings. He rarely ever raises his voice, in point of fact, and suggesting he do so is, well, rude."

John Bell looked over at Adeline.

She lifted her eyes and sucked in a breath.

"You should go," she whispered.

"If I do," he grumbled, "he's like to kill me dead. Now, I'm not afraid to go talk to this son of a bitch, but I need to know you'll do what needs doin' when it comes down to it."

She lifted her hand, fingers drifting along his jaw.

"I've been ready to do this since the day I was taken."

"Then we'll see it happen."

John Bell stepped around Hoke, who reached out to grab his arm.

"You be safe," he mumbled through a trembling voice.

John Bell nodded before descending the ladder.

He wrestled with the bolt on the front gate, lifting it clear of its hasp and shoving the gate open with his shoulder. As he stepped out into the open road, the emissary trod forward. Up close, John Bell caught a better glimpse of the man's face. He was young, far younger than his voice belied. His features were soft, elegant, his lips and eyes painted in some fashion of makeup.

The emissary smiled. "Good man. The Holy Father does detest being made to wait."

He motioned toward the sedan and stepped aside. Another bike rider moved around the back of the sedan to open a rear door.

John Bell looked up to Adeline on the wall, whose eyes were red and streaming.

He gave her a nod and walked over to the sedan. Peering inside, he found the back seat empty.

"Get in," the bike rider growled.

John Bell hesitated, then complied. The inside of the car was warm. Heated air spilled over from the front seat, heavy with the aroma of sweet incense and leather. John Bell took a seat, which plushed beneath him, as the escort closed the car door.

The driver, a rotund fellow with pasty skin and a ridiculous beanie cap gave John Bell a glance from the rear view mirror.

"All set, sir?"

John Bell shrugged.

The driver steered the car in a U-turn, aiming back down the road. As the sedan passed the flatbed, John Bell caught a closer look at his people tied to their own barrels. The nearest, the older of the Sawyer boys, was alive at least. His chest heaved under mighty breaths, trembling either from crying or from pain.

The driver gave John Bell several more glances as the sedan slipped down the hill toward the Red Mesa encampment.

"So, uh... did I hear you right?"

"Hmm?"

"Do you people really have the woman?"

John Bell shifted in his seat. "What woman?"

"The one what escaped the Holy Father," the driver stammered.

"Is... is that what he's here for? I thought—"

"You thought we was here for Ragmund, huh? Well, yeah." The driver sniffled. "I suppose that's a bonus, then?"

John Bell grimaced, gripping the edge of the leather seat.

They had come for Adeline. They knew she was there. The truth sniffer... he must have sensed her. They were doomed from the moment those advance scouts had left, and it had nothing to do with Ragmund whatsoever.

"We can trade," John Bell murmured.

"Whuh?" the driver gobbed.

"Ragmund. For... for..."

"For what?" the driver asked. "Your town? Look, sir, I hate to be the guy what says it out loud, but you people are dead."

"No. We have Ragmund."

"Yeah. So, maybe the Holy Father will like that. So, who knows? I could be wrong."

He smiled at John Bell from the rear view mirror as he pulled the sedan into the midst of the convoy.

The truck beds were mostly unpacked. Enormous arms fashioned from old construction cranes stretched out from behind the truck cabs, with baskets of cargo netting strapping lashed to each opposite enormous cubes of concrete.

Trebuchet.

The driver killed the engine and stepped outside to open John Bell's door. He moved out into the middle of the Red Mesa minions, all of which had halted their business and watched the scene before them with an eerie reverence. Their painted faces dropped into expressionless masks as the driver trotted up to what appeared to be a dog-eared Airstream camper.

"Come on, sir," he shouted at John Bell, who stood paralyzed in the midst of the wolves. "Oh, don't worry about them. They're more afraid of me than you."

John Bell blinked a few times, then looked over at the driver, who snapped his fingers. Shortly thereafter, someone opened the door to the Airstream from inside.

"It's you," he whispered. "You're... him?"

The Holy Father winked once, and stepped into the RV.

The gathered Red Mesa minions began closing around John Bell. He trotted up to the Airstream and rushed inside as they closed the gap.

He was met with a loud pop, and a rush of foam arcing into the air just before his face.

"Welcome, sir," the Holy Father bellowed while pouring a flute of champagne, guzzling it almost as quickly as he'd poured it.

He motioned toward a tiny seat near a laminate fold-out table. "I'd offer you some, but I don't like you very much."

John Bell shook his head and took a seat.

Beyond the Holy Father sat a line of three women, each half-clad in white linen draped over just one of their breasts. Their eyes were sunken, fatigued, and haunted. Their wrists had been manacled together in one long chain.

The last woman sat limp, her head hanging loose to the side, though it was clear she was breathing. Fresh bruises covered her face and shoulders.

John Bell recognized her.

Miss Suzette.

Holy Father followed his glare, and nodded before gesturing at her with his champagne glass. "I pulled her from the rest of your dirt-digging crew. I find myself light on wives, these days. This one is a bit long in the tooth for my tastes, and maybe a bit thin. But I can solve one of those problems myself. The other... well, I'm no spring buck myself." He guffawed and poured himself more champagne.

John Bell's stomach twisted.

The Holy Father set down the glass, took a swig straight from the bottle, and hunkered down onto the table behind John Bell.

"So, you've probably pieced it together by now. I've come for the woman."

John Bell nearly replied, but the Holy Father made a dangerous noise, and John Bell held his tongue.

"I'm so glad you're the one what came down to negotiate. I've wondered many times who this Johnny was. You see, she spoke of you. Yes. Which was dangerous, because I'm a jealous man, don't you know?" He stood and moved in front of John Bell. "And now, here you are. I have to say, I am impressed. You have this... squarish quality. Like an old cowboy. An old cigarette ad. Frontier man! Ha! Yes, Adeline likes the men with more gristle..." He pinched John Bell's bicep. "And less chewin' fat." He slapped his own belly.

"Don't," John Bell rasped.

The Holy Father stood stiff, and leaned in slowly.

"Don't? Don't... what? Hmm?" He sniffed at John Bell's ear. "What shouldn't I do, Johnny Boy? What in the entirety of the Badlands is there that I am prohibited from? What is there that you can deny me?"

John Bell tensed his arm. The man hovering over him was slow, slovenly, and probably not expecting John Bell to grapple with him. It could be easy, just a quick lift of his arm, grab this filth by the neck, and parade him out of the Airstream with a shattered champagne bottle held to his face. Then... then he'd have real leverage to negotiate.

The Holy Father snickered. "And you'd lose everyone on that flat bed."

John Bell looked up at the Holy Father with wide eyes.

The man chuckled and stepped away, lifting a finger to his own temple. "I know, it's off-putting. And I'm not entirely sure I believe half of what I pick up. It's... it's like a notion. Like a prejudice, but not my own. Sometimes I catch it from a distance, but most of the time I have to be right up close to hear people thinking. And, shee-it, you are one loud thinker!"

John Bell's fists melted, and he slumped as all hope drained from his stomach.

The Holy Father continued, "Ain't an exact science, but it helps. So, anyway. I am taking Adeline back. You've figured that, by now. And, since I just threatened you with killing your people, you've probably figured I have no designs on razing your lovely town to the topsoil. And there's a reason for that, and that reason is Ragmund."

John Bell looked up at the man.

The Holy Father's eyes grew distant. "I did love that woman. Her name was Mia. Lovely name. She was, well..." He cast an eye to the women shackled behind him. "Mia was a true wife. She loved me back. We'd talk. Holy shit, did we talk! She would walk with me, eat and drink with me, fuck with me. The woman was insatiable, and I loved that about her.

"Then Ragmund comes amblin' up with that stupid wagon of his. Vitamins, m'lord! Sold us vitamins dissolved in water! Supposed to straighten out the scurvy, the black cough, even the old 'cannibal shakes.' Hell, I admired the balls swinging on that man alone, to come up on our colony, and just look me in the eye and tell me I needed something he alone possessed." He crouched back down in front of John Bell and whispered, "And that he would sell it to me. Not give, like I couldn't just take it from him anyway. The bald-face gall, I swear to Christ, it gave me full steel, Sheriff!"

The Holy Father took several gulps of champagne, and tossed the half-empty bottle over his shoulder to let it rattle around on the floor, spilling its contents.

"And... and it killed her. That water. That miracle water. She died slow, too." The Holy Father's eyes reddened. "Puked her insides up. She wasn't even awake when she finally let slip. Yes. I want that man. Oh, the things I'm going to do to that man." He ran a sleeve over his eyes, then smiled. "So, your people get to live. Most of them. The ones I haven't already damaged, the ones hiding in your cellars. They're going to keep living, provided they survive the winter. And they can take heart that Ragmund's death will have been slow, agonizing, and humiliating."

John Bell lifted his chin, and after a couple attempts, said aloud, "And what of me?"

"You? Hell, son. I figured you'd want to die. I'm taking your woman." He leaned close once more. "Again."

"She won't stay. She'll escape."

"No, Sheriff. She will not. See, I've taken pains to ensure my lesser wives are kept secure." He gestured at the shackled women. Another had fallen unconscious. "No more escape. Not ever."

As the Holy Father stared at the women, John Bell took a long, deep breath. Ragmund's words echoed through his brain. Language of the Beast.

Language of the Beast.

John Bell cleared his throat, and muttered, "Well, then, you can have 'er."

The Holy Father smiled and leaned back. "Cute."

"I ain't kidding. If it gets my ass clear of this, then have her back. Her and Ragmund. Just leave the rest of us in peace." John Bell winced. Peace wasn't the right word. "Just... leave us to die."

Holy Father laughed. "Don't think I can't see through your bullshit, boy. I can, you know."

"Then, you know it ain't bullshit. I don't wanna die. That's obvious."

"You're the good type. You can't give up your wife like this. You're not a useless, dust-caked piece of Badlands flotsam like the rest of these so-called people. It's a play, Sheriff. I can smell it all over you. She's your wife. Least, she was before you considered her all contaminated. And you actually feel noble about that." He sneered. "I actually feel sorry for you."

John Bell mustered his will, screwing it as tight as he could. "She ain't my wife anymore, thanks to you."

"Is that so?"

"She won't let me lay hand on her. Hasn't since she escaped you people. Whatever you done to her, it stuck with her. So, here I am, playing the part... but she's just hanging around, haunting me like some kinda ghost. You take her, and it'd be a kindness. Put her body back where her mind stayed behind. Then I can move on, is what I'm sayin'."

Holy Father sneered at him and shook his head.

John Bell urged, "If you're sniffin' my brain, then you're sensing my feelings. Sure. I have feelings for Adeline. But I'm not... I'm just not gonna die for her. Hell, maybe without her I'll finally live."

The words washed over Holy Father without a response, and John Bell balled his fists in his lap.

A low chuckle emerged from the Holy Father at last, and he crouched in front of John Bell. "Now, that's using your pasta bowl. It's smart thinking, which is what worries me. And what worries me more is that I can't rightly tell if you're lying to me or not." He ran a finger under his nose. "So, either you're lying to me, but in trying to bargain for your sorry-ass life you've stumbled over one hell of a hard truth. Or... you're just the kind of good-when-it's-convenient scumbag that thrives in the Badlands. My kind of scumbag."

Holy Father paced back toward the women. He ran his hand through the first one's hair, and paused to tap his fingers on her head. After a moment, he turned with a lifted finger. "I'm feeling adventurous. Tell me, Sheriff... if you were to apply this same rigid rationality to, say, a monthly tribute to Red Mesa. Would that fit comfortably within your conditional morality?"

John Bell held a breath.

"All those lives, save for this one"—Holy Father pointed at Miss Suzette, still leaning limp against the wall—"your woman, and Ragmund. I take those lives for my own pleasure, but leave yours intact. And if you survive the winter, whoever's left will grow for me. Produce for me. Manufacture for me. And should occasion arise, make your people available for the comfort of my men." He approached John Bell with a half-smirk. "We don't venture this far south too often, so I doubt you'd be worth the trip. But we do need food. Food and other material goods. So, what do you say? Is that worth your life, and the continued existence of your sweet Jericho?"

John Bell released his breath, focused on the notion of leaving that Airstream to breathe fresh air again. "Yes."

The Holy Father glared at him for a long, tense moment, then clapped his hands, causing John Bell to leap out of his skin. "Then we have an accord, Sheriff!"

John Bell exited the Airstream with one final look over to Miss Suzette. Her chest wasn't moving that he could see. It may have been too late for her. The gathered Red Mesa brutes watched in confusion as John Bell returned to the sedan.

The Holy Father emerged from the Airstream and pointed to one of his men. The chosen stepped up to the car and slipped into the driver's seat. As the car pulled away from the camp, John Bell watched the teams loading enormous hunks of twisted steel into the trebuchet cargo nets. This would have to work. He'd have to find some way to make this work.

He'd have to find some way for this not to be his only choice.

RAGMUND STEPPED CAUTIOUSLY OUT OF THE JAIL CELL AS JOHN BELL stood aside. He watched John Bell's face with gathered concern, pacing his way toward the exit.

"You... you spoke with him?"

John Bell nodded.

The man pressed, "And he's made gestures?"

"Like we thought. You were enough to keep him from leveling the city."

Ragmund shook his head. "Doesn't sound like him. He usually just goes straight for the throat."

John Bell crossed his arms. "There may have been conditions."

"Conditions?" Ragmund blurted with lifted brow. "What conditions?"

"Why do you care? Come tomorrow morning, you'll likely be flayed alive and hung by your eyelids from some damn thing or another. And I'll be planning for a starving winter, so there's no real winners in this deal."

Ragmund shook his head.

John Bell scowled. "I'd expect a little more britch-pissing and a little less dour-faced vinegar. You do know what's about to happen to you, right?"

"Just don't understand it."

"What don't you understand, exactly?"

Ragmund huffed and uncrossed his arms. "Just don't like surprises."

John Bell reached for his desk to grab his rifle, and took a swing at Ragmund's head. The stock made contact with the back of his skull, sending him flying into the door, which flung open under his weight as the hinges gave way.

The man dropped into the dust of the main road.

John Bell strode out into the open, wielding his rifle like a club. "Who are you?"

Ragmund sputtered as he rolled over onto his back.

John Bell bellowed, "You're with them!"

"C... calm down," he wheezed.

Adeline trotted around the corner of the old post office, pausing to take in the scene. "What's going on?"

John Bell thrust a finger at Ragmund. "He's one of them."

"One of who?" she demanded.

"Red Mesa! He's in with them. Don't know how, but he's not sweating this. At all. Should be quiverin' in mortal terror at the prospect of bein' handed over to those animals, but he looks more groused that they ain't tearing us to pieces."

Adeline sighed. "Johnny."

"He said this is a surprise. How's it a surprise, Ragmund? A surprise because you done this before, right?"

He pulled his knees up to his chest and rolled up to a seated position.

Adeline trotted over to put herself between the two. "Johnny, what did he say?"

"Ragmund? He said—"

"No. The Holy Father." She squinted at him.

Ragmund coughed and rubbed the back of his head. "I was wondering that, myself."

John Bell took a step back. He wasn't prepared for Adeline. He'd hoped for more time, but now the moment was upon him.

"Nothing important. About what I expected."

Adeline put her hands to her hips. "He cut you loose. So, he wants something."

"Yeah. Him." He pointed to Ragmund.

The man sneered. "And what else?"

John Bell tightened his lips, then shook his head. "Nothing."

"And for that," Ragmund prodded, "he'll leave you be? I refuse to believe that."

"See?" John Bell barked at Adeline. "He's like a man without a map. Why's there a map, is what I want to know!"

Adeline shook her head. "What else, Johnny? He's right. Holy Father won't leave us in peace. Or... did you really believe him?"

Tears sprung to John Bell's eyes.

Adeline stepped closer. "It's me, isn't it? He knows I'm here."

Ragmund looked up at Adeline, then back at John Bell. "What?"

John Bell gave him a kick.

Adeline reached out with both hands. "Johnny? Does he know I'm here?"

"He... he knows everything. He's one of them psychic types, too. Can read minds."

Ragmund scowled. "He told you that?"

"What's it to you?"

He mustered his way to his feet, brushing off the road dust. "Because no one knows and lives to tell about it. It's his deepest secret."

"If it's such a damn secret," John Bell growled, "then how are you so intimate with his comings and goings?"

"Well, that's a complicated, tragic story," Ragmund chuckled.

Adeline held off John Bell with one hand and gestured with another. "Please. We need to know."

He shook his head at John Bell. "Can you do it? Give her up?"

"Of course not."

"Then the Holy Father's coming for this town. You know, he reads—"

Both John Bell and Adeline cut him off. "I know."

"Then you also know he saw through your lie. If he wants her, he's coming for her."

John Bell stretched his neck. "I made it convincing."

"Only way to do that is to convince yourself."

John Bell glanced at Adeline. "I did what I had to do to get out of there."

Adeline pursed her lips, then stepped away. "What... what does that mean?"

Ragmund pushed, "It means he convinced himself that he could... no, would... give you back to Red Mesa. I truly wish you'd told me this sooner."

John Bell stood silent as Adeline crossed her arms.

"Is that true?"

John Bell didn't respond.

Adeline continued, "Because you've been so distant. It wasn't... I mean, I didn't ask to be abducted, Johnny!"

John Bell shouted, "You think I don't know that! I'm angry, Addie. I'm angry with myself. Hell, I tried! I tried to see you the same..." He couldn't finish his thought.

Ragmund folded his hands behind his head. "We've all faced vicious truths, my friend."

"Ain't your friend," John Bell grumbled. "You're as good as dead."

"I understand this. And I accept it. So, I ask again. Can you give her up?"

John Bell took a long breath. "I'll die first."

"Okay. Probably how it'll go down. What about me? You giving me up, too?"

Adeline gave John Bell a measured look.

John Bell answered, "Can you give me a good reason why I shouldn't?"

"Because they're going to torture me to death. Because it won't help you now. Because you're not a monster like those Red Mesa brutes."

"You think so?"

Ragmund smiled. "I know vicious, Sheriff. You're not vicious."

"You still haven't explained your role in this."

Ragmund sighed. "Fine. I'm here to die. To suffer and die. That's my purpose. My 'role' in this, if you insist on calling it that."

John Bell wrinkled his brow. "That don't make sense."

"I suppose it wouldn't. I'm a slave to the situation. Afraid I can't shed much more light on it."

Adeline stepped in front of Ragmund. "We can help you."

"No," he replied with intensity. "No one can ever help me."

Adeline exchanged a glance with John Bell before finally running a hand over her head. "Okay. Holy Father either expects you to hand the two of us over, or he's expecting you to renege. He has ten of our people, and he's ready to execute them. That's our situation."

John Bell nodded.

She cast a glance up the main street, then back to the front gate. "Well, I'm not going back to Red Mesa. If that's a variable at all, then you're going to have to shoot me."

John Bell blinked.

Adeline continued, "I'm serious. If there's any lingering doubt that I'll survive it, you can forget it. I haven't told you everything about what happened there. Really, I haven't told you anything."

"Addie..."

"Johnny, I'm going to shoot myself if I have to. But if it comes to that, then I want to give my life for Jericho. That's our only option. Me, and Ragmund. If we can somehow unhinge the Holy Father, then that's exactly the way we need to—"

As she spoke, John Bell raised his rifle, aimed it mere inches from Ragmund's forehead, and pulled the trigger.

The sound cascaded off the adjacent storefronts, ringing like a bell before the distant echoes answered in counterpoint against the mountains to the west.

Ragmund's body listed sideways and crumpled at Adeline's feet as she stood rigid. Her eyes moved along the corpse, then lifted to John Bell, who had already checked his rifle and slung it back over his shoulder.

Adeline took a breath. "What... why?"

"It was a problem," he whispered, lips twitching. "I... I couldn't find a way out of this without handing him... he... there was no way they wouldn't take him." He wiped a tear from his eye. "They were going to hurt him more than I can handle. This was quick. Painless."

Adeline took a step away and nodded solemnly. "And me?"

"Like I said," he answered with a longing glance at her reddening eyes, "I'll die first."

"Then we have to think quick. He's watching. He's coming for us."

John Bell gripped his rifle stock and stared at the ground. "Well, I have a notion on that."

THE HOLY FATHER'S SEDAN LED AN ARROWHEAD OF VEHICLES FOR Jericho's front gate as John Bell watched from the parapet. The plume of dust settled once the motorcycles came to a halt, their riders dismounting with weapons drawn. The sedan sat toward the back of the phalanx, motor still running, as the Holy Father stepped out.

The man surveyed the front walls of Jericho before his eyes settled on John Bell. He took a long march, swinging his arms and taking up as much space as possible as he approached the gates to the settlement.

With a dramatic clearing of his throat, he declared, "My good Sir John Bell! We have come to our crossroads!"

John Bell stared at him.

The Holy Father's mirth melted rapidly, and he sneered. "The woman. You want to give her up. I know that. I felt that. You also want to save the people of this settlement more than you value your own life. I have no judgment on that fact. And, indeed, I wish you well with your devotion to your tribe."

He stood awaiting a response, which John Bell refused to give.

Holy Father's sneer devolved into a grimace.

"You give me the woman!" he thundered. "And that sack of shit, Ragmund! You do it now, and I'll consider not leveling your pathetic hovel!"

John Bell turned, took several slow steps, then turned back to face Holy Father. "You want Ragmund? Okay."

Old Hoke's head emerged from the parapet, alongside Billy Dan's. Together they hoisted Ragmund's limp carcass up and over the side of the parapet. It landed in a wet slap at the front of Jericho's north gate.

The Holy Father stared at the mass of flesh lying a few yards from his feet. His chest heaved a couple times, then erupted into a spate of laughter. He sucked in a mighty breath, then continued as he gestured for his armed thugs to observe and join in the joke which only he seemed to understand.

At length, Holy Father collected himself and straightened his spine to speak up the wall at John Bell.

"Well... that, that is something. I declare, you are a man of great worth." Holy Father motioned over the corpse as he approached it. "I'd spent many hours dreaming up the perfect retribution over this foul creature. But here he is, devoid of life and sensation, and I have nothing to show for it. You have, indeed, asserted yourself, Sheriff!"

John Bell stood motionless.

Holy Father's glee once again quickly melted. "So, you know this means I have to take it all. Everything. Brick by brick. Stick by stick. I won't stop until see it leveled to the ground."

Again, John Bell remained still, eyes bearing down onto Holy Father.

"Alright," Holy Father chimed, "I'm about done with you anyway." He lifted his hand and made a beckoning gesture with two fingers.

And nothing happened.

He glanced to his nearest thugs with irritation. They stood stiff for a moment, then turned to the west.

John Bell made his own gesture. Old Hoke and Billy Dan emerged from the parapet, heaving a weight over the side of the wall. The load fell at the feet of Holy Father, whose eye twitched as he stared down at the corpse of the sniper he assumed was in the hills.

At last, John Bell announced, "You get one chance to leave. This is it."

Holy Father looked up at John Bell, eyes shifting in rapid thought. "You're serious? Did you miss that whole brick-by-brick speech? That's going to happen."

"Suit yourself."

John Bell looked up to the hills and nodded once.

The ground at the Holy Father's feet popped with a spray of dust and chips of stone, and a half-second later, the faint echo of a rifle shot rolled around the nearby hilltops.

Holy Father skipped a step, then turned to run for his car.

"Shit," John Bell grumbled as he hoisted his rifle.

Another shot from the hills nicked the top of Holy Father's car as he plunged inside. His nearest thugs scrambled for their bikes. One lifted a pistol at the top of the wall, but Old Hoke plugged him before he could get the shot off.

Holy Father had already closed his door and had swung the wheel around to begin a tire-spinning U-turn when the rear passenger window shattered from a third rifle shot.

John Bell took aim and punched a hole through the windshield as the Holy Father's sedan caught traction and swung a heaving arc back toward his encampment. Billy Dan popped off a couple shots, one of which stabbed a hole in the trunk.

John Bell slung his rifle over his neck, gripped the nearest support beam, and hoisted his leg over the side of the outer wall.

Old Hoke shouted, "What'n hell are you doing?"

"Just keep them off the flatbed!" John Bell shouted, flinging himself over the side of the wall. His stomach lurched as he tumbled through air and landed on the side of the last motorcycle thug. When he crashed into the man's body, shooting the motorcycle to the side, pain lanced through his leg. He sucked in a breath and rolled over his shoulder, tilting aside as his leg shifted from pain to numb, then back again.

The thug kicked at the bike folded over his body, engine still revving.

John Bell pulled himself up onto one knee and unslung his rifle. He threw his bolt, took aim, and hoped the weapon wasn't damaged.

The rifle hammered against his shoulder, sending the Red Mesa warrior's head back into a spray of blood. John Bell tested his leg, finding it unable to hold his weight. So instead of running, he hobbled in a crouch toward the fallen thug's motorcycle.

Screams pierced the air, and John Bell looked up to the flat bed. Red Mesa men had pulled knives. The Sawyer boy gurgled as his throat was slit.

A gunshot cracked overhead, and the knife man wheeled from Old Hoke's bullet. The thug gathered himself, gripping his bleeding arm.

John Bell trusted Hoke and Billy Dan to deal with their kindred on the flatbed. He pulled the bike free of the dead thug, powering through the pain in his leg enough to throw it over the motorcycle. He tucked the bum leg up onto the side and cranked the throttle. The bike wobbled under the acceleration, nearly throwing him before he'd straightened it out.

The Holy Father's car was already halfway to the Red Mesa encampment. John Bell leaned into the motorcycle, tucking his head against the wind. Over the noise of the air and the screaming ethanol engine, he could hear the Holy Father hammering his horn. The first of the catapults began to pivot toward Jericho.

The bike advanced quickly on the sedan, which swerved along the dirt road. Either he'd made contact with his shot through the windshield, or the glass was too ruined to easily drive. John Bell took advantage and accelerated alongside the passenger side.

The Holy Father shot him a sweaty glance.

Was it close enough?

"Sniff this, you bastard," John Bell grunted as he pictured the Holy Father, and indeed the entirety of Red Mesa, burning alive. The thought of their pain, the sudden jolting image... John Bell trusted that he was, in fact, a loud thinker.

The sedan jerked further off-road, the front wheel catching a tall, flat boulder. The entire vehicle lurched with a thunderous crash, spinning trunk-forward as John Bell swung clear of the wreckage.

He eased the motorcycle to a stop, turning back to survey the damage. A billow of steam emerged from the sedan's crumpled hood. Holding himself upright with his good leg, John Bell pulled his rifle from his shoulders and chambered another round. He held his breath to take aim.

The Holy Father emerged from the driver's window, face covered in blood. His head bobbled as he writhed free of the car.

"This is for Adeline," he whispered.

And he pulled the trigger.

The Holy Father jerked, sat upright for a moment, and slumped backward limp.

John Bell exhaled, bringing down his rifle. Holy Father was dead. Finally... dead.

A crash from the encampment jerked John Bell from his reverie. He looked up to see a dark mass hurtling through the air with a whining rush of wind. It arced overhead, descending to crash somewhere behind Jericho's north gate.

John Bell turned to the Red Mesa camp and held up a hand, as if the gesture would call their attention to their slain leader. However, as the second trebuchet swiveled on its hydraulic base to launch another load over his head, he realized the vandals were unconcerned with his stretch of the mountain road.

He slung his rifle back over his shoulder and jammed the bike to life with his good leg, wincing as his crippled leg strained under his weight. With a tug of the throttle, he spun the motorcycle to life against the gravel under his feet, and raced toward the rows of vehicles rounding the two truck-mounted siege weapons.

As he approached, a few of the forward thugs noticed and turned guns toward him. He had no choice but to simply hunker down and speed forward. A bullet stung his left arm. No way to tell how bad the wound was. No time.

He leaned for the nearest gunman and kicked out a foot. His boot slammed against the gunman's knee, snapping it backward as he rushed past the front perimeter of the camp. More gunshots sounded behind him, and gravel popped in spots along the ground in front of him. A sharp *clack* resounded on the bike beneath him, and the engine's timbre rose.

His rear tire wobbled with increasing wags, and he clamped down onto the hand brake, easing sideways into a long slide. The rocks on the ground bit at his injured leg. Or were they bullets? He tucked his head as the front wheel caught a large stone, slamming back upright. John Bell tumbled along with the bike as it somersaulted, spinning clear of the wreckage just as it threatened to pin him against the dirt. He rolled along his upper arm and shoulder, letting the rifle take much of his weight as it could.

When he stopped tumbling and cleared his head, he reached for his rifle dangling from a broken strap. He wrestled with the bolt, but it refused to budge.

More gunfire popped into the cloud of dust the wreck had stirred, and he took advantage of the screen to catch his bearings. The two trebuchet flatbeds stood in hulking parallels behind him. One of the improvised crane arms slammed upward, tossing its sling into the air. A mass of compressed metal, perhaps a crushed junkyard vehicle, rushed into the air toward Jericho.

John Bell squinted against the dust peppering his face and hobbled as fast as he could for the nearer flatbed. A thug hopped down from the cab of the truck, swinging a flat bar of aluminum at his head. John Bell ducked before it made contact, and rammed the stock of his rifle into the thug's ribs. He followed with jab to the thug's chin, sending him back against the truck.

The thug, dazed from the hits, fumbled with his weapon and dropped it. He swung wildly at John Bell, reaching for his belt.

John Bell rushed him, throwing his shoulder into the thug's midsection. At that moment, the thug spoke.

"My good Sheriff, I presume?"

John Bell sneered into the face of the emissary.

"You're gonna die," John Bell growled.

The emissary smirked. "Allow me to express a contrary opinion."

He shifted his hips, pinning John Bell's arm underneath his armpit as they hammered down onto the ground.

From his new vantage point, John Bell spotted a sheathed bowie knife on the emissary's belt. He reached for the knife and drew it free of the sheath.

The emissary clamped a free hand onto John Bell's wrist, muscling the knife back toward him. The struggle of strength tilted toward the thug, as the blade inched closer to John Bell's gut.

"Good night, sweet Sheriff. And may flights of angels sing thee—"

A string of pops along the cab interrupted the grapple. The emissary's arm went limp, and John Bell shoved the flat of the knife blade against his opponent's ribs. John Bell took a quick step away as the emissary slid down the side of the cab with a bleeding hole on the side of his head.

The gunfire continued. John Bell hobbled alongside the flatbed, reaching for the short ladder leading to the base of the trebuchet. He mustered his way up to find another Red Mesa brute jerking a handle on a control console. The crane arm eased a degree clockwise as the operator squinted toward Jericho.

The entire flatbed rocked under a sudden load, and a voice called out some unintelligible word at the rear.

John Bell gripped the bowie knife, took a step forward, and jammed it into the back of the operator's neck.

The man's arms flailed backwards in spasms as he coughed and gurgled.

John Bell gave the knife a twist, and the man's body went limp.

With a labored shove of his boot, John Bell cleared the body from the control console and set the knife along its surface.

Four levers. He tested the handle the operator had just pulled. The crane's hydraulics whined as it continued clockwise.

John Bell peered over the console at the trebuchet alongside, and its operators already re-loading the sling with another crushed car. Just beyond that flatbed rose the side of the mountain, running at its angle with its jagged, bare stone outcroppings up toward the ridge line.

Would it be enough?

It would have to be.

John Bell pulled the lever once more, sending the hydraulics into their complaining wheeze as the crane arm swung out over the side of the road, continuing until the entire mechanism was perpendicular to the next trebuchet.

Shouts of alarm and anger flooded the street behind him.

He surveyed the rest of the console. Lever, lever, lever... and one big red button.

His body jerked under a sudden weight, slammed sideways as a bright pain filled his midsection. He grabbed the console for support as the pain turned to blinding, searing heat.

John Bell reached for his side, pulling back a bloody hand.

Gunshot.

More pops all around him as bullets sprayed the flatbed.

John Bell closed his eyes, and thought about Adeline. The day they'd met, out on the open road in the Badlands so many years ago. The day they'd found Jericho, with its paltry citizens barely hanging on. The day she'd been taken by Red Mesa.

The day she returned.

John Bell coughed up a handful of blood, clamped down his jaw, opened his eyes...

...and hammered the red button with his fist.

The flatbed listed as the crane arm rushed up behind him. Its payload flung at an angle directly over the top of the other trebuchet, whistling in the air as it hurtled into the mountainside.

The ground rumbled. Dust filled the air more completely than it already had. The flatbed rocked under the tremors.

Shouts of alarm.

And no more gunfire.

The surface of the flatbed bucked under John Bell's feet, tossing him into the air as enormous stones smashed into the steel of the vehicle. The crane arm twisted sideways, mangled under a car-sized hunk of granite.

John Bell tumbled backward into free-fall as pebbles and dust and stones and larger masses pounded him on all sides.

He lost his breath, gagging against the blood, and quickly passed out.

JOHN BELL AWOKE WITH A GASP, BELCHING OUT A SPATE OF BLOOD. HIS side throbbed from the gunshot wound, but the drowning reflex had stirred him. His breaths came in shallow puffs, lightning bolts of pain filled his chest when he struggled to breathe. He tried to clear his airway with a reach to his throat, but his right arm was pinned underneath something heavy.

He opened his eyes and heaved what little air he could into his lungs. Or perhaps only a lung, if one had collapsed. He blinked away stone dust, and craned his neck to find a tangle of metal surrounding him: the crane arm, mangled, twisted, and acting as a cage to hold back the side of the mountain. Boulders rested against the steel members, mere inches from his broken body. Though for all its merit toward saving his life, one of the struts lay splayed against his right arm, holding him tight against the wreckage of the flatbed.

He lay there, trying to fight the panic of suffocation as he struggled for air. The wind whistled around the boulders. Aside from that... silence.

No voices. No gunfire.

Nothing.

If there was anything left of Red Mesa, they had to have been buried under the landslide, or had long since retreated.

A plan. He needed a plan, if he was going to survive this.

He tested his other arm. It rose weakly, then fell again. He had lost blood. Probably still losing blood. And with half his breath, how could he ever pull free?

He held his thoughts as footsteps approached. A survivor. Well, here he was, an easy target. He'd done what he could.

The footsteps wandered around the wreckage, past him, then back again, ambling about the scene. Finally, he heard a gasp, and the footsteps rushed toward him.

He blinked away more dust as he stared up at Adeline.

"Johnny!" she shouted, though her voice sounded distant.

"Addie," he wheezed.

"My God, Johnnie!" She reached for the stones nearby to try and give him space to pull free. Some of the larger boulders shifted, and she held her breath. "Oh no."

"Go," he muttered.

She looked down at him, scowled, then braced herself against more steel to shove the nearest boulder free of the crane.

John Bell felt warmth rush into his arm, and he flopped aside, rolling clear of the steel cage.

Adeline eased the stone back into place. Something clattered overhead, and a few more stones rushed down the side of the wreckage. She covered John Bell with her body, and he reached up to try and shield her head.

Once the last stones settled, she helped him clear of the mound of wreckage, sliding him along his back until he could face forward again.

Forward, toward Jericho. Its north gates had been smashed open by the last of the trebuchet strikes, but he could make out figures clearing the debris.

"How... many?"

Adeline smiled. "Most. The town survived."

"Who?" he asked.

A shadow of grief flickered across Adeline's face. "Old Hoke got hit. In the chest. It was quick."

John Bell reached for her and pulled himself to a seated position. He tested the gunshot wound in his side. It was moist, but the bleeding had abated. He cleared his throat again, hacking out another rheumy gob.

"We have... we gotta work...on your aim."

She snickered as she laid a gentle hand on his head, stroking the side of his face. "I've never used a scope like that before. Sue me."

He added, "I'm sorry."

"For what?" she whispered.

"After you came back." He coughed. "I stayed away. I shouldn't have. Not your fault. It was mine."

She shook her head and wiped a tear from her cheek. "Let's not talk about that. Not anymore."

John Bell nodded and tried to smile. Instead, he just stared up at Adeline's face.

She glanced up, eyes wide, lips drawn together into a knot of astonishment.

John Bell eased his head aside to find a dark figure standing against the setting sunlight.

"How?" Adeline gasped.

The figure took a few steps closer, and Adeline gripped John Bell tighter.

When the silhouette crouched down, John Bell could finally make out a face.

"Ragmund?" he wheezed.

Ragmund stared at John Bell with weary eyes. Dried blood drew a line down Ragmund's nose, trailing from a flat, unblemished forehead.

He rubbed his hands together as he addressed the two. "Well, looks like I'm done."

John Bell panted, "What are—?"

Ragmund clapped his hands once then lifted a finger. "It's a very long, complicated, tragic story. And I don't feel much need to burden you more than I have."

Adeline eased her hands from behind John Bell's shoulders and stood. "How are you alive?"

"Don't have much choice," Ragmund replied indifferently. "Let's just say that I'm late for my next encounter, and the Boss is not known for His patience."

John Bell asked, "What boss?"

Ragmund stared over John Bell... to the east.

Adeline followed suit.

When John Bell managed to shift himself enough to see what they were glaring at, he found another figure standing in the middle of the plain... too far to make out any features. The figure wore a duster and hat, much like a gunfighter of old tales.

A bolt of cold terror shot through the center of John Bell's chest. "The Sentience?"

Ragmund stood slowly, then nodded. "Yep. Time to move."

John Bell muttered, "Is that—?"

"Listen," Ragmund interrupted. "You hurt Red Mesa. Hurt them bad. Their colony is maybe three days north of here by vehicle. If you get yourself patched up, get your strength back, maybe you can hit them there. They have food and some medicine. If you get your people"—he pointed with his thumb at Jericho—"into the right mindset, you might survive the winter without further barbarity."

Adeline shook her head, but Ragmund held up a hand.

"You can only accomplish this if you embrace the Beast. The animal inside you. After all, Red Mesa didn't start off as some hive of hooligans. They were much like you, originally. And they grew strong. Strong, but stupid. It was their time to decrease. Such is the way of things."

Ragmund dusted off his hands and took a few steps to the east.

Adeline called out, "Why?"

"Why what?" Ragmund muttered over his shoulder.

"Why do you do this? This... you visit destruction on people. That's what you do, isn't it?"

He paused, turned to face them, and sighed. "Years ago, I had another life. A wife and a child. Son... I think. Hell, maybe it was a girl. It's hard to remember those days through His fog." He waggled a finger over his face. "People much like Red Mesa hit our settlement. Came for our food. Our women. We were too weak to stop them." He peered over his shoulder at the stranger in the distance. "And I knew we were too weak."

John Bell offered, "You ran, didn't you?"

"I did," Ragmund replied, still looking to the east. "And He saw what I'd done. I abandoned my family to save my own ass." He looked back to Adeline and John Bell. "He won't let me die. I can't tell if He approved of my cowardice, or if he's punishing me. He just keeps my carcass walking. On and on. Step by step. Town by town." He sucked in a breath, grinned, then nodded. "Like I said, not much choice in the matter."

He offered them one last nod, and began his stroll to the east.

They watched as he withdrew into the Badlands, the wind whipping at his clothes. And by the passing of a gust heavy with the dust off the plains, he vanished.

J.P. SLOAN

J.P. Sloan is a speculative fiction author ... primarily of urban fantasy, horror and several shades between. His writing explores the strangeness in that which is familiar, at times stretching the limits of the human experience, or only hinting at the monsters lurking under your bed.

A Louisiana native, Sloan relocated to the vineyards and cow pastures of Central Maryland after Hurricane Katrina, where he lives with his wife and son. During the day he commutes to the city of Baltimore, a setting which inspires much of his writing.

In his spare time, Sloan enjoys wine-making and homebrewing, and is a certified beer judge.

Links:
Facebook: https://www.facebook.com/JPSloanAuthor/
Twitter: @J_P_Sloan
Webpage: jp-sloan.com

4

PROPHET'S WAKE

WILBERT STANTON

He came for me at night. All hands and mouth. His breath smells of alcohol. His weight on my back and his callused hand over my mouth. If he didn't catch me by surprise, I would have slit his throat, but a whole bottle of whiskey left my head foggy. He wraps his free hand around my waist and drags me out into the desert. I struggle and kick, trying my best to catch his balls, but he has that liquid strength that comes with one shot too many. I catch a glimpse of the stars, they shine in that mocking way, they know tonight's my last night on Earth, and they can give two shits about it, much like the rest of the crew who are now conveniently sound asleep. My feet drag across the sand; bits of rock skin my toes and send heat running up my legs. Barefoot, hung-over, and all... what a way to die.

I'm tossed to the ground hard. A surge of adrenaline boils my blood. I'm on my feet and all about the fight. But again, whiskey, foggy head... a fist cracks me across the jaw and I'm down for the count.

Gibson stands over me, smug as always with his pretty hair, and sparkling eyes that promise lies. "I'm not happy it had to come to this, Cassie."

I sit up and wipe my nose. "Fuck you!"

"We already did that," he says. "And as much as it pains me, I thought we had something. I honestly had feelings for you."

"Then you're as dumb as this stupid crusade." I spit a wad of blood on his worn out leather boots.

There it is, that spark of anger. He runs a hand through his hair trying to seem cool and collected. He hates when I get under his skin. "When I broke you out of prison, whisked you away from the UCF, what was the first thing I told you?"

"That you'd make us all rich beyond our wildest dreams. It's been a year, Gibson. Ain't seen nothing but desert."

"Besides that..."

"Nice tits?"

He sighs. "No. I told you there was more to you than the murderer society labeled you. You had a fire, yes, an uncontrollable fire that if left unchecked could incinerate the world. That fire also gave you passion and strength. You were meant for more, Cassie." He kneels next to me and puts his hand on my shoulder. "Why won't you let me free you of the animal you used to be?"

"Cut the bullshit, Gibson! Let's put the facts out on the table, plain for everyone to see. You sold us all a dream about some magical Prophet that would make us rich. We followed you into this god-forsaken desert because it was that or rot in a cell. You talk a good talk, so some of us started believing it was true. It was all just a load of shit. And you know it. A year! Wandering like nomads, living like fucking wild animals."

"And what's wrong with this life?" He spreads his arms wide, as if embracing the desert like an old friend. "Has it not provided and given you all you needed?"

"I would prefer an apartment in West City, living off the riches you promised. But since you can't seem to find this magical girl, I'd take shoving a knife in your gut as second prize."

"Cassie," he says with sadness that I know he means. I almost feel bad for him, even though he's pulling a knife from the back of his pants. "If it was just you, it'd be fine. I could deal with it. Because, frankly, I think I love you. Unfortunately, you've been spreading your... disloyalty amongst the others. That I can't have. So I ask you—no, I beg you, give me a reason to trust in you again. Be honest with me."

I look off to the side and chuckle. My blood is boiling and screaming to bash someone's head in. "Honestly? If you don't kill me now, I'm going to slit your throat and drink your blood like fine wine. You know why? Because there's no fucking wine out in this desert!"

Gibson laughs. He laughs so hard spit flies freely from his mouth. He's practically hysterical. So why the fuck not? I laugh with him. We both have a good laugh. I'm so busy laughing I don't even notice when he lunges. I sure as shit feel the blade dig into my gut. I can barely belt out a scream before he covers my mouth with his lips. I want to rip out his tongue and spit it in his face. Only right now, I'm too busy getting stabbed, over, and over again. The pain explodes in wave after wave. I don't know when Gibson stops, because everything's gone dark. On my back, feelings slowly start to fade away as coldness sneaks its way into my body.

Darkness.

Well at least I am finally free of the Badlands.

THE DARKNESS IS COLD AND ENDLESS. A COMFORTABLE EMBRACE I imagine a child feels in its mother's arms. No pain or stress. Just peace. I let it take me and reach into the deepest depths of my soul. If this is death, I could get behind it. Except... there is something...

"Leave her alone," a voice says. Sounds like a small boy. "Look at 'er, she's a raider!"

"Someone stuck her good," says another voice.

"Good." The first voice. "Hope she dies."

"It doesn't matter!" It's a little girl, her voice is soft but commanding. "I have to take the hurt away."

"Why? So she can kill us? Dead raider is the only good raider."

There's a scuffle. Someone pushes someone to the ground.

"Just let her be. We shouldn't question the Prophet's ways."

"Stupid. Prophet is ours, not for raiders. Den, you like her huh?"

"Whatever, let's get going." Den says. "*Vamos*, Althea. Nalu is going to make trouble for you already. Don't make him angrier."

"Wait," says the girl.

Warmth grows within me. I can't place where it begins or ends, it radiates all over. No, no, no! This isn't what I want. My breathing steadies. I focus the warmth; it's on my stomach, small hands pressed against my wounds.

I open my eyes and see a blonde girl looking down at me with this tenderness, like she thinks I'm a hurt pet that she has to cuddle back to health. She looks younger than I expected, not even a teen. Her eyes are so beautiful, and painfully innocent, they have soft glow that almost warms my heart... almost... don't go going thinking I'm going soft.

Althea whispers in my ear. "You need to find someplace with food and water."

I want to grab her by the throat and strangle her, but my arms won't move. What part of left for dead didn't she get?

"Come on, she's waking up!" Den yells.

Althea runs a hand across my forehead. "I'm sorry. The Seekers think you will hurt us. I have to put you to sleep now, just in case..."

Fuck sleep, I'm ready to... my head feels foggy, and my eyelids are heavy... I just need to wrap my... hands... around...

Darkness.

I RISE WITH A NEW MOON. WHATEVER SHE DID MAY HAVE YANKED ME back from death's door, but it didn't feel like it. A cold breeze sends a chill down my sweat-soaked skin. Sore, everything is so fucking sore. That kid was the Prophet; she had to be! All those stories Gibson told, the ones about her having healing powers... he was telling the truth all this time, the idiot just couldn't find his own asshole without a Navcon waypoint. A whole year trying to find her, and she just happens to show up the moment I'm finally free. I swear when I find her... she'll wish she left me to die.

I fall to my knees and wonder how long it would take to die if I just lay here and wait. Unfortunately, the lights up ahead are making my survival instincts tingle. On all fours I crawl, digging my fingers into the sand, pulling my body behind. It's not the most dignified method of travel. But I guess heat exhaustion will do that to a girl.

"Plans for when I get better," I mumble to myself. "Kill Gibson—no wait, I should find the Prophet first, take her to meet Gibson... rub it in his face. Kill him—no, cut him up really good... have her heal him, wash, rinse, repeat." My legs give out and I decide to take a break. I roll onto my back and look up at the sky. It's so vast and endless, eternal darkness with little specks of light. Just like when I was almost dead. Is there anything beyond the darkness? Wouldn't that be something? Living a long hard life, trying to survive by whatever means, doing what has to be done just to reach that end that everyone faces... only to find darkness. It kind of makes the whole struggle seem pointless.

"Over here," someone yells. "Quickly!"

I turn over and think I'm losing it. Through the blur of fading sight, I can barely make someone out. A man... he's wearing a white robe, with a hubcap hanging from his neck, and a sad looking pope hat mashed on his head. A walking stick leads him towards me, except it's not a stick, it's an old fashioned TV antenna. Two others emerge behind him, wearing the same sort of robes, with scraps of metal and other pieces of junk tied to their bodies. Pope hat points at me, and I give him a middle finger salute before reality decides it's too much for me. Everything starts spinning. Voices reach me with no meaning.

"How'd you get here?" someone asks.

"Prophet," I say. "Where's the Prophet?"

WHEN I WAKE UP, I'M SURPRISED TO FIND MYSELF IN A CRAMPED shithole of a shack. I'm surrounded by random scraps of metal, tins, and crude tools covered in rust. The bed of coarse blankets I lay on smells like dog. Whispers draw my attention to the small window at the far wall. Some people are huddled outside, watching me as if they think they'll catch a nip slip or something. These guys are all about their robes and 'hubcaps for accessories' lifestyle; to each his own.

The door to the far right opens and a little boy rushes in. He looks at me like he thinks I might bite his head off. Doesn't want to meet my eyes and takes cautious steps in my direction. I would offer him a smile, but I'm not one for smiles, so why start our relationship on a lie? Instead, I try to sit up, which sets him on edge. He backs away, but gets tripped up and falls.

"Sorry!" he squeals. "The Elder said to check on you... I... I'm supposed to see if you need anything. My name is Navi."

My throat's so dry I can barely get a word out. I have to cough up a lung and bits of my insides before I can finally ask for the one thing I need the most. "Do you have anything with alcohol?" It hurts just to speak, but a sense of relief washes over me when Navi nods and runs off looking for my cure.

When the door swings open, I catch a glimpse of more people outside. I can feel the eyes of everyone on me. It's like being in a dark alley and knowing rats are hidden in every nook and cranny.

Navi returns with a goofy smile on his face. He hands me a dirty mason jar with a pale yellow liquid sloshing around inside. I grab the jar and he jumps back as if he thinks touching me will turn him to stone.

"Thanks." I take a deep drink. It's warm and tangy. It tastes like piss... I think it might be piss. Why do I know what piss tastes like? "Is this piss?"

He opens his mouth to speak, but clamps it shut when a scream breaks the calm outside. He shoots a nervous look towards the door. All of a sudden, I'm not the most important thing since sliced bread. I take another experimental sip of the maybe-piss drink. Navi pulls at my arm and points to an altar off to the side.

"What is that?" I ask.

He doesn't answer; he points and pulls, which just annoys the shit out of me.

I give the altar a closer look; candles send shadows cascading across dried flowers, odd trinkets, pieces of bones, and five shotgun shells, standing at attention between two skulls. A laced drape hangs over the altar, fluttering in the breeze coming in from the window. I have to squint to see better, but the drape is hanging from a shotgun.

Seems like Navi finally realized he was coming close to meeting my boot up his ass, because he lets go of my arm and runs from the shack. People are rushing past the window and a crowd starts to gather outside. I take a deep breath.

"Idiots!" I say to myself, because as far as I'm concerned, I'm the only other person around with brain cells. Scribbled on the wall above the shotgun altar, in handwriting like a two-year-old with chalk is: 'Hand of God'.

More shouting comes from outside, a woman screams, then crying. I sit back down and take another sip of the 'Maybe Piss' drink. More shouting... don't get involved. I chug the drink down; my throat practically closes up. I check myself and am surprised to find soft mended flesh where there should have been gaping knife wounds. More shouting. I wouldn't care, but I get the feeling whatever's going on out there will hold up the next round of drinks. I finish the last of what my jar has to offer and sigh. Another shout. Goddamn it.

I've had about enough of this, I can understand being preoccupied, but I dragged my half-dead ass across the desert, I deserved the five-star service. I head out into the street and am greeted by a group of robe wearing weirdos huddled up together, hugging and crying, generally looking like the saddest congregation in history. Mostly women, children, and the old, with only a handful of older guys sprinkled about. They all cower before a hunched over man covered in pieces of leather, short blades attached to his fingers, like our own personal horror show. There's so much leather I can barely see skin... a Nibbler. He's dragging a woman away from the crowd. Navi's screaming and crying, kicking and punching at the Nibbler, who just swats him away like a gnat.

"Hey!" I shout.

Everyone stops their theatrics and looks at me. The Nibbler tilts his head and smiles. What I can see of his teeth are shaved down to little pointy needles. Navi looks at me with this pathetic pleading look.

"I need you to stop screwing around with my hosts," I shout at the Nibbler.

He laughs and kicks Navi in the stomach. "Who... are... you?" Between every word, a forked tongue slithers out. I get the feeling he's going to be an asshole.

I shrug and head back inside.

"I hate assholes." I rip the drape off the altar and grab the holy shotgun off the wall. It feels good to have a weapon in my hands. Next, I crack her open and jam a couple of shells in her sweet spot. "That's right baby, take it."

I hide the shotgun behind my back and step outside. The Nibbler is standing around with this confused look on his face, like he can't believe I walked out during the middle of our conversation.

"Unwise... to... come back," he says.

The woman he's got a hold of spouts off one last scream to make sure I know she's there.

"Last chance," I say.

"Or... you'll—"

I swing the shotgun out and blow his head off in one quick motion. When the smoke settles, pieces of his brain and skull are decorating Navi's hubcap armor. The woman squeals and crawls away from the brand new pool of blood. "I hate Nibblers."

Navi runs to the lady and hugs her. She doesn't even care that he's getting bits of brain all over her. They start bawling and it gets awkward, so I turn away. The whole rest of the bunch are on their knees reaching out to me, mumbling a bunch of shit, thanks, and other slightly annoying things.

"Can someone just get me another drink?" I ask.

The Pope steps forward. He takes off his hat and rubs sweat from his brow; his hairline seems to have a problem with his face. He grabs my hand and drops down to his knees. "You can wield the thunder!"

I hold out the shotgun and everyone drops their foreheads to the ground. "This? Pretty sure any of you could."

He nods like his head's too heavy for his neck. "The Last Cowboy said one day someone would come and wield the thunder. He said only the chosen can hold it, an outsider who will protect us from the fiends out to destroy us."

"No." I push him off and start back to the shack, only now someone else grabs at my hand, kissing my knuckles, being a nuisance. There's a tug at my shirt and a couple of others are grabbing at the fabric. Soon, I'm surrounded. "Fuck me."

THINGS TOOK A CONSIDERABLE TURN FOR THE WORSE. THEY BATHED ME in a lake, a holy lake, where livestock bathed. My sins were washed away and I was anointed with oils or cooking grease, whatever. They sat me on a rusted old beach chair that must have had a front row seat to the bombs. They fed me fruits, the majority rotten, and pieces of meat that may or may not have been dog. Okay, it wasn't all bad. But the worst part came at night.

"We are the children of the apocalypse," The Pope says. "The Last Cowboy spoke to us, he told us of a time when a savior would come."

"A cowboy?" I ask, not because I'm interested, it just seems like the question to ask. "So this cowboy comes 'round and basically tells you guys to stick it out, someone's going to come, pick up that 'holy' shotgun, and make your lives better?"

The Pope looks over the crowd of disciples sitting around us. He needs help with this, but no one is willing to lend him a hand. "Well, he is one with the desert—"

"Of course, that makes it better."

"He knows all and sees all!" The Pope gets a bit of confidence going. "Some say The Last Cowboy is God himself."

"So God decided to put on some boots, spurs, and a hat? Maybe... everyone has their kinks. But wander the desert? Hard time believing that."

He looks off to his disciples again. "You question our beliefs and yet here you are, wielding the power of thunder and rescuing us from the fiends."

I shake my head and hold out the shotgun for all to see. "It's a shotgun! Not a magical holy relic. You just had to put the shells in, point, and shoot. There's nothing magical about it."

"When I found you, you spoke of someone," he says. "Who was it? How did you come to be here?"

"I came looking for the"—shit, this is only going to encourage him—"the Prophet... I was left for dead, she saved my life; it was a whole thing. Look, I know what you're going to say, you're going to twist it all up in your holy mumbo jumbo. It's just not like that."

He looks up at me and smiles. I wonder how long their hospitality will last after I shoot his face off. "You were led here by the Prophet?"

I sigh and take a long sip of water handed to me by a little girl, who stares like I'm some sort of rock star. "Look, I just wandered the desert until you guys found me. Sure, mostly I was looking for her. Thought maybe she'd come here. Do you know how long Gibson had us wandering around looking for her? It was like we became this weird pathetic cult... well kind of like you guys actually."

"What is a Gibson?" he asks.

"An asshole," I blurt out.

The assembled disciples all murmur amongst themselves.

"So..." I say. "Yeah. Gibson promised us all a life of wealth if we found the Prophet. That was a year ago. We traveled up and down the Badlands, leaving no stone unturned and couldn't find shit. Then he left me for dead —don't ask—and lo and behold, who shows up? The Prophet. So now I need to find her, for two reasons. One, so I can get rich. And most importantly, two, so I can rub it in Gibson's face right before I blow it off."

"How can you not see it? You were meant to come here and protect us. You were meant to rescue our people!"

"Wait, protect is one thing. Sure, if while I'm here, some asshole comes around and starts trouble. Why not? Like I said"—I point the shotgun at him—"load, point, shoot. No sweat. But never did I say anything about rescuing people. That sounds like it requires a journey. A journey that is most likely out of my way."

"But the fiends have taken our people!"

"And you should have protected them instead of letting a 'cowboy' tell you that someone will use a magical shotgun to protect you. It's called taking responsibility for yourselves." I wave the little girl over who brings a bowl of grapes. I pop a handful in my mouth and shudder at the sour aftertaste.

"She doesn't know!" One of the disciples stands up amongst the crowd. He's a handsome, lean, tall, and rough around the edges type, one of the only fit looking guys here. The white robes do little to hide his toned arms. Pope looks at him with cocked eyebrows. He seems hesitant but continues. "She doesn't know about the Prophet..."

"What do you mean?" Pope and I both ask.

The new guy approaches. With each step, he seems to stand taller and square his shoulders just a little harder. Soon he doesn't look as pathetic as the rest. "They took her."

I look to the elder whose mouth seems to be sealed shut.

"Who took her?" I ask.

"The fiends," he says. "You came here looking for her?"

"Yeah... but she said—"

"She sent you here, because she knew you were her only hope. When the fiends come, we must give them our own. They are taken to a camp, kept for food... when last they came; the Prophet was here. They mistook her as one of ours and took her. If you seek the Prophet, you'll find her at their camp. I will go with you and free my people—I will... take responsibility for my own."

"Okay, first of all, stop calling them fiends." I stand and size him up. "They aren't some sort of holy scourge sent to test your faith. They're amped up weirdos called Nibblers."

More than one of the congregation members tests the name on their tongue.

"Second of all, I'm pretty sure if you stepped outside this settlement, you'd die."

"Because The Last Cowboy doesn't want us to leave?" he asks.

"No, because you'd probably walk right off a cliff or something."

He narrows his eyes and clicks his tongue. One of the little kids runs off. "I'm the best hunter, the fastest runner, most skilled tracker, and best equipped for the desert."

"And yet you haven't been able to get your people back."

He bites down hard. The little kid comes running back with a bow and quiver of arrows. He hands them off to Mr. Best-at-Everything and joins the others.

"Oh how exciting," I say. "You have a bow and arrows. So, this is the part where you wow me with an example of how amazing you are, by shooting your arrow around the world, and hitting a fly off the top of the moon. Guess what? Not interested. If you want to come. Come. Just don't get in my way. Also, if you're about to get killed and me helping you means I might get killed, I most likely won't be helping you." With that off my chest, I sit back down and fold my hands behind my head.

To my surprise, a slow smile spreads across his face. He kneels before me. "My name is Finn and I am the next in line to be elder. I will not let you or my people down." He stares at me with a smile. I guess he expected me to bless him or something, because things get awkward when I don't. "Okay... well... I will gather some supplies." He runs off to get what I can only guess. Rotten vegetables, dog meat, filthy water, and piss for drink seems to be their major exports.

We TRAVEL IN SILENCE FOR MOST OF THE DAY, VERY MUCH APPRECIATED on my part. Finn keeps some distance ahead, tracking, or whatever it is he's doing. He seems almost like a child let loose in a toy store. He runs back and forth sniffing and inspecting every scrap metal, plant, and grain of sand he can get his hands on. He probably doesn't get out much. I can't imagine him surviving out here too long on his own.

The sun is murder on my skin, and he seems to gain endless amounts of energy from it. At least when I was running with Gibson, I had the luxury of riding around in the back of his buggy. Sleeping with the boss had its perks, but this walking, ugh, lucky for me I got brand spanking new pair of shitty way-too-tight boots. Maybe I can make Finn carry me on his back... he definitely has the muscles for it. I wonder if he's ever had a real woman... I'd probably break him.

It's midday when we decide to break. Finn caught some sort of rodent that looks like a cross between a rat and a mutant raccoon. It smells something fierce, but that doesn't stop Finn from slicing it open and skinning it with his bare hands. I sit across from him and watch as he works with surgical precision. There's something almost sexual about it. The way he handles the flesh and undresses it of its skin. He sets the meat on a skewer and starts a fire by smacking two rocks together. He may be more capable than I thought.

"How much further?" I ask.

"It's not too far. It's best we approach during the night." He's got a fire going and sets the meat cooking. "These parts are very dangerous. We have to stay alert. I know you wield the thunder" —he gives the shotgun a quick glance—"but we still need to be careful."

I lay back and rest the gun on my stomach. "Trust me, first sign of trouble, I'm out. This Prophet better be worth it."

"Why is she so important?" he asks.

"She's my ticket to a better life." I look up at him and the sun reflects off his eyes.

My gaze makes him uncomfortable, so he goes about checking the food. "You said she healed you, is that not enough?"

"Where I came from," I say. "It wasn't ideal... I did a lot of things that people didn't like. They kept me in a cell, you know? Prison." I sit up and stretch. "I would have spent the rest of my life there if Gibson hadn't broken me out. He had this scheme. Gather up a gang of the worst scumbags the UCF had laying around. Take us into the Badlands, free of the law, and hunt down the Prophet."

"Did this Gibson need healing?"

I laugh. "Fuck, no! He had a buyer, someone that would give good money to have her in his possession. Enough money to see all of us living the life."

He gives me that look, the one my mom used to give me. "You planned on trading your freedom for hers?"

"Yeah... well, you don't have to make it sound so negative."

"And you say you did things that made you deserving of being in prison?"

I give him my most annoyed sigh. "At least that's what society deems, yeah."

"The Prophet only wants to help people. But... she spends her life being passed around, kidnapped, and kept like a slave. She saved your life, didn't she?"

"Yeah, you could say that."

"And you reward her by hunting her down in hopes of selling her?"

I get up and heft the shotgun onto my shoulder. "Look kid, your elder is the one that claimed I'm all high and mighty. I've never lied about who I am. Cassie Black cares about one person—Cassie Black. That's how I've always lived my life, and that's how I like it. I'm a very bad person, and that's the way it's going to stay."

"You like the way you live?" He laughs. "All it's done is get you locked up, lost in the desert, and here with me..."

I aim the shotgun at his stupid face. Four left. Is he worth the shell? The bastard doesn't even flinch; instead, he takes the skewer off the fire and offers me lunch.

WE ARE LYING IN THE SAND ATOP A DUNE LOOKING DOWN OVER A CAMP of Nibblers. They number in the dozens; tents and campfires are spread sparsely throughout. There's a pen at the farthest side of the camp. I can see Finn's robbed brethren huddled up close behind bars. They look like cattle ready for slaughter. Mostly men, some women... but I don't see a little girl.

"Is the Prophet with them?" I ask pointing at the pen.

He gives a low nod. The kind that means his balls just shriveled up and retreated back into his stomach. I don't blame him, this isn't just a random raider gang, or a couple of Nibblers, this is fuck me sideways the odds are against us.

"So I'm thinking," I say calmly. "That we head back to your village, and tell them we gave it our all. Then you say 'hey, you know, Cassie is good people. We should continue worshiping and pampering her,' and we all live happily ever after. How's that sound? Sound good? Sounds good to me."

He shakes his head. "No we have to save them. I won't let my people die in there."

I grab a handful of his hair and aim his head at the camp of assholes waiting to rip us to shreds. "What do you see down there? That's not something we can just hold hands through, banking on the power of friendship and holy relics. They will kill us, capture us, and do things to our bodies. In who knows what the fuck order."

"We can't leave them!" He grabs my hand from his hair and pulls me in close. "You gave us your word. Don't you want to find your Prophet?"

"Hate to break it to you, but my word don't mean shit... and there's no such thing as Santa Claus. As far as the Prophet goes, I've already given up too much for her."

He shoves me. The bastard actually had the balls to shove me. "Well then go!" His eyes are intense. "I don't need you. Your Prophet isn't even here so what does it matter?"

"What did you say?" I ask very carefully, tightening my grip on the shotgun stock.

"You heard me. She's not here!" He takes an arrow from his quiver and nocks it. "The elder had me lie to get your help."

"Not only is that insulting and hurtful, but I've killed men for less." I lift the shotgun up to his chest.

"Go ahead!" he shouts. "Do it. You think I'm scared of death? The Last Cowboy will lead me into the after if it's my time. I'm meant to save my people. I don't need your help."

I laugh. "You're such an idiot, the whole lot of you."

"You think I'm dumb, but I look at you and see someone who has nothing."

As a parting gift, I kiss him goodnight with the stock of my gun. He's laid out and probably dreaming of cowboys when I walk away.

FINN AND THE REST OF THEM HAVE GOT TO BE OUT OF THEIR MIND. Nibblers, not even a small manageable group, a whole fucking nest! Those assholes have to be on something if they think I'm going to march in there with four shells and a dream. If Finn is dumb enough to think he can handle it on his own, more power to him. He'll learn that their Last Cowboy moseyed the fuck out of dodge a long time ago. I feel a little bad for him. He's young and naive, still idealistic. I can't remember what it was like to be that way. He hasn't been stripped and beaten by the world yet. Too bad, so sad. He's going to skip right over the heartache and jump ass backwards into painful death.

I don't know why I can't stop thinking about Finn and the others. Just got to keep one foot moving in front of the other. Me and the endless desert are going to be best friends forever. The sand makes it hard to walk quickly. Eventually, my legs get tired and I have to take slow steady steps. I think my eyes are playing tricks on me when a thick mist starts to raise from the sand. It blankets the whole desert for as far as I can see. A shudder runs though me and I know I'm not alone.

The mist parts, revealing a figure seemingly gliding across the sand. The lapel of a long coat wrapped tightly around his body flutters in the night breeze; it's black as oil. A black cowboy hat sits atop his head, slightly tipped forward, obscuring his face in shadow.

You got to be fucking kidding me.

I think the best course of action is avoiding this asshole at all costs. Fear runs through my body; it makes my legs feel like rubber. I haven't felt this kind of fear in a long time, not even when Gibson tried to end my life. I turn on my heels, but before I can make a break for it, I find him standing in front of me. I catch sight of his face, ghostly pale like the moonlight. His paper thin skin is all wrinkles. Black veins run up and down his cheeks.

"Listen," I say. "I've had about enough of this. If you're looking to kill me, don't think it'll be easy." I heft the shotgun from hand to hand so he gets the picture.

He pushes the side of his jacket open, a six-shooter hangs from his belt, encased in shadow and whispers. I'm drawn to it; I practically have to force myself from reaching out to touch it. I take a step back and turn, only to find him standing before me once again.

"For fucks sake!" I shout. "So you're him, then? The Last Cowboy?" I aim my gun at him; make sure he gets a good look at the barrel, even though something tells me it will have no effect on him.

"There's no need for hostility." He brushes my weapon away as if parting a bed of flowers. His voice is old and rough, like rocks on sandpaper.

"What do you want?"

"To ask you a question," he says matter of fact.

"And what would that be?"

"What is your purpose?"

I shrug. "I tend to think random acts of violence, drinking... I like drinking, and general misbehaving make up my resume. Most of all, I tend to watch out for myself at whatever cost necessary so if you're planning to—"

"Look how far you've come. From the girl who grew up on the streets of a Black Zone to this, a savior, and yet you're running away. Running to where? To wander the Badlands, to search for the Prophet, so you can what? Return to their so-called *civilization* and hide from the law for the rest of your life? I've given you purpose. I've given you a chance to live a life worthy of your skills."

"Oh you did all this, huh?"

"There are infinite possibilities and paths a person can take. Even the most minute choice can lead to a drastically different outcome. If I hadn't whispered in Gibson's ear, on that particular night, at that particular time, would the Prophet have come across your path? Would you have ever found my children if you didn't choose the path I set for you?"

"Whispered what in Gibson's ear?"

"That you'd betray him," he says with a smile.

"Why?"

"Because I can see your worth. If you stayed with Gibson, you would have amounted to nothing. I need you to find my children."

"So this was all for me to help them? Why didn't you just step in and help?"

"I set the pieces and watch how they play out. Did the God of old intervene directly in his children's needs? No, because what use would that be? Give a man food and he'll eat for a day... teach him how to hunt... and so on and so on."

"But all you've done is make them depend on me!"

"Is the lesson theirs... or yours?"

"I'm not that important... why go through all the effort?"

"I've put together this little game, with players who have no lasting effect on fate, easy enough to maneuver without upsetting the bigger picture, small enough to go unnoticed. What I wanted to see was how you would fare."

"Because I can take out the important people."

He nods; the light shines right through his flesh when he looks up at the moon. "Like the Prophet."

"What makes you think I would care enough to?"

"Don't you? You proved yourself to be more than capable of taking care of yourself, and you have little regard for others. My test just proved that. All those innocent lives left to die because you care only about yourself... surely you wouldn't have a problem killing a child if it was in your best interest. If you followed me, did my bidding, you could be so much more. You could usher in a new era of chaos upon the Badlands."

I think of Finn, that big idiot going up against impossible odds. I feel a bit of guilt, sure, but not enough to risk my ass. "Sorry, but when does this story get interesting?"

"Let me give you something to think over for a moment. Will you spend your life living like a rat, hiding in the shadows, barely surviving... or will you become more, walk in the light and bask in glory? Everyone wants to be something. I often wonder the limits of man; how far can they go before they choose the path of fight or flight. You see the falseness of their so-called civilization. You understand *true* strength." He tips his hat. "One last thing, I offer you a present."

He fades with the mist. I stare at the ground where his footprints still face me. The stars shine down on me, all judgmental and condescending. Why is it they seem to care now? The mist clears and I'm greeted by the familiar sound of roaring engines. Buggies kick up sand as their wheels cut through the desert heading straight for me. Gibson's crew. Four people, four shells. I can take them all out. The Cowboy is giving me revenge. Payment for me to be his. Fight or flight, fight or flight. Well flight has got me this far. I take a deep breath and run.

We meet half way, me with my arms spread wide waving them to stop. The first thing I notice is the disappointment on Gibson's face. He brakes hard. His buggy slides to a halt a couple of feet away from me. It could have gone worse. The other two stop in a semi-circle around me, each driver looks to Gibson for guidance, because they are all spineless cowards who can't think for themselves.

"Cassie?" Gibson steps down from his vehicle and takes a cautious step forward. "How are you..."

"Skip the meet and greet," I say. "I have something you want."

The other driver and passengers climb down and take their proper places behind him.

"I thought she was dead," someone murmurs.

Gibson runs a hand down his face. "She should be—Cassie, why aren't you dead? I went through a whole lot of trouble making sure you were dead, you know."

"I found the Prophet."

There's a moment of hesitation. No one knows what to do.

"That's bullshit," he says.

"How many times did you stick me?" I lift my shirt and let everyone get a good look at the soft pink flesh on my belly. "Think these healed all by themselves out here? I didn't have a stimpak jammed up my ass... you should know."

His eyes light up and he practically trips over himself running to my side. He drops down to his knees, grabs a handful of my waist, pulling me in close to get a better view. "Well I'll be damned! I stabbed you at least five times—maybe more, you had me in a real emotional state."

I shove him off and introduce him to my shotgun. "I should kill you right here."

"So why haven't you?" He doesn't flinch, instead his gleaming eyes burn a hole into me. "You obviously want something."

"You were right about her all along, 'cept she's a bit smaller than you think." I sigh. "I know the truth now... I wanted to tell you I'm sorry."

He opens his arms wide and gives me that cheap smile. My skin crawls as I take a step into his embrace. He smells like dust and death. "I did miss you. You know after I left you for dead I kind of regretted it."

"I missed you too."

BACK AT THE OVERPASS WITH NO SIGN OF FINN. LUCKILY, ALL THOSE freaks are still walking about like a regular Sunday afternoon. If he tried something, I'm assuming they'd be in a ruckus. Where, then, where are you? There! He's sneaking up alongside the outer perimeter of the camp, trying to make his way straight for the pen. He's got an arrow nocked like it'll protect him from all these freaks. He has some balls on him. Got to respect that.

"Cass." Gibson crawls up beside me. "You didn't say there's a whole freaking nest of them." Sweat drips down his brow. He takes a look at his crew, two big burly men, and Jane the crazy bitch with the knives. We know they won't be enough.

"I'm thinking we just drive right in," I say. "Rush them before they know what's happening."

"You sure she's in there?" He squints in the direction of the pen.

I punch him in the arm. "As sure as shit. You think I'd forget the girl who saved my life?" I point to a random girl in the pen. "She must be huddled between the others, they are kinda protective of her."

Finn is nearing the prisoners. My heart sinks when I see a couple of Nibblers on a path that will intersect with his. They'll be on him soon and that'll be the end of it. I get up and look Gibson dead in the eyes. "Look. If you don't got the sack to do what needs to be done, I'll do it myself."

"I just think we need to plan this out better," he says. "I mean she's safe and sound in that cage isn't she? We should wait this out."

I glance over at Finn, nearly about to be caught. "Gibson, you always were a coward." I crack my fist across his face; he spins and goes down. It's all I can afford to give him right now. I'll need my shells.

The others take a moment to process I just knocked their faithful leader on his ass. Jane the crazy bitch pulls one of her wicked knives and smiles, as if she's been waiting for a reason to gut me. I let her check out the nail polish on my middle finger for a moment, then take off running down the slope. Gibson's yelling bloody murder but I'm too busy running and falling down the slope like a madwoman, practically tumbling into the perimeter of the camp. It's only seconds before I'm spotted, a hunched over man in tight leather that covers his body and face catches whiff of me and snarls like a rabid animal.

Shotgun shell number two finds a new home in his chest. He crumbles in a mist of blood. I jump over him and let the momentum carry me deeper into the nest. The thunderous explosion of my gun alerted everyone else of my presence. Three shells left.

Finn's far off, but I catch a glimpse of him. He spots me and even from this distance I can see the shock on his face. Yeah, that's right, the Savior is here and I brought the thunder. I stick the tip of my gun into a screaming Nibbler's mouth and blow out the back of his head. Note to self: never attack someone with your mouth wide open. Two shells left.

Nibblers are everywhere, swarming me like a pack of wolves, except these wolves have a leather fetish and metal blades grafted to their fingers. Surrounded with nowhere to go for cover, what's a girl to do? I look towards the pen for any sign of Finn, but a freak show with rusted nails sticking out his face gets in my view. I angle my gun just right. Pull the trigger. After his head blows, a Nibbler behind him catches the spray and goes down with a hole in his chest. One shell left.

Growls, their growls are all I can hear. It's almost deafening. Finn's got the door to the pen open. He's leading his people out. The growls grow louder and louder... they sound like... dune buggies! I jump out the way just as Gibson drives straight through the madness. Bodies lay broken and bloodied in his wake. Another buggy follows, cutting Nibblers down to my right. Jane the crazy bitch jumps from the passenger side of Gibson's buggy; her blades move so fast I can barely see them. But the trail of bodies she leaves behind shows just how efficient she is.

Gibson's guys jump out of the other buggy and start firing. One by one, Nibblers drop. Gibson sidles up next to me, firing into the crowd. Teamwork, it didn't mean shit. As many as we put down, more step in. There's no sign of it ending. More importantly, there's no sign of Finn and his people; he got them out. I did my part. Stick a fork in me.

"How many shells you have left?" Gibson asks.

"One," I say. "No wait, none."

He looks at me with those big dumb eyes. "What?"

I jam the shotgun under his chin and blow him a kiss before I'm sprayed with a shower of blood. I don't even have time to take in my revenge before Jane the bitch comes at me all slice and dice like. I swing the barrel of my gun trying to knock her head off. I would have made a home run if a Nibbler didn't catch me in the side. I'm on the ground, the smell of old leather and sweat in my nostrils. Jane the bitch screams, soon it's cut off by the gurgling sound you make when your throat's ripped out.

Under the press of bodies, I catch sight of Gibson's remaining crew getting a rather violent facelift. That's when I hear it, the sound of flesh being ripped from bone. I hear it before I feel it. Unfortunately, once I feel it, it doesn't stop. Such incredible pain, it's as if every nerve in my body is on fire. On my back. I can't move. At least I can see the stars; they shine in that mocking way. They know tonight's my last night on earth. Only, I think now... I think they are a little bit more welcoming.

WILBERT STANTON

Wilbert Stanton was born and raised in New York City. From an early age, Wilbert decided he would either write books or take over the world; everything else was just a precursor to his end game.

Along the way, he has studied Psychology, English, and Computer Science. He's held jobs in a wide range of fields and met people from all walks of life. Wilbert is constantly learning and growing as a person, in order to solidify his dreams.

In the end, world domination was a bit tedious, so he decided to focus on writing books.

Links:

Facebook:

https://facebook.com/authorwilbertstanton/

Webpage http://www.wilbertstanton.com/

5

THE OLD CITY

MATTHEW S. COX

This story takes place within the Awakened series after the events of
Prophet of the Badlands.

H ome offered a sense of security that Althea struggled to accept.
Being alone in the house reawakened old worries. Though she
hummed to herself while stuffing empanadas for later, she
glanced at every shadow and found herself freezing still whenever the
building creaked. Over and over in her mind, she planned out how she
might react if someone did try to kidnap her again. She wouldn't let that
happen. Her spike of determination made her mash the spoon down too
hard, spreading filling over the side of the dough. She bit her lip and
grimaced, as if Karina would've seen her mistake and been disappointed
in her.

The city police wanted her to visit them for a little while today. She
shifted her weight onto her right leg and tapped her left big toe absent-
mindedly at the floor while scraping the stuffing paste into a nice lump in
the middle. Each excuse she tried to come up with for not going to see
them made her feel like more and more of a liar. Anything from the big
city took her back to being separated from her family, and made her think
sad thoughts. Still, the psionic police did help Querq as they promised to.
She had to keep her promise.

A few more empanadas, and she'd go see what they wanted.

Karina had made a mush mostly consisting of black beans and

shredded chicken, with some chopped up herbs. Her sister wanted to try some of the new 'spices' the city police had brought in. Even Father seemed pleased by sniffing the jar. Despite that the powdered seasonings came from *that* place, she couldn't argue they smelled good. The fragrance made resisting her urge to taste it uncooked difficult, but Karina had specifically made her say 'I promise not to eat any before they're done.'

Althea jabbed the large spoon into the bowl of filling and scooped out a dollop, which she plopped into the middle of a new dough square before leaving the spoon upright in the chicken-bean mush. She folded the dough to make a pillow and sealed it by pressing around the edges with a fork as Karina had taught her. After adding it to the tray, she glanced out the window at the position of the Sun. *Late afternoon.* At the time, she huffed a sigh that made her hair jump away from her face.

"I said I'd go..."

She draped a cloth over the tray of unbaked empanadas, another over the bowl, and eyed the sink. The Water Man had gotten the faucet working, a feat that most people in Querq still considered an act of magic. Althea didn't want to 'waste' the faucet water just washing her hands, so she ducked out the back door heading for the water pump. Despite the street empty of people, the sight of the place where Dean kidnapped her with a tranquilizer gun tightened her throat. Karina still didn't want her going off alone, but she no longer feared the stinging green needles. Now that she knew what they did, she could protect herself... not that she expected anyone to try that again.

Althea stepped into a warm puddle on the boards around the pump; an involuntary squirm climbed her legs and continued into her back at the sensation of mossy slime squishing underfoot. She pumped twice to get water flowing, and rinsed food and flour from her hands before rubbing them down the front of her simple white dress to dry them. It didn't hang as long as her beloved skirt had, stopping about halfway down her thighs. The white dress Archon made her wear had been longer; at least she could run in this one.

Wanting to get home as soon as possible, she ran past the pump to the end of the alley, and hooked a left on the street. Cool dirt gave way to warm paving. Despite the small group of city police, and the fancy things they brought with them, few cars drove through Querq. Only the Watch had working vehicles, three 'pickup trucks,' as Father called them... which didn't make a lot of sense. They couldn't pick anything up. She pondered that while walking down the centerline of an ancient strip of blacktop. Here and there, scraps of reflective paint glinted at her. She skipped from one coin sized spot to the next, grinning, daydreaming about what it must've looked in the before-time when the whole street glimmered yellow in the Sun.

Mrs. Alvarez wandered by, offering a wave and a pleasant greeting; her three grandchildren also smiled and yelled hellos. Althea grinned back at them, savoring the joy the woman had shown once clear of pain. Most of her bones had looked strange around the joints, and it hurt her to move at all. She remembered fixing the youngest boy's broken ankle once, and tending to the nine-year-old granddaughter, Belinda, when she ran through Jorge's scrapyard and got a hunk of metal stuck in her foot.

The grandkids broke formation long enough to hug her one after the next, and followed Mrs. Alvarez off to the street leading to their home. The odd machine smell in the place came back to her. She'd visited to mend the woman's bone sicks. Their home smelled like metal and the underside of a car. It had to be from whatever happened there before it became someone's house. Father said most of the places in Querq from the before time had been shops and such. Corinne and her husband lived in something called a 'pizza place.'

"Pee sa. Peetz uh." She tilted her head; the effort of thinking about a word slowed her walk. "Piza. Piz-uh. Bah."

Two blocks later, she emerged in the center of Querq, where the city police made their home. They'd even brought their own building, a rectangular metal box elevated off the ground on fat metal legs. Various small components on the roof glittered with tiny flashing blue or green lights. One emitted a continuous whirring. Some of the smaller kids could run underneath the city police's house without ducking. Althea bit her lip, feeling a twinge of shame at her reaction to the noise of the flying machine that had brought it here. It had taken Karina a good hour to talk her out from under the bed. Even though it had felt like their home would shake itself apart, she didn't want to come out.

Unlike the rest of the children of Querq, who all came running to watch the flying machine set the enormous box down in the middle of the city, she wanted nothing to do with anything that could make her home tremble. Two black sky cars sat near the long wall of the rectangular box, identical to the one she'd been riding in when Archon first appeared to her. From the outside, where they should've had windows, they had slabs of black metal.

Althea blinked, certain the one she'd been in had windows. People can't see through armored plates. She shook her head, dismissing it as 'stupid city stuff,' and gave them both a wide berth on her way to a metal staircase attached to the side of the boxy structure. She gasped as soon as she stepped on it, as hot as a cooking plate. With a yelp of surprised pain, she raced up the four steps and hopped from leg to leg while knocking, though her small hand didn't make much noise.

"Hello?"

She bounced on tiptoe to keep her feet from cooking for a moment, but no one answered. A small metal box perched on the wall to the right of the door. Looked like another tiny door, perhaps for mice. Figuring it more 'stupid city stuff,' she leaned her face close to it.

"Hello?"

When nothing happened, she stood straight and frowned. Annoyance got the better of her and she pounded her fists on the door, but made only a slight bit more noise than knocking. She screamed, "Hello!" at the little box. Seconds later, she opened the tiny door to reveal a glowing green square about as big as her palm. *Eep! Glowy!* She leaned away and slammed the small door. A few seconds later, the door split down the middle with a loud *pfshh. T*he two halves retracted into opposing walls, releasing a blast of freezing air.

"Eep!" She jumped back.

A man in a clingy black uniform with a silvery belt smiled at her from the doorway. Darkish skin and black hair almost made him seem local, but he didn't look like everyone else here. "Althea?"

"Yes, sir." She stood with her feet together, arms at her sides.

He backed up, gesturing for her to follow. "Come in. I'm Officer David Ahmed, but you can call me David if you like."

Having acclimated to the scorching metal porch, the inner hallway felt like walking on ice. Gleaming white walls caught the glow of overhead lights, forcing her to squint. Despite it being a clear day, the light inside seemed brighter than the sky. Teeth chattering, she gathered her dress as tight as she could around herself and followed the man through a short hallway to a square room with two desks at opposite corners. He glanced at one for a few seconds, chuckled, and went past it to a smaller room with two cushioned black seats catty-corner against the wall. Each looked a little like Father's sofa, but only big enough for two adults. He sat in one and gestured at the other.

Althea perched on the edge, hands on her knees, back straight and rigid. Her body wouldn't stop trembling from the cold. An odd sense tugged at her mind; she looked up at him, somehow knowing he attempted to 'read' her emotional state. Probably to figure out if her shivering came from cold or fear. She didn't fight him.

"Would you like a blanket or something?" He smiled and crossed to a small storage cabinet by the wall. "I'm sorry it's so cold in here. Lieutenant Franck, my superior, can't stand heat. That dress is so thin, and you've got no shoes."

"Is this going to take long?" asked Althea. "I have empanadas I need to finish making."

Officer Ahmed took a plain grey blanket from the cabinet and returned to the adjacent mini-couch. "I understand you've had a difficult time of it before you arrived in Querq." He handed her the blanket. "This won't take too long, but I would like to meet with you somewhat regularly to offer any help you might want coming to terms with what's happened to you."

Althea cocooned herself in the blanket, pulling her feet up under her on the soft cushion. She clutched two handfuls of plush fabric at her chest and waited a few seconds for the shivering to lessen. "What does it mean to come terms?"

He rested his arms over his knees and laced his fingers. "People react to traumatic things in different ways. I'm aware you don't fully trust Division 0, but my interest here is only to help you heal any mental or emotional wounds you've suffered from your ordeal. Coming to terms means reaching a point where bad things that happened to you in the past no longer affect you as strongly."

Her telempathy read genuine concern from him, without a trace of deceit or greed. Not like the old man back in the city... Burkhardt. He'd initially felt like a raider finding treasure, until he learned 'all she could do was heal.' He couldn't use her as a weapon, so he couldn't care less about her. She looked down at her lap; blonde hair draped down her front touched her legs. "Like how I wanna hide when the sky gets loud?"

"You're frightened by storms?" Officer Ahmed raised his right eyebrow a little.

"No." Althea brushed the blanket at her chin to chase away a minor itch. "I'm scared of fly machines. I like rain. I always go outside when it rains."

He nodded. "Are you worried that whoever is in the aircraft is coming to take you?"

"A little." She looked up, smiling. "But I can stop them. I'm scared it will break an' hurt someone when it falls. Metal boxes aren't s'posed ta fly."

"You can stop them?" He slid a flat bit of plastic, one of those 'datapad' things, into his lap and tapped at it. The surface facing him lit up blue and green, painting his features in colorful shadows.

"Yes." She flexed and relaxed her toes while staring off into nowhere. "I used to be scared to, but I'm not anymore."

"Afraid to protect yourself? Didn't it bother you the way people kept treating you?"

Althea's mind filled with memories of cages, rope, handcuffs, leashes, and locked doors. She pressed her arms to her chest, wishing Karina or Father sat at her side so she could cling to them. "The Wagon Man took me all over. Alla people inna Badlands know I can fix hurts and sicks. They wouldn't do bad to me. If I did mystic things, they'd be scared and wanna kill me." She slipped a hand out from under the blanket to wipe a stray tear. "I feeled good helping people, even if I hadda be in a cage."

He typed for a few seconds. "Sorry... that's no way to treat a child. I'm... You don't seem as traumatized as I'd have expected for a girl your age having spent so much time in captivity."

"I'm scared of being tied." Althea looked down again. "I don't like it." Silence hung thick between them for a little while before her mood lightened and she raised her head to make eye contact. "I have a home now. A family. I'm not scared to say no when someone wants ta take me." A spread of embarrassment warmed her cheeks. "I used ta always let people take me. I promise not to run away, an' I don' run away. That way, raiders don't tie me." She gave him a pitiful look. "Much."

"You've got to be the most potent telempath I've met... that Division Zero has ever recorded. *And* you've got a passable grasp of suggestion." He stared at the datapad. *If this kid wasn't so damn innocent, command would be losing their minds.*

Althea tilted her head. "I won't take away your commands' brain shapes."

Officer Ahmed chuckled. "Listening to my thoughts?" He let off a resigned sigh. "Normally, we consider that a breach of manners... but given the life you've had, I'm sure it's developed as a survival instinct. Also, considering your situation... it's probably best that you keep checking people out. For security reasons, of course. I don't mind if you peek."

Althea considered the mixture of pity and concern swirling around him for a second or two before peering into his thoughts. He seemed to have expected her to be more upset, constantly crying or wanting to hide from people. That she acted relatively normal both relieved and intrigued him. "I can make people not do bads. I used ta be scared people would hurt me if they knew I could." She recalled the image of a mystic, a scrawny man in a handmade skirt and wild-colored headdress who led a band of raiders against another tribe that had captured her, one that had kept those hand-cuff things on her legs so she couldn't run away.

Of course, being a mystic hadn't stopped an enormous raider from knocking him senseless with a pipe.

She leaked some of the memory of watching him scream and burn, chained to an iron beam, into Officer Ahmed's mind. The kind of fear that glowed from her captors at the mere sight of a mystic had terrified her. They believed they had to kill him by burning, or he'd just keep coming back from the dead. Rather than try to explain it with words, she sent a shade of her fear that if she'd done anything other than heal, it would've been her lashed to a metal post and lit on fire. Everyone knew her as the Prophet, the healer. They'd take her away—some groups would keep her tied, some would be nice and treat her more like a person—but she would never stay in one place for long. She'd been with the Wagon Man the long-est, but only because she hadn't been famous yet. Once the entire Badlands knew her, she changed owners every few weeks.

As long as her captors allowed her to heal people who suffered, she tolerated her lack of freedom. After all, back then she didn't have a home, somewhere she'd rather be. Wherever she went, she'd only get taken again. And so on.

Officer Ahmed shivered.

Her love for Karina and Father bloomed, an unintentional radiance made the city police man flash a dopey grin. Sensing her power running away, she backed off.

"I still did somes." She shifted in her seat and stretched her legs under the blanket. "I stopped real bads, like wifing. But"—she puffed up her chest—"I have a home now. I'm not scared."

He tapped again at the datapad thing. When he finished, he smiled at her. "Aside from holding you against your will, did any of the people who abducted you do anything to you that you didn't like or that made you feel uncomfortable?"

Althea looked him right in the eye. "You mean did they wife me?"

He coughed. "I'm sorry? Wife you?"

"Put boy parts in my girl parts."

Officer Ahmed blinked. "Umm..." Discomfort fell away from him in sheets.

She shook her head. "Not right 'cause I'm too young. Some raiders have harems. They make me help the women when they get hurt from wifing. If they were too mean, I sometimes made them stop." Althea fidgeted, thinking about Rachel's fear of being wifed... almost as strong as Althea's dread of it. "No one wifed me. I would not let them."

"You've witnessed, umm, women being..."

"Wifed?" She nodded. "Yes. If they were real scared, I'd take 'way the raider's..." Her face scrunched up as she searched for how to explain.

"Urge?" asked Officer Ahmed, a second after a tingle in her mind. "You... interesting. Dampened their desire."

"One woman wasn't even as old as Karina." Althea looked down. "He was gonna wife her, but she was so scared. I made him guilt. Strong. He helped her 'scape."

Officer Ahmed fidgeted and leaned on the armrest. "Well, I'm very happy to hear that nothing like that happened to you."

"I wouldn't let it," said Althea in a matter-of-fact tone. "I rather burn onna post."

He nodded. "I think I would too."

"Why are you surprised?"

"From what I've read here, you were taken by this guy with the wagon when you were five or six years old, and put in a cage for about a year... you've been kept prisoner on and off since, and been surrounded by violence more or less the entire time." He exhaled into his hands for warmth. "And that mess with Archon in the city... I guess I expected you to be more, umm... damaged. It's remarkable how unscathed you seem from a mental standpoint."

She tilted her head to the side. "Is that good?"

"Quite... but somewhat unsettling too. A child your age going through that... it's astounding me that you're not showing much mental trauma." He tapped and poked at the datapad again. "Perhaps knowing you had the ability to leave whenever you wanted to, and staying of your own choice helped?"

She opened her mouth to protest, saying they'd kept her bound or caged... but if she'd been less afraid of being thought a mystic, she'd had the power to force them to release her. In a way, she had chosen to stay a captive.

Althea looked down at the little tents her feet made in the blanket. "Before, I only wanted to help everyone I could. 'Cep for wifed, I did what they told me." She rolled a marble of an idea around her head, smiling to herself at taking more and more risks as she got older. She hated being tied up, and used her 'magic' to manipulate her captors to avoid it. Small pokes at their emotion wouldn't make them think of her as a mystic.

"Well..." He leaned back, smiling. "I'm honestly surprised and relieved that you're so resilient."

She stared at him, eager to get back home.

"I understand you've already given the Admin people back west a good idea about that Archon situation."

Althea frowned. "He's not a nice person. I don't wanna see him again." She looked down and to the side as Aurora's words floated in her memory. *The time will come when you will not save his life. You will watch him die.*

Officer Ahmed rubbed his chin. "It's distressing we weren't able to find him at the abandoned power station. Though, I'm more curious about the entity you mentioned, the one from the garden."

She shivered despite the blanket. "The Many... Bad." Althea shook her head rapidly side to side. "Not good. Hates everything."

"Some people think the reason we haven't reclaimed the Badlands to modern civilization is due to supernatural influence, though they're somewhat of a laughed-at minority."

"I don't know what you said." Althea narrowed her eyes.

"You've seen the city in the west."

She made a sour face as the urge to run home welled up within. "I don't like it there. You said I didn't have to go back."

He raised a placating hand. "You don't. Please calm down. I'm only saying that people think it's odd that modern technology hasn't spread back across the country. Before the war, people didn't live in two massive cities crammed against the coastlines." His datapad projected a map of North America, and he pointed out cities here and there throughout. "People are trying to understand why, since the war has been over for four hundred years, we haven't spread out again."

Althea looked down, speaking in a near-whisper. "Because he won't let them."

"That's what a few people say, but no one believes them. Most think it's due to money... it would be too expensive. There are still issues to be dealt with: weaponized mutants the corporations released during the war, runaway androids, environmental damage, and so on."

"He told me that he's made up of all the people who died. They're angry and want other people to suffer too." She looked up at him, eyes wide, searching. "I don't understand. Why does he want to make other people hurt just because they got hurt? Making pain doesn't fix pain."

Officer Ahmed gave a mild shrug. "I wish I could answer that. I don't think there is a good answer for that. Alas, being cruel is not an exclusively paranormal trait. Some people are like that."

"That's bad." She shifted to sit straight, moving her blanket-encased feet to the floor. "People shouldn't be bad... even if they're already dead."

He chuckled.

Althea smirked at him thinking her 'adorable,' but held her tongue. 'Aww how cute' didn't bother her anywhere near as much as 'ooh, the Prophet, grab her.'

"I find it interesting that none of the reported manifestations of equipment malfunction have occurred here since we've arrived."

She stared at him for a moment, blinked, and kept staring.

He bowed his head. "Sorry. It's oddly easy to forget you're ten years old."

"Twelve."

A sly grin pulled his lips to the side. "Maybe I'll meet you halfway and say eleven. Though we really don't know what effect such an overclocked accelerated healing would have on your body. Maybe you are twelve and you've been spending so much energy using your abilities on others, your body hasn't been growing. Maybe you've got a subconscious fear of being 'wifed,' and your power had been keeping your body childlike as some kind of defense mechanism."

Althea huffed. "I'm sorry. I didn't have the school. You are talking words I don't know."

"Forgive me; I was more muttering to myself there." He read from the datapad. "I wonder if your presence here somehow interferes with that apparition's ability to break machines. You are such an unusual case."

"I'm not a case. I'm Althea," she muttered.

He closed his eyes, smiling away the frustration.

"Sorry for making you upset." She scooted her feet back and forth to warm them.

"It's okay. What I meant is that you have quite a few psionic talents. Healing of course. Your telepathy is the strongest we've ever seen. Your eyes... you see in the dark, correct?"

"Yes. Bio... loom nis ant." She beamed with pride at remembering the word.

"They always glow blue." He tapped a finger on his chin. "We have seen astral sensates who can see in the dark by shifting their vision half into the spirit world, but their eyes radiate white light, and only while they are using the ability to see in the dark... or to see spirits."

"Spirits?" asked Althea.

"Ghosts? Apparitions of people who have died. Have you ever seen one?"

She shook her head. "Just The Many."

"Interesting. Well, psionic potential doesn't always translate to ability... like any other muscle, it needs to be developed. You've got a bit of suggestion, clairvoyance, and telepathy as well."

"If you say so." She shrugged.

"You can order people to do things sometimes and they do it?"

Althea nodded. "The woman in the bad city already told me 'bout it. I don' like doing that 'cause it's mean. Only when someone's gonna get hurt if I don't."

He radiated relief and pride, much the way Karina and Father felt when she'd finally gotten the fork to work. He thought about people being frightened of 'suggestives' the way people out here thought of mystics. Her hesitance at using it made him happy.

"Most psionics exhibit anywhere from one to three separate abilities. You've got potential in six, though your healing and empathy are by far the strongest."

Althea slipped an arm out from under the blanket and flexed her bicep.

"Indeed. A well-used muscle."

She grinned.

"Well... I can't say I was expecting you to be so well adjusted. I'm glad." He leaned forward and patted her on the knee. "I'm glad that you've found a light at the end of that long tunnel."

Her brow knit together. "I wasn't in a tunnel." As Officer Ahmed chuckled, she thought back to running away from those two raiders in the Lost Place. "Wait. I was... for a little."

"I see why everyone here loves you." He took her hand and squeezed it. "You make everyone near you happy."

She shifted her weight forward. "Can I go home now?"

He nodded. "Yes. Thank you for visiting with me. If you ever want to talk about anything that happened to you, or if you have any questions about your abilities, please find me."

Althea stood, letting the blanket fall to the cushions behind her. Cold air swam up under her dress, bringing a chatter to her teeth in less than a second. "Thank you for being nice. Sometimes I get bad dreams in my head, 'bout people who wanna take me, but Father said it will need time."

Officer Ahmed stood and patted her shoulder. "After the life you've had, a couple of bad dreams are to be expected. He's right. It will take you time to accept that you're safe here. Your dreams tell me you love your family very much and fear losing them."

"Yes." She smiled. "Father said the dreams will stop once I find a *confee onza*."

He chuckled. "Confidence?"

"That's not what he said." She blinked.

"*Confianza*." He chuckled. "It's Spanish. Means confidence."

She flattened her eyebrows. "I'm not stupid." That she'd been searching around Querq to find a 'confee onza,' made her blush.

Officer Ahmed pulled her into a brief hug and patted her on the back. "You are too much." He chuckled.

She shot him a confused look for a second until she read his mood. He didn't mean to sell her; he'd meant 'too much' as some way to say he thought her adorable. Eager to get home and finish the empanadas before Karina returned from her farm job, she waved at him and found her way back down the little white corridor to the door. A few voices murmured from a nearby room, discussing something about 'Gee-ball scores.' One woman thought of being stationed in Querq a bit of a vacation, while a man in the conversation felt it a punishment. The scent of coffee hung in the air, along with a fruity-sweet smell.

Althea couldn't imagine how anyone could *miss* being in that big, awful city. Every time she thought of the place, it made her want to curl up and cry. So many people so close together, how could they be anything but miserable? All in a hurry; always angry. None could even be bothered to offer a kind word to a lonely child. She wrapped her arms around herself at the memory of being pushed aside, called a pickpocket, and stuffed head-first into a trashcan. Before the tears started, she thought of Karina and how happy she'd be that Althea had finished her chore on time.

She stood at the exit waiting for a minute or two before Officer Ahmed walked up behind her.

"Something wrong, sweetie?"

"The door isn't letting me out." She pointed at it.

He smiled and pointed at a small green square on the wall to the left. "You have to push the button."

"I don't touch things that glow." She shook her head. "It's not safe."

"This isn't radioactive or harmful. It's an electric light." He gestured at the ceiling. "Like those, only smaller."

Althea raised a tentative hand and poked the green square with her finger. She cringed, expecting it to burn, but it felt neither warm nor cold. The door opened, letting the warm outside air fall on her like a comfortable blanket. She flashed Officer Ahmed a grateful smile, and hurried down the steps before they could burn her feet too much, and spent a few seconds basking in the sunlight, letting it chase away the chill.

"There she is," said a woman.

A group of ten or so people hurried over, forming a horseshoe around her. She didn't recognize most of them, though except for one blond man, they all resembled locals with sienna skin and black hair. All of them seemed about Father's age, and wore backpacks and gear that suggested they'd been traveling. Sensing no malice in their emotions, she decided to stand still and quiet.

They gathered closer, about half knelt before her.

"We have journeyed for weeks to see you," said a man.

A woman a little older than Father bowed so deep her hair tickled Althea's toes. Her clothes smelled like wood smoke. "Guide us. What shall we do?"

Althea's stomach knotted with unease. "Please don't bow to me."

The woman sat up. "As you wish."

"She is real." A man leaned closer and put his hand on her arm. "I can feel her power. She is the one."

"Blessed child." A man in the back raised his arms to the sky.

"Stop." She edged back a step. "I'm just Althea. I don't know what you think I am, but I'm only a girl who can help people."

"So humble," whispered a younger woman. "We should be like her."

Murmurs of agreement swept over the group.

"Please don't pray to me. I'm only a girl." She caught fleeting glimpses from their surface thoughts; they all thought she'd come from some place called 'Heaven.' A few thought her to be sent by someone named God, one thought she *was* him... or her. "Please, don't. I'm just a person like you."

"Beloved, believe not every spirit, but try the spirits whether they are of God: because many false prophets are gone out into the world," yelled a woman to the right.

Althea glanced toward the voice. A thick-bodied woman with a square-jawed face and a weathered tan ambled closer. She didn't look at all familiar. Her dress and boots appeared to be made of the same type of leather, fringed with goat fur. Numerous pouches and packs hung from her belt, and she carried a pre-war rifle over her back on a strap. A strand of pewter-colored hair hung over her face, the rest held back in a bun.

"Please don't call me that. I don't like Prophet."

The stocky woman raised a hand at the group. "Beware of false prophets, which come to you in sheep's clothing, but inwardly they are ravening wolves."

Not trusting the outsider, Althea scanned her thoughts. Fortunately, she did not intend to abduct her. This woman believed she wanted to hurt people, wanted to be worshiped, that Althea committed a great crime against the same 'God' person that the others thought sent her here.

Althea scowled. "You don't understand. I don't want to hurt anyone."

"Fools," said the woman. "This girl is lying. She is not of God, or of heaven. Do not be deceived by her false innocence."

"Why do you hate me?" Althea leaned away from the palpable emotion. "Do you need me to mend your ear-shapes, or are you just stupid? I *told* them not to bow to me. I don't want them to."

"Leave her alone," shouted a man.

The angry woman fixed her with a glare. Her thoughts swirled in confusion; she hadn't expected Althea to deny wanting followers. A scowl formed as the woman regarded her claim as a lie. *Of course, the Devil will claim it does not want what it wants.*

"She's not what you think she is," said a woman behind Althea.

Althea twisted around to peer at a Division 0 officer descending the metal porch, boots clanking on the steps. She stared at the nameplate, but the funny marks, the frozen word, didn't mean anything to her. The officer looked like a local, with caramel skin, a rounded face, and black hair, but her English had no trace of a Spanish accent.

"This one spreads false testimony, seeking to lure the sheep away from the flock," said the angry woman.

"Operative word there being *sheep*." The officer folded her arms. "If your magic sky daddy has a problem with Althea, why doesn't he pop down from the cloud castle and say something?"

Everyone, except Althea, gasped.

The angry woman closed her eyes and wagged her head side to side. "The Lord works in mysterious ways. It is not our place to question."

"Right. Easy to keep the mindless sheep obeying your bedtime story when they're trained not to expect to see anything happen." The officer put a hand on Althea's back, smiled, and filled her voice with concern. "Are you okay, hon?"

"Yes. These people are confused, and that woman hates me, but I don't know why."

"Maybe *He* sent her?" shouted a man, pointing at Althea.

Althea stomped. "No one sent me. I live here. I don't want... followers, or people bowing. All I want is to help people."

The crowd stood in silence for a little while before the angry woman scoffed at the man who'd suggested this 'god' person sent Althea. The would-be worshipers surrounded her and got to arguing about what this entity wanted. Amid their trying to shout over each other, all of them seemed to lose notice of her.

Althea crept off to the side and started to make her way home, but stopped as a telepathic voice entered her head.

You let me know if these people bother you again, hon. The officer winked at her. *These Cat-3 people can be dangerous sometimes.*

Althea blinked. *None of them have cats.*

The officer laughed, and hugged her. *Oh my, you are so adorable.*

Althea hugged back, basking in the affection. She loved Querq, and how everyone (well almost everyone) here treated her so well.

It's short for category three. It's a rating system for mental problems. Cat-3 is religious delusions, those who commit crimes and attempt to justify it with religion, or those who've detached from reality and allow their mythology to cause real harm. The law considers them to be suffering a psychological condition.

While the words mostly sailed over her head, she picked from the woman's surface thoughts to help understand. *How can made-up stories hurt people?*

The officer rolled her eyes. Contempt fell off her in sheets. *Oh, you'd be surprised. People used to kill each other for believing in the wrong fairy tale. Or sometimes people would believe their Easter Bunny would magically cure sickness and wouldn't take their kids to a doctor. They'd sit there and watch their own babies die expecting some made up 'god' to zap them fixed.*

Althea's eyes widened at the images in the woman's mind. Of course, it had been a long time since that happened. As far as the officer knew, few people in the area still paid attention to this 'religion' thing. Most of that occurred in other parts of the world. The officer regarded 'religious' people with almost as much contempt as the angry woman had for Althea. She didn't *hate* them the way the woman regarded Althea as some kind of evil thing; the officer thought them stupid and primitive.

In a brief moment of dark logic, Althea wondered what The Many would think about the idea of a 'god.'

I should go home. Althea offered a pleasant smile.

The officer nodded. *Okay, hon. I need to stay here and watch these idiots so no one gets shot.*

Althea's eyes widened. She did *not* want anyone to get hurt because of her, or because of an argument about 'religion.' She stared at the arguing group and projected a wave of calmness. A shouting man cut off in mid word, staring dumbfounded at the angry woman as if he couldn't remember why he'd gotten so worked up.

Satisfied, she left them to exchange confused glances, and walked back the way she'd come. It struck her as silly to argue about a 'sky-man' who may or may not exist. The officer did make sense in a way. If this 'god' person really did have an opinion, why didn't he show up and say so? The Many had no trouble appearing to torment her. If such an entity did exist far above the clouds, it either didn't care or approved of things.

She shrugged, and let daydreams of fresh empanadas replace pointless thoughts. She walked about three blocks before pausing at the sound of someone running up behind her.

"Althea!" yelled a boy. "Please, help!"

She stopped and whirled around.

A pair of boys, both shirtless and in jean shorts, sprinted out of an alley. Santiago, on the left, had waist-length straight black hair and a thin build that often got him mistaken for a girl from behind. His best friend Diego kept his hair short by decree of his mother. They rushed to her side, both standing more than a head taller than her. A thick layer of grey dust covered them, as well as dozens of small cuts and scratches on their forearms and legs below the knee. Diego also appeared to have broken a toe, though it didn't affect his walking. Something had scared him good.

Her heart sped up as she realized Pedro wasn't with them. The three friends had always been together whenever she saw them, and the look of fear on the boys' faces got her worrying.

"What happened?" she asked. Her gaze dropped to a trail of blood running down Santiago's left leg. She took a knee and pulled up on his shorts, exposing a deep cut a hand's width above his knee. "Stay still."

"Pedro's hurt. He needs help," said Diego.

She touched his leg near the wound, despite the pair of them tugging on her. Her mind linked to his body. Amid the darkness of her closed eyes, his life shapes appeared one by one. Bones as lines of white, followed by muscles and the inside bits. She directed her attention at his leg, where a blank spot in the muscle form revealed a puncture wound deep enough to swallow her whole index finger. Small black lines and smudges appeared in place of dozens of small cuts and abrasions.

A quick mental nudge disabled his sense of pain, and she willed his body to mend itself. The minor hurt sealed in seconds, a trivial exertion.

Diego pulled her to her feet. "Althea, please... He's dying."

Her eyes snapped open. "Where? What happened?"

"He fell through the floor in Old Town," said Santiago.

Althea gasped. "We're not supposed to go there."

"Please don't tell anyone," said Diego. "But can you help him? I think his leg broke."

She put her hands on her hips and sighed. "They told you not to go to the Old City, didn't they?"

Santiago bowed his head. "Yes."

"Yeah," said Diego.

"Well, then, you *should* get in trouble. If you listened, Pedro wouldn't be hurt." She gestured at the alley they came from. "Let's go... Take me to him."

"I thought you weren't gonna go, sayin' we were told not to." Santiago jogged off.

"Someone's hurt because you broke the rules," said Althea. "Going to help them isn't breaking the rules."

"Oh." Diego hobbled along to keep up.

She waited for him and took his hand as soon as he got close enough to reach. Eyes closed, she linked to his life essence, concentrating on the broken bone shapes in his foot. The second and third toes had both snapped, and one of the muscles along the arch looked fatter than it should be, with a small rip. It took her about ten seconds to force his body to mend itself, and a small growl came from his gut.

Hers answered.

"This way," shouted Santiago.

She released Diego's hand and sprinted after the long-haired teen. He raced down the alley, hooked left at the end, and darted across a street into another alley. Althea had little trouble keeping up on the run, barely feeling the exertion by the time the boys stopped, winded, beside a building that made up part of the eastern wall.

Althea looked up at the walkway upon which the Watch patrolled. Blue-painted steel covered by mismatched awnings and stretches of fabric supported on poles passed over the roof of a two-story brick-shaped structure with three garage style doors on the right, and a normal door on the left. The roll-top doors appeared welded closed, and what had once been an office had large metal plates secured over a giant window. A row of small bricks surrounded a dirt strip by the wall that likely used to have grass.

"You climbed the wall?" asked Althea.

"No." Santiago gave her a cheesy smile. "The metal cracked." He grasped the knob and yanked open the door.

Althea followed him in to a room empty save for a cluster of ancient papers on the wall, bearing images of women. At first glance, they seemed naked, though a triangle of bright yellow covered one's 'girl parts.' She stared for a second, confused why anyone would bother wearing clothing so small. It wouldn't do anything for warmth.

Scratches on the floor suggested where a desk or some heavy piece of furniture had been dragged to the entrance. Santiago crossed the room and headed past an interior doorway to a large room full of old mechanical junk well advanced into the process of becoming a single heap of rust along the far wall. Hulking metal frames took up most of the middle of the room, separated by pushcarts littered with junk. Scraps of yellow and red plastic flaked on the ground by a few fragments of snipped copper wiring. Matching insulation decorated nubs on one of the carts, suggesting someone had scavenged wire. Aside from empty steel shelves, and a small window peering back into the first room, blank grey cinder blocks surrounded them on four sides, darkened in mold-covered trails where water had leaked in.

"Watch out," said Diego from behind. "There's traps in the ground."

Althea started to turn to look back at him, but his arm slid past her face, brushing her nose, as he pointed ahead. Three rectangular pits in the floor lined up in front of the garage-style doors. Santiago headed across the room to the most distant one, and sat on the edge.

"Don't fall," yelled Althea, while running over.

"Come on." Santiago eased himself off the edge and wound up standing on something inside.

She bit back the shout of alarm and rushed to a halt at the edge of the pit. He stood on a wheeled ladder/cart that left him at about eye-level with her. It wobbled and creaked as he made his way to the floor inside the pit. She didn't trust it, but if it held his weight, it didn't seem likely to break under hers.

Diego offered his hand. She held it and stepped from the floor to the top panel of the ladder, which held a wide, shallow pan. She squeezed his fingers as the cart shimmied underfoot. After a second to find her balance, she let go and climbed down the steps to the concrete. A scattering of small white cylinders littered the floor between her and Santiago, who waited up ahead. The front end of the pit, opposite the garage doors, connected to a walkway that linked all three chambers, and continued off to the right.

Santiago bounced on his toes by the tunnel. "Come on... hurry."

Her foot clipped one of the cylinders as she rushed ahead, which had a lot more weight than she expected. Althea gasped and limped for a few steps, trying to rub her ankle and run at the same time.

"Ow."

The boys ran down a narrow passageway lined with more empty steel shelves. A short distance later, it opened into a square room with yet more empty shelves and a number of pallets stacked against the wall. Santiago went straight to a concrete stairway that led up to the ceiling, and a metal cellar-style door. He gave it a heave, and the doors opened with a grating screech.

She followed him up the steps and out into the Old City, in the shadow of Querq's wall. Althea regarded the metal hatch with worry. "Does anyone else know about this door?"

"No," said Diego.

"Hurry... please." Santiago jogged backward down the street, away from Querq.

Althea pointed at the entrance. "The Watch needs to know about this way out."

"You can't tell them," whined Diego. "If they know, they'll close it up and we can't go exploring."

Althea leaned at him, imitating the way she'd seen mothers act. "If we can go out here, bad people can come in here." She gestured again at the cellar door. "Do you want raiders sneaking in at night? People could get hurt. You should have told the Watch right away." After a quick look around, and up at the wall, she sighed. "Where is Pedro?"

"Two blocks over. In the big place." Santiago took off at a sprint.

Althea ran after him, boosting her stride and endurance with a small psionic tweak. Diego let off a startled noise as she left him in the dust and overtook Santiago in seconds. She slowed to keep pace with him. He didn't look back, but sped up a little as the clap of her feet on pavement came up behind him. They passed two cross streets and cut diagonally through an intersection of a third before he clambered up a severe hill onto the grounds of an enormous three-story building. It sat adjacent to a sprawling field containing the decaying remnant of some manner of coliseum. A fork-shaped pole stood at either end of a field of fake grass, some of which had peeled up in sheets.

A shiver took her at the sight of it, picturing raiders and bandits jousting with motorbikes or unwanted slaves forced to fight each other. She forced the image of a severed hand flying overhead out of her mind and chased after Santiago, who had disappeared into a double front door.

The room contained numerous wood-framed cases, lined with jagged bits of long-broken glass. She stepped with care, mindful of debris in case any of the shards remained in her path. Whatever had happened to the shelves must have been long ago, as the floor appeared free of sharp dangers.

Santiago raced through another set of double doors and jogged past doorway after doorway on both sides of the corridor. He hooked a right perhaps sixty yards in and went down another hallway lined with narrow vertical doors. Most hung open, or simply didn't exist, revealing chambers she probably could've squeezed into. Padlocks secured the few doors that remained. She cringed, wondering what sort of horrible person made such cramped cages for children... and so many of them. Though they had air holes, she didn't want to look for fear she'd find skeletons. Maybe the war that ended the before-time had been a good thing after all.

"In here." Santiago paused with his hand on a doorjamb. The distant wails of another teenage boy echoed from beyond. "Be careful... the floor just fell out below us."

She nodded.

He crept in.

Althea followed into a large room with a ruined wooden floor. Loose narrow boards peeled up in places, and several holes in the ceiling revealed the upper level, with more holes in its roof. Dirt and debris gathered in dried whorls left behind by past rain. Thick yellow ropes hung like a forest of slender trees a short distance away, over cushioned pads. She grasped one of the ropes to brush it out of her way, and her hand clenched tight. The muscles in her back and legs locked as her mind leapt back to another time.

The rope extended past her face, close to her chin. Her arms and shoulders ached, the insides of her legs burned from where they gripped the rope. The overwhelming need to climb flooded her thoughts; fear of ridicule for failure built stronger and stronger. An indistinct man below shouted phrases like 'move your ass, Adams,' 'come on, boy. The rope won't climb itself,' and 'you're halfway up, come on, couple more feet. Pull!'

Fear built to a peak. She gazed out of the eyes of a memory, an emotional imprint in the rope, at a crowd of adolescent boys all pointing up and laughing. The climber looked down and got dizzy at the floor so far away. Hot ran down his legs; the laughter got louder. Terror paralyzed him; he couldn't climb up *or* down, and burst into tears. The shouting man turned soothing, beckoning the boy down. His grip failed, the rope fell away, and Althea snapped back to reality.

She shot a stare at the floor, and breathed a sigh of relief at not standing in a puddle. It had felt so real; she squirmed.

A distant wail of pain pulled her attention to the right. The boys hadn't gotten too far away; the vision must've only taken a second or two. She took two steps after them before Pablo's screaming changed tone from pain to terror.

Althea sprinted in the direction of the screaming, heedless of the small bits of wood jabbing into her soles. She zoomed past the boys and stopped short at the edge of a hole large enough to swallow one of the Watch's trucks. The floor below looked deeper than single story, though not quite two. Pablo lay amid a mess of debris, likely what remained of the floor that gave out. His right leg twisted at an unhealthy angle, and he struggled to drag himself back while screaming out for his mother.

A man-like being with dried, mottled dark green skin shambled toward him, growling and emitting a shrill whining sound as if trying to scream despite a jaw he couldn't open. It had no clothes, but also no man-bits to cover. The creature radiated hatred, directed toward Pablo.

"There's stairs over there," said Santiago.

She concentrated for a second on toughening her legs... and jumped.

Both boys behind her yelled in alarm.

Her toes hit the floor first, and she let herself fall into a somersault that dumped her on all fours; a dull ache spread through her left foot, though nothing felt broken. Pablo ceased screaming, staring in awe at Althea. She rose to stand, grasping hold of the creature's emotion and pushing its hatred aside. It lumbered to a halt a few paces away. From here, the armor-like texture of its scabrous skin confirmed her suspicion. Scrags called them 'ghouls,' though unlike what some of the legends claimed, they hadn't died and returned.

"You don't have to hurt anyone," said Althea.

It emitted a confused moan.

"*Mi pierna está quebrada,*" wheezed Pablo.

Althea turned toward him, but kept half an eye on the ghoul. "Sorry. Too fast. Broken? Oh, your leg. Yes."

The ghoul advanced a few inches, reaching toward Althea. Its right eye widened, though the left remained a veritable slit.

"Run," screamed Santiago from overhead.

Althea swallowed; her toes gripped the old concrete. She'd never been so close to one of these beings before. Always, raiders or settlers, whoever had kept her, had shot them from afar, fled, or sometimes risked a close-in fight. From the aftermath, mending shattered arms and crushed bones, she knew the ghouls had strength greater than the biggest raider juggernaut. Letting it get so close unsettled her, this person-thing who could crush her with ease.

"Hi," whispered Althea. "You don't have to hurt anyone. Maybe I can help you."

"Get away from her," shouted Diego. He threw small hunks of wood or concrete from above at the ghoul.

It ignored the pelting.

"Help," whined Pablo.

Althea took two steps sideways to the right, toward Pablo, her gaze locked on the ghoul. "I don't want him to hit us when I fix your hurts."

The ghoul's anger began to return. She quashed it and probed deeper into its mind. Its armored skin hurt whenever it moved, a burn as though inflexible plates ripped away from muscle. Althea raised her hands.

"Don't hurt me. I want to help you." She bit her lip, wondering if she could do for this creature what she'd done for the canid.

It remained motionless as she crept up to it and put a hand on its dry, scratchy chest. The skin didn't feel at all like that of a living creature, closer to the vests some of the Watch wore while standing post on the wall. Despite its hardness, her attempt to link to its life essence worked, proving she touched living skin. Life shapes unfurled in her vision, close to that of a man, but some of the inside bits didn't look right. The ghoul had two heart shapes, low in the belly where the bean-shaped blobs usually belonged. Lighter smears surrounded the inner bits, not quite as pale as bone. A few seconds' probing revealed a dense coating around some of the organs, similar to a thick fingernail.

She couldn't guess where to begin to make it human again; the change—if it had even been changed and not born this way—seemed too drastic. Would de-growing the armor around the inner shapes hurt it? Should she force the heart shape back where it belonged? And what about the second one?

Her fingers went cold. The life shapes glided away from her as if pulled back by an unseen force. At once, she felt the presence of The Many. The Sentience, as Aurora called it.

He is mine, child. You cannot save him.

Althea scowled despite her closed eyes. *Did you do this to him?*

Dry chuckling circled around her mind. *No. But I sustain him.*

She tried to force her power into him again; a faint hint of his life shapes appeared far away, drifting closer.

You cannot help him, child. He has been a weapon of war for centuries. There is no mind left to save.

She emitted a faint snarl. *I don't believe you.*

Again, The Many chuckled. *You may think me evil, but not everything I speak is false. Look into his mind for yourself.*

Althea opened her eyes and gazed up into a pair of pale yellow spheres. Where perhaps once a human's eyes had been, the ghoul had orbs of a single, solid color, which emitted a weak glow. Reflected blue from her luminous stare glinted off smooth patches of its facial armor. She opened a telepathic connection to the ghoul's thoughts. At the surface, it tried to comprehend why it wasn't bashing her to death. It hadn't hesitated out of hope, pity, or curiosity. It simply couldn't understand why it had stopped.

Little of any memory existed beneath its surface thoughts, only the need to kill anything that moved, and attempt to feast upon whatever remained after.

I speak truth, child. You can only help this wretched creature by ending its sad excuse for a life. Go ahead, child. Kill it.

Althea stared at her hand against the creature's abdomen. The dense, hard plate of skin rose and fell with wheezy breaths, flooding her senses with the stink of rotting-meat. She wanted to pull away, but couldn't bring herself to. The Many had attempted to trick her before. It wanted her to kill someone. She had killed a bonedog, but the alpha had melted away into shadows. Was it a real dog, or had it been The Many in disguise? Perhaps she hadn't taken a real life? She thought back to the millipedes, too simple for her to manipulate, too stubborn for fear to work on them. Bugs didn't count. Especially mean bugs that wanted to eat people.

"I can't kill him."

So, you would choose to leave him to suffer an eternal agony? He will never die from old age. He will spend years and years in constant torment. Many years after you are no longer here, this creature will remain, still suffering. You could spare him that.

Althea looked down. "I... It's wrong to kill."

Is it? The Many laughed; though the sound existed only in her mind, her bones shook from the deep timbre. *If a raider was about to kill Karina, and the only way to save her life was to kill him, would you?*

Tears streamed down Althea's face as an image overwhelmed her thoughts: walking into her bedroom, a man on top of Karina, knife at her throat, about to kill her after wifeing her. A gun in Althea's hand. Seconds to react. Anger welled up inside her. Anger like she'd felt toward Hector.

Ahh, there it is. You would do it after all.

Althea wept. *You are awful! Why did you make me see that? Why did you show me him wifeing her?!*

I did not show you that. I showed you her after.

She let off a rageful scream in her mind.

A spidery caress passed across her shoulders as though The Many walked around behind her, tracing his fingers across her back. *It is nothing you have not witnessed before.*

But not Karina!

The Many appeared in her thoughts, smiling. The ancient man in a leather duster coat, cowboy hat, and boots offered a resigned shrug with upturned palms. *Of course, I wanted to hear you say you'd kill him, to feel your anger. Even one as innocent as you is not free of wrath. I had to give you the proper motivation. If Karina was in endless pain, would you take her life to stop her suffering?*

Althea snarled. *No. I'd make the pain stop.*

An exasperated sigh scratched across the back of her mind.

"Althea?" asked Santiago, sounding close. "Pablo is hurt."

Kill this wretched creature, or you own the rest of its suffering.

She looked up at the ghoul. Still, its surface thoughts held a battle of confusion. It wanted to smash her, but couldn't summon the urge to do so. That it couldn't left it bewildered. Pablo's moans of pain crept into her consciousness as the essence of The Many receded. As much as she hated to admit it, the dark spirit had not lied. This creature, she couldn't help. She pondered commanding its heart-shapes to stop beating, but couldn't see it as anything but killing.

The ghoul snapped out of its stupor and raised its fist, its jaw opening and shifting left with a sharp *snap*. Thick saliva trailed off its teeth, fluttering in a bellow that wafted the stink of fetid carrion across her face.

Santiago let off a high-pitched shriek.

Althea gathered her fear at imminent death and threw it forward, filling the ghoul with dread and amplifying it. For an instant, she felt like the boy on the rope, a hair's breadth from wetting herself. The tone of the ghoul's roar shifted to terror; it fell over backward, flipped onto its hands and knees, and dragged itself across the room as fast as it could crawl. Some thirty or so feet away, it dragged itself upright and sprinted through a doorway, howling.

She took a deep breath and held it. *It's gone. Calm. Calm.* Her heartbeat slowed back to normal. With the ghoul distracted, she rushed to Pablo's side and knelt. He looked up at her with adoration in his eyes. The way his leg had twisted, she expected it to have broken in at least two places.

"I'm sorry."

He shook his head. "I understand. It would've killed us if you looked away."

Althea put a hand on his bare stomach, and commanded his body to stop feeling pain. "I need to move your leg. It won't hurt, but you shouldn't watch." She took hold of the rubbery limb and pulled it out straight, unsettled by the lack of rigidity.

Santiago doubled over and vomited while Diego stared with fascination.

She linked her mind to his life essence. The bone-shapes in his leg had become a scattering of small fragments in three places. His hip had broken, as well the bones below the knee, and his ankle. Althea poured energy into him, commanding the splinters to move back in place and stick to each other. Shard by shard, his leg came together. A minute or so later, she directed the blood shape back where it belonged, and mended some rips in the muscles where the sharpened bits of bone had cut.

By the time she opened her eyes, a thin layer of sweat covered her.

Pablo sat up and wrapped his arms around her. Despite being bigger, he clung like a boy to his mother and cried. She smiled, sensing his tears came from happiness and relief.

A loud *smash* echoed from the hallway where the ghoul had run off. Hissing and moaning followed.

"Time to go," said Santiago.

Diego grabbed Pablo's arm and helped him stand. "I got you, man."

"Is okay." Pablo bounced on his feet. "She is amazing. It's like I never broke it." Overcome, he hugged her again.

Althea allowed herself a second or two to enjoy feeling loved before she squirmed away. "He's right. We need to go back to Querq before the ghoul finds us."

As if on cue, the ghoul let off an anguished wail.

Diego glanced in that direction, shaking his head. "That didn't sound good. I don't think 'dat ghoul be findin' anything."

She stared at the doorway where the ghoul had run, more than a few feet in, the corridor turned black and white. A cloud of dust obscured the view, likely from whatever had caved in. She didn't trust this building not to fall on their heads. Scratching, skittering, and hissing echoed off the walls. The ghoul roared and wailed. A wet, squishy *crunch* followed. Diego edged up beside her, transfixed on the hallway as well.

Pablo studied the hole he'd fallen in from. "How are we going to get out of here?"

"There's a stairway." Santiago pointed off to the side.

Scratching grew louder in the hallway.

"Come on." Diego pulled on Althea.

She glanced to the side; the stairway Santiago wanted to use sat ten feet to the left from the corridor full of scary noises. They'd have to walk *closer* to go up. Diego and Pablo didn't seem to care much about the crunching and scratching, and started walking toward it.

A long tubular shape emerged from the dust, weaving toward them.

They froze.

"Somethin's movin' in there," whispered Santiago.

"What's that?" asked Diego.

A giant millipede spattered with greenish ooze slithered out of the darkness into the large chamber. Althea had seen ghouls shot before—green blood. This millipede looked larger than the ones that had attacked her when she'd been in the desert with Rachel and the escaped harem. Its body looked thicker around than Shepherd's thigh. She lashed out with fear as a reflex, but her telempathic assault didn't faze it.

Three fourteen-year-old boys hid behind her.

"Scare it off," whispered Diego.

"Can you kill it?" whispered Santiago.

"It's poisonous," said Pablo. "The pincers are red tipped."

Gleaming black shell plates undulated as it propelled itself closer.

Althea closed and opened her empty hands. Even if she had a spear, she doubted herself strong enough to break its shell. The giant millipede fit right in the middle of the category of 'bug.' Worse, *stubborn* bug. She wouldn't have hesitated to smash it, but lacked the means. Her left foot tingled with the memory of venom paralyzing it.

"I can't scare it. It's too mean." She locked stares with it. "I'll make it come after me. I can run faster than it. Go. Get help."

Diego put a hand on her arm. "But—"

Althea poked it with anger. Venom exuded from its mandibles and it hissed at her. She channeled her power inside, strengthening her legs and fortifying her endurance. The instant it surged forward, she darted to the right. Her feet clapped the old wooden floor like tiny gunshots, echoing off the bare walls. Scratching and hissing followed her. She barely noticed the boys' shouts and the creak of a metal door in the distance.

The millipede slid wide to the right, its pointy legs scraping on the bare concrete, as she cornered to head for an opening on the side of the giant room. A pile of blue padded mats twice her height blocked her path. She leapt onto it and climbed, grabbed the top of frayed canvas, and hauled herself up to stand on top. When she tried to jump to the floor, her feet squished down into the spongy obstacle, reducing her great leap into a near-fall. She scrambled for balance after landing, waving her arms about to keep from wiping out.

Knowing the millipede would be on her if she tripped, Althea squealed in fright and forced herself to run as fast as she could. Smears of grey walls, dark blue paint, and debris shot past her. Seconds later, everything went black and white, a sign she'd run into darkness. Maybe the millipede couldn't see without light? She glanced back over her shoulder and screamed at finding the enormous insect barely ten feet behind her, and showing little sign of slowing.

Her gait took on a bounding deer-like quality as she further strengthened her leg muscles. Althea leaned forward, pumping her arms, trying not to think about the clicking, scratching horror behind her, and focused entirely on the end of the hall thirty yards ahead. Twenty yards. Ten.

"Aaaaaah!" she screamed as she dove between a set of ancient steel double doors.

She whirled about and tried to slam them closed, but the creature got its head in the gap. Althea rammed the slab of metal against the bug, trying to crush it, but succeeded only in pinning it. The fifteen-foot long monster thrashed and whipped about in the hallway outside. Venom dribbled from snapping mandibles inches from her face.

Her bare feet couldn't gain purchase on the dusty polished wood; the harder she pushed on the door, the more she slid away. Althea grunted and struggled to keep from letting the millipede shove its way in. It gained a few inches, carapace scraping on steel.

"No!" she yelled. "Go away!"

It hissed, wrenching itself in a rotating back and forth motion. Althea pressed harder into the door, her feet pushing clean smears through the dust. She didn't like whoever had decided to cover the floor with such slippery shiny stuff.

"Go away!" She strained, grunting

When its tail pincer punctured the door an arm's length above her head, she screamed, high, loud, and clear.

The millipede didn't react to her terror. This creature felt no hatred, nor particular animosity. It wanted dinner. It didn't know anything other than eating and defending its territory from things it couldn't eat. She stared at the twitching mandibles. Her throat dried out. She worked her legs, walking in place, barely able to keep up enough resistance on the floor to prevent the creature from barging into the room.

Althea twisted, bracing her shoulder against the door. Wide-eyed, she stared at the millipede's 'face,' dreading touching it. Out of desperation, she sent a surge of blood and adrenaline into her left arm.

And pounded it on the nose.

It emitted a sharp shriek and recoiled; the door slammed closed. She bowed her head to exhale with relief, and spotted a small metal stake that looked as if it would slide down into a hole in the floor. She kicked at it until it locked. A matching one near the top of the door hung out of reach. While she stared at it, the door rocked with a loud *slam*. Althea kept pushing it closed.

Mandibles pierced the door at thigh level.

She screamed and jumped back. It tore the holes wider as it ripped itself free of the door. Seconds later, it bit through again, a little above the push bar, striking with a *slam* that shocked the air in her lungs. Again and again, it attacked the barrier; Each time it crashed against the steel, it seemed as though the entire building shook.

Althea padded backward, unable to stop staring at the thrashing horror. She drew her hands together at her chin, and cried out with her mind for Father. When that awful man had left her tied to a post blind-folded for the night, she'd called out the same way, and the canid found her. Knowing that Father would sense her beaconing for him lessened her fear. Back in Querq, he'd get a feeling that she needed him, and he'd come running. Hopefully, the feeling would guide him to her instead of leaving him wanting to find her and not knowing where to look.

The millipede rammed itself into the door four more times, its mandibles making holes big enough for Althea to stick her arm through, and causing the metal to bow inward. By the time the creature gave up, it had riddled the door with so many gouges she had a clear view into the hall. She shivered at the sight of the massive black-shelled horror slinking off into the distance.

She deflated to sit on the floor and slouched, gasping for breath while staring at the boards between her legs. Like the room with the climbing ropes, the floor had so much polish it appeared to have a layer of glass above the wood grain. She traced her fingers over it, wondering what kind of stupid person would want to make a floor slippery.

A moment of terror came and went as she pondered what might've happened to her if it had caught her. Involuntary tears and sniffles broke the heavy silence. Althea trembled for a few seconds until she felt gratified that the boys had managed to escape unhurt. Once her heart stopped racing, she looked up.

Painted lines adorned the wooden floor from wherever padded blue mats didn't cover it. A little ways behind her stood a strange little bridge made from a pair of metal frames holding a thick beige bar off the ground. The span had a smooth top and rounded sides. More pads surrounded it on the floor. She stared past it at a large row of bleacher style seats, covered in dust and debris from the collapsing ceiling. Curious, she stood and walked over to the purposeless bridge. The surface hovered about at her shoulder level. Maybe someone built it to cross the holes in the floor? But why would they make a bridge so narrow a person had to put one foot straight in front of the other?

The second her fingers made contact with it, her mind filled with a vision.

People filled the bleachers, dressed in strange clothes she'd never seen before. A line of girls about her age stood off to the side, in bizarre garments that covered only their arms and bodies, leaving most of their legs bare. She looked down at herself, finding a similar garment wrapped around a body that didn't belong to her. The girl who had left the emotional imprint had skin of a rich chocolate hue, and a much curvier shape despite being close in age.

Althea hovered like a spectator in a body moving on its own. The girl climbed up and stood on top of the spar. Flashes of light came from the crowd, snapping from random places. The cheering audience reminded her of the arena where Vakkar made men try to kill each other. A clench of worry filled her heart; did these people make young girls fight to the death?

The girl on the beam tried to keep herself calm, though the emotion left in the bridge said otherwise. She thought of the spar as a 'balance beam,' and had to do 'moves' on it to make her parents, and someone called Coach happy. Such intense nervousness at being in front of so many people left a permanent mark on the beam. She hated being watched by the crowd. She wanted to go home and be alone. The girl splayed her arms to the sides, brought her hands together, and bent forward, tumbling into a cartwheel. As the familiarity of a well-rehearsed routine set in, confidence overtook nerves, and the imprinted emotion faded.

Althea blinked away the vision, a hand on her belly to swallow the anxiety she'd picked up. As worried as the girl had been about falling off, Althea wondered what would've happened to her if she failed? None of the people in the vision appeared to have weapons, and no one looked angry or hostile, yet the girl seemed as nervous as those men who the raiders made fight.

Althea grinned and pulled herself up to stand on the beam. She walked back and forth twice, face scrunched up at how people could think the task difficult. In a moment of adventurousness, she mimicked the girl's motion and rolled into a handstand.

Her dress fell down around her head.

She brought her legs down slow and found her footing after a little feeling around blind. She eased her weight from her arms to her toes and stood, smoothing her dress back in place.

"I guess that's why they didn't wear dresses." She fidgeted with discomfort at the idea of those odd garments being so snug between her legs. Except for being pretty and shiny blue, they didn't cover enough to have been meant for warmth or protection. She scrunched up her nose thinking of the little yellow scrap the woman on the wall of the other building wore. It made no sense at all why they would wear something so tiny. Why bother with it at all?

She shrugged. Perhaps the girls who played on this beam wore those things for decoration? They seemed to be putting on some kind of show for everyone watching. *They're too young for a harem... what did I see?* She scowled. *The before-time is strange.*

Althea folded her arms, trying to make sense of what she'd seen. She walked back and forth on the beam, cartwheeled once more, and shrugged. "Is this supposed to be hard?"

She bit her lip and used the edge of the beam to scratch the underside of her foot. Those girls didn't have her gifts. Maybe they didn't grow up having to run and hide to stay alive. Elders had told her that life in before-time was quite different. People lived in relative safety. Perhaps anyone nimble enough to do something like this had been rare enough to be worthy of being a spectacle. Sometimes settlers would dress funny and dance for amusement. Maybe that's what these girls had been doing? Some kind of festival.

The millipede had evidently given up for good, as it hadn't returned... though she'd only spent two or three minutes playing on the beam. *I'm not helping anyone now. I should go home. I'm not supposed to be in the Old City.*

After hopping down, she turned in a circle, searching for a way out. She didn't want to go back through the ruined door toward the millipede. Fortunately, another double door offered an alternate exit on the opposite side of the enormous room.

Althea walked past two more beams, and a set of smaller ones much higher up at two different heights. Those looked like they might be difficult to walk on, but she didn't bother playing. A glint caught her eye from the floor about halfway across the room. She stooped and brushed at the accumulated dirt and silt, exposing a silver disc on a rotten red white and blue ribbon.

As soon as she picked it up, another vision came to her.

Her perspective changed to that of a girl standing on a small platform to the right of another girl, on a somewhat higher platform. She looked down at a skin-tight white and red garment like the others had worn, only this one covered the backs of her hands, connected to a fabric loop around her middle fingers. The girl peered down at the silver disc hanging around her neck. Shame crippled her, mixed with dread. Pale fingers caressed the silver amulet. She'd come in second. She didn't win something. Her parents were going to be angry. So much so that she stared at the medallion she'd won, and contemplated not even going home after the tournament. She would run away. The idea of never seeing any of her friends again felt better than going home to face her parents' wrath for *merely placing second*.

Althea gasped and dropped the medallion, backing away from it as if it were an evil thing unto itself. She melted to her knees and wept into her hands, overwhelmed by the shame and sense of worthlessness the ancient twelve-year-old had imprinted on the lump of metal. It took her a moment to gather herself enough to stop bawling. She wiped her face, hoping that the girl hadn't run off. She couldn't imagine *wanting* to be separated from her family. She scooted a little farther away from the medallion, lest it make her feel that way again.

How had the medallion remained here? Did the girl who won it leave it behind, disgusted with herself for merely doing great as opposed to perfect? Did the war start while they were in here? She clambered to her feet and jogged around it, heading for the door. It didn't matter why it wound up here; that girl would've been dead hundreds of years ago, even if she'd lived to old age.

Reading that girl's desire to flee her family made Althea want Father and Karina more. That millipede could come back and attack the door again at any moment, and from the amount of damage it had done, if it tried hard enough, it would break through.

She couldn't be here when it returned.

Althea ran to the other door, raising her hands to the push bar. She intended to ram it aside in a hurry, but changed her mind at the last second, and pressed it gently. Old instincts returned. Noise meant death. She eased it open and peered through into another plain hallway lined with white-painted cinderblocks.

Benches along the side appeared grey to her, as did peeling paint on the walls that formed words she couldn't read. Father wanted her to learn how, but so had Archon. The idea of 'school' learning made her think of him, so she'd done all she could to avoid it.

She took the first left, some thirty feet in from the door and found herself standing between two rows of those narrow vertical cages. Unlike the ones in the other hall, these seemed smaller and all had their doors. Only two hung open, though they contained some folded clothing rather than the skeletal remains of a young prisoner.

Althea looked down, feeling a touch stupid. The before-time people hadn't used them for cages; they put stuff in them like closets. She approached one and tugged the door open. A scrap of cloth hanging from a hook fell apart as soon as she touched it.

"Everything here is dead."

She sighed and moved to the end of the row where another doorway led to the right. She hurried to it and let off a disappointed moan when she walked into a dead-end room covered in white tile. The outer wall consisted of numerous individual segments, each with a faucet mounted high on the wall. She made confused faces at them for a little while before remembering seeing similar things on walls elsewhere, but still couldn't figure out why people would put faucets so high up or fail to include a sink.

Althea turned on her heel and headed back out, passing between two different rows of the small metal cabinets. In one open door, she spotted a twelve-inch plastic doll. The too-skinny false woman wore the same kind of clingy garment the girls she'd envisioned had on. She stroked its hair and puffed dust off it. Maybe she'd 'rescue' it and take it home.

"Are you lonely?"

She peered into its plastic eyes and felt the tug of an imprint. The city police had called it clair voy ants, but that didn't make any sense. *That's silly. Bugs aren't sigh-onic.* She hesitated, fearing another awful memory like the medallion, but curiosity got the better of her in a few seconds. She closed her eyes and opened herself up to the psychic energy embedded within.

A girl about Karina's age with a larger bosom cradled the doll to her heart like a girl much younger. She cried and rocked it side to side. Althea got the sense this girl had brought the doll with her to competitions for years, believing its presence somehow gave her luck. The emotional imprint held worry and love for her father. A war seemed likely to start soon, and he would probably have to go fight. The teen sat on a bench, crying harder while clinging to the doll. She dreaded having to leave her home, this school, her friends, everything she's ever known because of the danger. Her mother wanted to move west, trusting the government's promises of a safe zone, while Dad thought they should stay since he'd gotten a great new job.

She tried to put her anxiety aside so she could compete tonight; her thoughts turned toward getting into something called college in two years. To do it, she needed to win tonight. After a moment, she kissed the doll on the head, asked it to give her luck, and tucked it in the locker where Althea had found it.

The room seemed to age four centuries in seconds as the vision faded. White paint became grey, cracks appeared, and lights went from glaring bright to smashed and missing. Althea looked around. *This was a school? It's bigger than Querq!*

She frowned.

"No it isn't. I'm just lost and frightened. It only feels big."

A faint man's weeping emanated from the hallway outside the locker room. She tiptoed to the end of the row and peered out. A couple paces left of the opening, a man in a baggy grey uniform slumped on one of the benches, clutching his hands to his armored vest. Blood seeped through the fabric of his jumpsuit. For a foot or two on either side of him, the benches appeared blue, before fading to grey.

Althea rushed over to him. "It's okay. I can help you."

He didn't react until she grasped for his bare hand, and gripped only air.

At her attempt to touch him, he looked up. Dirt and blood caked around his mouth; his expression twisted with great anguish, though not from any physical wound. This close, Althea noticed the wall appeared through him; his body shimmered like one of those holler-grams the city police made.

After a brief mournful stare, he disappeared. The bench faded to grey. He must have been emitting light.

Althea took a step back. The corridor hung heavy with an eerie presence that hadn't been there before. At first, she blamed her fear of millipedes, but the longer she stood in place, the more she felt that man watching her.

"Are you still here?" she whispered.

Sorrow thickened the atmosphere. It seemed as though he wanted to make her sad, but she didn't allow it to affect her. Officer Ahmed said she had 'astrals,' but she'd never seen a ghost before. What else could he have been?

Althea clenched her fists in determination. That man needed help. An odd compulsion deep inside her made her want to do something for him, but she couldn't tell where he'd gone. She thought about wanting to see him. After a moment of squinting, concentrating, and probing around in her head, he reappeared—only he no longer looked transparent. While the bench, and the corridor around her remained in black and white, the man looked normal—and in color.

She figured him for a little younger than Father, perhaps in his early or middle thirties. He had short brown hair, had gone a couple weeks without shaving, and wore the most sorrowful look she'd ever seen on the face of a grown man. His black armored vest had a small patch with a word on it, a red mark to the left of white letters. He carried a handgun in a hip holster, and she recognized magazine pouches for a rifle around the side of his belt.

"Who are you?" wheezed the man. "Have you seen Madison?"

"I don't know anyone named Madison." Althea shook her head. "You've been shot." Again, she tried to touch the man since he looked so solid and real, but her hand passed through him, as if she'd stuck it into a cloud of that 'air conditioning' again.

He exhaled. "You're talking to me. No one else talks to me. No one else has seen my daughter. Bob won't tell me where she is."

"Who's Bob?"

"My boss. He's not answering the radio." The man sniffed. "You have to help me find Madison... my daughter. She'd be seventeen by now."

Althea stared at him for a moment. "You were in the war?"

"Yeah. What are you doing here, kid? It's not safe."

"I know. But the war is over." Something welled up inside her, and she knew this man did not belong here. "You don't need to be here anymore. I'm sorry... but you died."

He looked down at his chest. "Madison..."

"I don't know what happened to your daughter, but she can't be alive anymore."

"What?" He reached for her, but his hands passed through her shoulders. Grief shifted to anger. "What happened to Madison!? Tell me!"

"The war ended a long, long time ago. Couple hundred years." Althea shook her head. "She probably got old."

"Hundred years?" He stared into space for a little while. "Madison went to this school. Is the war really over?"

"Yes." Althea put on her most sympathetic look. "For a long time." She took a breath. "Why did people fight?"

"Companies disagreed with the government about taxes. They didn't think we needed politicians anymore. They were right." He waved disgustedly to the side. "Bastards in Washington just sit there like fat leeches sucking money out of everyone. The rich keep getting richer and the politicians keep bullshitting us. Yeah, the corporates are just as bad, but why have both of them sucking us dry? Government took our money because they could, and didn't do anything. Sure the corporates are rich fatcats, but at least they ran business and made jobs and stuff."

"You fought the gov-mint?" She blinked.

"Yeah." He chuckled, shaking his head. "Though, I guess 'fought' isn't the right word. Verizon hired me as a security guard. I got the job like three months before things got bad. I should've quit when they gave us armor and military-grade weapons, but they paid so god damned much. A hundred and fifty thousand bucks a year to sit on my ass watching security screens. I couldn't turn that down. Madison needed to go to college."

She scrunched up her face. "They gave you deer?"

The man laughed. "Yeah kid, sure. So, things got worse and worse. The telcos were the first ones to tell the government to go f—orget themselves." He glanced to the side, muttering, "damn kid."

"I'm sorry you died."

"Never saw it coming. I don't know what Bob was thinking. They never even trained us or anything. Couple hours a week on the range... fu—ming special forces guys hit us. We didn't have any warning. I didn't even get a hand on my gun before I died. Heh." He laughed. "Now that you reminded me I bit it, it's all comin' back to me. After they took me out, I watched the whole thing. They killed thirty of us in two minutes. Not one of 'em said a damn word. Like a machine. We didn't have a god damned chance." He leaned his head back, tears streaming out of his eyes. "My daughter... I never even got to say goodbye. She went to this school."

Althea held up the doll. "Was this hers? You appeared right after I touched it."

"That doll..." He reached for it. His body became transparent again, and he grabbed the plastic woman as though he'd become solid. "Yeah. We got her this when she turned seven. She was so into gymnastics... took this doll with her to every practice, every competition."

"For luck," said Althea.

"Yeah." He stared at her. "How did you know that?"

She clasped her hands in front of herself, fidgeting with her dress. "She left her 'motions in it. I saw them. I'm sigh-onic. She was scared you would have to fight, and she didn't want to leave home."

"What's sigh onic mean?"

She smiled. "I guess it means I can do stuff."

"Like what?"

Althea shrugged. "Like talk to ghosts."

The man bowed his head with a sad chuckle. "We decided it would be better for them to go. Debbie couldn't be reasoned with. She trusted the damn government. I decided to stay with my job, send them money when I could. The pay was too high to walk away from... stupid. Stupid. Stupid."

A twinge nagged at Althea's soul. An urge blossomed into action. She raised her arm. "You don't have to stay here anymore. They are waiting for you." She reached at nothing, and pulled aside the air like a curtain, revealing a shimmering silver doorway. Part of her mentally leapt back in shock, though the energy emanating from the opening bathed her in security, as welcome and reassuring as the scent of Father's house.

"Dad?" A woman's voice floated out of the silver rectangle. Seconds later, a thirty-ish woman with short auburn hair appeared. "Oh, God, Dad..."

"Maddie?" The man stood. "You're so... young."

The woman laughed. Another woman, a little older, appeared behind her. "I made it to ninety-four, Dad. I passed on in my bed, surrounded by grandchildren. Appearance is all in your head on this side. I think I looked my best at thirty-two. Everyone's here waiting for you. It's been many years..." She smiled at Althea. "You found Gina, my doll." Madison looked downcast. "I never did compete again after we evacuated. I always told Mom it was because I'd forgotten Gina, but that wasn't the real reason. Gymnastics always made me think about Dad." She beckoned her father to follow her.

"Thank you," whispered the man. He walked past Althea into the doorway of light, which closed like a theater curtain behind him.

For a few seconds, the sounds of an emotional family reunion echoed in the hallway.

Althea breathed a sigh of relief. She held on to the doll and hurried down the corridor, wondering what the heck just happened. Maybe she would talk to Officer Ahmed about it, but she'd have to ask Father first. She expected ghosts to scare or unsettle her, but something about meeting that man made her feel *right*. A part of her seemed at ease with what she'd done.

She rounded a ninety-degree corner and took the first door on the left, finding a large bathroom. Sensing a dead end, she pivoted on her heel to leave, but froze at the sight of herself in a huge mirror over a row of sinks. Her eyes glowed bright white, not their usual blue.

"What?"

Althea crept up to the sinks and stood on tiptoe, hips against the edge. She leaned close to the mirror, studying her phosphorescent eyes. They no longer appeared to have pupils or irises, resembling eye-shaped holes filled with pure white energy.

"What's happening to me?"

She reached out to touch the mirror beside her reflection.

The room shifted; decay, mold, broken tiles, and dirt vanished. Four hundred years ago, a girl sat on the sink shelf, bawling hard into her hands. She looked about sixteen or seventeen, and had a small, but telltale swell of a baby. The boy she loved had told her to go away and never come back. She didn't want to tell her parents she had a baby coming, afraid they'd make her leave the house. She worried about something called 'finals,' and dreaded being a mother would ruin her school.

Althea squinted, trying to understand how getting wifed would make someone do bad at learning. She forced her way out of the vision, and pictured the girl's emotions in a box, which she kept at arm's length. Whatever happened to that poor woman happened too long ago to get upset over. Her baby could've had a baby who had babies who'd grown old already.

I need to go home. Father is going to be worried.

She stared at herself in the mirror, afraid she'd broken herself by making her eyes change color. The instant she wanted her eyes normal again, they changed back to their usual azure glow. She blinked in surprise, but grinned at the elation of not doing something bad. Perhaps that—why they changed color—would be a question for Officer Ahmed.

Althea headed out into the hall and turned left. It hadn't been *too* long. She could still finish the empanadas before Karina got home from the farm. She rubbed her belly, looking forward to eating. Mending Pablo's leg had left her ravenous. The hallway went for some distance, and turned another corner. Alas, nothing looked like a stairway.

A rattle high and left made her look up. Less than a second after she glanced at a ventilation duct near the roof, the millipede burst out of it, hissing, swinging its head side to side in a searching manner.

Althea screamed her lungs empty.

As soon as the giant insect lowered its front end to the floor, hundreds of legs gripping at the wall, she took off at a hard sprint. She cleared to the corner at the end in a few seconds, and screamed again at the sight of a cave in. Before her brain could kick in to process that she ran *toward* the creature, she doubled back for the nearest doorway, fortunately one made of steel. She ducked past and slammed it a second and a half before the millipede crashed into it.

Two mandible points pierced. Venom dripped from the tips as they wiggled, testing the door. With a grinding screech of stressing metal, the millipede closed its jaws, scissoring the door. It couldn't fit through the inch-high slit it made, but it wouldn't take long to eat the door.

Althea backed up and whirled around.

Her heart fluttered in her chest. She'd found a room with no other way out save for a tiny window near the ceiling in the back. From the amount of shelves in here, she assumed the space had been used for storage. Her body twitched each time the millipede crashed against the door, piercing and tearing.

Again, she beaconed for Father. She couldn't stop shaking. During her years drifting around the Badlands, she'd been comforted by the knowledge everyone regarded her as too valuable to hurt. As long as she obeyed, even the meanest raiders would protect her. She had never known true terror but once, when bad-Shepherd wanted to smash her. This creature, this millipede, was one of those monsters that didn't care about her being the Prophet. It would kill and her with as little remorse as settlers killing Squealers for food. No one thought much about killing the enormous prairie dogs. She rather enjoyed the taste of their meat as well.

Being the meal, however, horrified her.

Althea ran to the wall under the window and sucked in a breath to scream for help, and choked on dust. Her heart seemed to synchronize with the millipede's assault on the door, thudding in her chest each time the monster slammed its face into the failing barrier.

She glanced back; the door had warped in, shredded in long gouges wherever the creature pincered slashes into the metal. The Many had to be laughing at her. It wanted her gone for reasons she couldn't guess. But that's what evil creatures do: they want innocent people to die. She held back the want to burst into tears and scream, and forced herself to look around. It would take too long to get up to the window and escape; the creature would eat her before she could get away. She had no choice but to stand her ground... somehow.

Sticks protruded from a huge box on one of the shelves. She considered arming herself, but they looked too long and thin, with a weird L-shaped bend at the end. The box next to it held hundreds of rubber discs about an inch thick. She grabbed at the next box, which held decaying head-sized balls with white and black panels.

A loud groan of protesting metal stalled her frozen. She glanced back over her shoulder. The millipede forced a flap of the door inward, wriggling through the hole it had made. Inch by inch, the creature squeezed into the room with her.

Althea yelled in surprise and pounced on the next box. Small hard, white balls with red stitching. She pulled it out of the way, sending them scattering on the floor toward the creature. Maybe they would slow it down. The next box filled her with hope. Wooden clubs.

She grabbed one and pulled it out, grasping it with both hands. Another one caught her eye, metal. She dropped the wooden one and drew the metal club from the box. Black tape flaked off under her grip, but the weapon itself felt solid.

Holding the club high, she took a wide stance in the middle of the room, and concentrated on the muscles in her arms and back. As the millipede worked its way in, she channeled psionic energy into her body. Her biceps swelled; her already sinewy arms grew more defined. She moved her right foot back, watching the creature, waiting, pouring more and more energy into herself.

The millipede got enough legs in contact with the ground to gain traction. It dragged itself forward, its strength and mass bending the flap it made in the door with a wail of stressed metal. It spilled into the room and rushed straight at her, its head rising, mandibles poised to take her head off at the neck.

Althea let off a war cry and brought the metal club down with every bit of strength she could milk out of her tiny frame. The impact of metal on chitin jolted her fingers with a painful shock, but rewarded her with a wet *crunch*. Yellowy ooze sprayed on her face and chest.

The millipede waved itself side to side in a spasmodic, repetitive motion. It slithered backward over itself in a continuous spiral motion, unwinding, and coiling again. She backed up, holding the club in a ready position, but the creature kept thrashing about as if it had forgotten entirely how to control its body.

She stooped to pick the doll back up and darted past the writhing millipede to the door, but the warped metal slab refused to open. She eyed the jagged hole and considered trying to crawl through, but didn't trust making herself that vulnerable near the millipede in case it snapped out of the daze.

Althea raced across the room to the shelf by the window and climbed.

Much to her surprise, the metal-and-glass pane opened inward with little difficulty. She stretched her leg across the open space between two shelves, straddling the gap below the window with a foot on either side. The opening led out to an alley, only a few inches above the paving. Her momentary amplified strength made pulling herself up and out a triviality. She crawled into the alley, rolled onto her back, and gulped down lungful after lungful of fresh, dry air.

She lay there for a few seconds trying to catch her breath. Her arms and back muscles spasmed as they shrank to their normal size and strength. A dull ache came on after, but she smiled, thrilled to be alive.

Home.

With a grunt, she sat up and got to her feet.

A moan behind her made her whirl, raising the club.

The same ghoul, torn up and bleeding in several places, stumbled out from behind a large metal dumpster and glared at her. Millipede mandibles had ripped great sections of its armored skin away, but new tissue bubbled up already, growing over the wounds.

Althea sighed.

She thought about making it afraid. *It'll only go hurt someone else.*

She eyed the club and considered... killing it. *I... can't.*

She considered attempting to 'heal' it. Perhaps instead of making it human again, she could permanently disable its ability to feel pain? But it's mind had seemed so simple... that might not even help. The brain between those hardened green ears made the canid mutant seem like the town doctor.

Unable to decide what to do, she bolted and ran when it charged her.

Her sprint came to an abrupt halt as soon as she reached the street at the end of the alley. A strange metal truck with six huge wheels, as tall as a man, sat in the road. Four people in dark blue jumpsuits with rifles similar to the ones the city police had given the Watch spun around to look at her. Three men, one woman.

They smiled and waved.

The ghoul, moaning, came shambling out of the alley.

Althea dropped into a ball and plugged her fingers into her ears, knowing what would happen next.

All four of them opened fire on the ghoul. She winced at the icy feeling of a departing life, and frowned. When the gunfire ceased, she opened her eyes and looked up. The people lowered their weapons and again smiled at her. A reaction one might expect from normal people finding a lost child.

She stood and returned a friendly wave.

"Hey sweetie," said a pale man with black hair. "Would you like to see inside our fancy rover?" He pointed at the strange vehicle.

She opened her mouth to politely decline, but stopped at the notice of a symbol on his chest. A round octagonal letter with another letter inside it. She remembered Archon's learning datapad enough to recognize a G with an I inside it. The image haunted her for some reason; time seemed to freeze.

Her memory leapt back. Framed by a haze of grey fabric, her vision contained the chin of a blonde woman, viewed from below, as if the woman carried her. Pale skin caught the reflection of blue light, and the same GI logo sat upon the woman's chest, near Althea's face. The world jostled in a rapid back and forth; the woman ran.

That's me... I'm a little baby. My mother... She blinked as reality came back. *How can I remember that? No one remembers being a baby.* Althea reached out a psionic feeler; all four of them radiated eagerness, the same sort of eagerness raiders always had when they found The Prophet.

She took a step back. "No. I'm going home."

"Real smooth, Ed. You might as well have tried, 'hey little girl, want some candy?' Idiot," said a dark-skinned man with short, curly hair.

"Bite me, Joe." Ed took a silver pistol from the back of his belt and pointed it at her. "We've been looking for you for a long time. Come on, sweetie. You don't belong out here in this shithole. Please don't make me dart you. This is for your own good."

Althea poured herself into his thoughts. They worked for a corporation... Gravion Interstellar Incorporated. These must be the 'corporations' the city police warned her about. The reason they let her live out here in Querq. She frowned at the little silver gun. They didn't use money to hurt people; they had guns too. He thought of it as a tranquilizer. Something that would knock her asleep.

"You're bad. Go away."

The woman quick-drew a similar gun and shot her in the chest. Althea peered down at a two-inch metal dart with green fuzz at the end. The delirium of drugs encircled her mind, but she'd readied herself for it. A seconds' worth of concentration sent a stream of chemical running down her leg to the road. She grasped the dart and pulled it out with a twist.

"That wasn't nice." She glared at them, tossed the dart aside, and leaned forward in an aggressive pose.

Before the confusion of how the drug hadn't done anything could wear off, she released a blast of sorrow.

"You hurt my mother!" she screamed.

The four adults crumpled in place. Ed and an Asian man who hadn't spoken burst into tears. Joe stared into space, as did the woman. Althea's lip twitched with a light snarl. This corporation already took her away from her mother. She would *not* let them take her away from her home.

"I'm sorry," whispered the woman. She dropped the dart gun and reached for a larger pistol. The slowness of her motion made Althea hesitate until the woman lifted the weapon to her own head.

She backed off the sorrow and clubbed the woman with calm.

Her gun arm went limp, the handgun clattered to the road.

Althea stood tall. She forced her way into their minds. None of them had any memory of her mother beyond reading files explaining that 'an employee' had run off with 'an unusual child' that the company had expressed interest in studying. Her mother had refused to let the company doctors touch the baby, and fled. A 'recovery team' proved unsuccessful in locating the infant. Althea growled with desperation at their lack of knowledge as to her mother's fate.

In Ed's mind, she found a memory of him sitting in a meeting where a stern-faced woman with caramel skin told the four of them that Gravion Interstellar had maintained a facility in the Badlands which had suffered an unexplained catastrophic failure eleven years ago, in which forty-six of fifty-nine personnel died.

Althea looked down at her feet. *I guess I'm not really twelve.*

After a few seconds to process that—being eleven made her feel like a 'child' more than calling herself twelve had—she shook off the somberness of wondering about her mother, and glared at them. She radiated dread, a slow, building sense of ominous doom rather than 'scream-and-run' fear. These people would remember Querq; they would believe that something *horrible* would happen to them if they ever came near the place again. They would fear it so much that they would tell their whole company never to go here.

"Go away. Don't come back and try to kidnap me. I'm not the Prophet anymore. I won't let anyone take me away ever again." She stomped toward them, making all four adults cringe. "Querq is my home, and you aren't allowed here."

A final blast of dread sent them scurrying back into their six-wheeled machine.

"Here!" a man shouted in Spanish from the end of the street.

The large vehicle lurched into motion and lumbered past her heading north.

Two blocks down, a man wearing the telltale blue denim of the Querq

Watch waved. In seconds, six more men as well as Father rounded the corner and came running toward her. Overwhelmed with joy at having a father to run to for protection, she dropped the metal club and sprinted into his arms. He mumbled in Spanish too fast for her to understand, something about Santiago and the boys... and how worried he became out of nowhere.

"Thea...?" He patted her back. "Did you call for me?"

"Yes." She nodded into his chest, and explained about the millipede and getting lost in the building.

The Watch decided to leave it be, figuring she'd likely killed it already, and headed back toward the gate.

Althea snuggled into Father's embrace. She cradled the doll to her chest, and basked in the feeling of being held by a loving father.

"The boys told us about their secret door," said Father.

"I told them to."

He made a noise part way between grumble and laugh. "I thought so. They also said you came out here to help Pablo."

"Yes. He'd fallen and his leg broke. I'm sorry for running off without telling anyone."

"You worried he might have been dying, but you could've sent one of the boys to get the Watch."

"Yes, father."

He brushed her hair back and looked at her. He exuded relief that came after a brief period of intense worry. "They also said you lured the 'pede away from them."

She gave him a guilty look. It had seemed like the right thing to do, since she could outrun it, but she'd been *so* scared.

Father hugged her to his chest and carried her in silence for a minute more.

Althea got the sniffles from thinking about the ghoul.

"It's all right, Thea. You're safe." He rubbed her back. "Those 'pedes scare me too."

"I'm not crying about that." She wiped her face. "I couldn't fix the green man."

"Those mercs must've shot the ghoul," said Alonzo, at their left.

Luis, at the front of the group, called up to the Watch above the gate. Soon, the belabored whine of an electric motor started, dragging the great doors open.

"You cannot fix everyone," said Father, his tone somber. "But you wouldn't be you if you didn't try." He kissed her atop the head.

Althea smiled as he carried her past the gates of Querq—her home.

Karina raced out of a side street about three blocks from the house. She rushed over and pawed at her. "Thea, what happened?"

"I'm sorry!" Althea looked back and forth between Father and her sister, awash with as much guilt as if she'd accidentally burned down the house.

"What? What for?" asked Karina.

"It's all right." Father patted the older girl on the shoulder. "She's had a scare."

"Not that," said Althea in a small voice. "I didn't finish the empanadas."

Karina and Father exchanged a glance, and burst into peals of laughter.

After a second or two of feeling foolish, Althea grinned and laughed as well.

6

STANCE-NO-STANCE

ROBERT J DEFENDI

I t was always about family.

Yoshimi Daichi removed his loose haori jacket and watched the kid. The boy's sword shook slightly in his hand. He couldn't afford a Nano-katana, much less a vibro-blade. He was about seventeen, with wide eyes, a shaking hand, and sweat pouring into his black clothes, loose in a style almost like a gi.

"What is your name, child?" Yoshimi was only twenty-nine, but that would seem ancient to a seventeen-year-old. Yoshimi's neuralware provided him the answer even as he asked the question, but he already knew. He asked because he desperately looked for a way to end this confrontation with the boy still alive. Questions meant time, and time meant options.

"I don't want to fight you!" the kid said. "I want to fight *him*." He pointed at Fujihara Okura.

Yoshimi looked over at his lord and adopted father, standing to one side of the wide, open lobby. "That is Fujihara Okura. Daimyo of Security for White Orchid Corporation. You are the dust and he is the moon. He would not duel you even if his body was able." But it wasn't, and so Yoshimi had the job as Fujihara Okura's professional duelist. It was more than a poor, adopted boy had any right to expect. More so because of Fuji-hara-sama's position.

"He must fight me!" Tears poured down the kid's cheeks. His shoulders shook with grief. The boy couldn't even afford a mourner to express his grief. How low did one have to fall before he had to express his pain himself? Yoshimi didn't want to think about it. Even a peasant deserved the dignity of a mourner.

Yoshimi looked over at his Daimyo. Fujihara Okura stood tall in a haori jacket of pink flowers, his hair salt and pepper, his stance slightly skewed, favoring an old injury. Whatever had caused the wound, Fujihara Okura bore it with shame. Surgery or cyberware could probably correct it, but some wounds one wore with honor and some wounds one wore *because* of honor.

They stood in the middle of the cherry wood and marble lobby of the White Orchid building, security guards surrounding them, looking to Fujihara Okura for their lead. The old daimyo must have shaken his head, because their submachine guns and swords hung at the ready, but no one brandished them. They wouldn't interfere with a duel of honor.

"You haven't told me your name, child," Yoshimi said. He knew it, of course, even without the reference library of Fujihara Okura's allies and enemies in his head. Yoshimi had never witnessed a seppuku before the boy's father's, five years ago, making his connection to this boy more intimate than the boy would ever know.

How would he get this boy out of this alive?

"Wada Maki," the boy said.

"Wada-kun," Yoshimi said. He's almost called the boy by his given name instead of his family name, but adding 'kun' was already familiar enough for a near-grown man. He wanted to show respect, while defining their relative status. Also, the suffix carried a certain fond overtone. You called someone above you 'sama.' You called your equal 'san.' You called a cherished boy 'kun.'

"Don't call me that!" The boy sniffled and brandished the sword. "You don't know my shame! You don't know my pain!"

But was the weeping really necessary? "Control yourself, Wada-kun," Yoshimi said. If some security officer decided he or she wanted to earn a promotion by saving the life of the daimyo, they'd shoot the boy where he stood. Best not to give them an excuse.

If he didn't duel this boy, Wada Maki had about ten minutes left to live. This situation *required* violence, and Yoshimi didn't trust any person other than himself to keep it from getting out of hand.

He drew his vibro-katana, the blade bright and terrible in the morning sun. The finest swordsmith in the employ of White Orchid had crafted it. Most vibro-katanas favored modern composites over ancient craftsmanship. Yoshimi would stand for none of that. In over three-hundred duels, he had only turned it on three times. It was too easy to kill with the weapon turned on, so even inert, this blade had to sing.

The boy fell into the first fundamental, the middle stance, the blade held at waist level, the tip pointed at Yoshimi's face. The shaking subsided. The boy's gaze and breathing steadied.

The boy had studied. If the stance and posture were any indication, he'd studied three to four years. He held his arms like a person who rarely suffered counterstrikes, so he probably trounced everyone in his class.

According to Yoshimi's reference library, Wada Maki had left the White Orchid Prefecture and lived in one of the more 'modern' Western-ized Prefectures. Yoshimi would never have met someone from his school, but it was obvious they started with a solid Five Rings set of fundamentals, with just a hint of Kendo corruption. Probably a master two or three generations back had studied Kendo and Kenjutsu, and hadn't cleaned up the lines of his feet. Something else corrupted the lines too. Maybe just a hint of NSK ninjutsu in the set of the boy's shoulders. Again, something that had bled into the art some generations back.

"Are you going to fight me?" the boy demanded.

"Your left foot is muddy," Yoshimi said.

The boy glanced at the floor.

"*Chikusho!*" the old Buddhist curse burst from Yoshimi's lips. "Don't look *down*." He pointed at his eyes. "Look at me. I am death. There is nothing more serious than what you're doing now."

"But you said my foot—"

Ha. The boy thought he meant literal mud, tracked on pristine floors. Even facing his death, the boy had some Japanese left in him. "Your *stance* boy." Yoshimi fell into the first fundamental as well. Not his preferred choice for meeting the middle stance, but this had never been a battle of blades. Blades could only take a life, not save one.

The boy responded, used to taking orders from a sensei. Maybe he sensed the death swirling around them like white mists on a hilltop. Maybe he knew instinctively that Yoshimi was the only person within miles that wanted the boy to walk out of this lobby alive.

"Look at my feet," Yoshimi said. The boy didn't. Good. He learns. He's Japanese after all. "I give you permission."

The boy looked at Yoshimi's feet and Yoshimi imitated the boy's stance. It felt like too-cold sake. "This is you." Then Yoshimi settled into a proper stance, and it felt like the embrace of Izumi-chan. When he saw her again, when he told her this story, it needed to end with the boy alive. "This is me. Do it."

Yoshimi liked him. The boy shouldn't listen to his enemy during a duel, but the boy carried just enough Japanese inside himself to follow a master. Not *enough* Japanese to expect treachery. The boy hovered a breath away from a thousand terrible deaths.

But one didn't harvest bamboo during the wet season. Figure it out, Yoshimi. You can *save* this child.

The boy's stance settled into something a little less embarrassing. Yoshimi's master would have only beaten him affectionately for that stance. Still, it was too rigid. The art of stance-no-stance, the ability to move between fundamentals fluidly and without thought, appeared to be beyond him.

"Are you ready, Wada-kun?" he asked.

The boy answered by attacking.

And time slowed down.

Yoshimi didn't intend to use cybernetics in this fight. That would be like using a katana to shape bonsai. Possible, but what are you trying to prove?

Still, a single piece of cyberware, a Mishiro Systems 'Ikusa,' engaged. The effect was involuntary. The cyberware detected an imminent attack and boosted his perception, cranked up his reaction time, thrummed in his bones and muscles and wires. To Yoshimi, the boy slowed to half speed, and Yoshimi stepped to one side, his smart-soles holding the floor despite his mass and physics remaining unaltered in his accelerated state. He effortlessly bypassed the blow, bringing his deactivated vibro-katana around and making a tiny cut on the boy's arm.

Time returned to normal and the boy stumbled through where Yoshimi had been standing. The Ikusa only gave a temporary boost to reaction time. Just enough to survive a surprise attack.

"That is blood, Wada-kun," Yoshimi said.

The boy looked at him, surprised. He probably thought the attack had missed. A single drop of blood fell from his right forearm, splattering on the floor.

"I have won," Yoshimi said. "Honor is satisfied. Go home. Respect your mother. Your father can rest knowing his son is a man with an old soul." Don't attack me, child. Don't push this fight to the death. First blood is enough.

Wada looked at him, tears coursing down his cheeks again. All around them, the security officers would be watching, but all other spectators would have turned away. The grief before had been unseemly, but something about these tears spoke of genuine, soul-deep anguish. They deserved respect and privacy.

"It can't be over." The boy sobbed. He held the sword up, shaking. "I can't have lost. I had to satisfy my honor." The words were barely intelligible, and every breath in Yoshimi's body ached to turn away, to give the boy privacy, but if he turned from this emotion, the boy would attack, and there would be nothing Yoshimi could do to save him. So he faced the grief. Looked it in the eye. This was so much harder than killing.

"We have privacy now," Yoshimi said. Don't do this, boy. Accept the loss. Stand down.

The boy glanced at the security, standing in a ring around them, about seven meters out, but Yoshimi shook his head.

"They do not count," Yoshimi said. "They watch but they do not see."

"It can't be over." The boy sobbed again. He tensed to attack. Yoshimi was going to have to kill him. He was going to lose this boy. Don't let this happen. You can't lose one. Strike now, before the boy can attack.

"Do you know how your father died?" Yoshimi asked. A duelist could strike with a sword. A *man* could strike with a question.

The words drove the boy to his knees. He let out an involuntary cry, spurred by some memory. Yoshimi steeled himself against the emotion and fell into a crouch a meter away, so they'd still be on eye level. Grief was a monster. A Japanese man didn't face it. He hid it and hid *from* it. He hired mourners to carry it. He did not look it in the eye.

But Yoshimi looked away from no enemy. He stared the grief in the face and he forced himself to remain calm. The boy needs your calm, or he will attack. His blood cannot be on your hands.

"Do you know what your father did?"

"He betrayed the company." The boy's voice ripped raw from his throat. He'd probably never admitted that before. Only in defeat could he realize that he'd really lost this battle five years ago, when his father placed blade to belly in a large room, upstairs.

"Yes," Yoshimi said. "He betrayed the company. He stole our secrets and sold them to the highest bidder. My lord"—and father—"discovered that. But that's not what I meant. Do you know what he did in death?"

The boy sobbed. "No," he whispered, his need to strike was so powerful a stone could feel it.

But he needed the story more. Yoshimi counted on that. The boy wouldn't know the truth if he died now. Yoshimi could use that need to keep the boy alive for one more breath. Yoshimi would take it. Then he'd figure out how to get the boy to give him the next breath. And the next.

"When confronted with his crimes, he attacked." *A man, dark in anger and dishonor, screaming as he drew a sword, launching himself at Fujihara-sama.* "My predecessor, my master, intervened. I was his student, and so I was there. I saw it all." *A man in sky blue silk, his vibro-katana inexplicably turned off. He struck, slicing the attacker's hands, causing the offending blade to fall to the floor.* "Your father lay defeated." *The man shaking on the floor, naked in shame before Yoshimi's own adopted father, Fujihara-sama.*

"And then your master ordered his seppuku." The boy whispered.

"No." *Fujihara-sama looking at his wife, a great and unseemly tenderness there, then back at the shamed man.* "He asked, 'Do you have a spouse?'" *The man sobbing that he did.* "'And a son?'" *The man no longer shaking now, numb with the realization of all the lives he's ruined. Fujihara-sama looking back at his wife. His love couldn't be more evident if he wore it as a mon.* "'Then I give you a gift,' the daimyo said." *Fujihara-sama looking at Yoshimi's master. The greatest swordsman and the greatest Buddhist who had ever lived. Fujihara-sama nodding and Yoshimi's master kneeling before the man, offering his wakizashi, wrapped in cloth.* "'I give you their futures, this wife and child.'" *Yoshimi's master circling around behind, into the position of the second, turning on his vibro-katana so there would be no pain.*

"You're saying he *offered* seppuku?" the boy asked. "He didn't demand it?"

Ah. Yes. There is just enough Japanese in you boy. Despite the westernized Prefecture and their corrupt, modern morals. Just enough to understand the difference.

"Yes. He offered it."

Because if Fujihara-sama had *ordered* the seppuku, that would be capital punishment. Capital punishment left the shame of dishonor on the entire family. Seppuku committed *willingly*, on the other hand, was a gentle spring rain. It washed all clean.

The traitor looking at Fujihara-sama, and Fujihara-sama's beloved wife and Yoshimi's cherished adopted mother taking a step forward, her pride in her husband a brilliant beacon behind her composed face. Fujihara-sama isn't looking at her, but he stands before them all, far more than just the man she loves. He is the man she can respect.

"My father's seppuku?" the boy's voice held disbelief.

"It was voluntary. His act cleansed you of all dishonor. His treachery does not stain your family. He gave you that in the end." Yoshimi finally let himself look away, his voice very quiet. "I'd like to think that he might be clean too, but that is for the ancestors to decide." Yoshimi shrugged. "I think your mother was too shamed to tell you the story."

"Why?" The boy looked up. The tears had stopped. "If he'd done it willingly, if none of us were shamed, then why did she flee? Why take me away?"

"No man or kami can convince a person to set down their shame if they won't let go," Yoshimi said.

The traitor pressing the wakizashi against his belly for the ritual suicide, one hand holding the protective cloth on the blade, one the hilt. He is pressing the blade against his belly, but before he can draw blood, Yoshimi's master does the second's work, taking the traitor's head from his shoulders before he can suffer the dishonor of making a squeak of pain. He was supposed to wait for the cut, judge when the pain would be too much for the man. He did not.

Yoshimi held out a hand and the boy took it. He helped him to his feet. For just a moment, Yoshimi glanced at the stunner implanted in his own palm. If he hadn't talked the boy down with words, he would have stunned him. Anything to get the boy out of here alive. Yoshimi never entered a battle without multiple win conditions.

"I apologize, Fujihara-sama," the master is saying to the lord, looking at the traitor's undamaged belly. "I struck too early. It appears I didn't give him time to make a cut. I fear he felt no pain at all."

"Go home," Yoshimi said to the boy. "Respect your parents. Find a girl. Love her like your father loved your mother."

Wada nodded and stumbled from the lobby. Yoshimi wiped his blade clean and sheathed it with one motion. Fujihara-sama walked over to him. Behind him followed a professional mourner. Fujihara-sama's wife and Yoshimi's mother, dead a week now. Yoshimi had buried those feelings of grief, but his adopted father had not. Typically, the mourner left employ as soon as the funeral was over. After one week, the presence of the mourner, expressing the daimyo's grief, had begun to disturb the other daimyos.

The mourner sobbed, quietly. "My wife," he whispered, because the old man couldn't. "How will I live without her?"

Fujihara-sama's features were placid. "You didn't kill the boy."

"No, Fujihara-sama. And all those years ago, you didn't execute his father."

"Indeed," he said. "Why did you choose to be a duelist if you're a pacifist?"

Fujihara-sama raising a hand. "You struck before he could make the cut, but that was not his fault. The dishonor is yours, not his. He tried to commit seppuku. His family is clean." The daimyo starting to turn away, then stopping. "But your dishonor, I think, is a small one." Then he walks away.

"Why do you insist on hiring pacifists to be your duelists?" Yoshimi said.

The old man smiled. "Was your master actually a pacifist? He took that traitor's head."

But he did it before the man knew the agony of driving a sword into his own belly. He did that even knowing that you could punish him for striking too soon and stopping the man's seppuku. The second's job was to take off the man's head and end his pain. It wasn't to stop the pain altogether. My master defied you, so that a traitor wouldn't suffer.

"Is a surgeon committing violence when he uses a scalpel to take away your pain, Fujihara-sama?"

A smile almost appeared on the man's lips. "Maybe, but the violence, I think, is a small one."

YOSHIMI SAT IN THE *SEIZA* POSITION, KNEELING BACK, HIS REAR-END resting on his heels. He'd moved his sword to his right side to be more difficult to draw, a symbol that he was still ready to defend his lord, but saw no threat inside the inner sanctum of the White Orchid Corporation.

Cherry wood and panels of linen art made up the walls. Paper lanterns containing pseudo-flame lights hung from the ceiling, but most light came from a long, wide series of windows in the wall, bathing the carpet with a blush of yellow.

Yoshimi meditated next to the reception table where a receptionist in a traditional kimono also knelt in *seiza*, monitoring and responding to three large holo-monitors, projected to hang in the air under a roof painted in branches and leaves. In one corner, a painted Sun shone Amaterasu's radiance across and through the ceiling beams.

The door slid to one side and Yoshimi opened his eyes, rising easily to the standing position and bowing as the daimyos left the boardroom. They exited, but instead of gathering on the other side of the room where Yoshimi could have ended his bow and waited for one to approach, one of the daimyos led the group to stand near him.

Now he would have to hold the bow until acknowledged. The Receptionist bowed briefly, but one of them must have given her the nod and excused her, because she lowered herself back into *seiza* and went to work. Meanwhile, Yoshimi bowed, his back muscles tiring, then aching, then burning. His legs throbbed from standing in that position, straining to watch for the return bow in the shift of their legs, the movement in the edges of his vision. While he was too polite to actively listen to a conversation of his superiors, part of his conscious mind noted that Fujihara-sama tried several times to end the conversation, but several of the other daimyos refused to finish the pleasantries. No, Yoshimi didn't come from a highborn family, and worse than that, he was an orphan. They often took the opportunity to remind him of his place, usually in the most torturous ways possible. On his Mind HUD, the clock ticked away minutes.

Finally, Fujihara-sama managed to break up the conversation and bowed to Yoshimi, who straightened with relief. Fujihara-sama's eyes smiled a bit as he finished, his face otherwise without expression. Next to him stood Urabe Jiro, hatamoto and second in command of the company, in the red silk of glorious rebirth, patterned in cranes and moons. His eyes friendly, his hair the color of honed steel, and his face exactly as smooth as the sand of an unraked garden after a hard hailstorm. He moved with an ease and precision found in twenty-year-old martial arts savants and old men with about a million credits worth of cyberware.

"You will be sending Yoshimi?" the hatamoto asked. No honorific on his name, but considering the difference in their stations, the omission carried no insult. The hatamoto couldn't be expected to take the time to add the neutral 'san' to the name of a samurai as low as Yoshimi.

"I will," Fujihara-sama said.

"Good." The hatamoto walked away.

Yoshimi kept his face calm. The compliment, coming from the hatamoto, stunned with its volume.

While the company was *ruled* by Kitsune Imoru, known as Kitsune-heike by everyone of lower station (meaning everyone), Urabe-sama was his hatamoto and actually ran everything. Highest of the daimyos, Urabe-sama ruled like a sword wrapped in silk. He didn't need a dueling champion like Fujihara-sama, maybe because he offset his age with cyberware, but more likely, because no one in the company possessed enough status to duel him. Or rather Kitsune-heike could, but he had ruled the company for more than ninety years. He was more of a distant god than a man now.

Yoshimi shifted his gaze back onto his master and waited for the old man to speak. Fujihara-sama nodded to him and then gestured for him to walk. "I have a matter for you."

"Yes, Fujihara-sama."

"The daimyos have told me resource expenditures are up throughout the company. No one can track why, but we suspect someone is funneling funds from all departments into a black project. Urabe-sama does not know what this project is, and that means that Kitsune-heike does not know what this project is."

"That is not possible, Fujihara-sama." It wasn't an argument, just a statement of fact. One could not hide from God.

"Hmm," Fujihara-sama said. "You are correct, of course. Kitsune-heike surely knows more than he's telling, but maybe such matters are beneath him."

Like the emperors of old, Kitsune-heike had surely gained a little of the divine. Some suspected that his long life wasn't the result of any technology, but the direct blessing of Amaterasu herself.

"You wish me to look into it, Fujihara-sama?" It wasn't unusual for Yoshimi to do his master's bidding out in the world. He had the entire security division of the corporation to serve as bodyguards, and sometimes the daimyo of security needed to investigate personally. When a daimyo used his powers as a lord to send an agent to do his bidding, that agent was, for all intents and purposes, acting as the lord.

"Whoever is doing this is working with knowledge of the company's internal procedures." The old man grunted. "Our cyber-defense group are the most likely suspects. Someone neutral should investigate."

"I see, Fujihara-sama."

"I believe you still have that"—he cleared his throat—"*extra*-corporate friend?"

He meant extra-legal. "Ido Norio. Yes, Fujihara-sama."

"It is time for him to show the quality of his character."

Ido had once hacked the corporate mainframe in an attempt to find records of Yoshimi's parentage. Fujihara-sama, in a display of undeserved affection for Yoshimi, had made the entire matter vanish. Fujihara-sama's late wife, may the kami cherish her, had affectionately accused him of being a 'sentimental old fool' after that one. Yoshimi had been standing guard on the other side of a paper wall during the conversation, which of course he had not, in good honor, heard.

"I will investigate at once, Fujihara-sama," Yoshimi said.

"Very well. You are dismissed."

Yoshimi rode the elevator down out of the executive level, dialing Ido-san. A virtual holo-panel appeared in his field of view, bearing his friend's avatar, a large, yellow smiley face.

「Yoshimi, baby, how are you?」 Ido-san tried to sound like a westerner. It was perverse.

"I need you find some money for me, Ido-san," Yoshimi said.

「I knew you'd come around, Yoshimi, my pal. What do ya need? A million? Two?」

Yoshimi forced down the insult to his honor. Ido loved to provoke people. Yoshimi wasn't sure if he associated with the man because he genuinely liked him, or because he upset the duelist's center of balance. Yoshimi was a better man for the challenge.

「Hmm. I just received an email from... How the hell does Fujihara know my address?」

"Fujihara-*sama* knows everything."

「Well that's a tick right in the ol' pee hole. All right. No, I see what I'm tracking. Ooh! Fujihara's special access codes. This will be easy. I'll get back to you in... two hours? Go have a drink or something.」

They said their goodbyes and the elevator door opened as the illusory display screen faded. Yoshimi stepped out into the lobby. Afternoon light shone through the windows, but the place was otherwise the same, minus the crowd.

Yoshimi's best friend, Sen Satoshi, stood guard at one of the side offices, young and handsome in dark blue and black silk. The only other professional duelist on permanent duty, his daimyo must have already started a new meeting down here. It wouldn't do to bother him on duty, so Yoshimi just nodded at him and left the lobby.

Two hours. It wasn't often Yoshimi had two hours to himself; he typically worked twelve to sixteen hour shifts. He turned on the sidewalk outside the building, calling a car on the comm link installed in his neuralware. A moment after that, he placed another call and let Izumi-chan know he was on the way.

The car arrived and he hopped into the primary seat. The automated vehicle launched, taking him into the skies over Okinawa. Yoshimi closed his eyes and tried to find his center.

For some reason, he couldn't.

"HE WAS ABOUT SEVENTEEN YEARS OLD," YOSHIMI WHISPERED, kneeling on the tatami mats, his eyes closed, the smell of the woman all around him, like lilacs and rosewood. Her kimono rustled as she cleaned up the tea ceremony. You could carve a lobe out of your brain and Tanaka Izumi could still center your chi with a tea ceremony. She was magic in motion and silence in a whisper.

He took a deep breath and opened his eyes. The woman was petite, her skin porcelain under the makeup, her lips red as cherries, her hair up. Her eyes looked down as she cleaned up the tea service in red and blue silk.

She must have sensed his attention. She looked up and met his eyes, smiling. She only acted this boldly when they spent time together without other company and the expression caused his chest to burn with warmth. Was this love? "You didn't kill him."

"No," Yoshimi said. "But it was close. I have to duel for Fujihara-sama up to three times a week. I'm going to lose one." An opponent, of course, not a duel. He never lost a duel.

Izumi-chan finished gathering the tea service and rose, carrying it to a side table. She turned back and considered him, her danna. Her patron. A teasing smile played upon her lips. "Do you want me to dance?"

"No." His expression cracked, slightly.

"Do you want me to sing?" She grinned and looked up to the roof daintily as she glided toward him.

"No."

She stopped in front of him, her figure that perfect cylinder of feminine perfection, every vulgar curve expertly smoothed by her kimono. He wondered distantly how much padding she used to maintain that perfect figure.

"Whatever could you want?" She moved behind him and descended smoothly into *seiza*, kneeling, her rear end resting on her heels. She put her arms around him.

A man couldn't show weakness after his *genpuku*, when he left childhood behind. Not to his father or mother. Not to his siblings. Not to his lord. Certainly not to his wife, if he had one. A man's weakness could only be known to himself.

And his geisha.

A geisha stood on the lowest rung of society, sharing it with the unclean eta, both non-persons as far as society cared. But although a geisha was a perfect, pristine expression of art and beauty, they lacked even the station of the half-people, the peasants. No matter how he felt personally, by the definition of the law, a geisha was not a person—not even half of one. Their word carried no weight of law. Anything a geisha said, by all legal accounts, was untrue if contradicted by even the lowest peasant. Fujihara-sama's cat had more of a legal identity.

And that meant that no matter what Yoshimi said or did, he could not shame himself before a geisha. This was the only place in the world where he knew no dishonor.

She drew him into his arms. The terror and helplessness of the day rose up inside him. The boy alone, sobbing, the guns all around. Yoshimi's words falling on what he feared were desperate, deaf ears. He had barely felt it during the event, and now it overwhelmed him.

And he wept.

His shoulders shook and great heaving sobs tore from his throat. The boy, fatherless like Yoshimi, his life cut off and sent adrift, like Yoshimi's had been. The boy, so full of rage like Yoshimi had been as a child. So lost. So broken. So desperate.

"They were a heartbeat from killing him." Yoshimi sobbed. "If I hadn't seen his father's death with my own eyes, he wouldn't have stopped. It was that close." His jaw quivered and his entire body spasmed. "I almost lost him." Izumi-chan rocked him back and forth, whispering to him reassuringly. "I almost lost him."

She smoothed his hair, kissed his tears chastely. Surrounded him with warmth and safety and protection. "You must have been terrified. I can't imagine how you kept your head. Your resolve. There, there." Her tears fell, landing on his forehead. "I'm here. It's all over now."

He would lose one. One day. He wouldn't have a choice. It would be duty versus his honor. His soul. His self. His Buddhist core. It was inevitable.

"Do you know that you're the greatest duelist alive?" she whispered after he quieted.

"Maybe." He didn't know, but so what? What in the world was more pointless than being the best killer in a world?

"Do you know *why* you're the greatest duelist in the world?" she asked.

He had slumped over now, his head in her lap. He met her gaze and she stroked his face, her expression perfect, chaste, and loving.

"Practice?"

"Aren't there men who practice more?"

Sen-san practiced more. It took all of his effort to be three quarters the swordsman as Yoshimi. You knew that kind of thing about your best friend, but kept the secret in the fortress of your heart. "Yes. There are."

"But they are not as good." She gently stroked the line of his jaw.

"No." She seemed to be getting at something, so he asked. "Why?"

"Because you don't have a choice," she whispered. "Because no one else can do this for you."

He wanted to kiss her perfect red lips. Was this what love felt like? Rumors said some samurai slept with their geisha. More than rumors. Just one kiss.

"I can't do it."

"That is the majestic glory of Yoshimi Daichi," she said. "You are right. The weight of this burden is too much, even for you." She smiled. "But you will bear it anyway. Because no one else can."

"I'll lose one."

"Maybe," she said. "But not the next one. Or the next." She cupped his face. "Not, I think, even the one after that."

She wanted him to kiss her, didn't she? She had to. He'd been her danna for years now. What was he waiting for?

His comm buzzed. He looked away, the moment over. He sat up. "Yes?"

"*Yoshimi!*" Ido's voice said. "*I have it.*"

Yoshimi rose smoothly to his feet. It might have been his imagination, but Izumi-chan looked disappointed. "I'm on my way."

He said his goodbyes and had ordered a car before he'd reached the street. By the time he sat in the primary seat, the car's little specialized AI lifting them into the air, Yoshimi had donned his mask and Ido briefed him.

"*So all the funds have been routed to the clinics. There seems to be a major research project going on there, draining massive funds in trickles from every department.*"

"How do you drain massive funds in trickles?" Yoshimi said.

"*How do something as tiny as raindrops make up a typhoon? You have a giant ass-load of them.*" Ido sprinkled imported western profanities into his language like hedonists used soy sauce.

Okinawa spread around him, the metropolitan sprawl reaching as far as he could see, the buildings silver and black here, gray and brown in the distance. The car arced into the air with the perfect curve of a sword strike, the acceleration pulling down on Yoshimi's stomach.

"So these are clinics, not hospitals or offices. Only peasants?"

"*See, this is weird. It's only the* eta *clinics.*"

The non-people. Biologically the same as samurai, with souls that had been reborn into the lowest caste due to their crimes on the karmic wheel. Who better to experiment on? No one cared about eta. The celestial order had declared them 'worthless' for the crime of being born to eta parents. They were as low in caste as geisha.

"What are their side effects?" There had to be records, even for eta.

"*That's the thing. There were several outright deaths at the beginning, but nothing for more than a year. From the resources, I think they were working with nanites. I don't know more than that.*"

"So whatever it is, they perfected it."

"Look, The Great and Powerful Fujihara didn't give me these special access codes for nothing. So I went back over all the clinics and hospitals again. I know you bastards don't think eta are people, but maybe this thing, whatever it is, could, you know, jump species." The disdain rang clearly across the comm link.

"It's not like that." Yoshimi's heart wasn't in the argument, his stomach churning as he defended the most monstrous of the Japanese dogmas. Even civilization had its terrible warts. Yoshimi had to force himself not to rage against this one.

"I know you think that." Ido-san's voice managed to convey exasperation and impatience at the same time. *"But we'll fight about that later. It's what I found. An uptick in the peasant clinic expenditures."*

"I thought you said they weren't doing the project in the peasant clinics."

"They aren't, but the only other change I can find, outside a statistical norm, is with the peasants."

"What's the anomaly?" Yoshimi asked.

"Fertility treatments. Exams. Consultations. The peasants have stopped having babies."

Yoshimi blinked. *"Chikusho!"* he cursed after a moment.

"I couldn't say it better myself. Well I could, but you'd lecture me for ten minutes."

"How bad?"

"Live births are down nine percent. Pregnancies fifteen."

"Miscarriages?"

"No statistical change. I think that fifteen percent will perfectly match the live birth drop in nine months. We're watching an increasing arc move through a nine-month timeline. The birth rate shares its normal proportion with the conception rate, just nine months ago."

"Give me an eta clinic," Yoshimi said.

Babies. Children. There was no better way to strike at the heart of the Japanese. While civilization was strict to the point of brutality to adults, those same adults doted on children. Cherished them. Indulged them. The family was so revered that Kitsune-heike had decreed, some ninety years ago, that adopted children like Yoshimi could never inherit, not in the samurai caste, where it mattered. Kitsune-heike wanted to refocus the Okinawan family on children and childrearing. He was sickened by the way they'd been relying on traditional adoption to find the perfect heir.

Family.

Yoshimi's hand started to shake. His throat grew wet. He tried not to think of his childhood. Of the plight of that boy this morning. He held up his hand and focused his will until the shaking stopped. Good. That had been unseemly.

The car landed fifteen minutes later. The clinic took up the bottom three floors of a dilapidated 120-story building. Scattered weeds and rocks surrounded the place, a stark reminder of station compared to the sculpted shoulders of the walks around samurai buildings. Weather had pitted the filthy, cheap chrome of the building's fittings. As he approached the front door, it didn't open for him, despite his status. He was forced to push it open with his actual hand.

He stepped onto institutional carpets worn five years past their planned obsolescence. He called the elevator, which answered at least, and rode it to the third floor, where the directory on his NetMini said he'd find the administrative offices. The elevator queried his NetMini, identified him as a samurai, and let him up. One couldn't have the eta working their way up to the administrative floor. That would be the refuge of the highly trained peasant doctors and bureaucrats.

The moment the door opened, Yoshimi drew his sword reflexively. The place was quiet. The smell of propellant gasses hung just under the conscious register, and it took him a moment to identify it. Someone had used a chem dart gun on this floor, and from the volume of air on the floor of a typical building, they had either used it frequently or they had used it very near the elevator.

He slid out into the hall, institutional green walls on either side. The doors all hung open, as if someone had been searching the rooms. The whole situation reeked of an NSK attack. But what would the central Japanese trade organization want here in an eta clinic?

His cyberware registered the attack before he did, and time dragged to an instant crawl. Yoshimi spun around, raising his blade to defend as a small, athletic woman sped in; he managed to deflect her vibro-katana. His mind barely had time to register that it wasn't a ninjato, the straight-bladed preferred NSK weapon.

The woman spun and reversed her attack. Yoshimi's speedware took over, turning on when his Izuka turned off. They heated up inside his augmented muscles as headware cranked his time perception and error correction to all-time highs.

A picture fell from the wall, creeping toward the ground in the sloth-like grasp of gravity.

The NSK was the closest thing to a Japanese central government and a clearinghouse for assassins and spies, but they also had cyberware that

White Orchid couldn't dream of producing. She moved at least twenty percent faster than him.

But a sword fight wasn't only about quickness, and Yoshimi struck back at the blurring form, his speedware heating steadily under his skin. Hers would go longer before burning her, and he had to finish the fight quickly.

He parried, slid, and countered, the smart soles on his shoes binding him firmly to the ground as his arms produced counter forces nature hadn't designed the human body to handle. He had to be careful not to fight acrobatically as he still had the same mass, and gravity the same acceleration.

He thrust and slashed and riposted. They exchanged fifteen, maybe twenty blows before he established his pattern of attack enough to fool her. Then he telegraphed a strike with his shoulder, reversing as she moved to block it, slicing his blade straight for her knees with all his speed and strength.

The strike wouldn't connect, not with the cyberware she packed, but it forced her to make the most critical of errors. She jumped.

The picture finally finished its fall, shattering on the floor.

His stance remained solid, but she flew into the air, helpless to do more than minor readjustments until the smart-soles of her shoes could grasp carpet again. Yoshimi struck and her parry started her spinning. As soon as she rotated away from him, he drove a palm strike into the back of her head, activating the stunner built into his hand.

She fell to the ground. Yoshimi stepped down his speedware before it overheated.

"*Well,*" Ido-san said over the building's speakers.

Yoshimi nudged the woman's body, wrapped in plain peasant clothes, with one foot. She didn't move. He knelt down beside her. She wasn't dressed in a sneak suit. She carried a katana instead of a ninjato. But she had to be NSK.

"*So. Now you've enraged a ninja clan,*" Ido-san said. "*Yay, you!*"

YOSHIMI TIED THE WOMAN TO A CHAIR. IF THE STUNNER HAD rendered her unconscious, it would be difficult to judge how long she'd be out, but it had only wrecked her motor control, so she'd be functional in ten minutes or so. He pulled up a chair across from her and was still waiting when it occurred to him to ask:

"Ido-san. Why didn't you warn me about her?"

"*I didn't know. I was trying to call you on your comm link, but I lost you when you went through the door to the building. Took me a minute to hack security.*"

Yoshimi tried to dial out on his comm link. 'No signal' flashed across his mind HUD. "Why don't I have a signal?"

"*I don't know, but I had to come in on a land line.*"

Yoshimi pulled out a hand scanner, but it glowed green. "I don't register a jammer."

"*Check her for electronics. She's NSK.*"

The Nippon Shogyo Kumiai was part trade organization, part neutral moderator for all the prefectures, and part espionage organization for hire. They had better tech than any corporation in Japan, hired assassins for inter-corporate wars, and held a monopoly on trade on and off the island.

Yoshimi had already patted her down for weapons, but went over her again until he found a small, button-sized device in her pocket. It had a single blinking light that appeared to double as an activation stud. He pushed it and the light went off.

'Signal restored.' Flashed on his mind HUD.

"Whatever it is, it can block my signal and isn't detected by my equipment."

"It's a counterwave device," the woman said.

Yoshimi glanced up to see her considering him carefully from the chair. "Good morning." He bowed politely. "I am Yoshimi Daichi and my esteemed companion on the PA is Ido Norio."

"*Yo.*"

She nodded, since she couldn't bow. "So you didn't kill me, Yoshimi-san. My name is Miko Rimi."

"Miko-san." He bowed again. "No. It didn't seem appropriate."

She squinted at him. "Yoshimi-san, you find an NSK operative working without clearance inside your corporate domain, and you don't kill her?"

"*He's like that.*" Ido-san said.

Yoshimi shot an annoyed looked at the nearest ceiling camera. "I may, in good honor, eliminate freelance spies and assassins. But you don't fit that description, do you?"

Now she really squinted at him. "But you had plausible deniability."

"That is not the same as proof," Yoshimi said.

"*I told you, he's like that. You get used to it.*"

"Besides," Yoshimi said. "I trust my instincts."

"*He had a hunch,*" Ido-san said helpfully.

Yoshimi gritted his teeth, but didn't give his friend the satisfaction of another glare. "*You* did not kill the people on this floor." He'd had time to check one or two. The chem darts contained a sedative, not a poison.

She considered him from her seat. She was pretty, although her peasant clothes were a little too form-fitting to be flattering. Her eyes, though... While they tried to pull him in, something hard and flinty hid behind them. He'd seen swordsmen feign weakness often enough to recognize the trick. She assumed he was a backward sexist. Play the helpless, coquettish captive, while no doubt calculating a half dozen ways to kill him without rising from that chair. She might not be dressed in a ninja gi or modern sneak suit, but he couldn't forget what she was.

Then a shift behind that calculated, inviting expression. A change of tactics, as fluid as any expert in stance-no-stance.

"*You're* investigating this clinic too," she said. "It's the only thing that makes sense."

Yoshimi smiled. His instincts were correct. What she was doing might technically be corporate espionage, but she just wanted the truth. She wanted the traitor in White Orchid as much as he did. They were on the same side.

"Go on," he said.

"If you were here to cover it up, if it was *endorsed* by White Orchid, you could only be here as an enforcer, and finding a NSK operative—"

"*We prefer the term, 'ninja.'*"

"—An NSK operative inside your facility without being under contract... you would have had to kill me."

"You use logic to deduce what I merely understand," Yoshimi said.

"Was that a compliment or an insult?" she asked.

"*You can never tell. I like to add the phrase, 'in my naughty parts,' to the end of everything he says. It helps. Trust me.*"

"You can take it however you like," Yoshimi said.

"*See?*"

She grinned, looked away, then burst out laughing. Yoshimi had lost control of this interrogation.

Did he dare trust her? The NSK had to be as worried about large-scale fertility manipulation as he was. And she hadn't killed any of the peasants here. That made her at least a *little* trustworthy, didn't it?

"I can always kill you later, Miko-san." He drew a knife and cut her bonds, half-expecting Ido-san to whisper "No he can't" over the speakers—the man would certainly think that was funny. But it was one thing to mock him and show him disrespect. Ido-san would never actually betray his trust. The man had almost died to unlock his birth records, after all. Sen-san might be Yoshimi's best friend, but Ido-san had earned his trust.

Miko-san rose slowly, rubbing her wrists. "I take it this is your way of suggesting we work together?"

"I think that would be agreeable."

"*Sometimes I change it to, 'to my naughty bits'. You know. Whatever works.*"

She bit down on a grin.

"We should continue our investigation."

"*Or 'of.'*"

"Together."

Ido-san's laughter burst from the speakers, and Miko-san turned away, too polite to laugh in his face. Yoshimi bore down on the shame of it. Ido-san might be a west-loving malcontent, but he understood people. He could charm an oni. Yoshimi was willing to play the straight man if it meant he didn't have to kill this woman. Let Ido-san play the monkey king. Yoshimi could withstand nearly any indignity. He was the rock and Ido-san the surf.

He waited patiently for them to control themselves. Finally, Miko-san straightened and faced him again.

"I'm sorry." She bowed. "That was uncalled for."

"Laughter is the salve that cures rich and poor alike."

"*Sometimes I think he's Chinese.*"

"Fortune cookies are a western invention," Miko-san said with a slight tone of disapproval.

Yoshimi controlled his smile. Maybe the two of them could find common ground after all. He met her gaze and bowed. She returned it.

"*Are you two having a moment? It sounds like you're having a moment.*"

One of them needed to be the first to reach out. If someone experimented on eta, and it had crossed over to the peasants, this transcended petty formalities of whether or not White Orchid had contracted the NSK or if her presence here had been at the behest of a rival corporation.

"We have been tracking misappropriated company funds," Yoshimi said. "Peasant fertility anomalies. They led here."

She nodded and considered him a moment. "We study your fertility records regularly and found some red flags. I suspect a nano-virus."

He squinted. A nanobot plague? That wasn't the most distressing thing in her statement. "The NSK hacks our fertility records?"

"Yes."

What honorable reason could they have to spy on fertility records? Yoshimi's hand twitched to reach for his blade, but no. She couldn't be *permitted* to tell him that. She'd made a gesture. A confession. He had to accept it. Do not strike the hand of courtesy.

"I understand," he said. "And that led you here?"

"We backtracked here," she said. "We ran a statistical analysis and a social net matrix and found the peasants in question had very little direct connection. The only leaps we could track led through their sanitation records."

"Ah," Yoshimi said. "That makes sense."

"*I didn't follow that*," Ido-san said.

She looked up at the ceiling. "Your culture says that no one other than an eta can touch the unclean, correct? Morticians. Butchers. Leatherwork-ers. All eta."

She was an outsider, Japanese but not Okinawan, not brought up under the rule of White Orchid Corporation. She'd barely understand the differ-ence between a peasant and a samurai, how could she grasp what it meant to be eta? The NSK was too 'modern,' too western to understand the old ways. The celestial order. The karmic wheel of death and rebirth.

"*Oh, I get it. Only eta can go hip deep in shit.*"

"We tracked the various sanitation workers and they all came back to a few clinics," she said. "This one seemed key. I came here because I'm not good enough a hacker to compromise their systems remotely."

"*Really?*" The incredulity might as well have been a slap in the face, but Miko-san didn't react, and Ido-san quickly moved past the implied insult. "*Well, I have special access.*" He didn't mention he could have hacked this place with a bargain deck and open-source software. Saving face for her. "*I've scanned the systems here while we've been talking. They've been scrubbed clean.*"

She nodded. "Then step two."

"*What's step two?*"

"We interrogate the staff," Yoshimi said, but he didn't like it. Eyewit-ness evidence, from peasants? What good could that do? Still, they didn't have any other options, and they might be able to find actual evidence later.

They gathered the staff and made them comfortable in a threadbare conference room. When they groggily came to, one by one, Yoshimi and Miko-san interrogated each in turn. The staff knew of the project, a nano-virus after all, but didn't seem to know its purpose. Only one person, it seemed, had, but...

"They killed him," Yoshimi said an hour later, in the hall with Miko-san.

She nodded beside him. All the peasants agreed. The director of the clinic, a minor samurai of a disgraced family, had been the only one who knew the truth. He'd turned up dead five days earlier. Heart attack.

"I'm looking at the autopsy right now," Ido-san said. *"Have I mentioned that I love Fujihara's security access? It's like having the cheat codes to life."*

"And?" Miko-san asked.

"They've been altered. I have no way of knowing how, but the tampering is obvious."

"You can't rebuild them or something?" she asked.

"I'll do a deep sector scan of the storage systems. It's possible that I'll rebuild the originals, but not likely. They would have used intelligence-grade scrubbers."

"*Chikusho,*" Yoshimi spat the harshest curse word a proper Japanese man would utter. A reference to being reborn as an animal. He was ashamed to have said it in front of a woman, and Miko-san considered him sideways for a moment before clearing her throat instead of answering.

"So they made sure not even a peasant could expose them," she said, "and they killed the only samurai who could bring testimony."

"Yes," Yoshimi said.

"So we're done," she said. "I've got nothing left."

No. She was just too modern to understand. Too western.

"That depends," he said.

"On what?"

"On whether you want evidence," he said. "Or just the truth."

THREE ETA KNELT BEFORE THEM, ARRANGED IN FRONT OF THE HOUSE OF the late director: the sanitation expert who fixed the sewage pipes, the mortician who had handled the body, and the gastroenterologist who had treated the director for an unmentionable 'dissolution of the bowels.'

The day had turned cloudy and they shivered in their thin, but thermally efficient, clothing. They dressed to look like eta, but in the high-tech temperature-controlled smart fabrics, the shivering could only come from fear.

"You three were all in the director's house the night he died," Yoshimi said. "Tell me what you saw."

"We saw nothing," the plumber said.

"I wasn't even there until after," the mortician said.

The gastroenterologist just looked away. Miko-san stepped close. A breeze rustled their clothing.

"It's barbaric, the way they treat you," she said. "I know. I understand. The NSK took me against my will when I was a child. I understand oppression. You can talk to me."

Ah. She assumed because he was eta, he must hate samurai, that just because her loyalty was mandated with a kill switch, that they resented their lives as well. It was easy to think in absolutes when you stood outside a system looking in.

And it didn't work. The eta stared at her, puzzled a moment, then shook his head. "You understand nothing." He wrinkled his nose as if he could smell the western stink on her.

She sighed and rose. "Even your eta are bigots."

"You mock the unfamiliar," the gastroenterologist said. "White Orchid brought us food and shelter and protection after the nuclear fire. They brought us safety and homes. Security. Warmth."

"They brought you slavery," she said.

"They brought social order," the gastroenterologist said. "But did you know that the lowest eta in Okinawa has a higher standard of living than the best slums of Sapporo?"

She raised an eyebrow. "You would give up your freedom for food?"

He stared at her as though she were slightly insane. "For my children? For my wife? Are you joking? Of course I would."

She shook her head, but Yoshimi hadn't come here to watch an eta match her in a battle of wits. He'd come because no one cared what an eta saw. Like a geisha, an eta had no legal status. He could witness any crime, but unless another eta committed the crime, his testimony held no weight. An eta wasn't worth the effort it took to silence him.

"You *know* something," Yoshimi lowered himself into a crouch. He didn't care if that put him on the same level as an eta. He only cared about the next words. "Not something you saw. Something he told you."

"A man develops a bond with his doctor," the eta said. "Even if that doctor is eta."

No. *Especially* if the doctor was eta. "I understand."

"I don't," Miko-san said.

"He couldn't afford a geisha," Yoshimi said. It was all fine to have discipline, strength, and power, but no man could contain it all. Eventually, even the most stoic man had to talk to someone. No one could be alone all the time.

"I still don't get it."

「Let him do his thing,」 Ido-san said over their comm link. He had them in conference mode.

"He was in pain," Yoshimi said. "You were the only one who could help him. His sickness made him unclean."

"He felt great shame," the eta said. It didn't matter. His words couldn't cast an ill light on the dead. He was just an eta.

"But it wasn't just the physical shame," Yoshimi said. "They must talk to you. You're already talking to them about the most shameful breakdowns a body can have. They must be dying to talk to you about the other shames they carry." He smiled sadly. "You must carry so many burdens for your patients."

The eta looked away for a second. "I know who was giving the orders. I didn't see them kill him, but he told me who it was."

"And who was it?" Yoshimi asked quietly.

"Urabe Jiro," the eta whispered.

The hatamoto of White Orchid. The second most powerful man in the prefecture, after Kitsune-heike. Possibly the most powerful *mortal* man in the world. Yoshimi's gorge rose in his throat. Urabe Jiro. Fujihara-sama's lord. His head pounded. Urabe Jiro. The most untouchable man in Okinawa.

⌈ Look on the bright side. We have hearsay testimony. From an eta, even, ⌋ said Ido-san.

Miko-san didn't bother with the sarcasm.

"*Chikusho*," she spat.

"Everything about this prefecture is ridiculous!" Miko-san said, pacing back and forth in Yoshimi's apartment, an hour later. "Your culture is a walking human-rights violation!"

"This from a group who places nanobot kill switches in their recruits to keep them from defecting?" Yoshimi asked quietly.

But she ignored him, pacing on sky-blue carpet, silhouetted in front of floor to ceiling windows. "You don't think that this is what the Edo period was *really like*, do you?" She gestured wildly with her hands, like a vulgar westerner. "You don't think that geisha, locked away in those pleasure districts, actually refrained from selling sex? You don't think that duels of honor were more common than a knife in the back, that your code of bushido was anything more than an excuse to brutalize the helpless?"

"I do not know what was," Yoshimi said. "I don't believe it matters."

"This isn't ancient Japan!" She finally managed to get her hands under control. "This is some romance-novel version of ancient Japan. The ancient Japan of bad movies. This is the hundred-yen version of Japan."

Yoshimi knelt in *seiza* on a mat, considering her as she paced, the projectors in the living room dark on the wall behind her, save for panels of slanting light filtering in from the tall windows. Her passion flared, too vulgar to be Japanese, of course, but one couldn't argue that her personal honor motivated it. There was nothing more Japanese than that.

"And yet, we are happy," he said.

"Are you?" She turned to him, her face a mask of frustration. A strand of hair fell over her eyes. She blew it back.

He smiled peacefully. "Yes."

She slid to the ground, kneeling, and remained quiet for a moment. "I know. I know that after the bombs, this country was a mess. I can't imagine how bad it was in Okinawa. And White Orchid offered peace. And prosperity. And a place." She looked out the window. "And even though you control the flow of information, your company has kept the highest standard of living of anywhere in Japan. Even the hackers can't deny just how good the citizens here have it. I've been to Sapporo's cyber-slums, seen people freezing to death, stealing food and knifing each other for purified water." She shook her head. "I've seen how bad it can be."

"It is our love of order that makes us who we are. White Orchid taught us that, centuries ago," Yoshimi said.

"And what did you do with the dissenters?"

"I believe you've met Ido-san?" Yoshimi said.

She smiled and looked down. "And my group dresses up in black and call ourselves ninja. We don't care that the black-suited ninja was invented by the theater because the audience was already trained not to see stagehands."

Now it was Yoshimi's turn to smile. "Your *ninja* are dressed as *stagehands*?" She was going somewhere with this. He decided to see where.

She laughed a little bitterly, a little ironically. "Ridiculous, huh? But evidently a person dressed in the black outfit of a stagehand, in the theater of old, was literally invisible to the audience. And if a person dressed like that and played an assassin, when he struck, he seemed to appear out of nowhere. So that's how they dressed their ninja. Real ninja probably dressed like whoever would be standing around their target. To blend in."

Ah. She reached out to him. Accept it.

"So we are all a little silly," Yoshimi said.

She considered him out of the corner of her eye. "You're a bit of a rock, you know that?"

He shrugged. "I'm a Buddhist."

"So am I."

"I, however, am good at it."

The laughter started low, then burst out of her in a completely unlady-like fashion, her shoulders shaking, her head thrown back. It might be uncouth, but it appealed, in a raw way. But then again, he was perverse enough to have Ido-san as a friend.

Yoshimi moved from a slight smile to a fuller one. He could let his control slip to unseemly degrees as well.

"So," she said. "Urabe. What do we do?"

"There is not much we *can* do about Urabe-sama," Yoshimi said.

"We are *not* calling that bastard 'Urabe-sama'," she said. "He's killing people."

"He isn't killing anyone."

"He's making sure they are never born, that's the same thing."

Yoshimi shook his head. "You're jumping to conclusions."

"There's only one reason to turn off the fertility of people, and that's to kill off entire genetic lines. And he's beyond our touch. No law can stop him. No court can convict him. There's only *one* way to stop him." She looked out the window, then back. "We have to kill him, right?"

Kill him. Yoshimi's chest tightened at the thought. Kill him. Of course she would go there first. The man was an inconvenience. So get rid of him. Why would she think any differently?

But, no, he needed to stop thinking so uncharitably. Urabe-sama might be many things, but he posed a far greater threat than a mere 'inconvenience.'

"We can't kill him," Yoshimi said.

"There's no other way," she said. "He is the most powerful man in the prefecture, after Kitsune, and our intelligence people aren't entirely sure the old fox is even still alive. It was Urabe's people who declared that stupid rule about adopted children not inheriting, wasn't it?"

"That was Kitsune-heike," Yoshimi said, his resentment sparking in his chest. He took a deep breath and forced it down. "It was after he lost his own children, early in his time as shogun. And it only applies to the company; peasants can do what they want."

She stared at him. "You don't see the connection there, between his children and his 'law?'"

"He did it out of grief, that's what you are saying?" He scoffed. "Nonsense. It is wise to disallow adopted inheritance." Yoshimi lied. He couldn't let an outsider sense the pain that rule caused him. "You must keep family as family. You cannot corrupt it with the likes of me."

She squinted at him in anger. "Do you know the average age of adoption in Japan?"

"No."

"It's thirty-seven. In the other prefectures, people adopt their second in command so that the person inheriting the family business will be the best person for the job. Children are a gamble. A Japanese businessperson picks the best of the best to be their heir, and grooms that person for years. It's considered a tremendous honor to the former families. It's one of the things that makes Japan great."

Yoshimi frowned. He knew that people used to adopt specifically to gain an heir. He didn't know that the rest of Japan saw it as a good thing. "He was trying to maintain the bloodlines. What happens if a person can adopt their successor, and not raise children of their own?"

"People don't stop having children, Yoshimi," she said. "It's an actual biological imperative."

So why cut off adopted children from inheriting? He'd always assumed —"But the old ways..."

"Fostering and adopting have always been traditions here. I tell you, this isn't real ancient history you're aping. It's something else. Something romanticized and convenient."

Why would Kitsune-heike do that? What wisdom did he have that the rest of Japan couldn't see? He'd assumed it was to ward off western influence. If adoption *was* a Japanese tradition, what did that say for Yoshimi's place in life?

"Yoshimi-san." Miko-san leaned forward as if she were going to lay a hand on his, but thought better of it. She settled back. "Anywhere else. In any other time, lords would have dreamed of adopting a man like you. They might have come to blows for the privilege. Yoshimi-san. You don't *believe* this, do you?"

Yoshimi looked away from her. This matter took them to the core of who he was, but he could only speak of such things with his geisha. He couldn't let her see.

"I feel like my words are causing you pain, but they aren't are they? My word just brushed over a pain you've been carrying your entire life."

Kitsune-heike couldn't be wrong about the bloodlines. If Yoshimi pulled at that thread, what unraveled? His determination to be the best swordsman, certainly. His honor? His beliefs? His need to be the perfect Buddhist? The best friend to Ido-san and Sen-san?

"I will think on this, Miko-san." But he would not. That way lay only madness. He needed that pain. It made him who he was. "Your words do me great honor, but I think they do you more."

She squinted at him, as if unsure how to take that. Then she looked out the window again.

"We aren't going kill him, are we?"

I'll lose one, eventually.

"We cannot."

"No court can convict the hatamoto," she said. "Even if you had testimony, no testimony would stick. Maybe all the daimyos together, but none of them know; I'm sure of it."

I'll lose one, eventually.

"We cannot kill him," Yoshimi said. If he pulled *that* thread, what would unravel? His honor? His self? His very soul?

"Then we'll keep thinking," she said.

I will lose one eventually. But not today.

AN HOUR LATER, YOSHIMI STOOD IN THE GARDEN BEHIND HIS apartment building, the wind rustling his clothing, carrying the smell of chrysanthemums and tree pollen. Around him stretched pebbled paths and flowerbeds. Just out of sight, water giggled like children in a fountain. The wind shifted and mist from the spray kissed the skin of his face.

Miko-san and Ido-san were in a deep conference in the apartment, but thinking had never been Yoshimi's strength. His strength had always been in understanding. One couldn't understand through brainstorming and debate. The more one talked, invariably, the less one understood. One could only understand through meditation and reflection. And listening, of course, but only in listening to one who already understood.

So he sought peace out here. Among the flowers and the bees. Inside lived chaos and disruption of the status quo, where samurai and ninja plotted the downfall of a powerful lord. Utter madness. Here, among the garden and the bees, was order. The drones like eta. The workers like peasants. The queen like the shogun. Funny. Only the samurai had no purpose in nature. When he understood the implications of that, he would no doubt hold great wisdom.

"The great Yoshimi Daichi," a voice said behind him. "Is he meant to be a warrior? Is he meant to be a poet? Is he meant to be a monk?"

Yoshimi looked over his shoulder to see his best friend, Sen Satoshi, carrying two bokken and training masks. He smiled an easy smile, his hair long and beautiful, like the wife of a daimyo's, but loose and hanging to his lower back. Sen's eyes always sparkled, and today was no exception.

"Perhaps Yoshimi Daichi was meant to be a beekeeper?" Yoshimi said.

"Or a gardener."

Yoshimi smiled genuinely. "Oh, I would know great joy as a gardener."

Sen-san looked him up and down. They had been friends ever since Sen-san had been hired as the duelist of another daimyo. He couldn't hide his thoughts from Sen-san.

"It was good to see you today in the lobby." After he'd been lightly tortured by the daimyos.

Sen-san smiled, but he examined Yoshimi carefully. "I know that look. You are in one of your moods."

"And what mood is that?" Yoshimi said.

"That I'm-a-brooding-warrior-Buddhist mood." Sen-san handed Yoshimi a bokken. "I am a river of conflict and pain, wrapped in a miasma of meditation and peace." He smiled. "It's your defining characteristic."

"Oh, please," Yoshimi said. "Do not hold your tongue to save *me* face. If I cannot get the truth from my friend, where can I get it?"

Sen-san laughed and fell into the stance of the third fundamental, the lower stance to draw Yoshimi in. Yoshimi fell into the fifth, his sword laterally to the right. "You knew I'd be here for training? I should be occupied with my duties."

"You didn't know that you came out here to train?" Sen-san asked. "It's 6 p.m., the hour of training."

"I came out here to think." Yoshimi watched his friend's lines. He'd always been good, and he'd been working on the rigidity of his back leg. Good.

Sen-san moved from the third fundamental to the fourth, fluidly, with the ease of a delighted breath. "You understand many things, Yoshimi-san, but Yoshimi-san is the thing you understand the *least*."

Yoshimi smiled. "Enlighten me."

"You came here to train because it's 6 p.m. You might have made an excuse, but that's why you are here."

"I didn't even know the time."

"Your subconscious discipline is better than any clock." Sen-san struck.

Sen-san had never beaten him in training, but he did well today, and

Yoshimi couldn't shake that last sentiment. If Yoshimi really had come out here because of the hour, not because of his need to get away, what did that really say? An eta could laugh and love and eat meat. An eta, being the lowest caste, had no power, but also no responsibility. They had to play in waste, but they could tell their wives and children that they cherished them. They could embrace a friend. They weren't duty-bound to stop a man who could have them executed with a gesture. They didn't need to hire a professional mourner because their private hours at night were not enough time to release the tears and the shattering grief of losing a wife.

The word samurai literally meant 'servant.' In the end, who was the slave, and who the free man?

"I know the answer to your question," Sen-san said an hour later, after he'd graciously accepted his defeat.

"What is my question?" Yoshimi asked.

"I don't think that you can, in good honor, tell me. And I don't think that I, in good honor, can know."

Sen-san had a bit of understanding himself, it seemed.

"And what is my *answer* then."

Sen-san stepped in close, too close for propriety. So close Yoshimi could smell the soy on his breath. His voice whispered. "Kill him."

Years of discipline barely kept Yoshimi's face calm. "Kill who?" he whispered back.

"I don't know, but I can see it in your stance. In the way you fight. You weren't aiming for my arms or my chest or my neck. You were aiming past me."

"So?"

"So for the first time in your life, you are practicing to kill. Whether you know it or not, you ready yourself for an execution."

"And you think I should kill someone. Without even knowing who?"

"A proper dog cannot bite the hand of a child or his master," Sen-san said in full voice and stepped away. "When a proper dog seeks violence, it is only from defense and loyalty, and purity of purpose."

"And you think I am a proper dog?" Yoshimi asked.

"What are you?" Sen-san smiled and picked up his jacket from where he'd thrown it earlier. "What am I? We are all dogs, tarted up and displayed for show."

He left the garden.

Well that hadn't helped at all.

He still stood there ten minutes later when his comm link buzzed. The caller ID read 'White Orchid Executive offices.' He answered.

「Hai,」he said.

A woman's voice spoke in his ear, or in the hearing centers of his brain more accurately, a direct connection though this neuralware, speaking in that high-pitched singsong of all secretaries. 「I have a call from Kitsune Imoru.」

Yoshimi hit his knees before he realized that she couldn't see him. Kitsune-heike. He took a deep breath, centering his chi. 「I understand.」 He lied. There was no day under sun and moon when Kitsune-heike would spend a breath on him.

「Please find a secure comm room. His call will follow in five minutes.」

"Hai!" he shouted and sprinted for his apartment.

He shot past Miko-san, talking to Ido-san over the comm link like a lunatic conversing with the voices in her head. Yoshimi didn't say anything, he just ducked into his communications room and sealed the door behind him.

Four minutes later, when the call came, he already stood in the bowed position, inside the featureless white box of a room. The blandness of the place made it more difficult to plant listening devices. When the shogun of White Orchid appeared, the lights dimmed and he flickered into existence in the center of the room, projected up as a hologram from the floor.

He stood perhaps five-foot-two, although the projection digitally represented a man who had long ago been replaced with a robotic doll avatar. In other words, he appeared five-foot-two because he wanted to. He wore a green haori jacket and yellow pants, unadorned. Not the robes of divine emperor used for his official appearances. He'd have calculated all of these as messages. All messages, but Yoshimi reeled, stunned, and couldn't decode them.

Kitsune-heike bowed with the slightest gesture of his balding, white-fringed head. Far deeper than Yoshimi warranted, but he probably didn't want there to be any confusion over what constituted a bow. Yoshimi straightened, hovering between the desire for perfect posture and the need to slump shorter than his shogun.

"*Yoshimi-san.*" The old man's face was smooth, but he had to be 120 years old or older, so however he'd extended his life, he could probably look any age he wanted. Another message? "*You are investigating a matter of great import to me.*"

So he was aware of the funds. He hadn't gotten involved before. Why wait until someone as lowly as Yoshimi had the task. A fourth message? A fifth?

"*You may speak.*" Kitsune-heike smiled sadly. "*I have found one sided conversations more trouble than they are worth. The wisdom of age.*"

And divinity? Many people thought that Kitsune-heike had refined his chi until he just sort of vibrated his way out of the mortal world.

"Yes, Kitsune-heike."

"*I will watch you,*" Kitsune-heike said. "*You will be my eyes. My hands can only reach so far. My voice is old and weary with age. Cherry blossoms do not fall because they are lovely. They fall because the old steps aside to make way for the new.*"

But he *hadn't* stepped aside, so his analogy— Oh yes. He didn't embody the cherry blossoms. He embodied the tree. Timeless. But talk in riddles? That didn't make sense. One didn't break their silence to say nothing. Another message hid there, and he just couldn't see it.

Either that, or Kitsune-heike was half-mad.

"*The rains water the fields. The laughter nourishes the ear. The light, ever-bright and new, feeds the rice.*" He considered Yoshimi a moment. "*Do you understand?*"

No, but one didn't argue with a man older than some family lines. "I will seek understanding."

"*Then I have one less burden on my heart.*" He started to turn away as if ending the conversation, then stopped. "*The law of adoption is inviolate. I will not give you your hearts wish. No matter what.*"

What? His heart pounded. His stomach sank. Yoshimi closed his eyes, as if struck, and when he opened them again, he found them slightly damp. Why would the shogun say that? Why remind him of how helpless he truly was? Cruelty? An alien misunderstanding of the human spirit?

No. Even across an insurmountable chasm of age and station and distance, Kitsune-heike could see into his heart. He could give Yoshimi anything he wanted. He was divine, in station if not in reality. And yet he would not. Had he seen into Yoshimi's heart and found him wanting?

"What I do, I do because I am your servant."

"*You are the servant of the peasants and the eta and the celestial order. That is what samurai means.*"

"Yes, Kitsune-heike."

"*But in this one thing, you may be my hand as well.*" His smile was ancient and full of painful, bitter wisdom.

"Yes, Kitsune-heike."

The shogun of White Orchid vanished, the room's holo-projector dark in an instant. The lights returned to normal and Yoshimi fell to his knees, then gathered himself into *seiza* and tried to center his scattered chi.

What had just happened? To be granted grace and denied hope in one visitation. Yoshimi could barely think straight. His skin grew clammy. His eyes grew wetter.

No reward. Just eternal, hopeless service. Why? Why even call to tell him that? Why feed him nothing but despair? Riddles. Hopelessness. Then again, why did Yoshimi occasionally talk to a dog? Because attention from his master rewarded a dog enough.

Yoshimi stood against the most powerful mortal man in the prefecture, and the only word from on high told him that he would not find succor. That he served for service's sake. To remind him that neither privilege nor responsibility came with thanks. He should have known. He had always known. In his heart.

But he hadn't understood.

He had never had hope.

He and his father served a thankless god under the yoke of a cruel and monstrous man. He sat in a brutal social system and he met genuine complaints with unspeakable violence as his actual purpose. For years, he had seen society as manifestation of the karmic wheel of life and rebirth. For years, he'd seen his life as a metaphor for truth and life everywhere, but what if it wasn't? What if it was all just ashes?

The comm rang, the holo-projector in the floor flashing.

"Hai," he said to answer it.

Urabe Jiro appeared before him. Hatamoto of the White Orchid. Second only to Kitsune-heike. The man who had created a nano-virus that destroyed the fertility of the lower classes. Towering. Disapproving, filling the room to the ceiling with light and presence, wearing the finest silk prints of doves and flowers. He stood easy with his cyberware bolstering his age like the braces on a dam. He stared down and crossed his arms.

"*Yoshimi Daichi?*"

Yoshimi bowed, and Urabe-sama returned the bow as a nod. This whole thing seemed too much a contrived. What was going on?

"Yes, Urabe-sama." *Chikuso.* Urabe-sama just had to order Yoshimi to commit seppuku right now, and it would all end. Urabe-sama did not need a reason. From the moment he'd started this, Yoshimi could only hope Urabe-sama wouldn't decide to act until Yoshimi had a solution. Now that all vanished in the sparkle artifacts of holographic line noise.

"*Are you my good and faithful servant, Yoshimi?*"

Without proof of a crime, he had to be. He had less freedom than the eta. Than the drones. Than the earthbound rice, drowning in the fields.

"Yes, Urabe-sama."

"Then I have decided to grant you a boon."

What? Yoshimi looked up at his lord and he blinked. "A boon, hatamoto?"

Urabe-sama's expression beamed, the perfect countenance of mercy and generosity. He reached down, as if scattering coins on the lower castes. He nodded. *"I would like to give you your birthright. I would return to you your inheritance."*

Yoshimi blinked again. "With respect, lord. That isn't possible. The law of adoption is inviolate. I cannot inherit."

"Not from your adopted father, no," Urabe-sama said. *"That is not the inheritance I intend to grant you."* He gestured, his arms encompassing the room. *"I'm going to grant you your original birthright. The one denied you first."* His grin was the picture of placid, Buddhist peace. *"I'm going to tell you who your birth father is."*

YOSHIMI STOOD IN THE ELEVATOR AT WHITE ORCHID HEADQUARTERS, watching the floor readout flash larger numbers as the lift hurtled him toward the top floor. He closed his eyes. Could he do this? Was he about to throw everything away?

Miko-san stared at him in shock. Yoshimi turned away, unable to meet her eyes. Over the comm link, Ido-san said, "He offered you what?"

"He offered to tell me who my father is."

Yoshimi shook the thoughts out of his head. He took a steady breath, sought the peace of the garden. The peace of the kata. The peace of the perfect strike, flawlessly executed. He could do this.

"We have to kill him," Miko-san said. "He wouldn't have made the offer if he didn't think you were close."

"You don't understand," Yoshimi said. "He didn't have to make the offer at all."

"He's trying to buy you."

"Obviously. The only reason he could possibly have called then is because he has my lines tapped. He heard Kitsune-heike's denial. He made a counter offer.

"He's too dangerous."

"We can't kill him."

"Is this your pacifism talking, or are you planning on taking the deal?" She stared

at him flatly. She knew. He couldn't hide his lack of strength from her. His flaws would shatter him, leaving everyone else to sweep up the pieces.

The elevator decelerated and dinged as he arrived at the top floor. The doors slid open.

A woman in a pink and white kimono stood waiting for him. She smiled prettily and gestured for him to follow before walking away with tiny steps. Yoshimi followed.

"Tell me, Yoshimi Daichi," Miko-san said. "Tell me. Tell me you'll let me kill him. It's the only way."

"No," Ido-san said.

"What do you mean 'no?'"

Ido-san continued, "I mean you're wrong. You can't kill him. Yoshimi can't kill him. This is what Yoshimi has always needed. He needs to take the deal."

Miko-san turned away.

A man took Yoshimi's sword and the woman in the kimono gestured for him to enter the office. Yoshimi activated his comm and transmitted to Miko-san and Ido-san, back at his apartment.

「I'm going dark. I will call you if I survive.」 His voice went over the network straight from his mind, so only they could hear. He turned on the NSK counter-frequency device. That would block their scanners, and their jammers. With that active, Yoshimi could record Urabe's confession.

If he could just get him to confess.

Through the door, he found Urabe-sama kneeling behind a desk, holo-displays flickering all around him. The man saw Yoshimi and smiled. Yoshimi bowed. The hatamoto nodded and rose.

"My boy. You've come."

"Hai, Urabe-sama."

The hatamoto strode around his desk, gesturing with his head to someone in the corner behind Yoshimi. Yoshimi looked over his shoulder as two men stepped forward, one with an electro-stunner pointed in his direction. The other with a scanner.

The man with the scanner studied the display as he played it up and down Yoshimi's body. Looking for listening devices and recorders, no doubt. It would be an obvious plot for Yoshimi to come in here and try to trick the hatamoto into recording a confession.

"He's clean," the man said. "Nothing."

"You can't kill him," Yoshimi said to Miko-san.

"I have to."

"I mean that you cannot, not that you shouldn't." He stepped up to her and looked down into her eyes. "If you go in there, you are not getting anywhere near him and

you are not coming out of there alive. But I am not taking the deal. You were taken by the NSK, not born to it, right? That means you have a kill switch. Obviously, the NSK has ordered you to resolve this, so if I did and you let me, you'd be directly disobeying them, and the NSK could activate your kill switch.

"They probably wouldn't kill me for that, even if they did think I had disobeyed them. I have a history of success. They'd just punish me."

"I can't imagine that's ideal either. No, I have to do this. You'd push it too far and likely die in the attempt. I'm not losing you. I'm not losing anyone. No one dies on this mission."

Unless it's me.

"You've come to accept my deal," Urabe said.

"Yes, Urabe-sama." Yoshimi cast his gaze down, on the floor.

"And if you do, you will tell me everything you know?"

"Yes, Urabe-sama."

"And you will do my bidding?"

"Yes, Urabe-sama."

Urabe-sama smiled, the wrinkled face tight and fragile, like armored skin, poorly concealed. Which it might very well be. He nodded at the men and they walked toward the door. Urabe faced the window and Yoshimi tried not to let the elation show on his face. It had worked. They had fallen for it—

"Wait." Urabe-sama raised one hand. The men stopped at the door.

"Yes, Urabe-sama?"

"When you said he was clean, you just meant of anything suspicious, correct?" Urabe faced them now.

"No, Urabe-sama. Completely clean."

Urabe-sama frowned. "But he has cyberware. Your scanner detected cyberware."

No. No. No.

"No, Urabe-sama. No electronics of any kind."

Yoshimi cranked his speedware to full, the wires throbbing under his skin, but the guard probably had cyberware as well. Even if Yoshimi owned better enhancements, they couldn't beat a readied trigger finger. He managed to dodge mostly out of the way, but the delivery element of the stunner clipped his arm.

The stunner overloaded his nerves with agony. A direct hit dropped a man before he could feel pain, but the stunner only a grazed him and Yoshimi went to his knees, his stoicism shattered as a scream of absolute bone-throbbing pain burst from his lips. A flood of pain. An ocean of pain. A typhoon of pain.

"Search him. With your hands this time."

Yoshimi thrashed in unspeakable horror as the men pulled his arms tight and patted him down, ripping his clothes until they found the NSK counter-frequency device. One of them shattered it with a gun butt and the other ran the scanner over him again.

"He has a recorder, a transmitter, and a full duelist's suite of cyberware," the man with the scanner said.

"Are the jammers in place?"

"Yes, Urabe-sama. He cannot call out."

"Any recording *cyberware*?"

"No, Urabe-sama."

"Take the recorder and the transmitter. Destroy them."

By the time the agony had dropped from world-ending to merely blinding, they'd stripped him of his ability to record or transmit a confession. At some point, he'd lost control of his bladder. He lay in the stink of his urine. Helpless. Like an incompetent. Or an eta. He couldn't bear the shame. He'd lost, and the kami had decreed he'd be humiliated as well as defeated.

Urabe-sama had returned to his desk and the two men stood above to either side, far enough away to use the stunners again. Finally, Yoshimi, soaked in urine, shaking on the floor, regained control of his body, but not his shame.

"I had such high hopes for you, Yoshimi."

"You were going to turn me against my lord," Yoshimi whispered. "My father." *Don't smell it. Ignore my dishonor. Please.*

"He is not your father, though, is he?" Urabe-sama *tsked*. "Not in a real legal sense. More a guardian, and a bad one at that. He can't even fight his own battles."

Yoshimi didn't dare move, so he lay on the floor. Defeated. Hopeless. The stink of his urine his entire world.

"You're killing the peasant lines," Yoshimi said. "A nano-virus, infecting the eta, spreading up into the peasants. Something smart that you can control. Select your victims. That's why the peasants are affected, but the eta aren't anymore. It is composed of nanobots, so it is a virus that you can turn on or off on a victim by victim basis."

"You think you have learned so much, my boy. But you have learned nothing." He shook his head sadly. "It's pathetic, really. Did you think through what would happen if I stopped the peasants from reproducing? Our entire society would collapse. From the bottom up."

Yoshimi looked at the man. Of course. It would be stupid to take out the lower castes. The peasants had never been the target, just a convenient testbed. The peasants were necessary. Without peasants, who would keep the city running?

"I knew that I needed to do something when Kitsune-heike called you," Urabe-sama said. "It was time to move."

Why was he still talking? Why wouldn't he just let Yoshimi die—

Wait. Why *was* he still talking? Why *hadn't* he just ordered Yoshimi to kill himself? He had the power. There would be no consequences.

Unless there were. But what consequences could possibly stop Urabe from exercising his casual control over life and death?

And why had Kitsune-heike spoken in riddles?

No, he knew that one. Kitsune-heike must have known Urabe might be listening.

The real question was what did the riddle *mean*?

I have found one-sided conversations more trouble than they are worth.

Urabe-sama had heard the whole thing.

You are investigating a matter of great importance to me.

Kitsune-heike hadn't spoken in riddles because he was mad, or out of touch with reality.

The rains water the fields. The laughter nourishes the ear. The light, ever-bright and new, feeds the rice. Do you understand?

Life and rebirth? Rain to grow. Light to give strength. And there was only one time, outside of his geisha's rooms, where a samurai freely heard laughter and didn't find the emotion just a little too vulgar.

The law of adoption is inviolate.

Children. Heirs. Urabe-sama wasn't trying to take out the families of the peasants.

"You're taking out the family lines of the other daimyos," Yoshimi said. "Your nano-virus. It's meant to prune each and every one of the great samurai family lines."

"Except mine?" Urabe-sama—no—*Urabe* said. "Is that what you're thinking?"

"You're a monster," Yoshimi said.

"Do you really think that Kitsune's heirs all just *happened* to die after he took control? No. He made sure there was no one to succeed him. Even then, he always planned to be immortal." The man didn't even bother with an honorific for Kitsune-heike anymore. He scoffed. "Murdering children is the oldest and most time-honored of samurai traditions." He smiled. "I walk in the shadow of giants."

Urabe was behind it after all. He hadn't confessed directly—he wouldn't make that mistake—but Yoshimi couldn't mistake his meaning.

And even if it had been a direct confession, Yoshimi still had no course of action. The room awash in jammers. Yoshimi's recording device shattered. He could only put his word against the hatamoto's. A samurai of equal rank might be able to call that a confession, but Yoshimi was as the dust.

"Bring in the old fool," Urabe said.

One of the men stepped out of the room and Urabe looked down upon Yoshimi, like Lord Moon in the heavens. He scowled. "Pick yourself up you filthy bastard."

No one had ever dared say that word to Yoshimi before, Urabe didn't lie, did he? The obvious conclusion on why he'd been abandoned by his parents. He couldn't deny it.

Yoshimi rose to his knees, the smell of his shame sharp in his nose. Behind him, his adopted father stepped into the room. Yoshimi recognized the sound of the man's limp. Don't let him smell it. Don't let him know my shame.

"Give him his boy's sword."

A rustle of clothing, but no words from his father. What could he say? They all knew what would come next.

"Give it to me," Urabe said.

They didn't have to be told what. One of the men handed him Urabe Yoshimi's own wakizashi and a folded cloth. The hatamoto wrapped the cloth around the blade, just below the hilt and stepped up to Yoshimi. He presented the weapon.

"You will now commit seppuku as punishment for your crimes," Urabe said. "Your father will second you, but he will not be absolved from your shame. You have betrayed your daimyo and your hatamoto."

"What is my crime?" Yoshimi asked.

"Your crime is too unspeakable to utter," Urabe said.

He wouldn't just kill Yoshimi. He had to discredit him. No. He had to discredit his *father*. Without Fujihara-sama, could the daimyos muster enough power to stand against him? Without Fujihara-sama, would they have the courage?

Defeated. Urabe had won. For the first time in his life, Yoshimi had only one path to victory, and it had crumbled.

Yoshimi opened his kimono and took the blade, grasping the hilt in one hand, the protective cloth in the other. He placed the point against his belly. Behind him, his father turned the vibro-motor on.

"No," Urabe said. "Turn it off."

Not even the daimyo of security could refuse the hatamoto. The blade turned off.

"You will not take his head until he makes five cuts." Urabe leaned in to Yoshimi. "You hear me, bastard? Five. You will know every agony for your crimes before you die. Do you understand?"

"Do you understand?" Kitsune-heike had said.

Yoshimi stared down at the blade, his hands shaking. His father stood behind him, and there was no way the man couldn't smell the shame of Yoshimi's emptied bladder. Yoshimi closed his eyes. He needed to compose a death haiku. He would die with *that* much dignity.

Five cuts.

No one could withstand crying out for five cuts, and that would be more shame. Yoshimi shamed. His father shamed twice, once as his family, once as his failed second. They'd lost. Seppuku as capital punishment. No dishonor would be absolved.

"Do you understand?"

"Don't make us force the matter. Make your cut," Urabe said.

"Do you understand?"

"No. But I will seek understanding."

Understanding.

Yoshimi opened his eyes. He hardened his voice. How had me missed that? "No."

Urabe seemed too startled to even be angry. He looked at his men, as if to see if he'd heard correctly. "What?"

"No," Yoshimi said, but he made no threatening gestures. They wouldn't stun him for saying no. If they stunned him, they couldn't force him to commit seppuku. They'd just guard him and if necessary call for more men, to force the blade into his hands, into his belly. Stunning him would just make everything take longer. They'd save it for a last resort.

His only power here was to make it inconvenient for everyone else. Unseemly. But what was worse to a samurai than unseemliness?

"Not until I ask my father a question," Yoshimi said.

Urabe considered Yoshimi's adoptive father. The man would be too powerful to kill without good reason, the other daimyos would object, and he hadn't damaged their power yet. Even if he *did* plan on killing off the family lines, he'd have to deal with them for the rest of his life. This plan would always have been about the hatamoto's grandchildren. The plans of a proper, civilized person were generations in the making. The foolish westerners never understood that.

All the daimyos together could cause him problems. He shrugged and pulled a pistol from his sash, pointing it at Yoshimi's head. Not a stun gun. Yoshimi stared down the barrel.

"Be *very* careful what you say to him."

"Father," Yoshimi said. "Did you get my message and listen to it?" Ido-san had insisted. Always have a backup of your data.

"Yes," Fujihara-sama said behind him.

Urabe looked like he almost pulled the trigger, but now he had to know what message Yoshimi had sent. If he pulled the trigger too soon, he'd have to kill the daimyo of security right after, and that might force the daimyos' hands.

"Then testify to these people the last thing Kitsune-heike said to me," Yoshimi said.

It took his father a moment to respond. Yoshimi hadn't understood the importance himself and so he hadn't planned for the situation. Fujihara-sama probably didn't remember instantly. From the expression on Urabe's face, he was trying to remember as well. They'd been speaking of how Yoshimi's purpose as a samurai was to serve the people below him. And then he'd said...

"But in this one thing, you may be my hand as well."

Urabe's face went white and his gaze flicked up to Fujihara-sama then down to Yoshimi. He pulled the trigger, but Yoshimi had already dove to one side and the bullet missed. Yoshimi rolled and came up, the world slowing as his speedware kicked into full power, catching the old man flat footed, driving him up against the wall even as he pulled the trigger over and over, firing harmlessly into the ceiling.

"I never confessed. I never said the words," Urabe hissed. "I never said I did it! You are a man of honor, and I know you won't bear false testimony!"

"That, Urabe, is why I'm challenging you to a duel," Yoshimi said.

"You could deny my son," Fujihara-sama said. "But I don't believe you can deny the hand of your lord, Kitsune-heike."

And Urabe's eyes said he couldn't.

Yoshimi nodded to Sen-san as he limbered up in the middle of the executive atrium. A fountain and zen garden dominated the center of the area, which rose in tiers to the edges of the room. Couches and chairs sat under potted trees and a skylight bathed the area in light from the roof. It smelled of freshly polished wood.

「Are you ready?」 Miko-san asked over the comm link, their communication reestablished.

「I am,」 Yoshimi replied.

Sen-san nodded in his direction and made a short gesture with his hand. The meaning was clear: kill him. Yoshimi held his gaze long enough for his friend to know that the message had been received, then turned away.

Fujihara-sama stood to one side, on a high tier, in navy blue silk in sun patterns. He didn't look crippled when he stood like that, his hands folded in front of him, his face a masterpiece in zen calm. Meanwhile, the professional mourner no longer appeared grief stricken. Whether words had passed between them or the man just understood how to read a room, he studied Yoshimi closely, wringing his hands in terror.

The other daimyos watched on, some sitting, some standing. Assistants and lesser executives filled the rest of the tiers, dressed in colors like the plumage of a shogun's aviary. Which, in a way, this was.

Yoshimi's sword rested easily in his hand, the vibro-blade buzzing with the oscillations of the motor. He closed his eyes a moment, letting the peace of the fountain and the trees enter him, wash away the stain of civilization, of doubt, or of stress. One by one, his muscles released. His heart slowed. His mind found the calm center.

He opened his eyes as Urabe entered the room.

The man wore a light kimono top and hakama pants, to conceal the movement of his legs no doubt. His face was like gray steel, beaten into a scowl by a frustrated sculptor. He entered under a cloud of anger, not even trying to maintain appearances.

"Let's finish this," he growled.

"There is one other spectator, Urabe-sama." Yoshimi might not add the -sama honorific in his mind but he would not give the man the satisfaction of dropping it in public. Such a raging display of disrespect would be... unseemly.

"Who?"

As if on cue, the elevator doors opened and Kitsune-heike stepped out into the room, looking like Confucius in a pink jacket. He glided in as all around them, Daimyos bowed and executives fell to their knees.

Yoshimi bowed.

Urabe must have bowed behind him, because Kitsune bowed to the Urabe, the hatamoto, then in a spectacular insult against his second in command, bowed just as deeply to Yoshimi. He then settled himself on the highest tier, on a couch that lived just this side of 'dais.'

「 How did you know he was coming? 」 Miko-san asked over the comms.

「 He didn't, 」 Ido-san said, 「 But I would have bet money on it. I haven't seen the old fox take a personal interest in a matter like this in fifteen years. You don't set this up and then miss the final show. 」

Yoshimi faced off against the hatamoto. They had only bowed to the shogun, so they bowed to each other, and Yoshimi fell into the third fundamental, the lower stance, to draw him in.

Urabe attacked and time crawled to a halt. Yoshimi pivoted, smart soles compensating for the poor friction of the floor as he twisted at something like four times the speed of an unaugmented human, dodging down and around, and striking for the bottom of the man's arms.

Yoshimi had caught Urabe off guard in the office, suggesting his cyberware suite must have been different than Yoshimi's, but the old man still had speedware. While the room and the crowd slowed to a halt, Urabe appeared to move normally. His cyberware was just as high quality as Yoshimi's, but no faster.

Urabe countered and the blades met, the oscillation of the two weapons almost counting time in their super-enhanced state. They clanged, the hum of the motors throbbing up Yoshimi's arms in strange interference patterns, like a pond after the disruption of two stones.

The old man fought in a traditional style, but he'd allowed the forms to be corrupted slightly by various street fighting techniques. They'd probably served him well in the past, a dirty move or two worked wonders against a duelist who had only sparred, but Yoshimi had fought far too many duels to fall for them, and they served only to blur the purity of his strikes.

His Mind HUD told him they've been fighting for six seconds and the wires of his speedware heated under his skin. He struck, dodged, weaved, and parried around the fountain, the blades beating and transcribing arcs in the air.

A fight wasn't like a dance. It *was* a dance. The rhythm of the strikes, the movements of the duelist's legs, the flow and spins and counters. The push and the give. The beat of the swords, like the heart of a powerful beast. The sweat, the pain, the exultation.

The old man was good. At one time, he'd probably been better than Yoshimi, but he hadn't been challenged in decades, even though his reflexes were those of a young man. As the speedware heated until it burned, the hatamoto's strikes and parries became a hair out of control.

Yoshimi hammered on his defenses and the weft and weave of the man's guard parted. That alone might not have been enough to beat him, but Yoshimi could see it eating at Urabe's calm. The man had indulged too many passions, been denied too few desires. His discipline was about ten years past a fine honing.

As Yoshimi pulled away from an exchange, his speedware burning to the point he feared a glow showing through his skin, his augmented muscles shaking with fatigue poisons, the error correction software that supplemented his strikes redlining to correct his movements, Yoshimi looked the hatamoto in the eye.

And he smirked.

The whisper of a smirk. The suggestion of a smirk. The essence a smirk leaves in the room when it passes, like the perfume of a geisha two hours past. No one in the room could have caught that smirk.

The strike landed true on the center of Urabe's calm.

The man attacked, not wildly, but a bit off balance, out of center, his control that of a ten-year duelist, not a forty-year one. He struck, his feet sloppy, and he didn't quite compensate for the acceleration of the speedware. His lines were as dirty as roadside snow, and Yoshimi danced around the strike, his movement a lover's whisper in the dark.

His thumb switched off the vibro-katana just as the blade sliced across the forehead. The man stumbled through his lunge and the blood bloomed and poured from the wound.

Five more exchanges, each a half dozen blows, and the hatamoto stumbled, blind from his own blood. Three more and Yoshimi controlled his opponent's movements as if he were a child. Two after that and the hatamoto's katana clattered to the floor.

"I believe that was first blood," Yoshimi said, knowing the man wouldn't take the out.

The Hatamoto lunged, and Yoshimi slid to one side and applied the stunner in his palm to the hatamoto's head. The strike landed true. The old man collapsed before he could feel pain.

One day. One day I will lose one.

But not today.

Fujihara-sama's security people took over, removing Urabe's weapons and guarding the body until he came around. When he was himself again, they helped him into a kneeling position and faced him toward Kitsune-heike.

Miko-san called him the old fox, a play on kitsune meaning fox, but Yoshimi suspected that there was more to it than that. The man carried more years than any two people in this room put together. He'd known that Urabe had tapped the call he'd made earlier. He'd carefully laid out all the authority and clues that Yoshimi had needed to weather the confrontation with the hatamoto. Had he known all this from the beginning, or had he merely suspected? Had he really moved beyond the realm of the mortal and into the divine? Miko-san and Ido-san would both certainly insist on a more prosaic answer, but looking up at the shogun, Yoshimi wasn't sure any answer would be wholly true. Truth was a pale reflection of enlightenment anyway. It only rarely came with wisdom.

Kitsune-heike didn't rise to give his pronouncement, and everyone in the room looked on expectantly as the man spoke.

"Yoshimi-san," he said. "Do you have a cloth?"

"I can get one, Kitusune-heike."

"Do so now."

Yoshimi went to Urabe's office and retrieved the cloth he'd almost used to commit seppuku. Anticipating Kitsune-heike's request, he folded the cloth and was ready when the shogun spoke again.

"Urabe." No honorific. "You have violated one of the most sacred trusts of our people. A strike at the family is a blow that cannot be blocked or weathered." The old man looked at Fujihara-sama's hired mourner, then back. "It is a bond so sacred that ninety-one years ago, I enacted the law of adoption so that it would never be cheapened. You do not warrant mercy. Or respect. Or honor."

Urabe snarled at the shogun, but didn't speak. Instead, he smoothed his face and raised his chin, considering the room haughtily. Yoshimi drew his wakizashi and carefully wrapped the cloth around its blade.

"It is my wish that you be ordered to commit seppuku."

The crowd didn't react. This could end no other way.

The shogun looked down a moment. "However, I will not mete the same punishment to your children as you tried to mete upon the daimyos'. Yoshimi-san, would you kindly *offer* Urabe your sword."

Yoshimi bowed to the shogun and then offered the wakizashi to Urabe. The man took the blade, his reserve slightly shaken. He placed the blade against his belly.

"This human being is a monster," Kitsune-heike said. "He deserves no consideration. I ask, however: will anyone second this man in his death?"

Yoshimi raised his chin. "I have never met the children of Urabe-sama." He still couldn't drop the honorific when speaking out loud. "But I will do them this courtesy, if it is the will of the shogun."

Kitsune-heike nodded and Yoshimi stood behind the man. The now-former hatamoto raised the short blade to his belly and opened his mouth, probably to recite his death haiku.

Yoshimi turned on his vibro-katana and struck the man's head from his shoulders.

He looked down at the body for a few seconds and up at Kitsune-heike. He carefully composed his face in a look of horrified embarrassment. "My apologies, Kitsune-heike. I appear to have struck his head from his shoulders before he made a single cut. I'm afraid he didn't suffer."

The shogun smiled ever so slightly. "You no doubt thought that he was about to cry out when he opened his mouth. Standing behind, your view would be unclear, no?"

Yoshimi just bowed.

"The dishonor is entirely yours," Kitsune said. "I will not punish the children of Urabe for your misjudgment."

"Thank you, Kitsune-heike; you are as merciful as you are wise."

The shogun rose and left the room.

The daimyos glared at Yoshimi. While none of them had wanted to hear that bastard's death haiku, they would be furious that Yoshimi had killed the man without suffering, after the crime he'd attempted. Still, they'd always disliked him. He could bear this small additional burden.

"Why do I insist on hiring duelists who are pacifists?" Fujihara-sama asked as he stepped close.

"Why did you give your adopted son to be trained by one?" Yoshimi said.

"Just, 'son,'" Fujihara-sama said and walked away without expression.

The mourner stopped as he passed in the man's wake, and bowed, smiling. He followed Fujihara and left the room.

YOSHIMI MET MIKO-SAN IN HIS GARDEN. THE WIND BLEW GENTLY AS she approached, fluttering her clothes about her. Maybe her figure wasn't so vulgar after all. He could appreciate the simple beauty of a person at the peak of human fitness.

She tucked a black hair behind her ear, considered him, and smiled. "You did it."

"*We* did it," he said. "I never could have succeeded without your signal nullifier."

"That failed quite dramatically."

Yoshimi shrugged. "It didn't need to play out the way we intended. It gave him a plan to root out. It didn't matter that at the time it was our only plan."

"You pulled it through in the end."

She stared into his eyes, and for a moment, he felt a flush of guilt. He looked away. He needed to visit Izumi-chan. His geisha would be worried.

"The nano-virus?"

"The White Orchid labs have finished analyzing the nano-virus. We were all infected," he said, "but the unactivated virus doesn't do much except spread and reproduce. Mainly, it just interfered with nanobots that it found threatening."

"Nanobots?" she frowned.

He nodded. "It would hunt down any that it felt might try to deactivate it. It would multiply. That's about it. It would identify its host for further instructions. That was about it. If the signal had been sent with your or my genetic profile, it would then slightly alter our body chemistry to wreck our fertility. It didn't actually cause damage. Damage could be detected and repaired. There was no test to detect this particular virus, and no reason to invent one. What would Ido-san call it? Security through obscurity."

But she still looked distracted. After a moment, she rallied and met his eyes again. He wasn't used to women looking him in the eye. He found it disconcerting and invigorating at the same time.

"It's time for me to go home," she said. "I'll miss this."

「Me,」 Ido-san said over their comms. How long had he been eavesdropping? 「She means she'll miss me. I get that a lot.」

Yoshimi contained a smile. He bowed to Miko-san. "I wish you great honor in your endeavors."

She bowed back, straightened, and walked away, stopping at the door to the garden.

"Urabe. He offered you your family back. You didn't accept."

"No, I didn't." Urabe had been disingenuous anyway.

"Why?"

He didn't know why he told her. He'd never told anyone in his life. But somehow, this felt different. Maybe because if she wanted to know the truth, she could just find out using NSK resources. Maybe something more. Maybe he didn't have a reason.

"I've always known who my birth father was," he said.

「Wait! What?」 Ido-san said. 「I was arrested trying to find out your father's name.」

"I always told you not to do that," Yoshimi said. It wouldn't have mattered. He had no way to restore Yoshimi's inheritance; he'd just assumed Yoshimi hadn't known that.

Miko-san faced him and her eyes searched his face. For a moment, he thought she might ask who. If she had asked, and if Ido-san hadn't been listening in, he didn't know what he would have answered. Why would he have the urge to tell his deepest secret to an NSK operative?

Maybe because she was the type of person that *didn't* ask. "All nanobots?"

"The nano-virus?" he asked. "Yes it attacked any nanobots it found threatening." Why was she focused on that?

"Huh," she said, then they bowed again, and she left.

「You've known your birth father? All this time? You've never told me?」

"It is not my secret alone." Yoshimi sank into *seiza*. He closed his eyes to meditate.

「Your adopted father almost had me strung up for that hack.」

"He was putting on a show. You were never at risk. I think he always respected your loyalty," Yoshimi whispered.

「Seriously? You aren't going to tell me? Seriously?」

Ido-san droned on, but as Yoshimi had said, it wasn't just his secret.

Because his birth father was also his adopted uncle. When Fujihara-sama had discovered his older brother had fathered a bastard son with an eta woman, it had almost destroyed the family. It had ended in a duel, the older brother's seppuku, and a wound that shamed Fujihara-sama so much, he would never have it corrected.

Fujihara-sama had found the child, covering up his birth records with the false name Yoshimi Daichi. He'd mentored Yoshimi under his duelist and bodyguard, so that the older man would never have to be parted from his adopted son and birth nephew.

Fujihara-sama had inherited the position of daimyo of security, where it might have passed to Yoshimi if not for the shame, the secrecy, and the eta parentage. Yoshimi didn't mind. Fujihara-sama had been better to him than any other father could.

It was always about family.

A man was supposed to find peace in meditation. Yoshimi, in the garden, found something beyond peace. A smile crept across his lips.

And then vanished. His eye shot open. Ido-san still droned on, but Yoshimi forgot himself and interrupted.

"Ido-san?" he said sharply.

「Because I know you better—What?」

"The kill switch they place on NSK operatives? The one that keeps them in line? That's delivered in the form of nanobots, isn't it?"

「Yeah, why—Oh. That's why she kept asking about the effect of the nano-virus on nanobots.」

Yoshimi laughed out loud. The emotional outburst was unseemly.

But, he thought, the dishonor was a small one.

ROBERT J DEFENDI

Robert J Defendi was one of the writers for Savage Seas for the game Exalted. He's worked on Spycraft, Shadowforce Archer and the Stargate SG-1 roleplaying game. He wrote the current incarnation of Spacemaster. As the publisher of Final Redoubt Press, he designed and released the critically acclaimed setting The Echoes of Heaven. He was featured in Writers of the Future XIX, and When Darkness Comes. He's the author of the successful podcast audiobook Death by Cliché. He's featured in Space Eldritch, Space Eldritch II, and Redneck Eldritch, as well as Actuator 3: Chaos Chronicles and the Curiosity Quills: Darkscapes anthology.

Death by Cliché was his first published novel.

Robert J Defendi was born in Dubuque, IA (in accordance with prophecy). He reads voraciously, if you consider audiobooks reading (which you shouldn't). He has yet to find, conquer, and rule a small Central American country (but I think we all know that's inevitable). He is neither Team Jacob nor Team Edward (he is sympathetic to Team Guy-Who-Almost-Hit-Bella-With-A-Truck). He shamelessly stole that last joke.

It's Bob Defendi when he writes comedy. It's Robert J Defendi for all other writing projects. No period after the J. Because he's an ass who likes to make things difficult for publishers, that's why.

Links:

http://www.robertjdefendi.com/

7

THE CONTRACTOR

MARK W. WOODRING

"What's this thing got?"

The shopkeeper looked almost annoyed as he picked the handgun up from its case.

"This is the MARS Devastator III, semi-automatic pistol. Clip holds thirty, one in the chamber. This thing'll even fire SNDERs. Comes in class four and five."

"MARS?"

"*Multi-Ammunition-Response-System*. Although, in my opinion, if you're using this thing you're not *responding* to shit; you're starting some."

The dark-skinned man looked slowly across the counter, then reached for the weapon. Turning it over, he traced an ebon finger across a small, triangular pattern inlaid on either side the grip. Raising his head only slightly from its examination of the weapon, he asked:

"E-T-I? Really?"

The man fanned his thumb over an identical triangular shape in his right palm. Enhanced-Target-Interface had seemed so promising when it had hit the market over a decade ago, designed to work with a human's nervous system and project a set of cross-hairs onto the retina, but it never quite lived up to the hype. Then the m3 plug had hit the scene, rendering the ETI a digital appendix. Now, some folks were even going wireless. Almost nobody bothered to use ETI anymore, except some old timers.

Like him.

The clerk sighed. "I know it's a legacy feature, but I think this is the last model that's going to carry one."

"Sometimes I miss the old days, when a man had to really *try* to kill you, instead of letting a computer do the work."

"Whatever, pal. I don't build 'em, I just sell 'em."

The man didn't seem fazed by the clerk's attitude. Instead, he pulled a nondescript credstick out of his pocket, one of his emergency sticks, a holdover from his working days. Pre-loaded with enough credits to let him disappear for at least a week, it also came in useful for keeping his buying habits private.

"I'll take two, class five, three mags each: two with boom-boom, one Indirium. And an extra box of each."

The clerk's eyes widened. "That's pretty heavy stuff right out of the box. You must be doing a job." He looked around the store conspiratorially, although there was no danger of anyone else being close enough to hear them, not at this time of day, and not in this little hole-in-the-wall of a shop on the fringe of a grey zone.

"You're doing a job, aren't you? Who you working for, hmm?"

The dark-skinned man raised his head. If he had not been wearing polarized lenses, the clerk would have seen a glance that said it all.

"Don't bother to wrap them. I'll wear them."

The clerk muttered something about "crazies," and proceeded toward the back of the shop to complete the order.

A moment later, the man emerged from the store and swung his leg across the saddle of a waiting motorcycle. He slid a helmet onto his shaved head, leaving the sunglasses in place beneath the mirrored visor. A quick touch of the starter and the Yamaha *Wildwind*'s engine roared to life. In seconds, it was careening down the streets, throwing exhaust fumes behind it like a smokescreen.

It's been in storage too long.

The smoke faded as the engine heated up.

Just like me.

A quick glance at the battery indicator showed a nearly full charge. As much as he loved to run the machine using the engine, fuel was becoming scarcer and more expensive every day. Even his somewhat questionable source was proving less and less reliable. With an inward sigh, he flipped a switch to engage the hi-torque electric motors.

The sanguine whine of electrons flowing, en masse, to both wheels replaced the rumble of controlled explosions. A quick jolt as the front tire's drive engaged was rougher than he remembered.

I'll have to get Jimmy to look at that. The last thing he needed was to lose control of the bike at high speed.

After everything I've been through, to punch out in a traffic accident...

The man smiled behind the visor. He loved the speed the bike offered him, and in his line of work, it was essential. Speed often made the difference between getting paid and spending the rest of his nights in the morgue. He kicked the shifter again, picking up still more speed.

He smiled again, wider.

My line of work: that's a very eloquent way of putting it.

He liked to call himself an "Independent Consultant." Other people didn't use that exact wording, however; "info-thief" was the commonly-used term to describe people like himself.

It felt good to be on the road again, back in the game. He thought he'd done his last job three years ago.

He'd been wrong.

THE LAST OF THE GIN SLID DOWN HIS THROAT AND THE GLASS SETTLED back onto the bar with a gentle *thud*.

"You need another, Pat?" the bartender called from down the bar where he placed two beers in front of some sketchy-looking fellas who had wandered in a few minutes ago. They weren't regulars, and Patton had caught himself sizing them up as they approached the bar.

Not that there was much to size up about them. Average height, above-average build, light jackets—*it's fucking raining, asshat. Calm down—* still, something seemed off about them.

Fuck. Old habits.

He returned his attention to the synth-gin. He'd retired with a fair amount of cash, but it wouldn't last forever, and in order to make it last, sacrifices—like *real* gin—had to be made.

"Pat? You need a refill?"

The "Yes" caught in his throat as he looked down the bar. The man closest to him reached for his beer, gripping the bottom of his jacket to keep it from pulling up.

Old habits.

What are these guys doing? Robbery? Worse? Or are they actually here for just a drink and nothing more?

"Yeah," he finally choked out. "Gimme another."

You're too old for this shit, Patton. Go the fuck home.

"Thanks 'Naldo," he said, as the man refilled his glass. "Hey." He lowered his voice and waggled a finger at Reynaldo to come closer. "I don't want to start anything, but those two guys down there—"

"I know, Pat, I know," 'Naldo smiled at him. "It's under control."

"You sure?"

Reynaldo nodded, giving him a smile.

"Okay. This is it for me, though. Cash me out and I'll see you tomorrow."

"It's on me. I appreciate you looking out for me. Nice to know someone cares."

"Can't have my favorite bar getting messed up, can I?"

"Nope. Have a good one, Pat."

Patton shot the gin and stood. He patted himself down quickly before remembering he wasn't carrying anything but his NetMini.

Fuck, I must be getting old.

He made his way outside into a light rain. Despite the clouds covering the evening sky, the street was lit up as if it was high noon. Flashing billboards and neon lights identifying nearly every business on the street made it impossible to tell day from night unless you looked straight up between the towering buildings and airborne advertisements and saw blue sky or stars.

The rain had reduced foot traffic to almost nothing, but the few souls braving the weather clung to the walls of the buildings in an attempt to stay dry. Patton couldn't care less.

What's a little rain the face?

As he rounded a corner, he bumped between a couple of men who, like him, had no compunctions about walking in the rain.

Patton tensed. In this part of town, an accidental bump could escalate into a gunfight in seconds.

"Excuse us," said one of the men politely, barely breaking off his conversation with the other, as they continued walking in the opposite direction.

Must be my lucky night...

He reached his building and keyed the front door, entering the small lobby. Not a five-star, but not a complete dive, either, although a waterlogged teenager stretched out on one of the chairs with his eyes glazed over was certainly trying to bring down the overall aesthetic at the moment.

Patton kicked the kid's feet as he went by. The kid barely moved.

"Get out of here, kid," he said. "You slumming up the place. Go get wasted somewhere else."

The kid mumbled something unintelligible, but didn't move.

I don't have time for this.

With one eye on the kid—you could never tell when a junkie was going to just up and lose his shit with you—he waited for the elevator.

After a long minute, the doors finally slid open and he entered, punching at the buttons.

The lift doors opened on the twenty-sixth floor. Patton made a left and moved to the end of the hallway.

Keying the lock on his door, he moved inside and secured it. Nice building or not, he could only afford to live here because of his former job. It had paid well, but left him with a bit of a reputation in certain circles.

He pulled off his jacket and was about to hang it up when he felt a small bulge in the pocket. Reaching in, he pulled out a small, flat, rectangular piece of plastic, about the size of his thumb.

A data-stick?

How had it gotten in his pocket? It wasn't his, and his pockets had been empty when he'd left the bar.

Those guys in the street...

A BLINKING LIGHT ON THE CORNER OF THE GLOBE-NET TERMINAL THAT formed the glass desktop announced a message. Pulling it up, a thin smile crossed the reader's face, a frame of red hair outlining the face in the cold light of the display.

‹Contact made›

A purge program ran automatically when the message closed, overwriting data locations and burning circuits. There would be no proof the message had been received, or had ever even existed at all.

HE TURNED THE DATA-STICK OVER IN HIS HANDS. DATA-STICKS WERE basically obsolete, anymore. Almost nobody used them, unless—

What the hell?

He wouldn't risk connecting the stick to his NetMini. He glanced at the fixed terminal in his apartment.

I shouldn't even connect it to that one.

Throwing his jacket back on, he went back downstairs and walked three blocks, eventually spotting an unoccupied public terminal. He jammed the stick in as fast as he could find the socket. As soon as it synced, an auto-execute ran and spat out a dozen or so lines of text on the display. At the top of the screen, a countdown began.

30... 29... 28...

He scanned the screen, and paused at the second to last line: *500k.*

7... 6... 5...

He rescanned the list, as his finger hovered over the final line:

‹*[ACCEPT] / [REJECT]*›

2... 1...

THE BLINKING LIGHT ON THE GLASS DESKTOP REAPPEARED. A LIGHT touch confirmed what the reader knew would be the case.

‹*ACCEPT*›

The purge program ran again. There would be no link between the reader and the contractor.

There never was.

PATTON PULLED THE DEAD STICK FROM THE TERMINAL, SNAPPED IT, AND dropped one half down the nearest sewer grate, and threw the other in a trash can five blocks from his apartment as he took a roundabout way home.

Five-hundred-thousand credits? That had been as much as he'd retired with three years ago.

I shouldn't take it. It can't be that simple.

He kept walking, the rain beginning to pick up again.

I'd have to be a fool to pass it up.

THE DOOR SLID OPEN AND A SLIM FIGURE STEPPED INTO THE SMALL, dimly-lit room, barely large enough to contain the desk, the office chair behind it, and the two chairs in front of it. A second figure sat behind the desk, checking the GlobeNet, occasionally tapping the holo-panel to page forward through whatever subject matter currently occupied his attention.

The door slid closed, and a soft, feminine voice said, "We have procured a contractor, sir."

"Another repeat, or someone new? I've noticed quite a few call-backs of late. I don't need to remind you—"

"—Of the necessity to insulate ourselves from the contractors? No, sir. This is a new contract. He was one of the best before he retired three years ago."

"Is that by reputation or personal knowledge?"

"Both. His name is good on the Net, and I can vouch for his ability. He's the one who hit Division 5 a few years ago. He got them to send a squad into the grey zone as a distraction for a smash and grab a couple blocks away. He convinced them there was an illegal 'borg fighting ring planning to expand into a couple city blocks on the edge of the zone. D5 boys were there in a heartbeat. All they found was a 'bot-fighting gang, low-tech, low-credit, no threat. By the time they sorted out what had happened, he was gone."

"How do you know it was this person, if he was so good?"

"Who do you think he was smashing and grabbing for?"

"Not for this office." It wasn't a question.

"No, it was a personal project as a favor to a friend. Don't worry. I didn't use any of the Office's assets."

"Good. It would be a shame if something as trivial as a favor cost you your position here, don't you think?"

"As you say, sir."

Fingers drummed on the surface of the desk in contemplation. "Very well. You can return to your duties, but keep me apprised. The timetable is short on this, and we don't need anything to go wrong."

"My loyalties are with the balance, as they always have been. Have a good evening, sir." A swish of medium-length red hair trailed her out the door, leaving the room's occupant alone with his thoughts as it slid closed behind her.

Something so small, to have such an influence on things so important, he thought.

Sighing, he heaved himself up from his chair and moved toward the door. It had been a long day, and the next few weren't likely to be any shorter.

PATTON PULLED THE BIKE INTO A SMALL GARAGE IN A NEIGHBORHOOD he would normally have preferred to drive straight through. It wasn't technically in a black zone, but he could piss on it from here. An electronic eye cued a mechanical *ding* to alert the garage occupants someone had entered. He killed the motors, and the whine slowly died away as a man in grease-stained coveralls walked toward him from the back of the garage.

"You still own that thing?"

Patton removed his helmet and smiled. "You know it, Jimmy. It's not going anywhere. When I'm dead, I'm leaving it to you."

"Great. More shit for my junk pile." Jimmy smiled. "What do you need?"

Patton looked around, and convinced they were alone, said, "I picked up a job."

"Thought you retired?"

"Was. Call it a command performance."

"Money that good?"

"Oh, yeah."

"What can I do to help?"

"Well, first I need you to look at the bike. The front motor seemed a bit grabby when I kicked over to the electrics earlier."

"Simple enough. But you really need to just shit-can the combustion on this thing, or get a new one outright. How do you even afford the fuel for that anymore? And where the hell are you getting it?"

Patton smiled. "You aren't my only friend, you know. I know a guy. Yeah, it's pricey, and yeah, it's not really gas, but there's nothing like it. I fought forever to not upgrade this with electrics in the first place, Jimmy. You really think I want to get rid of the engine? Shit. I gave up real gin to pay for gas."

"Whatever. What else you need?"

"Where's Tig?"

"Last I heard, she was living in a shithole that barely qualifies as Above, jacking-in for whoever's got money to pay her do whatever it is they need her to do."

"Give me the address. How long before the bike will be ready?"

"Well…" He pulled a small box from his coverall pocket and plugged it into the maintenance port on the bike. "It looks like"—some text scrolled by on the small screen—"you are"—he punched a few buttons —"good to go." He unplugged the device and stuffed it back into his pocket, smiling at Patton.

"Just a quick calibration sequence. You let it sit too long. Electronics like to work, not sit. Once you're retired again, don't forget to take it for a spin once in a while."

"Thanks, Jimmy." Patton slid the helmet back onto his head. "Grab a beer next week?"

"Only if you're buying."

"You got it. Thanks."

The electric motors sprang back to life and Patton pulled smoothly away from the garage. Nobody like Jimmy to fix his machines.

PATTON SLIPPED OFF THE *WILDWIND* AND KEYED IN THE SECURITY CODE before moving to the run-down mini-scraper—only 87 stories—where he hoped to find Tig. Hopefully, she was in good enough shape to do it.

Thankfully, the lift was working, though it took two full minutes to get him up to sixty-six.

Good thing I'm not in a hurry or anything.

The doors opened, ejecting Patton into a corridor which could generously be called a disaster area. What few overhead lights worked flickered, but even that couldn't disguise the disgusting nature of the place. Worn carpeting, stained with things Patton didn't want to think about walking across, and more than one rat carcass mixed in with the various trash and other detritus of life in the grey made Patton glad he'd retired when he did.

He picked his way down the hall, finding the door he sought about halfway down.

He knocked—loudly—to make himself heard over the thumping, repetitive beat of whatever was passing for music beyond the door.

The thumping got marginally quieter, and he took the opportunity to knock again. "Tig! Open up! It's Patton!"

The sound quieted more, but didn't cease: shuffling came through the door.

"Patton?" It was, theoretically, Tig's voice. "What're you doing here?"

"I got a job. You interested in making some money?"

The music stopped. Something slid behind the door, and it opened a couple of inches. In the dim light beyond, Patton could just make out a pair of haggard brown eyes and pale skin.

"Tig? Shit. Forget money. You interested in some sunlight? Maybe some food?"

She didn't look this bad last time.

"Yeah. Food." She closed the door, only to open it a moment later. A five-foot tall stick-figure in denim pants and a black hoodie hurried past him in the direction of the elevator, hefting a backpack Patton knew contained her deck onto one shoulder.

Patton pulled the still-open door closed as he turned to follow her.

"THAT'S IT? THAT'S THE JOB?" ASKED THE BLOND-HAIRED TEENAGER sitting across the table from him. Her hair was pulled back into a loose ponytail, and her eyes darted around the room, never settling on anything for more than a second.

Net-induced paranoia. Too much time on the Net, without external sensory stimuli, and the "real world" started to become a difficult place to function for hard-core surfers like Tig. They lived most of their lives online.

That's why I hate jacking in. She's been doing it her whole life.

"Yep." He sipped what passed for coffee in the diner Tig had led him to without a word. "That's it. Clean, simple, in and out."

The waitress arrived and set two plates of food in front of them. Tig dug into her meatloaf, cutting it and coating it with the mashed potatoes. She wolfed down the OmniSoy facsimile with abandon.

Probably hasn't eaten in days, except for the occasional protein bar when she comes up for air and to take a piss or something.

Patton had known some hackers to hire nurses to insert IVs and catheterize them so they could stay on-line longer for mega-hacks. Bedpans, too.

Shit's disgusting, but this job should only take a couple of hours.

"It's just a smash and grab," Tig said around a mouthful of the faux-meat. "What do you need me for?"

"I think it's going to be a little more complicated than that, but I don't like going into places blind, you know that," he said. "I need eyes so I know what I'm getting into—"

"You can jack yourself in. Why do you need me?"

"—*and* I also like to have someone watching my back in case things don't quite go according to plan. Somebody I trust to take care of the Ones and Zeroes while I'm busy." He rapped his knuckles on the table in front of her plate, drawing her eyes to his, her jaw stopping mid-chew.

"So? Can I still trust you?"

She slowly started chewing again, her eyes locked on his.

I think I preferred it when she wasn't *looking at me*.

"I left my apartment, didn't I?"

Her gaze returned to her meal as he considered his next move. Finally, he swiped a cred-stick at the terminal and stood.

"Finish your food and then do some recon. Get back with me ASAP. I want to go in tomorrow night."

A muffled *mmm-hmm* and nod was the only response he got.

"YOU IN YET?" PATTON SAID SOFTLY FROM HIS PERCH ATOP THE *Wildwind* across the street from a garage door he knew didn't lead into HansoTec, but close enough: the business next door.

"Almost, boss," Tig replied in that creepy, semi-asleep tone being jacked-in lent to her voice. "Their security is pretty basic, but they were at least smart enough to layer it four deep."

"You have thirty seconds before I find a new deck-jockey."

"You wouldn't do that. Who are you going to get?"

"If you don't hurry the fuck up, I'm going to jack in and do it myself, and you know how much I hate doing that."

Silence echoed across the comm as Tig considered her next words.

"Copy that. Ten seconds."

All business now, *aren't you?*

Nine-and-a-half seconds later, the garage door slid silently upwards for a moment, then stopped.

Patton swung off the bike moved across the street at a leisurely pace, trusting in Tig to monitor the surrounding traffic cams to alert him to any unwelcome companionship. As he neared the door, his eyes narrowed, mentally measuring the opening.

"You sure I'll fit through there?"

"Unless you've gotten fat in the last hour. It's sixteen inches. Even your equipment should fit."

"Bite me, you little shit," Patton muttered as he dropped to the ground and shimmied under the door. As he pulled himself upright, the slab of steel slid down again, though he noticed a sliver of light coming from beneath.

"Safety margin?" he asked.

"It's an inch I won't need to raise the door if you leave in a hurry. It's not visible from the street, so I figure it'll be okay."

"It had better be, or I'm kicking your ass."

"Get a move on. You've still got work to do."

Patton jogged through the cargo area toward the front of the building and found himself in a sterile-looking room filled with dozens of self-contained workstations with computer terminals and flat-screens, all in sleep mode. The faint twinkle of LED indicators sprinkled throughout the workspaces gave the impression of twilight in a forest of translucent Plexiglas walls.

Cube farm. I think I'd shoot myself if I had to work in one of these things.

Hurrying through the perimeter aisle, Patton located what he was looking for.

Where, to be more precise.

A door: exactly where the plans had indicated it would be; a miracle, considering all the modifications some businesses liked to do to their facilities. Behind it, he found a room perhaps ten-foot square containing the air handling and control functions for this building.

This *half* of the building, anyway.

He moved to the wall separating him from his target: HansoTec.

"Hurry up, old man." Tig yawned.

"You need a nap?"

"THE PLAN IS SIMPLE ENOUGH," HE HAD TOLD HER EARLIER AT HER apartment. "You get me inside FujitaZee, and I'll go through the utility spaces to get into Hanso. By the time I make my entrance, I expect you to have their security down."

"It'll be down." She picked her teeth with a scrap of wire she pulled out of her hair. "But why all the fuss about this? HansoTec hasn't developed anything important for at least six years. Mostly, they just find applications for second-tier tech."

"Well, maybe somebody in there got lucky and invented something worth a damn," he replied. "It's not my job to know what it is, just to get the information out and make sure nothing is left behind for them to replicate it with."

"Whatever, boss. I don't see any problems with my end of it. I don't even have to leave the apartment."

"Good. Let's get to work." He glanced at his NetMini. "We have three hours before we go."

"I'm gonna grab a nap."

"If you sleep through this, so help me, God, I will kick your ass."

"*One* time. I fell asleep *one time*..."

PATTON PULLED THE COMPACT VIBRO-SAW OUT OF HIS PACK AND WENT to work on the wall dividing FujitaZee from HansoTec. Hopefully, the building plans he'd plucked off the Net were accurate and the wall wasn't any more reinforced than he'd planned for, and that the noise from the saw wouldn't alert anyone left in the building at this hour.

He hoped the utility room would drown out any unusual noise.

Ninety-seconds later, he finished the Patton-sized hole.

Stowing the saw in the pack, he readied himself to clamber through. "How are things looking in there?"

"All the Ones and Zeroes are playing nice, if that's what you want to know."

"Thank you," he said, climbing into the hole. "Was that so hard?"

He exited in a mirror image of the room he just left. He put one hand on the door and the other on the latch. Leaning in close, he listened for any surprises that might be waiting for him.

"I'm getting ready to move out. Are you in their system yet?"

"Yes, but it looks like they have better security than Fujita. If your information is right, they've got the data you need locked down behind some serious firewalls. I can see it, but it will take me forever to get through it from outside."

"Dammit," he murmured. "Am I going to have to do this myself from in here?"

"Check the outside pocket of your bag. I packed a little something special, just in case."

He felt around in the pocket and pulled out a data-stick.

"What's this?"

"It's a bologna sandwich. What does it look like? Find a terminal and plug it in so I can do my job."

"Touchy, much?"

"Heard that."

Patton opened the door an inch and peered through, but found only a hallway lit by standby lighting. Jogging in the direction he knew from the building plans would take him to his goal, he stopped long enough at the first terminal he passed to plug the data-stick in.

An almost-sigh came across the comms.

"Was it good for you?" he asked sarcastically, continuing through the building.

"I've established an interface that mimics an on-site terminal, but lets me access it from here."

"I'll assume that means it won't take forever to get through the firewalls now?"

"Ding-ding! We have a winner."

Tig had locked down the security protocols at least, so the next sixty seconds were uneventful and Patton found himself in front of a clear door. Beyond it was a small, airlock-type space, with a door on the far side opening into a large lab.

Clean room.

He eased open the door and slipped inside. A *hiss* of air over-pressurized the room. His ears popped.

"You get access to an inventory or anything, yet, to tell me where I should be looking?"

"Look for Red Section. I'll have the exact location in a few seconds."

"Right." He moved through the interior door.

"They're going to have to hire a cleaning lady tomorrow," Tig said in his ear. "You are one contaminated—"

"Think real hard before you finish that sentence."

"Red, forty-two, shelf three."

"That's my girl."

A small flashlight gave him enough light to navigate the morass of workstations and racks of equipment.

"This isn't like any tech lab I've seen," he said.

"What do you mean?"

"They've got bio specimens and hardware stations set up next to each other."

"Um, hello? It's not like we haven't been integrating the two for a few years."

"Yeah, but the labs are always separate. They develop the hardware, then figure out the integration with the wetware. This looks like—"

"Not to be a nudge, or anything, but who cares? Not our job, remember? Smash, grab, and sterilize, right?"

"Right."

I was never this curious when I was younger.

Finding a section of storage shelves and cabinets obnoxiously painted red, he skimmed his way to forty-two, opened the cabinet door, and looked on the third shelf from the top. He stopped and stood straight up.

"Well. That's kind of anti-climactic."

"What? What is it?"

He reached carefully in and removed the only item on the third shelf. About the size of a Petri dish, he could tell this wasn't growing any sort of culture. He glanced at the label before reading it out for Tig to verify.

"PRME-3-U5."

"That's it. I've located the files; as soon as you say call it, I'll run the transfer and destruct protocol."

"You sure the data-cleanse will be complete? No chance of recovery?"

"Not a single One or Zero will be left standing. Those storage locations will never hold data again once it runs."

"Okay. Do a quick search and make sure there are no other samples to get rid of."

"Way ahead of you. There is nothing listed in the inventory anywhere. What you have in your hand should be all there is of... whatever it is."

"You didn't peek at the data? I find that hard to believe."

"It's encrypted beyond anything I break into quickly. And we don't care, remember?"

"Right, right." He moved back toward the airlock. He closed the inner door, listened to the air *hiss* down to normal pressure again, and opened the outer door before bending down and removing a small, metal box about the size of a pair of shoes from his pack.

I don't want to be here for this.

He opened the box and set the container inside. After the latch clicked closed, he removed his glove and thumbed the front edge. A small blue light glowed in response to his touch.

"Time to go, Tig. Get ready to purge the system." Patton closed the door behind him and glanced back long enough to see the blue glow spreading from where he had placed his thumb, slowly encompassing the entirety of the box.

He ran for the utility room. He figured he had about a minute before the bio-organic compound fully activated and consumed everything inside the box.

And caused a minor explosion in the airlock.

He hit the hole in the wall in thirty seconds, knowing there was no one in his path, and Tig had made sure there would be no audio or video record of his presence. The only thing they'd find was the hole, and they might not find that for a day or more.

Plenty of time.

Tig had Fujita's door up by the time he got there, and as he rolled underneath, he said "Purge it, Tig!"

As he ran for the *Wildwind*, he heard her say, "Bye-bye!" and the comms cut out.

"Tig?" He reached the bike and keyed the start sequence to roll away from the curb. "Tig?"

There was no response.

Shit.

PATTON NEARLY LOCKED UP THE FRONT BRAKES ON THE *WILDWIND* AS HE pulled up in front of Tig's building. Without even keying the security for the bike, he jumped off and ran for the door. Luckily, some weirdo was exiting the elevator as he entered, and he jumped into it, stabbing the button for sixty-six and paced nervously around the small enclosure at it crawled upward.

Finally, it jolted to a stop and Patton pulled the door open faster than it was designed to move. He ran down the hall to Tig's door. Barely rapping it with his knuckles, he tried the handle, only to find it locked. Glancing down at the re-enforced latch, he realized he couldn't force it open.

He pounded on the door with his fist. "Tig? Come on, Tig, answer the door!"

Silence.

A look at the control panel next to the door gave him hope. Reaching into his inner jacket pocket, he pulled out a short bundle of cable with a connector on each end. One he plugged into the open port on the panel, the other he oriented with the triangular ETI interface on his right palm.

Fuck. I hate this shit.

He snapped the connector into the ETI port. As soon as the building's system completed its handshake with Patton's bioware, he was greeted to a view of the web even Tig had never seen.

Instead of a computer-assisted set of cross-hairs running from an ETI-enabled weapon being projected onto his retina, a wireframe overlay of the computer systems he had just connected to radiated out from his palm, into the control panel, and traced the physical and virtual network connections that spread out like wild fire. Unlike traditional hackers, like Tig, Patton never lost sight of the physical world; instead, he'd had his ETI software modified to ensure he would see both.

So he could watch his own back, if necessary.

As usual, it took a moment for his brain to adjust to the conflicting data coming in through his optic nerve, and he steadied himself on the door frame with his left hand as he found his balance. Finally, he could focus on the network and attempt to unlock Tig's door.

As soon as he shifted his focus to it, the overlay in his vision gathered a red tint, growing slowly more defined as his focus increased. Though the visual details of his interface weren't as developed as a pro like Tig, he was capable enough to know what that meant.

Firewalls. And not the building's normal firewalls, either. Tig doesn't like visitors, and I'm not good enough to beat her security.

Backing off, he shifted his focus again and followed the network back to the building's central security server. He had to hope it had what he needed.

Even though his skills were no match for Tig's, he knew enough to be able to exploit the maintenance vulnerabilities in the nearly non-existent security a building like this could afford. No wonder Tig had juiced her firewalls. An adjustment, a prod, and he watched as the maintenance override command shot back through the building's net, stopping as it reached the control panel, where the red glow extinguished in a shower of virtual green sparks.

Disconnecting himself, he opened the door and flew inside. It was dark, and he nearly tripped over a heavy box of—something—just inside the doorway.

"Tig!"

He fought his way around the box and found his flashlight. He swept the beam around the room, and his eyes finally settled on the back of a head, blonde hair pulled into a ponytail, a thin body slumped in front of a darkened terminal.

"Tig?" he asked, a bad feeling forming in the pit of his stomach. "Tig?" He reached out his bare right hand, so dark against her blonde hair and pale shoulder, almost afraid to touch her. "Tig?" he whispered, brushing her shoulder with his fingertips.

A low wheeze escaped her lips.

"Oh, thank God." He moved around in front of her and shone the light in her face.

Glassy eyes stared at—no, *through*—him, and a line of drool marked one corner of her mouth. Her breathing was raspy, but even.

What the hell?

He couldn't take her for help, not on the bike. He had to make a choice. Now.

He left the apartment, still shaking at what he'd seen, and descended to the lobby as quickly as the lift would take him. From the lobby's terminal, he placed a call to D1, hoping Tig's neighborhood wasn't too far into the grey for them to respond.

He bolted out of the building and rolled the bike far enough down the street to be inconspicuous, but where he could still see the entrance to the building.

In ten minutes—*Ten minutes? They must have been drawing straws to see who had to come*—a D1 cruiser arrived, and a pair of uniforms got out and strolled into the building.

No fucking hurry or anything, fellas...

A couple of minutes later, a MedVan came in to land behind the cruiser. The street was quiet enough at this hour for Patton to hear a call come over their radio as they got out.

"*...late teens...alive...maybe...kind of seizure...*"

The MedTechs grabbed their gear and entered the building at a slightly less sedate pace, but it was clear speed wasn't on their agenda.

Starting the bike, Patton crawled it past the Medical Unit and glanced at the display inside the cab. Its destination showed as Public Hospital 859.

Two blocks.

Somehow managing to keep his speed under a hundred kph, Patton parked and secured the *Wildwind* before walking into the emergency room waiting area.

He didn't have to wait long.

The heavy plastisteel outer doors slid apart and the two MedTechs rolled a gurney inside at a pace that pained Patton to watch. A nurse at the inner doors waved them inside.

Ok, she made it here. Now what?

Patton had no idea how to get beyond the doors. He couldn't simply barge in, and he couldn't claim her without a lot of questions he didn't have the answers to. This had never been part of the plan. For the life of him, he couldn't figure out what had gone wrong. The infiltration was solid, the acquisition was perfect, destruction had gone off without a hitch, and Tig had run the transfer and purge pro—

Oh, God...

A flash on the GlobeNet display summoned a finger to it. At a touch, a message expanded.

A sharp intake of breath broke the stillness as she read the message.

‹*Contractor intact. Sub-C wiped. Target received. Guidance?*›

Subcontractor? That was unexpected, she thought.

She idly twisted her red hair about her fingers for a moment before reaching for the terminal.

‹*Clear the books.*›

A moment passed before a reply came.

‹*Confirmed. Clearing the books.*›

The purge program ran again.

"Dammit," she said to the empty room.

After an hour of trying to figure out a way to get beyond the doors to see Tig, Patton left and went outside in search of a public terminal.

Someplace quiet...

He snapped his fingers, realizing where he could go. Privacy... a terminal... everything he needed...

Everything he needed was twenty minutes away.

Twelve minutes later, he pulled up to the closed door of Jimmy's. Barely a second later, the door rolled up, and Patton goosed the bike through the opening as soon as it was high enough.

He was off the bike and moving toward Jimmy's office before the electrics had even finished whining down. Jimmy keyed the controls to lower the door again and yelled at him as he went by, "What's the rush? Terminal ain't going anywhere!"

Already cabling himself into Jimmy's terminal, Patton's vision dimmed as the grid overlaid itself on his vision. Swimming past the moment of adjustment, Patton grabbed a data packet and rode it across the city until he found his destination labeled discreetly as "PH-859." He thought a moment how Tig would chide him for his primitive interface, and winced.

He jumped the ingoing data-stream and began running the map of the system. It took him only a few seconds to locate the patient logs; he found three entries for young females admitted within the last ninety minutes, and since only one was currently listed as "Critical," he targeted that file.

"That's Tig," His voice outside the grid said, as his virtual-self flipped through pages of medical data. Physical stats, vitals, blood work, EEG—

Patton stopped. Unrolling the virtual printout of Tig's brain scan confirmed his worst fear: she was basically a flatline of neural activity, and the constantly updating monitor showed that what little activity remained was diminishing—rapidly.

"No, no, *no*!" He slammed his unwired hand on Jimmy's desk, hard.

"Pat?" Jimmy poked his head through the door. "Obviously something's wrong. Bad?"

Patton yanked the cabling from his palm and hurled it across the terminal.

"Yeah, Jimmy. It's bad. It's real bad."

"Okay, calm down." Jimmy raised his hands as if to defend himself. "What can I do?"

Patton exhaled hard and collected himself. This wasn't Jimmy's fault. None of it was. It was his fault. *He* took the job. *He* recruited Tig. He thought he was untouchable.

"I shoulda stayed fucking retired, Jimmy," he finally said, softly. "I fucked up. Bad. Tig's gone."

"Aw, shit no, Pat. Say it ain't so." Jimmy put his hands down at his sides. "She was a good kid, Pat. She really was."

"I know. And because of me, she'll never be anything again."

He sat there in silence for a few minutes. He didn't even notice Jimmy back out of the doorway to give him some privacy.

Finally, he gathered up his cables and put them in a cargo pocket of his jacket. He hefted himself out of the chair, feeling every one of his years, and sighed.

This time I'm staying retired. As soon as I find out who did this.

He walked back into the service bay and found Jimmy standing by his workbench, organizing whatever happened to be lying around: a couple probes, his diagnostic unit, some loose cabling.

"Thanks for giving me a minute, Jimmy. I appreciate it."

Jimmy didn't look at him. "Anything for you, Pat, you know that. What now?"

"I think it's best if you didn't know, Jimmy."

"Then I already know. You were never the kind of guy to lay down and let something go unanswered."

"I suppose not."

Patton swung his leg over the *Wildwind* and slid his helmet on. Jimmy finally turned to face him as the electrics whined back to life.

"Hey, Pat? Be careful out there."

Patton's dark eyes drilled into Jimmy's before he slapped shut the mirrored visor of the helmet.

"Thanks, Jimmy."

He rolled the bike to the door, engaged the throttle, and the electrics whisked him into the street, the bike's LED headlamp clearing the darkness from his path, relegating the shadows into the alleys that seemed to make up most of the grey zone as he passed, only to spill out again behind him, a tsunami of darkness engulfing the street.

As he maneuvered his way out of the grey and toward his apartment building, he accelerated through smoother streets, weaving through what little traffic existed at this hour as though the city stood still.

Finding an empty stretch of road, he keyed the accelerator up. He needed to clear his mind. He couldn't go into this clouded. The display ticked up...80 kph... 100 kph... he keyed it again. He needed the rush. 120...140...160... Jimmy had the *Wildwind* moving like it was new.

The display ticked to show 180, and the front brake caliper slammed shut on the rotor as the front motor shut down. Patton stopped counting how many times he flipped in the air after four. He hit the pavement and slid another three-hundred feet to a stop.

The *Wildwind* had catapulted him ahead of it as it, too, tumbled down the road. It traveled farther than Patton had, slamming into him as it passed, finally stopping another hundred feet or so beyond his mangled body. A growing pool of crimson glowed black under the streetlights.

THE GLOBENET FLASHED A MESSAGE.

‹Books cleared.›

Purge.

THE REDHEAD KEYED THE ENTRY TO THE DOOR, ENTERING THE SAME dimly-lit office as before.

"Are we complete?"

Her red hair bobbed with a nod of affirmation. "We are, sir."

"Good. Now we can file this project away with the others. Some discoveries never need to be made, wouldn't you agree?"

"Yes, sir. Luckily, HansoTec wasn't even aware of what it had. It's a shame about the asset, though. He could have been useful in the future, with his skill set."

"Perhaps, but that's always the problem with contractors, isn't it? They provide us the anonymity we desire, but their loyalties remain their own. That is one thing we cannot have."

"Understood, sir. Have a pleasant evening."

A half-annunciated "Thank you," was the only reply she got.

She closed the door behind her and moved to the exit of the building, ready to clear away the mental detritus this job had left behind.

Perhaps some gin.

MARK W. WOODRING

Mark W. Woodring was born in central Pennsylvania before being whisked away to Texas (it's a whole other country) at the incredibly awkward age of 12. Graduating high school by the skin of his teeth, he joined the Air Force, where he spent 20 years traveling to such exotic locations as Austin, Texas, and Ogden, Utah (along with South Korea and Saudi Arabia).

After successfully reaching retirement, he completed his Master's of English at Weber State University. Mark is currently a technical editor for the US government while continuing to write and edit, while maintaining his blog (My Own Little Shadow) and a Podcast (the Visually Stunning Movie Podcast). He miraculously still lives with his wife and three incredibly demanding cats in Utah.

8

SPECIAL PROJECT

JAMES WYMORE

Min-gun gently bobbed, pushing forward and backward on one control stick, letting the hovercar rise and fall as he sat among the chaotic clump of vehicles crammed into the small parking space in the middle of Kangneung City. It was a small city by Korean standards, making it the ideal start and stop site for a race. Three story buildings, a mix of new and old in various stages of wear, surrounded the group. It didn't help the car prepare for the race to go up and down, but it put Min-gun in the right state of mind. Hovercars didn't run on normal 'engines,' but he liked to feel it responding to his touch. Once the cars left the ground, this event would only loosely resemble a ground car race, but he went through the same meditative mental preparations. Shin Min-gun always unplugged to listen to the car, feeling it with his heart, for a few moments during the calm before the storm.

He watched a cyborg of a man move from car to car after leaving him, manually plugging into each person and vehicle. The short man's black hair had been shaved on one side, giving way to a metal panel with lights and various plug jacks. His eye on that side had been completely replaced with a camera that had only a single red light behind the lens. It was unbecoming to trade so much of one's humanity for tech, but somebody had to make sure none of the drivers were using enhancement software to tweak their reflexes or enhance their control. He bobbed the car once more.

Then he plugged in.

Bzz-click.

Once the jack went in behind his ear, his peripheral vision filled with images of transparent gauges, since the car didn't have any physical ones. The tachometer, a graphical analog dial, not digital numbers, coasted gently up and down as Min-gun continued revving. The computer meshed with his brain, giving him detailed information on the state of the car's ion lifters, fuel reserves, altitude, and vital statistics. The software came standard with a Geiger counter, but he never needed it. For some reason he couldn't explain, he'd always been able to feel nuclear radiation intuitively. He had dozens of sensors he could access, but he kept only the vital ones open in his periphery.

Across the front of his gray metal hood, floated the back end of Han Hee-ran's latest Japanese import, painted hot pink. She didn't want anybody to miss her crossing the finish line first. Only an average driver, she had the money to buy speed most of these street urchins could only dream of. Since they regulated all the cars, that wouldn't help her much today. The rest were Korean speedsters, many with old-style racing stripes or fire over the wheel hubs. To Min-gun's side, his best friend from birth, Pak Young-ju, sat in his green Daewoo 420x with tasteful gold trim. His friend gave him a thumb's up, which he returned before tightening his gloves. On the other side, one car away, Kim Kang-dae waited for the cyborg to finish checking her neural implant. She drove a flat black Kia hatchback with tinted windows. The odds favored her to win today. Statistically, she was the best driver in the lot, so naturally Min-gun had a huge crush on her, despite her occasional off-putting airs.

An alley behind him allowed cars to drive into the parking lot, but none of them had driven there. Law required them to have wheels to drive on, but most hovercars used for racing had tiny tires so light and small that they barely held the car above a level road. If they drove over a crack in the sidewalk, these sleek machines would high center.

The image of a column of lights popped into Min-gun's head via the racing software uplink, causing him to tense with adrenaline. He gripped the control sticks tightly.

The top of four lights blinked red.

He took a deep breath.

The second light flashed red.

He nodded to Young-ju and gritted his teeth at the back of Hee-ran's pink bumper.

The third light flashed red, keeping the rhythm.

Min-gun took a deep breath and held it.

The instant the final light blinked green, Min-gun pushed the throttle full forward and gave it just a little lift. His car jerked as all the ion lifters for all the cars suddenly burst on at full strength, the combined sound, which was a quiet hum for standard hovercars, thundered below. All around them the ground glowed blue from the lightning sparks under each vehicle.

Min-gun ignored the vibrations in his seat and steering wheel as he tilted the pitch to full forward.

Most racers would wait until Hee-ran's car moved away first, but she wouldn't delay and he refused to waste even a tenth of a second. If he was wrong, they'd collide midair and either he'd push her forward or they'd both crash down in a ball of fiery wreckage. He wasn't wrong.

"*Sok-do*, let's win this thing," he said to the car. The only decoration he'd put on the bare gray panels were two Korean symbols, hand painted in black on the side doors. Sok-do: speed.

He blasted across the roof of the first building, eating the dust Hee-ran kicked up on her close pass. They lifted over the next row of buildings, cars spreading out around them to buy space as they increased speed. At two hundred kilometers per hour, Min-gun was still within spitting distance of Hee-ran.

Kang-dae managed to squeeze toward the front, of course. Yeong-ju rode less than a car length behind and to the side. Min-gun didn't think of these people as friends, crushes, or enemies anymore. He only registered cars, and he would be in front of them all before the race ended. He had to. He needed the first place prize money to finish his new hover racer. One he called *Special Project*.

The wave of vehicles moved north like a flock of fat birds that hadn't chosen a leader or arranged into a proper 'V' formation. Min-gun only glanced occasionally at his rear-view camera at the roaring mob behind him. He didn't let himself obsess about the few cars in front of him, either. Whatever you look at is where your car goes. He didn't want to go behind the other cars, he wanted to go in front of them. So he kept his attention forward as the Aebaek mountain range whipped by on the left. This race culminated in an obnoxious series of touch-and-go near-landings at each of the five peaks around Seorak Mountain, which lay one hundred fifty kilometers north of Kangneung. Most hovercars in the city maxed out below six hundred forty kilometers per hour. These customized racers usually did closer to seven hundred sixty. He had twelve minutes of straightaway.

As they roared across rice paddies, farm houses, and the occasional Buddhist temple built in defiance of the unhealthy radiation levels, Min-gun sensed several radioactive hot spots go by underneath. None of the racers swerved. They were going too fast to use the Geiger counters to avoid such spots. Since 2178 when Pak Kyong-woo decided to nuke Korea rather than lose to the South in a war he started, these zones became ubiquitous all over what remained inhabitable of the rural areas. North Korea became an unlivable blight. Seoul City took the worst of it. The radiation from nuclear bombs had gone through ten half-lives, getting to where most of it was inhabitable. Yet in Seoul, the radiation levels persisted. Nobody knew why. Despite the devastation, it had unified Korea again after so long. The majority of the remaining Koreans lived in overcrowded cities with clean air domes, mostly in the southern quarter of the former nation, but there were always a few who reminded everybody that if the Japanese could take it after World War II, Koreans could take it now. Min-gun always felt a strange attraction to these hot spots. He knew better than to go poking around in them, despite the inexplicable longing in his soul to explore them. Couldn't let that distract him now.

He set the altitude to a miniscule climb. The peak stood one and a half kilometers higher than the starting point. Some of the racers climbed early, looking to gain speed by going straight once they were so high up.

Hee-ran and Kang-dae gradually pulled ahead, making speed on pure tech. Despite the software velocity regulators, aerodynamics and reduced mass still gave expensive cars an edge. Min-gun didn't let it psych him out. Losing the advantage of bigger engines brought their cars down to a level he could beat with skill.

As the first mountain peak drew closer, he enlarged the transparent map in his mind. In order to avoid head-on collisions, they all had to go around the circle in clockwise order. The first peak was the lowest elevation, with tall coniferous trees rising around the bare rock on every side. Touching the rock would be suicide. Instead, they just had to get within two meters of the beacon mounted at the highest point for each peak. A single car could make a pass with ease, though they'd have to bring the speed down to below two hundred. However, with so many cars fighting for space, drivers often bumped into each other, sending the impacted cars careening in every direction. More than once, this race had been befuddled by a huge pile of crashed cars blocking any access to one of the beacons.

"On your left," Yeong-ju said through their personal comm link.

"Dae so," Min-gun said. *That's fine.*

Wherever possible, they worked together in races. Min-gun was just as happy for his best friend to win, although if that happened today, he'd make Yeong-ju loan him some of the money to get *Special Project* finished.

He drifted right, holding fourth place as he closed in on the first beacon. Hee-ran and Kang-dae were neck-and-neck in front. He hoped they'd get too aggressive and bump each other to the side. He didn't want Kang-dae hurt, but if they pushed each other away, they'd have to circle back around and lose enough seconds to be out of the lead for sure.

They didn't.

Some ugly blue car Min-gun didn't recognize went across behind them. Then he went over with Yeong-ju on his tail. He supposed it was a spectacular view with craggy mountains ringed by green sticking up out of the misty clouds below, but he didn't care. The instant his monitor signaled his car passing the first beacon, he was banking and lifting toward the next peak.

A pack of three cars came right behind Yeong-ju. A white Hyundai split between two running close together and knocked them both to the side. One overcorrected and ended up sliding sideways into a tall tree, scattering pine needles and crushing one of the ion thrusters from the side. It went down in a trail of smoke. The other looped around to pass the beacon again, losing seventeen places in line.

As they approached the next beacon, Kang-dae's black car tried to slip under Hee-ran's hot pink racer. It was a gutsy move, because if Hee-ran didn't notice, Kang-dae could use her hood to lift the back of the other car and cause her to go over the beacon too high.

No such luck. Hee-ran dropped altitude suddenly, pushing Kang-dae down into the treetops. They stripped the car of its speed, leaving Hee-ran in the clear lead. By the time Kang-dae recovered, four cars, including Min-gun, had gone by.

The third peak stood the highest, with the sharpest turn. Min-gun closed the distance to the blue Hyundai. No trees grew here, the rocks sticking higher above the timberline. As they approached, the blue car pulled a cheap trick and tapped his brakes, just before the beacon. If Min-gun overreacted, he'd be rear-ended by Yeong-ju.

Instead, he banked hard, dropping his altitude as the car flew sideways. Min-gun's ion lifters burned long black lines into the shiny blue paint as his thrusters forced the blue car off course and pointed Min-gun directly toward the next beacon.

"Nice!" Yeong-ju said. "Ah-ee-go!" A crash sound came through the mic. The white car had nudged Yeong-ju from behind, scraping the bottom of the green racer across the rocks. Yeong-ju corrected fast, coming up right next to the white hovercar, but losing valuable seconds.

The two of them created a short traffic jam, holding everybody else back a few seconds as they returned to race speeds.

Min-gun had an easy second place with only one car in front of him, but he wasn't about to let that spoiled rich girl take home his money.

Despite cutting it fine on both the remaining beacons, the pink bumper still flew in front of him when they straightened out and headed back to Kangneung City. With the mountain range on their right, they both pushed their ion thrusters to the limit. Hee-ran drifted to the side and lowered the altitude, letting gravity help her speed early on. Min-gun kept his nose straight, dropping incrementally as he kept all the thrusters on full. The engine temperature was high, but not enough to be a problem.

They both held their positions for the long straight run. Min-gun couldn't tell if his friend was in third. As they wore away the long straight race, new hovercars began approaching them at high speed from the side.

Cops.

Korean police officers learned long ago that their best move was to come in with sirens blaring and scatter the perpetrators, rather than sneak up on them. It was a much better strategy for anybody hoping to live until retirement. Most of the racers in the back scattered. They knew they didn't have any chance to take home prize money, so why risk getting their cars impounded? Three cars, including Kang-dae's black, Yeong-Ju's green, and the now black-striped blue one still fought for third.

Even without software regulators, the police cruisers had no hope of catching the racers. Min-gun just hoped they didn't have a barricade up to block the finish.

As he came down from above her, Hee-ran lost her lead. Having used up her elevation in an early sprint, her thrusters had to work just a little harder to keep up. Min-gun didn't want to shove her nose down the same as she'd done to Kang-dae, especially when that meant grinding her into a building. However, he wasn't about to be a gentleman if it meant letting her win. Besides, she could afford new paint. Wasn't 'vanity pink' the name of that color?

The race ended at another beacon. Whoever crossed two meters above it first would win. Only this time, if they were going hundreds of kilometers per hour, they would not live to spend the prize. They were both going the same direction, but it became a game of chicken. Whoever had the guts to hold their speed longest would cross the beacon first, but if that speed was too high, it would end with them smashing into a building and dying in a spray of burning battery acid.

Min-gun knew he had to cut speed. He saw Hee-ran slowing, too.

Technically, he had the lead, but his height made it about even. His peripheral vision began to flash red as the gauges detected an imminent crash.

One instant after the pink car's air brake flaps opened up, he threw the stick forward and dropped all his altitude. He already knew his car wouldn't come out of this. *Sok-do* had been a great hover racer, he would miss her.

His air flaps all opened as the vehicle fell from the sky. He reversed the ion thrusters and let the gray car drop onto the ground at full speed. As the small wheels smashed and the bottom of the car scraped horribly across the pavement, the last beacon on his display flashed green with the number 1 filling his vision. He cranked the controls to the side as the car wobbled and smashed into a concrete wall.

Hee-ran landed almost as hard, then disappeared in a blur of pink. Other cars landed and took off too fast for Min-gun to identify through the cloud of dust. He tried again and again to get his thrusters online, but they weren't responding. When red and blue flashing lights colored the walls around him, he pulled the jack wire to the car's gauges out of his head, released the seat restraints, jumped out the broken windshield, and ran.

SHIN MIN-GUN CLOSED THE HOOD GENTLY, TAKING A FEW SECONDS TO wipe smeared greasy fingerprints off the gold quarter panel he'd been leaning over. To the average eye, his new vehicle looked a lot like any other van flying around Taejeon City. A trained eye would easily spot the signs of a racer. He had a wide spoiler and side vents for steering in flight, both of which were flattened for better control at high speeds, something most hovercars didn't require. The stripped down brown leather interior had plenty of aftermarket gauges, but nothing to add a single gram he didn't need, including a passenger's seat. No radio, air conditioning, or luxury steadying gyroscopes. The car's computer didn't even have a monitor. Min-gun had allowed a small amount of mass for one extra security measure. If anybody jacked into his new racer with the wrong password, their head-circuit would be fried with electric feedback from the battery. He didn't know or care what it would do to the would-be thief's brain.

"All done?" Pak Yong-ju asked. He had his hovercar, the green Daewoo, up on the lift. He'd been hammering out dents in the lower casing from being pushed down on the rocks. Even after all that, he only came in fourth. Young-ju was a genius with car computers and electronics, but Min-gun had a better hand for body work.

"Yeah," Min-gun said. He took the hammer from his friend and started tapping lightly to round out the casing by one wheel. "I'm surprised they are going all the way to Seoul. That's more rads than are healthy to absorb."

"Afraid it will distract you?" Yong-ju scowled. "You've been weird about that stuff since you were a kid."

"I can't help it. I find it fascinating."

"You tried to take a bus to one of the hot spots when you were in elementary school."

"It's crazy, I know. It just draws me in. I can't understand it."

"Why not? You like anything dangerous. Hovercar racing is just a faster way to do what radiation poisoning does slowly."

"You think I have a death wish?"

Yong-ju shook his head. "No. But you can't help flirting with it. That's why you like Kang-dae."

Min-gun scoffed. He didn't think she was dangerous. "I don't know what they were thinking scheduling another race so soon."

"On a week night, no less." Yong-ju smeared orange hand cleaner on his fingers and began scraping grease off his skin. "Kang-dae will be angry."

"Why? It's not like she's still a student." Min-gun began washing his hands.

"I think she likes the easy money when rich high school kids show up to the weekend runs. Although it would be nice if she didn't show up."

"Give me a better chance to win again." Min-gun smiled and stuck out his chin.

"You don't always beat me." Yong-ju put his elbow on his friend's slightly shorter shoulder.

Min-gun grabbed a towel. "No, but I will next time for sure."

"Still believe in that *Special Project*?" Yong-ju made quotes in the air with his fingers. "You'd have been better off putting your money into a new car." Except Hee-ran, none of them could afford 'new' hovercars, of course. These were rebuilt ones they salvaged or bought heavily used. Some of the racers stole them, but Min-gun and Yong-ju weren't thieves.

Min-gun's smile dropped and his brow knit. "What's wrong with *Special Project*?"

"It's a converted taxi, to start with. It's a waste to keep putting money into mods for a spruced up people mover," Yong-ju said. They walked over to it together. "You don't even know for sure if it will work."

Min-gun popped the side door, revealing a huge thruster he'd salvaged from a fallen military combat aircraft, side-mounted so it pointed out the back. "It'll work. Everything is the same as the engines hovercars use, it's just a larger scale."

"You shoved a retasked VTOL motor from a crashed military vessel into the hovercar equivalent of a minivan." Yong-ju shook his head. "Even if it works, even if you don't blow up and fall to the earth in a ball of fire, the aerodynamics are impossible. There's no way a second hand airport shuttle is going to be able to take that kind of acceleration or speed. It'll spin and crash."

"Only if I do something stupid like turn at top speed." Min-gun closed the side door and inspected one of the custom scoops he'd cut into it where the window used to be. "Going straight should be no problem."

They'd been arguing about it for months now. Yong-ju kept helping him with the programming, steering controls, and electrical systems, though. Min-gun knew deep down, Yong-ju wanted to see it race, too.

"Before you die, it's your turn to buy dinner." Yong-ju smirked.

They peeled off their coveralls and locked the garage door.

THEY FOUND A NICE TABLE IN THE CORNER OF THE CLOSEST restaurant. Min-gun ordered a platter of barbecued beef and a table full of side dishes. "Can't depart this world with my best friend thinking I'm a cheapskate."

"First time in your life you had enough left over after parts to buy more than fancy Ramen noodles."

Min-gun smiled. It faded quickly when he looked to the far side of the room. Kim Kang-dae sat alone in the corner. Even with her brow knit, she looked gorgeous.

"Why don't you go over and say hello," Yeong-ju said.

"I don't think she's the kind of woman you just chat up in a restaurant."

Yeong-ju snorted. "They're all that kind of woman."

As their food arrived, several men in dark suits came in and sat around Kang-dae. She started chewing on one lock of black hair as her eyes glanced nervously from face to face. Min-gun couldn't even enjoy the savory sweet beef as he watched her talking quickly and then dropping her eyes when one of the men spoke back.

Another group of girls to one side began pointing and giggling. "Looks like I have fans even here," Young-ju said. He patted his friend's shoulder. "Do yourself a favor. Talk to her and get it over with one way or the other. Or else come with me and I'll make sure at least one of those girls takes an interest in you."

Min-gun shook his head, trying to read the lips of the men in suits. Soon after Young-ju went to the other table, the men talking to Kang-dae left. She hadn't even touched her food. Convincing himself he acted out of pity, he went over and sat across from her at the table.

"I thought you had me until that second peak," he said.

She looked up, almost as if she wanted to hit him. Then her eyes softened and she looked back down. "Congratulations. Sorry about your car. I heard they impounded it."

"Luckily, I have something better in the works. I call it *Special Project.*"

She looked in his eyes, wanting to be interested, but too distracted. "That's great."

"Something wrong? What's up with those men?"

She sighed. He'd always seen her as a fierce, independent woman. Now, he wasn't sure what to think. He still found her fascinating, of course. "Look, I'm sorry, but you really don't want to get messed up in my problems right now."

"I'm pretty sure I do. Why don't you give me a try?"

She sighed and looked up again. Some of her fire had come back. "Just trust me when I say there are no short cuts."

He didn't know how to respond. Before he could think of something witty, she stood and walked out.

"I..." He took a deep breath and watched her go.

Another group of girls came in. One of them gasped loud enough to draw the attention of everybody in the room. "Pak Young-ju! Wae keurae?" More words followed, but her fury made her voice go higher and higher until it all ended in one long screech. The girls he had been talking to looked both amused and angry.

The new girl, clearly one of Young-ju's ex-girlfriends, stomped forward, wielding her purse like she meant to decapitate him with it.

Min-gun jumped up and ran out the back, right behind his friend. As they hurdled garbage cans in the alley he said, "If one of your exes was chasing you, maybe you'd win a race for once!"

"IT'S READY." MIN-GUN WIPED SWEAT OFF HIS FOREHEAD WITH THE back of his coverall sleeve and smearing it with a line of black grease. "They aren't regulating top speed for this one."

"How are you going to stop this thing? You'll need a parachute or something. The air brake flaps are way too small." Yong-ju shook his head for the thousandth time.

"I don't need to stop it. The finish line is up in the air, so I can keep going as long as I need to slow down. But I see your point on the turn-around over Seoul. I'll probably have to keep up on the regular thrusters and only use the big-boy for the return stretch. I can't wait to see their faces when I go from dead last to first place."

"I can't wait to see their faces when you drive up in this thing." Yong-ju let his smile drop. "But seriously, I don't want to watch you die."

"Then keep your eyes on the road."

As MIN-GUN LOWERED THE HOVERVAN ONTO THE ROAD WHERE THE cars lined up, somebody behind him honked their horn. "You can't park that here. Take your delivery somewhere else!"

In his rear-view camera, the driver of the ugly blue car he'd beaten last race waved his fist out the window.

Hee-ran pulled herself out the window of her newly repainted pink racer and laughed when in Min-gun's face. "That's what you wasted your prize money on? If I knew that, I'd have let you win and saved myself the trouble of having to get my car fixed."

Min-gun just smiled and pointed behind with his thumb. "I think the front of the line is reserved for winners. You'll need to pull that eyesore back that way."

"One fluke win doesn't make you a winner." She sat back down and fastened her restraints, still laughing to herself.

The same cyborg came up and handed Min-gun two wires. One he plugged into his dashboard. The other he plugged in behind his ear. He didn't see or feel anything as the driver overwrote every program to leave only the basic gauges, map, and rules for this race. A few seconds later, the man took his wires to Yong-ju's car.

Min-gun watched as more than twenty drivers pointed at his van and openly mocked him. A new thirst for vengeance welled up inside him. He'd be doing the same thing if he traded places with them, but somehow it felt personal. Pursing his lips, he patted the dashboard. "I believe in you

Special Project. We'll show them what happens to people who can't think outside the box."

He smiled, then frowned as he realized how much his vehicle resembled a box at the moment.

Still unplugged, he began lifting and dropping the van. It felt different than his last car. The larger body absorbed more of the vibrations and the cavernous space behind him echoed. He kept looking at the red toggle switch on the dashboard that engaged the rear thruster. What would really happen when he flipped that switch? The back doors would swing open, the military ion thruster would kick on, and then...

He stopped himself. Don't get distracted. He focused on the feeling of the rhythm as he bobbed up and down. Then he plugged in.

Bzz-click.

Gauges came up in his periphery. He skimmed the race rules, checking to ensure no technicality existed that could disqualify him. They explicitly stated no limits on engine size or top speed. He nodded and checked the map. Two hundred kilometers to Seoul City from Kwang-ju, then back. No beacons this time. They only had to cross through laser grids. It looked like a simple there and back, but the people in the race would guarantee it wasn't simple.

The stack of lights blinked into his mind. He knew his eyes weren't seeing them, but they looked real with yellow paint on the metal frame and four black circles stacked.

Red.

He gripped the controls tight

Red.

He tipped the altitude up at a slight angle.

Red.

He took a deep breath.

Green.

Special Project shot forward.

Min-gun wasn't surprised to see Hee-ran moving ahead right out of the gate. Without regulators, her car boasted one of the highest acceleration rates available. Ten seconds later, the other cars edged past him, too. As they spread out and worked their way out of the city, the cluster of machines all out paced the hovervan.

Even at top speed, he'd be minutes behind the others when he reached the turnaround point in Seoul. He knew this logically, but emotionally, it was hard to watch the pack edge ahead of him, leaving more and more distance between him and the next slowest racer.

He accessed the real time ranking app. Hee-Ran and Kang-dae were leading. At least Yong-ju was in the top five. In all his time racing, he'd never looked at the ranking before. For the first time, doubts about *Special Project* creeped into his mind.

As they neared Seoul, he felt radiation streaming through him more and more frequently. He'd studied radioactive decay in depth. He knew there were unstable elements whose nucleus would split, shooting out various things like helium atoms or electrons and changing into a different element. These things could happen in chains with different steps of decay having half-lives ranging from very short to very long. Sometimes the new element was unstable, but instead of splitting, it would just emit a gamma ray, or high energy photon, to reduce the energy and stabilize the nucleus. Those gamma rays were the killers. They were small enough to chop up or mess with the DNA, which would lead to mutations that grew as cancer. In cases of extreme exposure, cells would die, leading to intense sickness or even death. But none of that happened to Min-gun. He'd been exposed to toxic levels more than once without any problems. It was strange that he could feel it at all. Another distraction.

Once he crossed the edge of what used to be Korea's biggest city, on par with New York, the devastation came into view. Everything here gave off every kind of radiation. Robots, sent to test the ground in various areas and clean up the mess, scurried around on the surface with the hope of someday restoring Seoul to its former glory. However, it still looked like a waste land of fallen buildings. A few weeds grew in less caustic patches, but most of it remained barren with rusty rebar sticking up out of broken concrete. The actual blast sites were huge craters with pools of black gunk in the center.

Twenty kilometers before the turnaround, Min-gun saw cars ahead of him. They weren't heading the other direction as he expected, though. They all stopped in a group.

He slowed, knowing it would take him a long time to stop completely.

A voice came through the comm unit. It wasn't Yong-ju. Somebody'd hacked in. "We have taken control of your vehicle. Do not resist or you will be shot out of the sky."

Min-gun noticed two columns of smoke rising from fallen cars. One of the wrecked cars had pink sides. They'd killed Hee-ran?

He tried to turn and drive away, but the software they uploaded gave them remote control of *Special Project*. The van slowed, lifting in altitude as it joined the large group of helpless cars. Over the top of the others loomed a large freighter sized hovertruck. It had guns mounted on the sides and people on hoverbikes came flying out of the large cargo space to the racers. They were stealing all the cars!

Min-gun realized he would be a sitting duck like all the rest. He hadn't even had a chance to use the huge thruster mounted behind him. He smiled and looked back. His little surprise wasn't connected to the regular controls. He reached forward and threw the red toggle switch. The back doors burst open. The jet engine kicked on. *Special Project* blasted forward like a rocket, trailing a fifteen foot stream of blue light.

The red collision detectors flashed in Min-gun's periphery as he picked up speed. He couldn't steer, so he couldn't use speed to escape.

"Stop or die!" the hacker said through the comm again.

Min-gun couldn't stop. Besides, leaving these drivers in the radioactive waste of Seoul without their cars amounted to a death sentence.

Guns, mounted on the side of the hovering cargo vessel cracked. One shattered his windshield. Min-gun popped his side door, and jumped. The wind blew the door closed behind him. Much faster and he wouldn't have been able to open it at all.

As he fell, he gazed up at *Special Project* driving flying into the open cargo space on the side.

Min-gun waved, in case Yong-ju or Kang-dae might be watching. He smirked as the large carrier tipped and fell from the sky, a trail of black smoke rising from one side. Radiation saturated his body, streaming through in higher and higher doses. Then everything went black.

GAMMA RADIATION IS SO SMALL AND ENERGETIC THAT IT CAN TRAVEL through the spaces between atoms. Even lead cannot shield against it. Some forces can affect it, though. It can be absorbed in different ways, even harnessed as energy.

Min-gun dreamed of being an ion thruster, fastened in the back of an abnormal hovercar. He didn't get his fuel from batteries, though. He collected it from the air around him, absorbing electrons and leaving behind charged molecules. So much energy built up, that he thought if he didn't discharge it, he might explode. So he overrode the dampener and blasted the car forward at supersonic speeds. As it flew up above the atmosphere, he felt cold. His motor began to shake and rattle. He could feel the mounting brackets coming apart.

When he woke, his teeth were chattering as the cold night wind leeched heat from his body. He lay in a puddle of thick black sludge in the middle of a crater. With shaking hands, he removed his gloves and felt his arms and face. No damage? He stretched and stood. Not even a broken bone? Why wasn't he in pain? Or dead?

Radiation continued coursing through him. Only now, it seemed to collect. Instead of punching through the other side, it built up. He coughed some gunk out of his mouth, which left a metallic taste on his tongue. Then he shivered. Without thinking, he felt his body convert the radiation into heat. It reminded him of a hot bath.

Impossible. He must be dead. He stepped forward and tripped, plunging both his hands into black muck. If he were dead, this might be hell, but something about tripping and falling felt all too mortal. He shook his hands off and sloshed through the muck up onto the edges of the crater.

A high layer of clouds blocked the stars, making the air feel as energized as he did. He heard a few distant robots, continuing their impossible task of cleaning up the radioactive city. Even those robots occasionally broke down because of damage the radiation did to their circuits. Then they'd have to be cleared by other robots.

Min-gun walked, feeling no soreness. He wasn't even tired. He trudged on, stopping at a blackened pile of metal. Here and there, bright pink paint from one of the car's panels showed through the ash. The other car lay fifty meters off, but he didn't know that driver. He knew Hee-ran. He wanted to cry. He wanted to scream that he would take revenge, but the shock and surreality kept him from internalizing his emotions.

He'd never heard of anybody trying to steal hovercars during a race before. It boggled his mind. He looked around again, focusing on the black shell of the cargo vehicle propped at an angle with the high end on a crushed building.

He approached it, unsure if he should be wary of more danger. The open side had roll up doors, like the garage he shared with Yong-ju. He walked up to it and scanned the wreckage inside where *Special Project* brought the behemoth down. The gun on the lower end was mangled, but the high end gun seemed to be intact.

The warehouse sized room inside remained empty except for the odd anchoring chain or overturned toolbox. They clearly expected to leave with a couple dozen high end race cars. This big transport probably had huge ion thrusters, he mused. He might be able to salvage one if he wanted to make *Special Project 2*. He turned to check on a low moaning sound from inside the carrier.

He walked to the low end where the platform touched the ground. "Hello?"

The crying grew louder and more punctuated. Despite the darkness he found a large tarp and a few shelves overturned in the corner. Min-gun jumped up and made his way across the floor into the darkness. He pulled the plastic tarp to reveal a young woman.

Gagged, she stared at him through crying eyes. When he stepped closer, her eyes went wide and the moaning stopped.

Kim Kang-dae.

He remembered her talking to the men in the restaurant. Had she somehow been involved in all this? That didn't make sense. Why would she enter the race if she knew there were pirates waiting to steal all the hovercars?

He pulled the gag from her mouth. Closer, as his eyes adjusted, he saw hers were bloodshot. She looked pale and sick.

"I'm so sorry," she said, her lungs rasping.

"Where's everybody else?" He tried to free her, but found the chain of her handcuffs went through holes at the corner of one of the metal toolboxes.

"They took my car and left me here to die, as an example." She coughed. Blood drooled over her cracked bottom lip. Healthy when they left her, she now suffered from acute radiation poisoning. Even after half a day, she would only be this sick if the rads were extreme.

"An example for what?" He found a hacksaw. Thinking better of trying to cut the reinforced steel chain, he tossed it in favor of tin snips to cut into the sheet metal of the toolbox.

"I promised to help them fix the races. They bought me the car." She choked and squeezed her eyes closed.

"So you were supposed to win or lose when they told you to?" He pulled the chain free of the toolbox.

She nodded. "I told them I could win. They lost big covering bets on the last race." She choked. Min-gun had to suppress a smile. People had bet on him to win? That felt good. "I guess they tried to cover the losses by stealing..." Another cough. "...cars."

"We have to get you out of here." He put one arm behind her, preparing to lift her. Despite everything, he couldn't help thinking how long he'd wanted to hold her.

"No." She shook her head, so he stepped back.

"Why. You can't stay here."

"Too late." She tipped her head. "You fell. How'd you..."

"I don't know," he said. "I just woke up. I didn't even break anything. The radiation, I think I have some kind of power. It's like the stuff makes me better instead of worse."

She looked at him with wide eyes. "I'm so sorry."

"It's not your fault. You didn't know."

He sat and tipped her so her head rested on his shoulder. He put one arm around her and just held her. She rocked a little. She coughed a few times.

"Thanks."

"My pleasure. I can't wait to see Yong-ju's face when he sees me."

"Must be wonderful." She convulsed. "People who care…"

"I care about you," he said. "I've been trying to ask you out for a long time."

She tipped her head and gave a faint smile. Then she coughed and blood drooled down the shoulder of his jacket to mix with the dried residue of the black sludge.

He hoped whatever had helped him could somehow be transferred to Kang-dae. Maybe the radiation could help her, or he could channel it. He felt her relaxing. He felt some heat moving, but it wasn't enough. She closed her eyes. Sometime later, she stopped breathing.

"No short cuts," he said softly to himself. None of the nearby vehicles could be salvaged. He would have to walk out of Seoul. Would he be dangerous to his friends? Would he have to live his life here in the radioactive wasteland? Maybe they could use his blood to find a way for other people to survive in radioactive environments. Only one way to find out.

As the sun came up, Shin Min-gun walked south toward Taejeon City.

JAMES WYMORE

Tall tales and imagination filled James Wymore's formative years as he moved around the American West. Constantly in pursuit of a gateway to another world, he failed to find a literal door to another reality. However, he learned to travel everywhere fantastic through writing.

As an adult, James voyaged to other continents, where new philosophies and cultures fed his desire to see life from different perspectives. He then immersed himself in studying nature, in the hopes of finding a loophole. Along the way, he continued creating stories about alternate worlds like the ones hiding just out of sight.

James finally settled in the Rocky Mountains with his pet wolf, Kilgore, and started publishing his work. With three books and six short stories in print after just one year, he celebrates the best supernatural portal he's found so far—the mind.

Search with him at
http://jameswymore.wordpress.com

9

FIELD TEST

PATRICK BURDINE

T he screaming really got his blood pumping. Primal, guttural. Tribal. It always had that effect on him. Cheers and shouts for one team, cries of derision at the other. Us. Them. He smiled and felt it all wash over him. The stadium was a home even for those times when he was sleeping on the streets.

His mom used to bring him here when he was a kid, back when he was Manuel, Manuelito in the earliest days. He changed it to Manfred in his late teens, hoping the Euro name might give him a better chance at getting one of the corp jobs. Most of the kids he grew up with had done similar name switches, Pedro was now Piotr, Jose went by Josef. Maria was one of the lucky ones, she got to keep the name of her birth. He scoffed when he thought about how naïve it had been to think it might make a difference. Their black hair, black eyes, dark skin, accents, movements; all of these would betray them, of course. But they'd been hopeful as only the young and poor can be. That hope had died as such hope always must. Slowly, painfully, leaving only bitterness for an epitaph.

Manfred, though, he understood hope was best as fuel for the engine of ambition and that it would never replace viciously hard work. He never complained, not even when he was given the lousiest assignments and the worst of the worst neighborhoods during his time as a security contractor. Eventually, his unique combination of work ethic and tight lips after the job had attracted one of the major sec-corps, Seguritek. They were so busy they turned clients away and their pay was top of the scale. They even offered a benefits package if you were willing to do the work. Most of it was dirty, but Mexico City wallowed in dirt, so he didn't mind it. Much.

He glanced down at his watch and then over at Sections 27A and 27B. By his estimation, they had about a minute left of life. He glanced at the digital scoreboard that ran the length of the crumbling AdobeCrete hallway and watched as Wilhelm Luger scored another goal for Dynamo, increasing their lead to 4-1.

Manfred had never been a cruel man, and it caused him pain not to say anything. More than trying to clear the sections before it happened, but also because he was a Dynamo fan, and they really needed the win if they were going to make the cup season. He sighed and leaned against the wall, pretending to check his WristCom like the rest of the moderately wealthy men and women crowding the hall. He didn't look for anything in particular, just wasted time until the firebomb exploded. He only had to wait thirty-eight seconds.

His ears rang in the immediate aftermath. A moment of shocked silence for the dead hung over everything and then the screaming started again, less raucous and devoid of joy. The wounded survivors and the panicked people left unscathed but terrified began a tidal rush out of the stadium. Manfred pressed tight against the wall and scanned the rushing crowd. He finally saw the target, Luis Marquez. He'd been easy to spot; everyone else kept checking over their shoulders, but Luis kept his eyes straight ahead. Other faces showed their fear, while he wore a grim mask.

People bumped and jostled Luis as he made his way to the edge of the hallway, away from the center to prevent himself from being crushed if he were to stumble. Manfred watched the bomber drop something into a trash chute nestled between a Cruncheros OmniSoy SnackShack and an automated Garza-Primatatek Phoenix jersey kiosk. Then the bomber peeled thin layers of synth skin from his hands, rolled them into small balls in his palms. He popped them into his mouth like gumballs and began chewing. Whatever fingerprints the bomb techs found wouldn't belong to Luis.

Manfred's heart pounded an angry beat and his face flushed as he watched the bomber. Dozens dead, hundreds more wounded and this guy couldn't care less. They called themselves liberators, but their actions proved time and again that murderers was a far more fitting title.

Manfred flattened himself against the wall and watched the river of humanity pass him by. Most of them feared another explosion, but Manfred knew not to worry. The ordnance Luis planted had all detonated as expected. Manfred wondered at his efficiency and the efficacy of the explosives. Most resistance cells used cheap, homemade devices but the group Luis worked for had better equipment and even some training. Manfred's main concerns were not being crushed by the crowd or failing his mission and losing the promotion that EVP Druss offered as reward for completion of the assignment.

As Luis approached, Manfred dove into the crowd and maneuvered like a man swimming along a heavy current toward his prey. When he finally drew up next to his target, he let himself be carried along shoulder to shoulder. Manfred kept an eye on the maintenance closet he'd over-ridden earlier. *Three, two, one.* He dropped low and shoved the bomber into the room. Luis stumbled over the bucket that Manfred had set up in the center of the doorway and fell hard.

Manfred stepped in and closed the door behind himself, drowning the room in blackness. The room's only light came from the glowing green indicator on the panel in the door frame.

"What the hell, man, watch where you're going!" Luis started to push himself up but Manfred kicked him in the side.

The hardplas toe of his boot cracked a couple of ribs. His breath left him with a pained whoosh and he fell back onto the AdobeCrete floor. Manfred reached behind himself and slapped the control panel, bathing the room in red as the lock engaged.

Manfred reached down and grabbed Luis's wrist and torqued it hard, flipping him over onto his belly and then dropped his knee into the bomber's back. The smell of piss filled the air and Manfred knew he'd bruised the man's kidney.

"You're making a big mistake," Luis called out through gritted teeth.

"I don't think so, *ese.*"

Luis struggled, but the damage to his kidney had sapped much of his strength.

"Look man, whoever you think I am, I'm not. My name's Jaoquin Ramirez, I work here delivering food to the seats. I don't have no money."

Manfred was already sick of this guy's voice. His stomach lurched at the thought of what he was about to do, but he didn't hesitate. He sat on Luis's back, cranked the right arm as far as it would bend, and shifted his weight around to grab the other one. He locked both in the crook of his elbow. He took a pouch of gel from an upper pocket, tore it open with his teeth, and squeezed the contents over the bomber's wrists. The StayGel hardened in less than a second, binding the man. Manfred rolled him over and grabbed a bright penlight from another pocket, shining it into Luis's face. His cheeks glistened with tears and a trickle of blood trailed down from one nostril. Luis squinted and blinked into the brightness. Manfred looked down at a mirror of the face he'd grown accustomed to over the last month.

He straddled Luis and drew the two paper-thin cords from their sockets embedded in his wrists. The cords twisted and writhed like living things as their simple programming sought their fleshy contact points.

"It's not your money I am after."

He reached toward Luis's face. When the cords came within inches of contact, they lanced forward at his eyes, boring in through the skin of his eyelids and slithering into the gap above the eyeball and socket. Luis screamed and thrashed for a full five seconds before going limp.

Manfred's head began to pound with the onset of a vicious migraine. He forced himself to steady his breathing and focus as he'd been taught. Unfamiliar memories superimposed themselves over the bomber's twitching head.

In the early days of the project, he'd tried to remember the images that flashed before him, thinking them somehow more important, but he'd come to realize he'd have greater recall if he just relaxed during the transfer process. This was his first time with a live subject, and the deluge of information stored over a lifetime overwhelmed him. A black haired woman smiled and started to speak, but before he heard the words, she'd morphed into his hands as he placed three bombs under the seats in Section 27A. The memory flickered and he found himself back in primary school learning math. Then his first job cleaning a stadium. This stadium. He had worked here, after all. The first time he'd made love to a girl named... named... the name eluded him. It would probably come, or maybe it wouldn't, but it was irrelevant. Another thousand memories mundane and monumental flooded over him and threatened to drown him with the life of Luis Martinez who called himself Marquez after a character in a crime vid he saw once. Luis himself had not consciously realized the reason he'd chosen that alias, but Manfred knew. Manfred saw his own surgically altered face leaning in close, a trickle of blood running from his nose. Tears washed his cheeks and a blood vessel in his temple throbbed visibly. He felt the fear of Luis's impending death.

Everything went gray as the MindThief finished its transfer and the safety protocols clicked on to prevent Manfred from following Luis too far into oblivion. Manfred, rested his weight on Luis's heaving belly, and wiped away tears with the back of his hand. The cords slid from the bomber's eyes, slick with thin blood and cerebro-spinal fluid. They hung flaccid like snakes who'd just eaten their fill and lapsed into torpor.

Manfred retracted them back into their housings under the flesh of his wrists with a twitch of his hands, and tried to catch his breath while he put his thoughts in order.

"I am Luis Marquez," he said to the room and was surprised to realize that he believed it. He stood, swaying slightly as his equilibrium returned. He walked to the rack of cleaning supplies and found the aerosol container he'd planted earlier. Returning to the twitching form on the concrete, he sprayed the man. The corrosive aerosol broke the original Luis down into an unrecognizable lump of biological slime. DNA testing could eventually reveal his identity, but the mission would be completed far before anyone saw the report.

He waved the access rod over the door lock and rejoined the exodus, letting his feet guide him without knowing where he was going. Outside the stadium, he stuck to the shadows, avoiding contact with the Citizen Management Officers and the medical aid arriving on the scene.

He followed a circuitous path to the FerroTrans station. The third train car was the one he wanted. He boarded and looked at the other passengers: three women huddled in quiet conversation at the end of the car, a group of tired workers wearing MexiFabrica uniforms, one snoring loudly, a couple of kids listening to music, and a woman wearing a tight fitting green shirt and black knee length skirt. Manfred walked over and sat on an empty bench across from her. She met his eyes and lifted her chin in acknowledgment at him. Magdalena.

The other passengers filtered off the train at their stops. Manfred and the woman didn't acknowledge each other further until the car was empty.

"How'd it go?" she finally asked him.

He shrugged. "You saw how it went."

"Are you okay?"

"Those people didn't do anything wrong. They didn't deserve to die."

She leaned across the walkway, touched him on the leg, and then sat back again.

"No, but they deserve to truly *live* don't they? Not just lease their lives, trying to pay down an account that grows faster than they can pay? I'd rather be dead than a slave to the corporations."

"I notice you didn't get a seat in 27a."

Her face hardened. "Feck off, Luis."

"I'm sorry. I'm just tired is all Maggie." He punctuated the sentence with a long sigh. "Do you ever think about being someone else?"

"All the time. It's why I do this. When this is over, we'll all get to be somebody different. I wish I'd been born up north. I'd be different then, but I wasn't, so I do the best I can."

He ran his hand over his face and felt the unfamiliar scars and two days' growth on cheeks he normally kept smooth. Opening his eyes, he noticed two small bloodstains on his sleeve.

"I think CorpSec is on to us," he said.

She sat up a bit straighter in her chair.

"Why do you say that?"

"Someone jumped me on the way out," he rubbed his knuckles and showed her the blood on his sleeves. "I killed him. Stuffed him in a closet and poured a bunch of solvent on him." Manfred had been counting on the confusion to cover up the murder, but couldn't be sure no one had seen him go into the closet. Besides, he'd never met a member of the resistance who wasn't at least a little paranoid.

She looked around the train. "You weren't followed were you?"

"No," he said. "I took the long way to the train. Almost missed it. I went by that taco stand we used to eat at." He remembered that Luis and Magdalena were recruited into the resistance at about the same time, nearly three years ago. They ran errands together for a while. Sometimes after a job, they'd grab a bite to eat. Once he'd thought maybe something would happen between them, but it'd stayed platonic.

"Anyway. We should probably let them know."

Magdalena nodded slowly. He let his eyes linger on her body and tried to remember Luis was attracted to her. All Manfred saw was a promotion. Eventually, he folded his arms, closed his eyes, and dropped his chin to his chest. Another hour or so, and Stage Two would begin.

He remembered his CorpSec briefing with Druss. The intel indicated that the Resistance had big plans. Bigger than a Frictionless stadium bombing. With the Annual Retreat coming up next week in Aztlanta, most of the stakeholders became nervous. The target had to be identified and the fallout mitigated. A lot of money was thrown around in the name of security to fast-track several projects. This cell had a *brujo*, and to get through the mind witch required more than just masking a face and a voice. Seguritek had been developing just the right technology for slipping through a psychic screen and that, in turn, had led to Manfred's assignment.

He'd almost drifted off to sleep going over the details for the thousandth time when the train juddered to a stop. He locked eyes with Magdalena; hers held a flash of panic that reflected his own.

"Sure you weren't tailed?" Magdalena narrowed her eyes.

Manfred's heart pounded in his throat and he had trouble swallowing. He ran the scenarios in his mind on whether his cover would hold better if he killed the security or Magdalena, or if they should just run for it.

A soothing female voice filled the train car. "We apologize for the delay. The tracks ahead have been damaged and a work crew is currently attending to the repairs. We expect no more than a three-hour delay. A limited supply of hovercarts have been made available through our partner TransporTech at the fantastic value of C750 per passenger. If you would like to take advantage of this offer, please come to the front car where an associate is standing by to take your order. Again, the price is only C750. TransporTech looks forward to serving you."

"Are they fecking kidding?" Magdalena grumbled and leaned back. "The entire ticket was only 250. See? This is what I am talking about. I bet the tracks aren't even messed up, or if they are, they did it themselves."

Manfred reclined on the bench, laying his head on his hand to hide the shaking. He slept most of the four hours it took to get moving again.

MAGDALENA LED HIM THROUGH THE WRECKAGE OF OLDTOWN AND INTO the warehouse district. He didn't have any knowledge of the area, nor did he have any stolen memories of it. The MindThief wasn't perfect, and the human brain simply contained too much data to absorb it all. He'd held on to enough that his guide had accepted him so far, but the dull headache growing behind his eyes let him know the memories would be as fragmented as a dream at noon within a few hours. Inside a day, Luis's mind would be as unrecognizable within Manfred's head as his body was back in the stadium.

"Pretty sure I've never been here," he said.

"That's the point," she replied. "Patrón wants it that way. Only two of us know where it is and we're bringing the rest in. The others should already be there, actually, thanks to the fecking delay."

"I'd have eaten if I knew it was going to take this long to get there."

"Not much longer, I'm sure you'll live."

I hope so.

She led him to a huge building of cracked AdobeCrete. A faded painting of a smiling pig offered a plate of CarnitaSoy and the slogan "It tastes so real, it's like I'm eating myself!"

"Maybe I'm not so hungry after all."

She snorted a half laugh that sounded almost porcine. "Terrible slogan, good food. We had it for special occasions when I was a kid."

A door clicked open as she approached it and she held it open for Manfred. He walked through and gagged, nearly vomiting on a terrible stench. He almost missed the sensation of feathers lightly dusting his scalp under his hair. The witch scanned his mind.

"Fecking hell, Ro." Luis's words spilled out of Manfred's mouth.

"Can't be too sure these days." A dark skinned man stepped out of the shadows holding a well-maintained prewar pistol at his side.

Six barrels of abandoned soy paste had been stacked up near the door.

"You're late; what happened?" The newcomer, Ro, looked at Magdalena for the answer.

"Train problems," she said, "or some alternative revenue grab. Whatever, I thought it was better to just stay on the train rather than leave a trail."

Ro and Magdalena locked eyes for couple of seconds. Ro eventually smiled and broke the gaze.

"Like what you saw?" She snapped.

Manfred didn't need to be a witch to feel her anger. "Does this whole place smell like this?"

Ro tucked the pistol into the waistband at the small of his back. "Nah. Come on, you're the last ones; we thought you might have been caught. Or compromised." His gaze lingered on Magdalena. He turned to Manfred. "You okay bro? You seem a bit off."

"I'm going to puke if we stand here much longer. How's that for off?"

Ro held his hands up. "Sorry, just had to be sure everyone was actually everyone, you know? Those face-shifting *pendejos* are everywhere. The smell throws people off their game, makes the scan easier." He nodded deeper into the cavernous building and Manfred led the way.

They navigated the trash littering the floor of the abandoned warehouse and to another smaller structure within the building. Management and security offices had no doubt been housed there during CarnitaSoy's better days. Glaring security lights lit the area, revealing graffiti tags covering the walls, layered thicker than the dust that settled on the abandoned conveyor belts. They also illuminated the only new thing in the place: a freshly installed security door. No amount of stolen memories would get him through the biometric lock on the door. He'd have to improvise. When he got near it, Manfred took a stutter step to a halt, grabbing his stomach and bending at the waist.

"Something wrong?" Ro asked sharply.

Gooseflesh formed on Manfred's neck as he felt the tickle of the scan.

Instead of answering, Manfred half swallowed his tongue and triggered his gag reflex, vomiting out the fluids from his stomach. Ro puked behind him as his body had a sympathetic reaction to Manfred's autonomic reaction.

"This fecking smell," Manfred said between coughing retches.

Magdalena pushed by him and walked up to the door. "It better smell better in there." She slapped her hand against the bioreader. The door unlatched and swung open. She stepped through and Manfred followed, wiping a string of spit and mucus from his chin as he did so. Ro followed and waited until the door closed behind him.

"Still hungry?" Magdalena asked.

Manfred shook his head.

"There's plenty to eat," a voice called out. "As long as you don't mind drinking it." Sarah Campbell walked into the room holding a can of Nutrink in each hand. "You're late."

"I'll take one," Manfred said and caught the can she tossed to him.

"Seriously?" Ro asked.

He shrugged. "I've gotta get that taste out of my mouth and the smell out of my nose or I'm gonna puke again."

Magdalena gave Sarah a hug and sipped from the other drink as she filled Sarah in on the problems with the train.

"Patrón is already here. He's upstairs, of course. Talking to Vincenzo." Sarah called out.

The fifth and final member of the cell. Manfred took a sip of the Nutrink. It had enough sugar in it to actually taste good. He glanced at the label and then around at the others in the room. He'd throw the can into Sarah's face then spin and punch Ro in the throat. Step past him and take his pistol, tripping him to the ground as he went, and then shoot him once in the head. The shock would start to wear off and it was fifty-fifty whether Magdalena would run for the exit or dive to the side. Either way, she'd be dead inside five feet. Finally, he'd finish Sarah off. It'd be too loud though; Patrón and Vincenzo might make it out. But that wasn't this mission. Not yet. Instead, he drained the rest of the can and hoped it would help the increasing pressure behind his eyes. He looked for a trashcan and then realized Luis wouldn't. He tossed the can into a pile of garbage in the corner.

"What are they talking about?" he asked.

"The weather," Sarah said. "The feck you think?"

"Is it still on?" Manfred starting fishing.

"Why wouldn't it be?"

"Because it seems impossible. And the retaliation will be..." Manfred trailed off.

"If you're scared, go back to your shitty little hab and watch the holos. We're going to be heroes. We'll be the trigger that fires the bullet of revolution." Sarah's eyes flashed.

"I'm just saying it's gonna be a *cabrón*. Those guys have security for their security."

"You got through at the game. Patrón planned it, got everything in place—"

"Like hell! *I* planted the bombs. I killed those people. When was the last time you went out and pulled a trigger for anything, *perra?*" Luis's anger drove Manfred's words.

"Enough!" a voice resounded from the speakers embedded in the walls. "If you are done bickering like children, come up here."

Magdalena finished her drink and threw it on the same trash heap. The can landed next to Manfred's and it was hard not to read it as a show of solidarity. She bumped him as she walked by and whispered, "I warned you not to sleep with her."

Manfred tried not to look shocked. Why didn't he remember that? It seemed recent enough that the MindThief should have picked it up. Or had it and the memories were fading quicker than he expected. The scientists who did the implant had advised him he'd have access to the memories for twenty-four hours. Or was it ten? Luis tried hard to remember the briefing. He couldn't quite find it, but he did remember his name was Manfred. Or maybe his cover was Manfred.

"You coming, Luis?" Ro was holding the door to the stairwell open for him. The *brujo* looked hard at him, but Manfred didn't have the sensation of a scan. "You're not going to puke again are you?"

He felt himself shaking and was glad for the cover. He decided to reinforce it to discourage Ro from scanning him again. "I shouldn't have drunk that so fast. I might." He rolled his shoulders, walked to the stairwell, and followed Ro up.

They climbed three flights of stairs to the top floor of the management building in silence. Manfred tried to imagine Sarah naked, hoping it would jar a memory, but he came up blank. He couldn't even remember what... what's her name looked like. The girl from marketing that he—Manfred—had been seeing for close to ten months. Julia? Yulia? Something like that. And the throbbing pain in his head didn't make it any easier.

The yawn of an empty doorframe welcomed them at the top of the stairs. Most of the walls had been knocked out as well, clearing virtually the entire floor. Echoes of the women's bickering carried through the open space. A very tall man stood quietly to one side. Luis was pretty sure this was Vincenzo. *Wait, Not Luis. MANFRED!* Manfred was his name.

Everyone was looking at him.

"Sorry, what?"

"Sarah questioned your resolve and that has Patrón worried," Vincenzo said.

"*Pinche* Sarah."

"Screw you, Luis."

"You weren't that good the last time!"

She slapped him.

The room was silent until a voice that neither Luis nor Manfred recognized spoke. "As much as I enjoy a good holo-novela, we have more important things to discuss."

He'd been standing there in the shadows the whole time; as he stepped into the light, an ethereal wind brushed against Manfred's face. Ro wasn't the only *brujo* in this cell.

"I'm sorry," Sarah said.

"Me too, Patrón," Manfred said, trusting the MindThief to hide his thoughts.

Patrón's blue eyes, the color of the Gulf from a painting, locked onto Manfred's. "Is it true? What she says about your devotion to our cause. To our people? Is your resolve weakening?" The voice was precise, notable by its lack of accent, neither Euro, local, nor other. It was a voice out of a holo and its owner could have come from anywhere.

"That's stupid. How much blood have I shed—and spilled? More than anyone here, and you know it. You all know it."

"Nobody is questioning your past deeds, Luis Marquez. It's more about the future. What kinds of things *will* you do? Will you strike a blow against the invaders? Open the door for a free future where we are no longer a client state, but a free state as we were before the war? Strong? Free?"

Poor, ripe for conquest, the thoughts rose unbidden to the front of Manfred's mind. Hopeful, proud. These were the thoughts that fluttered from the shadow of Luis's.

"You must be strong Luis for just a while longer. And you Sarah, and you Magdalena, and you Romeo, and you Vincenzo. It is no mere accident of chance that you five have come together and survived the crucible of resistance. You have become strong, like a fist. A fist that will smash the ACC's hold on us. It's our hope that the resistance will no longer exist. Will no longer be needed. And we will need the leaders to come from the resistance. Will you be the leaders of the new nation?"

Everyone answered an affirmative.

"Our target is a senior VP named Balthazar Druss."

Manfred's stomach dropped. He knew that name, but couldn't remember where from. Probably someone Luis used to know. Yeah, that seemed right to him.

"Gather round." Patrón motioned to the holodisk reader in the center of the desk at the far end of the room.

The cell formed up around the desk and Patrón activated it. The hologram flickered through several images of a man, which a recorded voice identified as Balthazar Druss, senior VP for Seguritek Industries, a private security company who held contracts with the largest corporations in Mexico. The mechanical voice began to drone on about his career path, his achievements in the name of the corporate identities.

A subsonic round passed harmlessly through the hologram of Balthazar Druss and impacted somewhat more explosively with Ro's left eye. A fraction of a second later, a handful of wounds cut a rough red pattern across Vincenzo's chest,. The sound of the DTF MP42 roared on the trail of the rounds.

Manfred reacted first diving through the hologram and rolling to cover behind the desk. Sarah took a round to the body and then two more in her head as she fell. Magdalena dropped behind the cover of the desk next to Manfred.

"Quick reactions, quicker than I expected anyway," Patrón's voice was calm. "This cell has been infiltrated."

"Wait!" Magdalena cried out. "Wait, I'm loyal! We're loyal!" She looked to Luis for backup. "*Dios!* Were you hit?"

Manfred's head pounded and his vision had acquired a reddish hue. He brought his hands up to his cheek and when he looked at them, they were slick with blood.

"I don't think so," he said. A thin trickle of blood like a tear crept down from left eye.

Patrón continued, "It wasn't Ro for obvious reasons, though you'll be interested to know he was looking to sell you all out to a coyote for smuggling across the badlands. Sarah was too full of holo-romantic revolutionaries. I thought it was Vincenzo until I got him up here to talk. So the infiltrator is definitely one of you two. Or, I suppose, there is a third option. The Seguritek agent may have been killed in the infiltration attempt."

Manfred looked at Magdalena and saw her face scrunched up in confusion.

She called out, "If you thought they were loyal then why kill them?"

"Because it was my job, of course. I'm overseeing this field test."

"Do you have any idea what he's talking about?" she kept her voice low.

"I do," he said, and shoved her out from behind the cover of the desk.

The stitching sound of the submachine gun rang out, and Magdalena's body jerked with the impacting rounds.

"What is your name, agent?"

"Lu-Manfred Braun." Manfred held his hands up over the edge of the desk, showing them to be empty.

The sound of footsteps coming up the stairwell echoed off the empty walls.

"Remind me to update my curriculum vitae holo, would you? I almost paused the entire operation to correct the title. I've been an Executive VP for half a year now." Balthazar Druss said as he arrived on the landing.

The pain in Manfred's head was nearly unbearable, and tears joined the blood leaking from his eyes.

"Are you sure that is the operative?" Druss asked.

"I believe so, but can't be sure," Patrón answered.

"Agent 2nd Class, Manfred Braun, do those hands peeking over the desk belong to you?" Druss called out.

"Yes sir, it's me."

"Confirmation code?" Druss asked.

Manfred's voice shook as he answered. The pain made it hard to concentrate. "AGWFCH423DGAE."

"Stand up and let's get a look at how you're holding up."

Manfred rose slowly. When he wasn't shot, his shoulders relaxed a little. "You know Patrón?"

"Know him? I hired him. It's occasionally useful to recruit some agitators and let them blow off steam before they become dangerous."

"Blow off steam? They've killed hundreds."

"Never anyone that mattered. Hmm, looks like he's rejecting the MindThief." Druss said.

Manfred looked from Patrón to Druss. "But you were the target."

"You don't think I'd get permission from the Board to use someone else for project Judas do you? And imagine if I did pick someone, and they learned they were being targeted for assassination. That's the sort of sloppiness that ruins careers. You're a bit slower on the uptake than I'd expect from a 2nd Class. Note that down as well as a potential side effect of the implant." He turned to Patrón and asked, "any giveaways?"

"He was a bit clumsy on circumventing the biometric, but got through the weaker witch okay. I wasn't sure myself and I was actually looking. Although, I think this whole" Patrón waved his hand around Manfred's face "bleeding from the eyes thing might make someone suspicious."

"When did it start?" Druss asked.

"I don't know, uhh..."

"Come on, quickly, before you have a brain bleed and are unable to provide any more useful data."

"Brain what?"

"Medical is already on the way. Out with it or I'll leave them standing under the pig!" Druss commanded.

"It started I don't know Luis was talking to me. And the game was on the holo. And I remember the rain, it was so cold but her touch was so warm. That's it! And her name was Jess."

"Who?"

"The first girl I had sex with. In the stands at the stadium. I put a bomb there! Why would I do that? I have to—" Manfred's eyes rolled up into the back of his head as the aneurysm struck.

"Damn," Druss said. "Set up another cell, I'll get this data back to R&D, and we'll iterate on the successes." He turned to leave then stopped and spun on his heel, smiling at Patrón. "It's good to see you, Stein."

"You too, sir. And don't forget to update that C.V."

PATRICK BURDINE

Patrick Burdine writes thriller, fantasy, and horror fiction as well as the occasional romantic comedy. He has collaborated with Amazon Best Selling Author Aiden James on the Lifeblood Legacy as well as the Nash-Vegas Paranormal series. In addition to his novels, he has written a number of short stories, novellas, and scripts. You can follow him on twitter @authorpb and visit his site at www.patrickburdine.com for some free content. He lives in Los Angeles with his wife and four children.

10

MAESTRO'S REQUIEM

MATTHEW S. COX

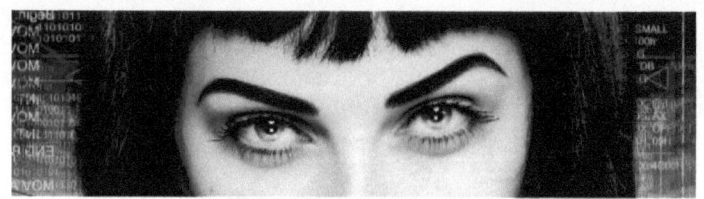

Methodical as always, Nina thought over the operation backward and forward while observing forty-eight-year-old Jerome Drummond in the green-on-green of a night vision scope. Seventeen days ago, GlobeNet sniffer programs tripped on a communication channel to Europe, a network address belonging to the Allied Corporate Council Citizen Management group—their law enforcement. Contents of multiple successive messages detailed the intent for a UCF corporation to purchase eight prisoners, orphaned children of rebel fighters who'd survived a raid on their resistance cell. The only problem was, no one had yet figured out how they'd been smuggled into West City, or where they were.

Many of the people working under her on this case hadn't slept a full night in seventeen days.

In her cross-hairs, the Senior Vice President of Osiris Biotechnic—chief of R&D—reclined in a massive black chair behind a desk of chrome and glass. He sported a sculpted flattop, white-collar shirt, thin tie, seventy-five thousand credit emerald cuff links, and an 'I own the world' smile. A holo-panel hovering over his desk bore the image of a stocky, square-jawed man of similar age, though far paler than the dark-skinned Drummond, who shimmered from the light it cast.

What is it about corporate types? They always leave the lights off when they ignore the law... or human decency.

For six hours, she lay prone atop the roof of another century tower, one full of office space owned by Halcyon-Ormyr. Five hours and forty-four minutes of waiting for Drummond to receive the call the network people said he would. The hovercar manufacturer would likely never become aware Division 9 had been there. If anyone happened to notice her, they'd probably decide to mind their own business: her sand brown longcoat and clingy black bodysuit screamed government agent. She shifted, attempting to evade an awkward lump pressing into her side. The layer of gel in the ballistic stealth armor could harden in a microsecond to stop bullets, but it didn't do much to protect against a roof covered in egg-sized 'decorative stones.'

Her jet-black hair blew in a wind her body could ignore when she wanted it to; synthetic skin and plastisteel didn't care about cold. She sometimes missed having it long. This body had come with a bob that didn't grow unless she triggered nanobots to make it longer, and so far, she hadn't seen a reason to beyond sentiment.

A wire connected a port at the back of her neck to a modified UCF-M22A7 assault rifle allowed its optics to interface with her eyes. Range and windage information appeared in tiny text at the lower right of her vision above a giant numeral 6 indicating rounds remaining. The rifle's boxy outer casing displayed a pattern matching the multicolored rocks, creating the illusion the weapon had been made of glass. Her mental command extended the motorized barrel out to its full five-foot length. Lime green cross-hairs and a hairline trajectory estimation arc centered on the executive's head as her vision zoomed in enough to perceive particles of dust in the gaps between loaf-shaped segments of cushion behind him. A faint whirr in her right ear announced a caseless round sliding into the chamber by her cheek.

If the intel's good, 12.5mm is too quick.

For more than two weeks, Nina and her team had been staring at 'arrest photos' of eight young children who'd probably watched their parents die. Grainy images, wide-eyed expressions of anguish and dread had etched in her memory. She, and everyone at Division 9 who'd gotten wind of this operation, wanted to kick down a door or two, but Osiris had five research facilities, three of which they'd tried to hide from the government. They all feared choosing wrong would spook the VP, and a potential rescue operation would become an eight-count murder investigation—if anyone ever managed to find bodies. Normally, Nina preferred delicate operations... but these were children. The waiting had been the second most unbearable thing she'd ever lived through.

Division 9 NetOps owned the Osiris Biotechnic network for the past two weeks. The audio feed patched in via her internal uplink brought her ears virtually into the room as though she stood at Drummond's side.

"I am glad we could come to an arrangement," said the man on the holo-panel, Gamedi Zharkov according to her case notes, a Director of Citizen Management in Minsk. The Allied Corporate Council ran everything, even their military, like another part of a corporation. "My associates tell me the merchandise arrived intact, yet we are still waiting for the payment."

Drummond's eyes flickered with irritation. "There should be no deviation from our deal, Gamedi. Two and a half million per unit. Fifteen percent up front, the rest on delivery. Doctor Rice has yet to confirm that nothing was damaged in transit and none of the petri dishes are contaminated with anything which could render them useless for our purposes. As soon as he tells me everything is as expected, you will get paid."

Gamedi's lips stretched into a wide line, not quite a frown, but not far from it. "We are short seventeen million credits, Mr. Drummond." His Russian accent thickened. "You are aware these castoffs could have been more easily dealt with locally, especially the ones too young to have adopted their parents' radical ideologies. It is a risk for both of us."

"Oh, come now." Drummond reached forward, resting his hand on the desk, one finger tapping the glass. "We both know your people have little regard for non-citizens no matter how old they are, and these were part of your little"—the man failed to conceal all of his condescending amusement—"resistance problem? I am curious, Gamedi, if your society is the superior one, why is it that your very own citizens have taken up arms in secret?"

"Unrest is universal, my friend. Regardless of who is in charge, someone will claim it unjust." Gamedi coughed into his fist. "The vermin are as you requested. Their families *were* criminals. There is no one to ask questions, no trails to cause problems. It is perhaps ironic that your company, within the great and noble UCF, conducts such unseemly business."

Jerome turned his hands upward. "If you find our research so distasteful, why then did you sell them to us? Could it be your stake in the research data? Hmm?"

"Need I remind you the sort of issues you may experience should your, how you say, 'NewsNet' receives certain recordings?" Gamedi smiled. "It would be not so pleasant for Osiris's stock, yes?"

Drummond flinched. "You should have received the funds by now. Perhaps some of them aren't quite as healthy and useful as you claimed?"

He waved a hand at his desk, summoning another holo-panel. "Give me a minute."

Forty-one seconds later, an exasperated middle-aged man with short silvery hair swept back over his head appeared on the second screen. A mixture of wailing children, one screaming in anger, and monkey-like whooping came over the new connection. "I'm very busy now, Drummond, dealing with your rush job. We were supposed to have another two weeks to prepare."

"Why haven't I received a message confirming receipt? Our friends in the east are expecting payment." Drummond had to yell to overpower the noise.

Doctor Rice's irritation deepened. "They're all usable, but it will be a few weeks of waiting for them to get back up to normal weight before we can start any tests. As of now, their systems are too stressed for any useful data collections. The weakest of the samples would likely kill them in hours. However, for purposes of the agreement, they are fine. I sent the confirmation message over twenty minutes ago. Now, if you'll leave me to my work."

⌈ Lieutenant Duchenne, this is DeWinter. Confirm trace on the remote facility. We're kicking the gates down now and securing their network. Physical location should upload to group Navcon in three seconds. ⌋

Hardin's virtual face offered a solemn nod. ⌈ Duchenne, proceed. ⌋

⌈ Roger, Ops. Net Team, lights out. One ticket to Miami. ⌋ Nina's voice over the comm channel set off a flurry of activity. Her boss shouted at a field squad to move on the lab where eight foreign children were about to face who-knows-what. The Vidphone calls to both Gamedi and Doctor Rice went dark, and a little red dot winked on beside the door of the VP's office as the mechanism locked.

She sent her voice over the GlobeNet to his holo-terminal. "Jerome Drummond, this is Division 9. Have fun in hell."

The man opened his mouth to shout; time dragged to a standstill as Nina's combat boosters kicked in. A handful of electrons raced down the wire into the rifle, setting off the electronic trigger so her finger didn't have to move. A spark tickled the electrode foil at the back end of a caseless block of propellant. Three relative seconds later, a massive 12.5mm slug came spiraling out of the barrel without a trace of muzzle flare. The projectile cruised across the street ninety-seven stories below and kissed the window of Drummond's office.

Bright silver lines raced a zigzag spider web away from the contact point; glittering diamond flakes followed the bullet into the room amid the slow-motion symphony of glass shearing apart. A split second of scream left the VP's throat, a low demonic sound in Nina's accelerated time state, as the spinning bullet struck the cheek ridge below Drummond's right eye.

The window turned white; long, jagged cracks flashed to a near-opaque crisscross of tiny fragments. Streams of blood squirted out of his ears, expelled by a pressure wave traveling through his brain. The majority of solid material within the man's head erupted in a blast of gore, which leapt onto the wall. Like snow, the suspension of glass fragments cascaded down, more than half raining along the side of the building toward the distant street.

She shut off her boosters; time returned to normal.

Drummond slumped in the chair, two vertebrae and a flap of skin all that remained above his shoulders. A cloud of diamond-like glass bits collapsed on the rug, and the door lock turned green. Hardin would probably grumble about speaking to the target, calling it a warning that could've increased the risk of the VP getting away. She didn't care. He had to know *why*. The recording of everything she'd seen and heard over the past twenty minutes went out over a shadow VPN few civilians even knew existed, back to the D9 system.

⌈I'm done here. Tell the site team I'm on the way.⌋

DRUMMOND'S CALL TO DOCTOR RICE HAD BEEN LIKE A BRIGHT NEON roadmap through the darkness of the GlobeNet, leading the Division 9 NetOps team straight to an unregistered R&D facility in Sector 7904, near the south edge of what had once been called Oregon. The lower-middle-class residential district sat one alley away from the wall on the inland edge of West City, seventy-five meters over an area known four centuries ago as Ashland, according to the archives. It surprised her they hadn't put a project like this out in the Badlands, and she wondered if educated people actually believed in all the stories about technology mysteriously failing out there.

She flicked her thumb at the hovercar's control stick, entertaining an idle memory of Shabundo Ghede moving souls between humans and machines. *I suppose stranger things have been true.*

Her unmarked black patrol craft rounded the corner of a steel-and-glass residence tower; the flight from the Osiris Biotechnic corporate office south had taken nineteen minutes at 618 mph. Sometimes, having a Class 3 doll body and far-beyond-human reflexes came in handy.

Already, a scattering of nondescript black hovercars, two vans, and four blue-and-white Division 1 patrol craft collected around the front.

⌈Network is clear. No automated defenses. Initiating file lockdown,⌋ said DeWinter on a voice only link.

A virtual holo-panel opened, bearing the face of a woman with short black hair and brown skin in a black Division 9 operator's suit, rubbery material straight up to her jawline. The ID widget under the panel read: Operative [O1] Padilla, R.

⌈Lieutenant. The facility is located two levels below street. The super says he had no idea it was there. All four elevators reach it, but only with a specific code and ID. You should be able to walk right in. Sanchez must've been sleeping in training. It took him fifteen minutes to get the damn front door open.⌋

Seconds later, Sergeant Sanchez appeared on a separate virtual window, holding up a middle finger.

Nina eyed the ground; the closest clear landing area offered a longer walk than she wanted to waste time on. ⌈I'm here. Is the site secure?⌋

⌈Yes, Lieutenant. No hostiles, but...⌋ Operative Padilla looked off to the side, somewhere between wanting to cry and scream in rage. A shrieking child and a repetitive *bang, bang, bang* echoed in the background. ⌈They're... these people. They're not even human.⌋

Nina's mental impulse caused her virtual avatar to nod. She hurried into a reckless landing between the building and a pair of tech vans, with less than two inches of clearance on all sides. Nothing an unaugmented person would've dared to try. The rapid descent made two Division 1 patrol officers scream and dive for cover, evidently expecting a crash.

She got out and stormed through the building's entrance, six feet from her car. A small group of civilians loitered about, curious at the police presence, but seeming clueless as to the reason for it. Ignoring the questions shouted over the helmets of more patrol officers, Nina headed for the elevator.

NetOps had hacked the touchscreen, adding a destination labeled 'Secret Illegal Research Facility' below the basement. *That's got 'Joey' written all over it.* She whirled to face the door and jabbed a finger into the screen, barely holding back enough not to shatter the glass.

Soon, the elevator doors opened to a lounge-like room with two purple couches, four vendomats, and a wall-mounted holo-screen showing a Gee-ball match. Two mirror-finished disc bots as big as dinner plates scooted back and forth over pristine white tiles, cleaning the floor. The same repetitive *bang bang bang* noise she'd heard over the comm link grew louder the farther she walked. She followed the sound of activity into a hallway leading out from the front right corner and strode past five offices and a conference room to a pinned-open double glass sliding security door.

She stopped short at the sight waiting for her.

Four Division 9 field operatives stood around a large room with medium-sized primate cages, four-foot cubes built into the left and right walls, stacked two rows high like tiny jail cells. Rhesus monkeys occupied four of them, as well as a lone black chimpanzee. The remaining non-empty cages contained dirt-smeared human children, ranging in age from around five to maybe ten, all of whom looked malnourished. A plastiboard box on a silver table at the center of the room held a mound of stained, ratty clothing that stank to the point a street vagrant would scoff at it. Next to it sat a pile of police-style zip cuffs, all cut open.

Myofiber muscles in Nina's arms shivered with imperceptible trembles of anger as she imagined the children being carried in, cut free, stripped, and stuffed into cages one after the next like god damned research monkeys.

In the first cage, left wall top row, a tiny blonde girl of about six lay on her back, stomping both feet against the bars of her cube-shaped prison, while screeching like the animal they'd treated her as. The cage had little reaction to her assault, though a hanging water bottle had already been shaken halfway empty. Next to her in the adjacent pen, a girl a year or two older with dark hair cowered, trembling, against the inner wall, back to the room and trying to cover herself as much as she could. The remaining six were all boys. Some sat like lumps where they'd been dropped, morose expressions of acceptance on their faces; the youngest sobbed, but tried to stay quiet. The oldest, a sandy-brown haired boy of about ten, knelt in the center of his cage, both hands covering his crotch, and stared at the Division 9 team with a look of guarded hostility.

A cabinet on the wall to the left of the kicking girl's cage held sedative autoinjectors and a five-foot pole mount. The scientists likely used it to spear the larger primates in their cages without having to open them, but the mere thought that some labcoat might use that stick to tranquilize a trapped child fighting against whatever they'd try to do to them made her knuckles creak.

She took a second to center herself with the reassurance that they'd prevented the worst-case scenario. *At least they're all still alive.*

One of the Division 9 agents fiddled with a little black device connected by wires to the electronic lock on the angry girl's cage. Nina figured him for Sanchez, even from behind. He seemed frustrated and poked and slapped the component in his hands.

The girl howled louder, pummeling her feet back and forth into the bars. She wheezed and gasped for air, as though she expected to drop dead if she didn't escape in the next thirty seconds.

"Sanchez." Nina walked up to him, catching a whiff of sour awfulness from the box of clothes: sewer, vomit, and urine. She almost considered they'd been stripped to *improve* their comfort, but seeing them all still dirt-smeared made it clear the scientists thought of them only as animals, expendable creatures they could do whatever they wanted with.

Taken by a spike of rage, Nina ripped the tranq cabinet off the wall and smashed it to the floor, sending green autoinjectors scattering over the floor. The loud *smash* of thin plastisteel stunned the field team in their tracks. The children all went quiet and watched her. The little blonde girl stilled. After a few seconds more of staring, she lowered her feet from the bars and sat up.

Nina's presence, the raw fury wafting from her eyes, caused the kids all to shy away... except for the blonde girl. She crawled closer, grabbed the bars, and pressed her face to them. A boy on the opposite side whispered to his neighbor, speaking Russian. An echo of his words followed in English at the back of her mind.

"Are they going to kill us now?"

The black-haired, maybe eight-year-old, boy didn't reply, his gaze locked square on Nina.

"Sorry, Lieutenant. I'm trying to get this open as fast as I can, but they've got some serious crypto here. It's separate from the network. Self-contained. You'd think they were teaching the monkeys how to hack security codes..."

As if on cue, the chimpanzee snorted.

The filthy, savage girl kicked the bars again before slapping them a few times and grunting, out of breath. She locked terrified blue eyes with Nina's. Droplets from her battered water bottle fell in trickles down her body, collecting dirt, and dripping black onto the lining pad below the cage floor. The girl looked as though she hadn't had a decent meal in months: her ribs were prominent, her hips and legs bony and bruised. Red marks on her wrists and ankles suggested she hadn't much cared for being restrained. Finger-shaped bruises on both her upper arms filled Nina with the need to hit someone, but those marks could've come from the Citizen Management officers who'd arrested the child.

Growling, the girl grabbed the bars and tried to rattle the door, but couldn't budge it. She seemed to sense Nina had come to help them, and her wild expression teased at a nervous smile. A whine escaped from her nose, the tone imploring, her expression asked Nina how people could do this to her.

"*Pozhaluysta otkroyte.*" The girl leaned her face between two bars, her voice fell to a pleading whisper. "*Pozhaluysta.*"

The ghostly child voice in the back of her head echoed, "Please open... please."

"Get someone in here with some god damned blankets." Nina pushed Sanchez aside, grasped the bars, and switched to Russian. "Back up, sweetie. We will not harm you. I'm going to get you out of there." The language came courtesy of a neuronal chip, a cortical copy of someone else's knowledge that after so many months felt no different from having learned it.

The girl startled, gawking at Nina as if shocked someone could speak. She scooted away, fingers and toes gripping the floor of the cage like a feral thing ready to pounce and sprint at the first chance. Waist-long hair, frizzed up into a lion's mane added to the effect. The transition in the eyes staring up at her, from abject terror to hope, made Nina sick, wondering what horrible things the girl had seen back home, and how terrifying it must be to not understand anything one's captors said.

Nina clenched her fingers around the bars. A quick tug snapped the plastisteel door from its hinges with a loud *pank,* and sent a blast of sparks spewing from the electronic lock panel. She rotated left and handed the door to Sanchez, who grabbed it before thinking and staggered to the side as the unexpected weight dragged him down to his knees.

"How did you do that?" whispered the child, crawling up to the open edge. "What are you?"

Three of the boys behind Nina, on the opposite wall, thrust their arms out between the bars of their enclosures, all hollering to be let out next. From what they yelled, some of which consisted of slang her chip missed, they all understood they were to be used for medical tests, and expected to die in their cages, never having been let out again.

Nina reached in and grasped the girl by the armpits, lifting her into a delicate embrace. The child clamped on, trembling. "I was hurt very badly, and they had to give me a new body so I didn't die." She looked toward the others, struggling to keep her mood out of her voice. "Please stay calm. We are here to help. I know you've all grown up scared of the police, but you are not in Europe anymore. You are safe now."

"I'm not a lab monkey, I'm Elizaveta," murmured the girl. The former ball of rage sniffled. "They were going to be mean to us, yes? To make us sick and see if their medicines work? To test the doctor machines. Treat us like mice in boxes." Her grip tightened. "Thank you for saving us. I don't want to die."

"Don't be frightened, Elizaveta." Nina patted the girl's back in an attempt to be comforting.

A woman in Division 1 armor holding a grey blanket open to receive approached.

Nina found it oddly difficult to want to let go of the girl, and the child's death grip didn't make it easier. "Can you speak any English?"

"No. What will happen to us?"

"It's okay, Elizaveta. This woman will keep you safe."

Elizaveta clung tighter and whined. Nina held her for a moment more, as the shouting from the boys grew louder and more insistent. The somewhat older girl in the next space kept quiet, staring ashamedly at the floor of her cage.

"Come on, sweetie. I have to get the others out, and I can't do that with you hanging on me."

Elizaveta trembled. After a bit of coaxing, Nina managed to hand her into the blanket-grip of the patrol officer. Burritoed in the warm fabric except for her head, the child peered at her, again seeming fearful. "What will they do to us now?"

"You'll be taken to a *real* doctor who will make sure you are healthy, then given to proper families here. We are not going to send you back to Europe."

Elizaveta bit her lip and rested her head against the armored shoulder of the woman holding her. She stared into Nina's soul as the officer carried her toward the corridor leading to the elevators. A second before they disappeared past the archway, the child raised a hand to wave.

I'm going to be seeing that poor kid in my dreams for the rest of my life.

Nina turned back to the next cage and grabbed the bars. The dark-haired girl continued to try to become part of the inner wall. She whimpered as she tried to keep herself covered with her arms. At the *pank* of the bolts failing, the child looked over her shoulder, her face bright red with shame. Nina hurled the cage door like a Frisbee, embedding it into a cabinet of electronic equipment.

The second girl remained quiet and still.

"Come on, sweetie," said Nina in Russian. "You don't belong in a cage."

She whimpered and made eye contact, but still didn't move.

"What's your name? I'm Nina. It's all right... you don't have anything to be afraid of anymore."

The perhaps eight-year-old kept staring at her, ignoring Nina's continued attempts to be comforting and coax her out, until a man in blue Division 1 armor brought over a waiting blanket. She inched backward a little and hid her face against her knees, remaining curled in a tight ball as Nina reached in, lifted her out, and handed her to the officer. Her hair reeked with a mixture of mossy earth and sewer.

"You're safe now," whispered Nina in Russian. "No one is going to hurt you."

As soon as the officer closed the blanket around her, the girl seemed to relax a little. She gathered the cloth tight at her chin and whispered, "Polina," before she burst into tears. The man carried the bawling girl out to the elevator lobby.

One by one, Nina tore the doors away from the cages, getting angrier and angrier. The field team scurried to find a place to stand clear of fifty-pound square shuriken flying about. By the fifth broken cage, the boys practically came out clinging to the doors, jumping to freedom as soon as they could fit. Sanchez had disappeared down an interior hallway, muttering something about not being needed here anymore. Nina freed Dimitri, Fedor, Ivan, Josef, and a five-year-old who seemed too terrified to speak. Pavel, the oldest, waited for Nina to clear the door and hopped down from his second-story perch to stand in front of his former prison, fists on his hips in the pose of a conquering hero.

"I am glad I do not have to kill you all." His bravado lasted all of three more seconds before another officer wrapped him in a plain grey police-issue blanket, and the tears came. "The police always lie. A-are you lying again? Are we really free?"

Nina grasped his shoulder and gave him a comforting squeeze. "You're really free."

He reached up and put his hand atop hers. "Thank you."

Operative Padilla approached after the officer carried Pavel out of the room. The chimpanzee screeched and slapped the bars, tilting its head at Nina with an expectant look. She seethed at the box of dingy clothes, a few small moldy sneakers, and one teddy bear that looked as though it had spent months in a sewer. She found herself transfixed on the pathetic stuffed animal.

"What happened to the staff?" asked Nina.

"Lieutenant." Padilla gestured at one of two hallways going deeper into the facility. "We've detained five individuals. We have two others in a separate conference room who had apparently suffered an attack of conscience. The woman's story is that as soon as they saw their new test subjects were human children and not actual primates, they attempted to stop it. When persuasion failed, it got violent. The woman suffered a non-fatal gunshot wound; the man is still unconscious from being hit over the head by a fire suppression unit."

Nina picked up the bear, staring into its plastic eyes. An air of moldy must exuded from its matted, crusty fur. *Every god damned day I see something worse than the last. Maybe Shinigami was right... we are all just circling the drain.* 「Hardin... are you getting this?」

Her immediate superior appeared in a virtual holo-panel courtesy of her electronic eyes. Pasty, but military-hardened face, tight curly brown hair looking like a dead beaver draped over his head. 「 「I am. Unbelievable. Are you okay?」

「I want Osiris Biotechnic shut down. If this doesn't warrant a dissolution order, I don't know what would. Fucking *cages*, sir. Like god damned chimps.」

「That'll be a month of inquest hearings, but, you're right.」 Virtual-Hardin sighed at the mountain of paperwork waiting for him, his expression grim. Brown caterpillar eyebrows rose together. 「 Oh, there's someone from Zero trying to contact you.」

Operative Padilla, unable to hear the back-channel communication, cleared her throat. "Lieutenant? Is everything okay?"

"If you have to ask that, you haven't been looking at what's going on here." Nina tossed the desiccated stuffed animal atop the pile of foul-smelling clothes.

Before Nina could think 'who is it?' back over the head-comm to Hardin, a commotion got her attention from the rear hallway.

Additional field team agents, all clad head to toe in black operator suits, their faces covered, escorted five handcuffed scientists in sky blue lab coats over business casual. A frightened woman in her mid-twenties with tan skin and dark hair kept her head down, mumbling repetitively. In front of her, a somewhat older woman with pale skin and brown hair maintained a haughty look of detachment, as though she expected the company lawyers to sort it all out within the hour. Ahead of the women walked three men, the farthest thirtyish and Chinese, the next a pale, gaunt, dweebish man who couldn't stop trembling. An annoyed fifty-something with a perfect neat coif of white-grey hair led the group in single file. She recognized him from the vid call.

"You're overstepping!" yelled Doctor Rice. "You're interrupting vital research! This is going to harm all of humanity. It is exceedingly unlikely that any of the subjects would have suffered any lasting detriment to their health. I'd be happy to show you the testing documentation if you don't believe me. They will merely be exposed to various pathogens and cured, or used to evaluate surgical techniques that *will* save countless lives once we perfect them. At worst, they'll have some mild scar tissue and perhaps some light nerve damage."

Nina stormed around the large central table and got in the way of the prisoner escort. "You put *children* in cages. Children who'd probably watched the ACC kill everyone they'd known."

Doctor Rice struggled at his handcuffs while trying to stick out his chin, searching for some modicum of dignity. "Yes, yes. Resistance. They should consider themselves fortunate not to have been killed over there. I'm afraid the whole thing came together on short notice and this was the best solution in the interim."

She glared at him, fists creaking tighter.

He offered a shocked blink. "What? Thanks to those bleeding-heart activists, primates have more legal protection than foreign children. Besides, they're a closer analog for the cures we're trying to find. They're about the same size as chimpanzees. If we tried to use monkeys, we'd have a thousand university students outside at all hours singing and waving little candles at us."

Nina tried to melt one of the empty cages with a stare.

He sighed. "Security is a factor—we can't have them carrying pathogens out into the world—and these conditions *are* better than what they had been living in." He tried to gesture, but the binders clicked. "Think about all we could have done for the advancement of medicine. Our schedule had seventy-four pathogens and fourteen experimental surgical procedures. Is 'ethics' worth tens of thousands of lives? These test subjects would've been shot in the street if not for our purchasing them. Osiris money *saved* them. Surely, you see the benefits far outweigh the negatives? Is it *that* distasteful for a handful of throwaways no one will miss to suffer a few years of discomfort for unimaginable advancements in—"

The man's voice needled Nina's brain beyond rational thought. She grabbed Doctor Rice by the shoulder and jerked him over sideways, slamming him downward with every ounce of anger and strength she could force out of her Myofiber muscles. The edge of the table met him at the neck, causing his skull to stop while the rest of his body continued to the floor. His head liquefied on impact with a dull *whump* that left a crimpled dent in the metal. The decapitated body's arms continued twitching for several seconds, rattling the binders around his wrists.

Operative Padilla, on the other side of the table, wound up covered in a spray of gore. One eyeball with a squiggle of nerve clung to her chest, which she flicked to the side.

"Holy shit," whispered Sergeant Cooper.

"Damn." Sergeant Romero whistled. "I don't think a Narcoderm's gonna dent *that* headache."

Nina glared at the remaining four scientists. "Would anyone else like to attempt to justify what you people were doing?"

The nerdy man and the younger of the two women urinated. The fortyish woman passed out, draping limp in the arms of the field agent escorting her.

"Y-You c-can't do that," stammered the Chinese man. "You k-killed him."

Nina fixated on the dark crimson depression in the mirror-like table. Blood pooled in the indentation, gooping over the side drop by drop. "The only reason I'm not performing a summary execution on all of you is so you can provide testimony about what was going on here during a dissolution inquest. Osiris Biotechnic has forfeited its right to exist." She snapped her gaze to him. "All of you will provide complete and true disclosure of everything that happened and everything that was going to happen to those children." A long blank stare came back at her. "Or I'll just save everyone the circle jerk and wasted time right now."

He babbled. "But... But..."

"This is a Division 9 investigation. You don't *have* rights. You don't even count as a human fucking being anymore." She grabbed him by the lab coat. After a half-second of serious consideration to cramming him into a monkey cage, she flung him at the hallway out with enough force to launch him off his feet. He sailed through the air, landed on his chest, and slid for a little farther before his legs hit the ground. "Get him out of here."

The field team picked him up and hurried away with the other detainees.

Operative Padilla looked down at her dripping suit and back up at Nina. "What about the other two?"

"The dissenters?" Nina clenched a trembling fist for a few seconds until her rage ebbed. "Consider them cooperating witnesses instead of suspects unless they give you a reason to do otherwise." She turned away from Padilla, scowling at the cages. 「You said something about Zero?」

The chimpanzee slapped the bars and howled. It pointed at her, pointed at the bars, and... smiled.

Four medtechs entered, trailing a pair of hover-gurneys behind them. Pale yellow light spots followed the floating stretchers down the back hallway amid the clatter of boots.

"Heh. He almost seems smart." Nina chuckled to herself.

Hardin's virtual face tinted green from the left side. ⌜Yes, Zero. That one you worked with on the moon. Agent Wren. She said she has an important message about something you'd asked her to look into.⌟

The chimpanzee gave her two thumbs up and tapped its head.

She blinked. "Don't tell me you know what I'm saying?"

It nodded, patted the bars, and made a praying gesture with its hands.

Nina twisted around to look at the rhesus monkeys on the other side of the room. They appeared to be acting like rhesus monkeys, oblivious to what went on in the room. Again, she glanced at the chimpanzee. "You understand English." It nodded. *I'm... wow. Whatever.* "Fine. Someone please deal with this... umm... creature." She popped the door off the cage and heaved it aside. It hit the ground with a heavy *thud* that rumbled in the floor.

The chimpanzee lowered itself out of the enclosure, ambled over to the table, and picked up a datapad. Within a few seconds, it had opened a word processing app, and typed, ‹I am Francis. I have extra brain parts. Electronic. I am not dangerous.›

"What will they do next?" Nina shook her head.

Francis flipped the datapad back to look at it, typed, and spun it around for her to see again. ‹Why humans put small humans in cage?›

"Greed."

More typing. ‹Evil. May I leave too? Do not like this place.›

Nina grabbed a random field operative and glanced at his chest. "Sergeant Cooper, please do something with"—she gestured at the chimpanzee—"Francis. Bring him to the university or something." ⌜Go ahead, sir. Patch her through.⌟

Francis gave a thumbs-up, tucked the datapad under his arm, and reached up with his other hand to hold Cooper's.

She paced around the table twice before needing to get far away from the box of fetid clothes, and headed to the 'lounge' by the elevators. The air hung thick with the smell of 'child,' but none remained, all likely en route to the nearest Amaranth medical building. The more time she spent with Division 9, the less idyllic her view of the UCF became. Things seemed a lot more like the police state the fringers claimed, but at least when it came to children, the government tended to bend over backwards and spare no expense. *Coddle the kids and they become loyal citizens I guess.* Still, police state or not, it beat starving in the sewers of Minsk, or whatever other cities they'd been rounded up in. ACC security forces tended to deal with dissidents in a rather ham-handed faction. *Damn miracle they'd survived at all.*

She closed her eyes, letting anger and sorrow wash over her. *Maybe I should've listened to Dad. If I knew what kind of shit I'd see in this job... Every damn time it gets worse. Soul-eating.* Nina stared up at flickering overhead lights that cast the lab in a baleful glow as though they drained the life out of everything they touched. *Can something go right for once? Can I feel like I am making some difference?*

「Nina!」 The smiling blonde, blue-eyed Division o agent appeared in another small virtual window, this one dead center in her vision and high. With only a bust to look at, the woman could pass for a young teenager. Her bright expression and naïve idealism didn't help that either. 「Sorry if this is a bad time, you look pissed... Uhh, you told me to let you know if any ghosts told me about, uhh...」

Though on an intellectual level, she knew her 'heart' was a mechanical device circulating blood for her living brain and spinal cord, Nina's body gave her the sense of it racing, pulse pounding in her head. *So easy to forget what I've become sometimes.* 「You... found *him*?」

Agent Kirsten Wren, Division o, I-Ops, bowed her head. 「I've got a spirit next to me who says she was killed five weeks ago by a huge aug with a curved blade for a right hand and a giant hammer for a left.」」

「The Russian.」 The walls closed in around her. Nina couldn't stand another instant of being in this place... of not racing off to find the man who'd almost killed her, the man who *had* killed her life, and her Vincent. 「Where is he?」

「Stardance said he wasn't Russian.」 Kirsten glanced left, muttering to someone. 「He was... singing something like Italian.」

Nina thought about the case file from the Division 2 detective who'd been killed trying to catch him. The suspect had a thing for classical music. Belted out opera sometimes while eviscerating prostitutes. She shifted her focus to Hardin's panel, her intention limiting outbound to only him. 「I've gotta deal with something.」 She opened the channel to Kirsten again. 「He isn't. It's his street name. Hammer and sickle. Real name's Bertrand Foster.」

「Nina...」 The corner of Hardin's lip tightened to a smirk. 「If you want this disillusion proceeding to hold, we've got to be thorough.」 His voice lowered, more 'sympathetic parental figure' than commander. ⌜I understand what you have to do, and won't stand in your way; if you can get that psycho, go for it... but those kids deserve your full attention first.⌋

⌜Wren, what's the situation? Can that woman find him at will, or are we looking at a limited window?⌋ Nina shivered with restlessness, but wandered back into the room full of cages.

"It's kids," muttered Sanchez to the blood-soaked Padilla, evidently assuming Nina had left. "All the chick doll operatives get like that with cases like this since they can't have any. Don't take it personally."

"Working on a psych degree in your spare time, Sanchez?" Nina glanced at him. "Maybe you should work a little more on your network skills so you can open a basic fucking lock."

Padilla stiffened, unable to make eye contact with her.

The room got quiet. Sanchez looked down. The field team got back to tearing the place apart file by file, room by room. Beyond the lab, two hallways full of offices and a dorm still waited.

Nina tried not to let her *need* to run off and find Bertrand result in rushing what she had to do here. She opened a playback window; her systems kept a continuous recording of the past two hours, more if she enabled extended logging. From it, she isolated a still close-up of the desperate, pleading face Elizaveta had given her as soon as the girl had realized Nina could speak to her. She left the 'please let me out of here' picture open in the corner of her sight for motivation and to take her mind off Bertrand. ⌜Ops, send a cleanup team over to the Osiris Biotech tower to scrape up Drummond. I want D1 there in the morning to detain everyone in the building until we find out who exactly was involved with this project.⌋

"Diaz and Simpson," said Padilla, "Do a complete clone process on Price's terminal. Hines, Romero, and Cooper, with me." She headed down the left hallway, deeper into the facility.

⌜Even their food service people?⌋ asked a man, on a voice-only channel.

⌜Does *anyone* have a brain? Osiris employees only. Leave the contractors alone.⌋ Nina glowered. Elizaveta's picture kept her from storming out.

The medtechs reappeared, pulling out a semiconscious man and woman hooked up to gel sleeves to perform field-repairs on bullet wounds. Peach-hued goo flowed through clear hoses with a constant, repeating *squish-click-hiss* from small pumps.

Kirsten finished a whispered conversation with thin air. ⌜She says she can find him whenever you want, but she's not the most patient spirit I've met.⌟

Nina patted the nearest medtech on the shoulder. "Thanks." She looked at Kirsten's avatar. ⌜This'll take a while. I'll vid you as soon as I can. Oh, and tell that ghost I know exactly how she feels.⌟

FOUR HOURS LATER, NINA CROSSED THE MAIN CONCOURSE OF THE Police Administrative Center, heading for the Division o wing. Psychobabble rattled around her head about how the communication barrier between the scientists and the non-English-speaking orphans made it easier for them to treat human beings as lab animals. As much as she couldn't sit still anticipating finally tracking down Bertrand after almost two years, she'd ordered a replacement teddy (fluffy and white) and stopped by the Amaranth hospital where the children were under observation. Her guess proved right; the rotting bear had belonged to Elizaveta, who lit up at the sight of its replacement.

Of the eight, only she and Pavel seemed unafraid of her. At first, she'd assumed the others feared she might hurt them after witnessing her display of anger and hurling cage doors, but Elizaveta had whispered the truth—they feared her position as a government police officer. None of them wanted to go back to jail. Despite Nina's best attempt at projecting sincerity while explaining they were safe in the UCF, the children proved slow to trust, so she'd kept her visit short enough to verify they'd all been declared healthy. The doctors wanted to keep them a few days on nutrient-supplement IVs and run them through psychological evaluations.

In a scary-calm tone, Elizaveta explained she'd seen people shot and die before, and wouldn't be upset if the same thing happened to the 'bad doctors' who'd put her in a cage. Nina had left it at telling her Doctor Rice had a skull-splitting headache. Still, the memory of the child's imploring blue-eyed stare refused to leave her mind. The scrawny six-year-old blonde looked much happier in a clean hospital bed, but couldn't hide her fear at what would happen to her. Being orphaned would've been frightening enough to a girl her age without being sent across the world and treated like an animal for lab testing.

Nina clenched her fists, wanting to kill Dr. Rice all over again.

The squeak of elevator doors brought her thoughts back to the present. Amid a sea of identical black patrol craft with narrow, clear bar lights on the roof, Kirsten stood waiting for her, flanked on either side by a faint thermal anomaly. The one closer and on her right registered fifty-two degrees, six colder than the other.

Kirsten pushed away from her car and stood as Nina approached. "Lieutenant."

"Agent." Nina glanced at the exit ramp leading up to street level, five lanes with security booths across. "Thank you. You're sure this is him?"

A faint noise, warbling, hinting at a feminine voice but too weak to form words, caused a sensation like muscles Nina didn't have in her neck tensed.

Kirsten looked at the less intense cold spot. She held her hand as high as she could reach to indicate someone huge, then relaxed and sighed with annoyance. "Sorry I'm short. He's... wow." She nodded at nothing before looking to Nina. "'Bout seven feet tall or so. Two cybernetic arms double the size of a normal person's, chest full of metal, mohawk, sword and a hammer for hands?"

"Wonder how he touches himself." A man's voice picked at the edges of Nina's electronic ears, sounding a hundred yards away yet speaking at a normal tone.

Kirsten's face went bright red. "Dorian!"

Nina couldn't find a scrap of humor under the weight on her heart, synthetic as it may be. "Yeah. That's him."

"Stardance is extremely angry." Kirsten grimaced. "That man... well. Be glad you can't see what he did to her."

Phantom burning pain speared into Nina's lower back. "I can guess. I got a real close look once. Tell her I'm sorry she's dead and I survived."

Ephemeral warbling.

Kirsten shot a scolding look at the non-space to her left. "That's not it at all... She'd already called in. Her backup was already on the way there *before* she got hurt. It's not that she was a cop and you're poor that..." She nodded at something. "Ready? She's angry enough to feel where he is."

"I've been ready for eighteen months." Nina walked around to the passenger side door.

A man's grumbling seemed to pass by her on the way to the back seat.

Kirsten half-smiled, seeming also subdued by the somber topic.

Nina stared off into space, watching images of that night play across her mind as the car rolled up and out of the garage before taking flight. A dark alley lit in shades of metallic blue, the vendomat flying, useless bullets striking a chest covered in two layers of subdermal armor. As long as she'd carried her MCP50, with 15mm slugs more than double the diameter of

MAESTRO'S REQUIEM | 299

the 6mm ammo her old Division 1 duty pistol had, she *still* had a mental hang up about guns. Despite the enormity of her Class 6 hand cannon, she expected it to bounce off whatever she pointed it at.

Buildings glided by on either side of the car. The occasional feminine murmur in the air came from the back seat. Every so often, a recognizable "left" or "there" came across in whisper.

"I can go in with you if you want." asked Kirsten. "Star's a little angry at me for making her wait for you."

"You know all those rumors you hear about Division 9?"

Kirsten looked over. "Yeah."

"I'm about to live up to them." Nina glanced through her reflection on the video display serving as a window at a decaying skyscraper. "Should've figured he'd be in a disavowed sector. Tell her thank you for waiting."

"She can hear you." Kirsten mumbled "yeah" at the back seat. "She understands."

The Navcon display on the dashboard showed the little yellow arrow indicating the patrol craft crossing into a blacked-out area of the map.

"From what Stardance's saying, this guy's more machine than human. I could flatten him with one mind blast." Kirsten cringed, bit her lip, and shrank in on herself. "Oh, crap. I'm sorry..."

"It's okay. I know what you mean." Nina tapped two fingers on the handle above the door in a repetitive motion, trying to be meditative.

Kirsten looked forward, and made a sudden descending left that came within a second of more murmuring from behind. "I know how that sounded. Thanks for not being freaked out that I have that power."

Nina spoke in a flat tone, her thoughts frozen on Vincent's last seconds of life. "Right back at you. Most normals look at me like I'm going to twist them in half if they breathe too much of my air."

"Great, so you could both kill each other without any effort. Fantastic." A 'clap' sounded right behind Nina's head.

Nina couldn't help but half-smile. "Heh."

Kirsten looked at her. "Did you just hear Dorian?"

"My ears are digital, remember? And sensitive. Guess that EVP stuff is true. The girl's indecipherable though."

Female murmuring, louder, and tinged with emotion came from the back seat.

"She's a lot younger as a ghost. She said he's in that alley." Kirsten gave her a mournful look. "Are you sure you don't want backup?"

The air by Nina's left shoulder got cooler as the man's voice returned. "She needs to do this."

"You probably won't want to watch." Nina looked out and down. "Which alley?"

Kirsten pointed at a gap between two buildings little more than steel skeletons with nuggets of concrete still clinging in spots. Holes in the floor slabs made it seem possible for someone to fall from the top story to the ground given a few lucky bounces on the way. Old furniture rotted in place, some hidden by tattered plastic sheeting hung by squatters attempting to live out here. Some of the upper levels had active campfires, and it had only been dark for twenty minutes.

"Descend to about forty feet, and I'll hop out."

"Okay. I'll hang back here. If you need me, just comm and we'll come running." Kirsten brought the car down to the level of the fourth floor.

Murmuring.

"What did she say?" Nina pushed the gull wing door on her side up, letting in a blast of warm, humid, garbage-laden air.

"She said she's going to watch and doesn't care if you don't want her to."

Nina looked at the back seat, focusing in on the warmer of the two cold spots. "No, that's fine with me. Come on. You deserve this too."

She jumped out, falling thirty-eight feet onto the top of a large boxy trash crusher. Myofiber muscles in her legs and back absorbed the force of the landing, imparting a slight dent to the surface of the cube, and sent a resounding *boom* up and down the alley. Pigeons exploded from everywhere, and a vagrant emitted a startled, drunken shout.

Nina stood, took one step, and dropped to the plastisteel ground without a noise. The cold spot hovered nearby. "I can't understand you when you talk, but I can see where you're standing because you're cold. Lead the way."

Feminine murmuring lasted three seconds before the amorphous area of chill drifted off into the alley. Nina followed at a brisk walk. A few Frags poked out of garbage piles or plastiboard cartons to give her curious stares. Most of the time, her body looking, feeling, and behaving so close to still-normal human was amazing, the only thing sometimes that kept her going. Two-point-three miles into the center of a black zone however, her slender, athletic looks and 'cute' French nose were the opposite of helpful.

She heard Joey's voice say 'cute' to describe her nose. She hadn't told him about this side trip yet. He'd have tried to talk her out of it, or wanted to come and help. More likely come and help... *Damn adrenaline junkie. No, Bertie, you're not killing another man I love.*

Three Frags, one with a cybernetic arm, emerged from the building on her left, assuming her a 'rich bitch' who'd gotten lost. It didn't seem to strike them as strange that she walked *deeper* into the black, and didn't look the least bit afraid. Their expressions promised at best rape and robbery, and at worst, murder.

As soon as the first man got within grabbing distance, Nina spun around and palmed his face in her right hand. She whirled into a kick at Metal-Arm as she hurled the first man headfirst into the ground. His skull burst like a rotten cantaloupe on impact; the other man crumpled over her leg like a bag of jelly and fish bones. The third man had barely registered the event in his expression by the time she'd recovered her stance and faced him.

He managed to suck in a breath to scream before she drove a palm strike into his sternum to avoid putting her fist in him to the elbow. A crunching squish emanated from his torso; he slapped to the ground on his back, legs in the air, and slid thirty feet before vanishing under a mound of debris. The pile of appliances, furniture, and random shit someone threw out of the adjacent skyscraper shifted and collapsed forward, burying him deeper.

That'll either scare the other eleven watching off, or they'll be back with missiles. Humanoid thermal signatures in the dark faded out as people scattered.

Nina whirled in search of the cold spot. It took a moment to find, and she jogged after it once she did. Three quarters of a block down on the left, firelight flickered out of a wide alley strewn with dead cars. Recognizable gouges from a curved vibro blade suggested Bertrand had set them up on their sides as a barricade.

She wandered through the improvised gate, and emerged in a section of alley that dead-ended in the hollow of a U-shaped building. The road descended a slight gradient to a loading dock, upon which sat the trappings of a crude 'apartment,' furniture made from scraps of whatever had been salvaged from the nearby towers.

A momentary fit of 'frightened little girl' panic froze her in her tracks at the sight of the man who, eighteen months ago, had killed her. The doctors, her superiors in Division 9, even her mother told her she hadn't died... but they didn't know what she meant. Nina Duchenne, the twenty-five-year-old idealist, died face-down in an alley an arm's length away from the man she'd wanted to marry.

Bertrand Foster, seven feet and change tall when he didn't slouch, hovered over a barrel-turned-grill. Legs, big by any male standard, seemed ridiculously thin compared to his torso. A mass of segmented steel tubes descended like dreadlocks from the back of his head, curving around and into the center of his back. Bulbous metal shoulders glinted in the orange firelight. Both of his cybernetic arms hung down to his knees; tiny (normal-human-sized) metal fingers unfolded from the side of the hammer, which had replaced his left hand. Rubberized hoses swayed from it, lines powering the hydraulic ram that could drive the striking head forward to pulverize.

For months, this man had been the star in her nightmares, and despite *knowing* her new body was more than capable of tearing him apart, the sight of him paralyzed her with the need to flee, to get away from him as far and fast as possible.

He painstakingly manipulated a large outdoor grill fork with his clumsy hammer-fist, turning bits of meat over on a grating. Faint music, something ancient and classical, leaked from earphones on either side of a head that sported a ten-inch lime green mohawk. Bertrand waved the fork about like a conductor's baton, leaning back and swaying as the music took him. His body shuddered, arms raised as if the ratty collection of bed, chairs, and small table were a prestigious orchestra giving the performance of their lives.

"Nina..." whispered Vincent out of her memory.

Fear, panic, and terror swirled. Nina looked down at her pale hands, clenched them to fists, and straightened her posture. Confident. Calm. Ready.

I've wanted to find this piece of shit ever since I finished acclimation training. What am I afraid of? She sighed out her nose. *I've already seen him. I'm going to have a wonderful dream tonight no matter what I do now.*

She walked up to within twelve paces of the gesticulating homicidal conductor. "Hello, Bertrand."

The man froze. His head tilted a few degrees to the right. For a moment, he stood like a statue, the alley silent save for the muted sound of music coming from his headphones. He stepped back with his left boot, still the same armor-covered, spiked thing she remembered on the ground inches from her nose, and faced her.

His huge chin, wide and square, framed giant, blocky teeth outlined in grey rot. His eyes, crude street-tech cybernetics, telescoped six inches away from his skull like old camera lenses. Each glowed deep orange like the coals of a demon's furnace. They whirred, shortening and lengthening as he focused on her.

"You're a hard man to find."

The same bloodthirsty grin he'd flashed the first time he'd seen her returned. She couldn't be sure, but it seemed a degree or two less wide. Perhaps the old, shorter, cuter Nina had been more 'appetizing.' Being short had made most people regard her as someone in need of protection even if they'd been younger than her. Granted, as a Division 1 cop, she *had* been a total failure.

"Remember me, Bertrand?"

The beginnings of a deep, grating chuckle stalled to a grunt of confusion. He reached behind himself to put the fork on the grill, and took a step closer. The glowing spots at the tips of his eye tubes widened as iris doors expanded inside. "You... I... do remember."

A voice she had so long heard in her restless dreams rattled her; deeper than a man should be, slow, over-enunciating every syllable, it belonged to the monster in the closet waiting to devour the part of her brain that still wanted to cling to Nix, her old stuffed rabbit. She didn't let it show, managing to find an amused smile instead.

Bertrand glanced at his hammer arm.

"That's right. I'm back from the dead to take you with me." Nina shook her head. "You didn't quite finish me off. You lost your arm that night, didn't you, Bertie?"

「Nina, are you okay? It's quiet down there.」 Kirsten's head popped in on a small floating holo-pane.

"I think I remember pieces of you landing on me when the explosive round shredded you. Honestly, I'm impressed you walked away from that."

「I'm fine.」

「Copy. Still up here if you need us.」 Kirsten's panel collapsed to a thin blue line, which shrank to one white pixel and disappeared.

"Finish." Bertrand's blade arm emitted a high-pitched scraping noise as the vibro-inducer came to life. "Smash."

"That's what I had in mind." Nina raised her arms. "I should warn you, I'm not the same helpless little thing you remember, but it won't matter. I don't really care what drove you insane. Whoever you were before, he's long gone."

Bertrand lunged forward, raising his hammer arm. Nina's speedware pushed the world into slow motion as she slipped to the right, grabbed his forearm, and jiu-jitsu flipped him over onto his back. He struck the metal ground with enough force to blast dirt and trash away, forming a clear spot six feet across. Time resumed with Bertrand skidding to a halt a few yards away. He let off a confused grunt and scrambled back to his feet. After a momentary bewildered glance at his arm where she'd grabbed, he charged.

He led with the scythe. Nina ducked to the left, letting the whining blade careen over her head. She grabbed his tattered excuse for an olive-drab jacket in both hands and shoved him into the plastisteel wall. The dull *clank* of his impact echoed up into the night, startling another wave of pigeons to wing. The tips of his elongated eyes left crescent-shaped dents in the metal. A pair of Nano claws popped out between the knuckles of her left hand, and she sank the ten-inch transparent blades into the small of his back before giving a twist and yanking them loose.

The synthetic diamond held an edge one atom wide. With the strength of a military-grade doll behind them, they sliced through implanted armor with such ease it felt as though she'd stabbed a block of ballistic gelatin. She meant the strike as a statement, not a kill, and backed away.

Bertrand howled, hooking his sword arm into the building, tearing a three-foot rent with an ear-splitting squelch of hypersonic edge against plastisteel. Roaring in rage, he shoved away from the wall into a spinning backhand with the hammer block. Nina ducked the *whoosh*, and popped back up in time to catch the bladed limb at the wrist.

She kicked at the elbow while pulling with her left hand. Bertrand's cybernetic limb smashed upward, the joint bent and broken past its normal range of motion. While the hit (to her surprise) hadn't torn the limb in half, it brought forth a cry of agony suggesting he'd felt it in his bones where metal grafted to flesh.

"Glorious…" His iris-door-eyes widened as far as they could. "You… I have rebirthed you in perfection."

Nina backed up as he raised one working, and one fused arm skyward.

"I have purged the flesh, and now you are one of us." The orange light in his lenses shifted chromatic. "Yes! *Yes!* You are as I am. The sin of the flesh is lesser with you… daughter."

She let off a furious scream and stomp-kicked him in the chest. Bertrand sailed a few feet back into the wall, denting it. Another tremendous *boom* echoed in the alley, something light and metal clattered to the ground inside the abandoned structure.

"I am *not* your daughter!"

Laughing, Bertrand stumbled into a loping charge and swiped at her with the hammer. She danced back, having little difficulty evading it. As she'd fantasized, this fight played out as one-sided as it had been the last time they met. Only tonight, *she* had all the advantage. She thought about how weak she'd been. Two years and some months as a patrol officer with Division 1, waiting for a transfer to forensics that she'd never get. Caught in some bureaucratic snarl. Killed, her life forever ruined by paperwork.

Bertrand came in again with a backswing. She caught the arm in a braced stance, stopping it cold. After a split-second 'I'm stronger than I look' smile, she spun into a flip and hurled him at the second story wall across the alley. He slapped face-first into false stucco tiles, and fell amid a rain of debris that exposed a patch of plastisteel.

His body hit a dumpster with a loud *whump*, amid his grumbling and growling. He dragged himself to the edge and slid headfirst to the ground, rolling onto his back. With visible effort, he forced himself to his feet again.

Ruined... She stared at the visage of Bertrand Foster, altered cheeks and jaw so large his face had become a parody of humanity, too wide for the top of his head. Saliva oozed between blocky teeth as he gasped for breath. *A version of a life I could have had.* She saw Joey smiling at her, reckless idiot he was, and put a hand on her stomach. *Maybe not ruined... but changed.* This body of Myofiber, silicon, and plastisteel would keep her alive and beautiful for as long as her sanity could hold, but it would never offer her the chance to be a mother. They'd supposedly kept her ovaries before cremating the twisted mess Bertrand had left of her body, but she hadn't been able to bring herself to have them checked. Sanchez's taunt had hurt because it rang true. Given the condition she'd been in, she doubted they'd even be viable.

Whatever adoration he'd shown before, his insanity seemed to shift gears back to 'it's got a vagina, kill it.' He wagged his hammer arm in an attempt to grab the submachine gun he no longer carried.

"Lose something?" asked Nina. "That thirty-mil cannon cause brain damage when it took your meat arm? How are you going to pull a trigger with a solid metal brick?"

Bertrand let off a foam-at-the-mouth, head-shaking roar. Veins in his forehead bulged. He spun, trying to pick up the trash crusher he'd landed on, but his scythe arm, now a fused, inflexible bit of metal, couldn't get a grip on it. Snarling, he whirled to face her and charged.

Nina leaned left to avoid a downstroke, and jumped away from a telegraphed side swing. He reared back in slow motion courtesy of her neuralware. The hoses on his arm all twitched, an insectoid muscle readying for a strike. The hammer head lanced forward on a hydraulic piston, headed for her nose.

She evaded with a quarter turn to the right, allowing the metal to pass three inches away from her face. The instant the *shhthonk* of it slamming out to full extension reached her ears, she grabbed the piston near the head; Nano claws sprouted from her left fist as she raked downward, severing the strut where it met the arm. Dark green hydraulic fluid sprayed in arterial spurts from the hole. Bertrand stared at the missing weapon, a look of horror warping his caricature of a face. On a whim, she brought the disembodied, sparking hammer around and buried it in his large pauldron of a shoulder.

Blue lightning flickered from the smashed armor sphere; his left arm twitched and jerked out of control and he emitted a snarl of pain. She grabbed him by the chest and pulled him down while driving her knee up into his gut; the strike launched blood out of his mouth. While he wheezed for air, she gave him a light shove back that sent him staggering and flailing to keep his balance.

"Payback's a bitch, Bertie... and her name's Nina." She stomped forward and punched him dead in the nose, knocking him flat to the ground in a nanosecond. He bounced ass over head and slammed against the wall, precipitating another waterfall of smashed tiles.

He grunted.

Damn. His entire skull must be plastisteel. A momentary switch of vision mode to metallurgical scan painted the world in black and white. A brilliant white skull showed within his head, a sure sign of it being metal. Medium grey bands highlighted the Myofiber grafts that let him keep his head upright with such weight. Wires in the neck became apparent, as well as the crisscross weave of fibers below the skin, including a flat, featureless groin. A mechanism in his side where urine and waste collected in removable baggies appeared in clear detail a few inches away from an adrenaline / stimulant pump near the kidneys.

Nina switched back to normal sight. While the man's skull might be metal, the brain inside wasn't, and he lay stunned, muttering, and apparently unaware of where he was. She pounced on his chest, grabbed his left arm at the elbow, and curled her right hand into a fist before deploying a pair of Nano claws. As soon as they locked at full extension, she sliced through the bicep. After discarding the severed limb with a casual toss to the side, she severed his smashed vibro-blade arm an inch shy of the shoulder.

"It's a violation of UCF law, Section CI-42 D, for a felon to possess a cybernetic prosthesis with a rating beyond rehabilitative." She chucked the other arm over her shoulder. "Furthermore, it is a violation of Section CI-11 B for a person with diagnosed psychosis to possess any cybernetics with combat capabilities. This includes, but is not limited to strength-enhanced limbs, and"—she punched her hand into his gut, grabbed the adrenal pump along with its nest of tubes, and tore it free—"combat grade boosters. Military spec targeting optics are a no-no as well, even if they're four generations old."

She tossed the bloody box and tubing aside before grasping his lens eyes, one in each hand. Bertrand moaned and squirmed as bloody froth oozed between his teeth.

"I'm afraid I have to confiscate these."

Nina braced a knee against his neck and, with a wrenching twist, snapped both mechanisms away from his skull, yanking a few inches of thin wires out of what he had left of a brain. Bertrand convulsed and drooled even more. He stopped moving, though continued breathing, mouth agape and tongue lolling. She looked over the crude optics for a few seconds before tossing one then the other aside.

"By the power vested in me by the United Coalition Front National Police Force, Division 9"—Nina reached under her coat and pulled her MCP50, before putting the barrel up to Bertrand's forehead—"I pronounce you guilty of the murder of Officer Vincent Montoya, UCF National Police Force, Division 1. Attempted murder of Officer Nina Duchenne, also Division 1, the murder of a prostitute named Stardance, and however many others you've killed, you sick, twisted fuck. For these crimes, you are subject to summary execution."

Boom.

Hot splatter rained over Nina's face. Contrary to her expectation, her massive hand cannon left a hole in the artificial forehead and blasted every ounce of bio matter out the back. She stood, took two steps back, and put seven more rounds into his chest. Azure muzzle flash painted the alley in quick snaps, and the echo-back of rapid gunshots combined into rolling thunder. Not that she could've ever used such a giant handgun before having a doll body, but it made her feel a little better to see seven clean holes.

Headlights washed over her as the Division 0 patrol craft landed a short distance away. Four bulges at the corners opened to allow wheels to unfold and make contact with the ground. A few seconds after touchdown, the bright cyan glow of ion engines faded out from under it.

Nina swapped magazines, reloading her pistol, and holstered it under her left arm before walking over to the car.

Kirsten paused with one leg out of the car, her face ashen while staring past Nina.

"Sorry," said Nina. "I told you not to watch."

"Not you. I've seen way worse than that guy." Kirsten bowed her head in reverence. "Did I ever tell you about Harbingers?"

"I don't think so." Nina took a tissue from her coat pocket and wiped some Bertrand off her face. She looked up with a sudden thought. "Is his ghost here?"

"Yeah... sort of." Kirsten twisted to her right and peered over the car, watching something drift away down the alley. "Not for long though."

An odd calmness became profound for a few seconds before fading.

Nina blinked. "Did something weird just happen?"

Kirsten took a second to collect herself, having choked up. "Stardance said thank you. She's moved on. You gave her the justice she needed. I couldn't have brought myself to kill him unless my life was in direct danger."

"Oh, don't worry. As soon as he got a good look at you, that would've been true." Nina stared at the traction-coated plastisteel at her feet, trying to stop thinking about her last night as a normal person. "He likes them short, cute, and terrified."

"I don't scare that easy." Kirsten nodded toward the patrol craft. "Want a ride back?"

"... crime scene crew... "

Nina looked at where she assumed Dorian to be. "Seriously? Out here?"

Kirsten grinned. "He said 'Not like we're going to call a crime scene crew.'"

"Oh." Nina got into the patrol craft. "Right."

SIX DAYS LATER, NINA SWAYED SIDE TO SIDE, AMUSING HERSELF WITH how her oversized sweatshirt brushed her knees. Three slabs of hydroponic chicken francese sautéed with a soothing hiss. She frowned at her toes and got into the same old debate about feeling silly painting false nails, no matter how real they looked or felt. A butterfly of nervousness swirled around her gut as she worried at the chicken with a spatula.

Crystalline wind chime sound filled her apartment. Nina glanced to her right at the floor-to-ceiling windows looking out over West City; a jagged skyline of black absorbed the deep reds and oranges of dusk. *Wow... he's actually on time.*

Nina patched in to the house computer, linking to the panel out in the hallway by the door. A virtual window popped up showing the corridor, and a weary-looking Joey in his cowboy hat and black trench coat. He'd let his black hair get frizzy and long, too many late nights in NetOps. She opened the lock and sent her voice out via the speaker. "Hey. I'm in the kitchen. Decided to cook tonight."

"Okay, that works…"

Nina took the pan off the heat and eased the three pieces of chicken onto individual plates. She'd about finished doling out pasta and pouring more of the sauce over it when Joey walked into the kitchen, eyebrow raised, thumb cocked back over his shoulder.

"What's up with the critter on the couch?" He sidled up behind her and threaded his arms around her.

Nina smiled at the food. "Her name is Elizaveta."

"*Privet,*" said a tiny voice from the doorway behind Joey. "*Eto vash muzh?*"

"Bad case. I picked her up this afternoon. I'll be fostering her… maybe more than that if things work out. She doesn't speak any English yet." She set the pan on a cool burner and turned around to kiss Joey. After, she smiled at the clean straight-haired girl in a neat white dress and purple-painted toenails, switching to Russian. "I have not married him… yet. Maybe I will." Nina winked.

The girl flashed a conspiratorial grin as she padded into the kitchen.

He took off his hat and coat, giving the child a narrow-eyed stare like a gunfighter about to draw on his nemesis. Long hair and a couple days without shaving left him looking more like a pirate captain than a cowboy. "Is it housebroken?"

Elizaveta climbed into her seat, wide eyed at the food. She looked up with complete shock on her face. "*Eto vse dlya menya?*"

"Yes it's all yours. Don't hurt yourself, but as much as you can finish," said Nina in Russian before smirking at Joey as she joined them at the table. "I know you're trying to be cute but… can you skip the animal comparisons for now. You heard about Osiris?"

He cringed and slithered into a chair. "Crap. She's one of *those* kids? Wow, I'm fried. I saw those files… Spent the past week balls-deep in Osiris's neuroprocessor cluster array. Didn't recognize her cleaned up." He watched her eat for a moment before a look of recognition appeared on his face. "Oh yeah, the aggressive little bugger who kept kicking the door." Joey shoveled a forkful of chicken and pasta into his mouth, chewing with exaggerated "mmm" sounds. "Oh, damn. This is great."

"First time trying this… Just simple instructions." She nibbled on hers. "Damn corporations… kidnapping across the ocean. What next?"

Elizaveta shoveled forkful after forkful in her mouth.

"Their whole system is more akin to the capitalist runaway that occurred in the years leading up to the war. Most of their population is shit poor, but the corporations over there are still concerned about bad PR. Odd to say it, but they'd be *less* likely to do something this scummy." He sighed, staring down. "They'd sooner just kill them and blame the resistance, or I guess they were too small to be thought of as a threat. Probably would've sent them to Mars to bolster a colony."

ACC Mars... Nina cringed. *They were safer in the cages. It's a damn mess up there.*

He chuckled under his breath. "So you wanted to keep one? No consult?"

Elizaveta whined, staring at about half a plate of food she seemed too full to eat—but *really* wanted to.

"I saw how you were with Hayley... I thought you'd be okay with—"

"We'll see." He leaned to the side and raised an eyebrow at the girl. When she looked at him, he switched eyebrows. She smiled. "Maybe we can work with this one."

"I have clingy parents. They'd adore watching her whenever we wanted 'us time.'" Nina sat straighter.

Joey forced a smile. "You sure you want to expose her to the creepy twins?"

Nina chuckled. "They're not creepy, and I can't believe Dad. He's warming up to them, even knowing..."

"Yeah." He winced.

Nina smiled. "I think she adopted *me* at first sight. Only one of the lot who wasn't afraid of me."

"Well you are pretty scary when you're mad, or got your mind set on something, or find a giant, knuckledragging bastard..."

"Oh." Nina set the fork down on her plate. "You watched my logs, didn't you?"

"Twice. With popcorn." He winked. "Extra butter. About that whole revenge thing... Do you feel better?"

She spent a few seconds watching the child attempt to eat just one more forkful while swaying her feet back and forth. Elizaveta still had a hint of wariness, as though someone might come up behind her and take the food away, but seemed... grateful.

Nina let her mind dwell on the memory of tearing Bertrand Foster's telescoping eyes out of his skull.

"Yeah." She exhaled past a smile. "I do. I think I can finally let myself live."

11

SINS OF THE FATHER

BENJAMIN SPERDUTO

MOSCOW, RUSSIA: DECEMBER 4, 2415

"Citizenship is more than a privilege, greater than a responsibility."

Dmitri let the statement sink in for a moment before he continued. He scanned the two hundred and thirty-one faces staring back at him from the auditorium's seating area, watching for any signs of wavering interest.

"It operates on a higher level than the old bonds between the state and its mindless multitudes. In centuries past, citizenship served to constrain liberty, shackling men and women the world over to a great, bloated leviathan that understood no language save tyranny and ruthless exploitation. Without the freedom of contract, that most natural and fundamental of human freedoms, the prosperous and the industrious were compelled by threat of violence to serve and sustain the idle and the indigent."

He waited for a hand to go up, maybe even an indignant voice raised in protest. Occasionally, he got a thinker. Not every time, but often enough to keep his mind limber. Most had the good sense to keep their mouths shut, at least until Dmitri launched into this particular soliloquy.

No thinkers here today, apparently.

He continued: "A monstrous ideology held an iron grip over liberty, like the calcified religious dogmas of ancient times. Theirs was the gospel of theft, a doctrine of illegitimate takings by which the world's great minds and brilliant luminaries surrendered the fruits of their genius to an undeserving and ungrateful world even as it scorned their industriousness and went on demanding 'more, more, more'."

A few smiles. Half-engaged nods.

They were listening, at least.

Did any of them hear?

"Until one day our brave founders resolved to endure these indignities no longer. They would be slaves no more, and in so doing they would forge a model for a new kind of citizenship, a new kind of freedom. And when they stood up as one to declare 'No more!', the despots of the bloated, parasitic state took up arms to compel them with violence. But our founders chose to protect their liberty. In defiance of tyranny, they stood together to form the Allied Corporate Council and ushered in a new birth of freedom with the War of Dissolution."

A full quarter of the class vanished before he finished his last sentence.

Dmitri glanced at the clock on the auditorium's back wall.

1530. Time to go.

Must be running slow today.

"That will be all for now." Another fifty or so students disappeared en masse as he spoke. "Be sure to review the vid file I've highlighted for an overview of the Dissolution. There will be questions on military and public relations strategy throughout the war. I'm sure I don't need to remind you that attendance is mandatory?"

Most of the students had logged out by the time he finished the spiel. The fifteen who remained stared at him with seemingly genuine interest as their avatars continued pantomiming recording the lecture he'd stopped giving several minutes ago.

"Forgot to set the timers, did we?"

Programming a false avatar to attend class was one thing; being careless enough to get caught was quite another. Dmitri waved his hand to bring up a display with a short list of names. He flagged each name, which caused cone-shaped hats labeled "DUNCE" to appear on the remaining students' heads.

One of the students vanished.

Dmitri smiled.

Too late.

He clapped his hands and the auditorium's walls lifted into the sky one by one to reveal a massive, pleasantly manicured courtyard. Lomonosov University's main building stood on the far side of the grounds, its starred peak towering several hundred feet over the rest of the campus. The rest of the university's famous structures occupied positions along the great courtyard's perimeter. Dmitri took in the sight, inspecting each building in turn before looking to the next.

The real thing must have been something to see.

A bell sounded, followed by a flashing circle that appeared in the upper right hand corner of his field of vision. He reached up to tap the circle, causing it to expand and reveal a block of text.

What's taking so long? Katerina's asking for you.

The message was from Inga, his wife. She never messaged him unless it was urgent.

Dmitri flicked his wrist to summon a glowing holo-pad. A few swift keystrokes caused the university grounds to dissolve into blackness. He floated in the dark for several seconds before weight and sensation returned to his body. The chair beneath him made his lower back ache, and the senshelmet's triodes chafed against his temples and forehead. After taking ten deep breaths to let his brain adjust to its surroundings, he removed the senshelmet.

The room he called his study was little more than a closet. He barely had enough space for his SetunTech Trinity deck and senshelmet rig, but it was the only area in the flat where he could have a measure of privacy. After shutting down his equipment, Dmitri unlocked the door and stepped out into the main hallway.

"About time you finished up," Inga said, poking her head through the doorway leading to the living room.

Dmitri shrugged. "I keep waiting for one of them to surprise me. Maybe next semester."

"Well, Katerina's been asking to see you all day."

"I know. I got your message. How is she?"

"Her headache came back this morning. She said it's even worse this time. I gave her something for the pain, but it didn't seem to make any difference."

That made four days out of the last five their daughter couldn't get out of bed long enough to leave the house. Dmitri wondered if her school might start asking questions.

"We really should look into taking her to a doctor, don't you think?" Inga asked.

"Let's give her another day. She's been under a lot of stress this year. Might clear up with a bit more rest."

Inga scowled, but didn't press him on the matter. Not yet, at least. She knew that even a cursory trip to a clinic would cost the family the equivalent of a month's pay. If the doctor prescribed medication, and they always prescribed medication, the cost might well double.

Paying the doctor was the least of Dmitri's worries, however. He was more concerned about the nature of Katerina's recurring headaches.

"I'll look in on her." He turned away from Inga to walk down the hall. Katerina's bedroom door stood slightly ajar, so he pushed it open and stepped inside. Horizontal strips of light filtered in through the metal blinds over the window, just bright enough to illuminate the tiny space. Although Katerina's fourteenth birthday was only a few weeks away, her room still looked like it had been decorated for a ten-year-old. A puppy dog motif adorned the walls and the dresser tops, and the shaggy rug covering the hard ceramic floor featured a husky with brilliant, sky blue eyes. The glowing lights woven into the fabric of those eyes hadn't worked for at least a year or two.

She always wanted a dog when she was little. Dmitri still remembered the way her slender body trembled when he explained that they couldn't possibly afford such an expense, even a cheaper synthetic animal.

"Papa?"

He jumped at the sound. Katerina lay beneath a mound of blankets on her narrow bed, but her voice carried across the room strong and clear. Dmitri sat next to her and placed his hand on her shoulder.

"How are you feeling, Katti?"

The girl shifted, rolling over to look up at him. She rubbed at her eyes clumsily.

"Papa?"

Her voice was labored this time, groggy.

She'd been asleep when he touched her.

"Your mother said your headache's returned."

Katerina nodded. Even that modest effort elicited a pained groan.

Dmitri glanced back at the door. Inga wasn't there. He leaned closer to his daughter.

"What about the dreams?" he asked. "Did they come back too?"

The girl bit her lower lip and nodded.

A dull, buzzing tone sounded from the apartment's main hall.

Someone at the door.

Dmitri wondered if Inga was expecting company. He patted Katerina's hand and stood to leave. "I'll be right back."

Katerina grasped her father's wrist. "Papa, don't..."

A tingling sensation shot up his arm, like he'd plunged it into a bucket of ice water.

The door tone buzzed again.

"I'll get it," Inga said.

Images flashed through Dmitri's mind: citizen managers in riot gear, the caseless round of a submachine gun clicking into the chamber, a woman with eyes like cold iron.

He heard the door open.

Then Inga screamed.

Dmitri wrenched his arm free from Katerina's grasp and rushed out to the hallway where a squad of four citizen managers armed with submachine guns poured in the front door to the living room. The first one to enter caught Inga by the arm and wrestled her to the ground.

"Remain calm, Citizen!" The CMO agent clamped handcuffs around her wrists. "This is a routine sweep."

Two of the citizen managers spotted Dmitri in the hallway and raised their weapons.

"Hands where we can see them, Citizen! Now!"

Dmitri did as they commanded. They closed in on him quickly. One manager kept a gun trained on him while the other forced him against the wall. After binding his hands, they dragged him into the living room and deposited him next to his wife. She looked at him expectantly, but he could do little more than shake his head in response.

The penalties for interfering with representatives from the Citizen Management Office could be quite severe. Although Dmitri's status as a citizen afforded him certain legal rights, refusing to cooperate with a CM sweep was not among them.

The fourth manager inspected each of the hallway's rooms while the others went about securing Dmitri and Inga. He stopped when he peered into Katerina's room and trained his submachine gun on the girl's bed.

"Here, Commander! She's in here!"

A blonde woman wearing a long, black coat glided in the front door. Her face had a certain ageless quality, she could have been anywhere between twenty and fifty. She glanced at Dmitri and Inga as she moved across the living room, her black boots clanking against the ceramic floor. Something about her eyes, cold and gray as weathered iron, made Dmitri shudder.

The woman's coat bore no patches or insignia, but even a fool could tell what she was by her demeanor: an *Otdel Neobyasnimii Yavlenii* agent, responsible for investigating "unexplained phenomena" throughout the ACC.

She strode down the hallway and entered Katerina's room. Nearly a minute went by before she emerged.

"Sedate her and bring her downstairs," she said to the nearest manager, her voice flat and emotionless.

Dmitri's mind raced, trying to muster some legal argument that might prevent them from hauling his daughter out the front door. If the ONY was interested in her, chances were good that she might not return.

"Wait!" he said. "You can't just take her like that! She's a citizen! What crime has she committed?"

The woman stalked into the living room and glared at him. "Your daughter is no longer a citizen. As of this moment, she is the property of the Allied Corporate Council."

"What?" Inga said, her voice wavering. "You don't have the right to—"

"I have all the right in the world, Citizen," the woman said, raising her voice only slightly. "Your daughter poses a potential danger to herself and those around her. Count yourselves fortunate that I'm choosing to over-look your failure to report her recent health irregularities. Your negligence could well have endangered everyone in this building. In light of Citizen Dmitri's outstanding history of service, however, I've recommended only routine surveillance until such time that loyalty can be affirmed."

Two of the citizen managers carried an unconscious Katerina out of her room, her arms and legs bound tightly. She looked so frail in their rough grip, so vulnerable, like she might snap in two at any moment.

Inga burst into tears when she saw her.

The ONY woman went on talking, but Dmitri couldn't hear her. Instead, another voice rang inside his skull, bashing against the back of his eyes like a hammer striking an anvil.

Help, Papa!

Rage and desperation wracked his limbs, forcing him onto his feet.

"No! Put her down, damn you!"

He took one step forward before the ONY agent calmly pressed her hand against his chest. A jolt of electricity surged through his body, causing his muscles to seize up and his jaw to slam shut so hard that he cracked a tooth. He withstood the searing pain for only a split second before he lost consciousness.

Somewhere in the blackness, Katerina's voice called out to him.

PODOLSK, RUSSIA: DECEMBER 13, 2416

The shelter's roof caved in during the night, crushing six people and badly wounding eleven others. What little heat the overworked generators produced escaped out the ruined ceiling, plunging the temperature inside well below freezing. By the time morning finally arrived, seven more people had died of exposure.

Dmitri was no structural engineer, but even he could see that the shelter would be a death trap until the roof was repaired. Several families left after sunrise, gambling that they could find space in another makeshift shelter before nightfall. Those who remained were already clearing away the wreckage and doing their best to patch together a temporary roof. Search parties assembled to go scavenging the surrounding neighborhood for materials while the children pulled rivets and screws from mangled steel beams. All the while, snow drifted down into the shelter and accumulated on every surface, promising to soak everything the next time they fired up the generators.

Inga was still asleep when Dmitri returned to their tiny space, wedged between a cement support column and another family's pile of weathered blankets. Their neighbors had gone to lend a hand with the repair efforts, leaving no one else within earshot.

Dmitri nudged his wife with his tattered boot. "Get up."

She rolled over, groping for the bottle she'd carried to bed last night. Dmitri reached over her and snatched the bottle up before she could find it.

Not that it mattered much. There was nothing left in it.

He tossed the bottle aside.

"Get up," he said, pulling her off the ground.

She swatted at him and muttered something unintelligible, but Dmitri eventually got her to sit up. A whitish film covered her eyes, and her breath smelled like spoiled milk.

"Pull yourself together," he said. "I need you to lend a hand here getting the roof fixed."

"Roof?"

"Yes, the roof. Part of it caved in last night, remember? If one of us doesn't pitch in with the repairs, they're liable to throw us out of here." Dmitri hoisted Inga to her feet.

She wavered, but managed to keep her balance. "You're not staying?"

Dmitri shook his head. "It's Monday, remember? They'll be looking for new workers down at the transit station." He leaned close, whispering into her ear. "If everyone here is working on the roof, I'll have a better chance of getting chosen. A good week's pay might be enough to get us out of this shithole."

Inga nodded, but her expression didn't change. "Right. Whatever."

"Inga, listen to me." He turned her head, forcing her to meet his gaze. "We can do this. We can do it together."

She sighed. "Right."

The look on her face made him sick to his stomach.

HUNDREDS OF MEN AND WOMEN GATHERED AT THE PODOLSK TRANSIT station every day in the hopes of finding paying work. A fleet of armored buses showed up at 0630 hours, followed half an hour later by hovercars carrying labor subcontractors. Aspiring laborers queued up to be assessed, and the lucky ones got to board the buses and be whisked off to sign a twenty-four hour contract to work in the city's factories. The paltry salary terms were non-negotiable, especially since anyone who balked at them had a hundred people in line behind him willing to accept any pay rate, no matter how small, if it meant getting a contract. After their contracts expired, the weary workers would be loaded back into the armored buses and paid as they staggered off back at the transit station.

If they were lucky, they might get home before getting mugged.

No one knew exactly what they would be asked to do until they signed their contracts, but the pace and conditions of the work were uniformly grueling. Workers who fell behind their benchmarks or made too many mistakes had their pay docked, sometimes to the point where they left owing the factory money. Anyone who failed to finish a shift due to injury or sheer fatigue could be arrested for breach of contract.

Mondays, however, were particularly hectic. That was when subcontractors from Moscow came to the transit station hunting for workers. They offered seven-day contracts for menial labor in and around Moscow, usually on construction or renovation projects. While the work sometimes proved just as dangerous as a job in Podolsk and sometimes paid even less, the promise of a solid week's pay was enough to drive desperate laborers to desperate action.

If the subcontractors didn't bring armed security forces with them, the crowd would surely consume itself in a bloody riot. An undercurrent of violence festered throughout the transit station, like a coiled spring ready to erupt with a dreadful, kinetic force. Fights broke out in the lines with alarming regularity, and every few days, a man might slit another's throat to move up in the queue.

Dmitri often thought about the classroom lectures he used to give about how worker demands and regulations crippled the economies of old. He wondered how many of his students accepted that narrative.

Did he believe it himself at the time?

He couldn't remember anymore. Living the last year as a non-citizen left little him time to ponder the true course and nature of the ACC's history.

Of course, he had other, better reasons for not thinking about the past.

"Next!"

Dmitri stepped up to the folding table where a Moscow subcontractor waited with a NetMini in hand. Two security guards armed in heavy riot gear and submachine guns flanked the makeshift workstation. A small camera device on the table whirred into motion to focus on Dmitri's face as he approached. The facial recognition scan would connect his face to his PID in the network database, which would deliver every scrap of information about his identity and personal history to the subcontractor's NetMini.

The Moscow man didn't look up from the holo-screen projection.

"Dmitri Saranov. You were a citizen until last year. Failed to cooperate with a routine Citizen Management investigation. That right?"

"Yes, sir."

"No formal charges or fines. Just a revocation of citizenship status. Sounds to me you got off light."

Dmitri said nothing. The camera's scanners were monitoring his metabolic rate and a multitude of involuntary facial reactions. He didn't want to give it anything more to work with.

"It says here you're fluent in German. Is that still true?"

"Yes, sir." He considered answering in German, but decided it best not to try the man's patience.

The subcontractor nodded and tapped something on the holo-screen. He didn't need to ask anything else; the camera's biometric scanner would tell him whether or not Dmitri had any health problems and update his PID file accordingly.

"It's your lucky day. We have a German firm building a new shopping center near the outer roadway ring. They need workers who can interpret for the ones who don't speak German. Your non-negotiable contract will run for a span of seven days, subject to renewal at the firm's discretion. Do you accept these terms?"

"Yes, sir."

The Moscow man waved another security guard over to the table. "Escort this one to bus seven. Next!"

Dmitri could hardly believe his good fortune. He'd never been selected for a long-term contract. The few times he hadn't been dismissed out of hand, his status as a former citizen eliminated him from consideration.

Trust was a hard thing to come by these days.

The security guard led Dmitri through the electrified fence separating the armored busses from the crowd of aspiring laborers. They walked past the busses bound for the Podolsk factories and toward the newer, less weathered vehicles at the far end of the station. When they reached the bus labeled "Moscow 7", the guard handed Dmitri off to another armed guard.

"Got another one for you," he said.

After a quick nod, the bus guard gestured to the door. "Get in. Seat 13B."

Dmitri dutifully climbed into the bus. Half the seats were already full, with the other workers packed into the rear section. He made his way down the aisle to find his seat. Each row had space for six workers, three on either side of the aisle.

Seat 13A would have been considered a window seat if the bus actually had windows. A young woman, probably no older than thirty, sat there drumming her fingers on her lap. She looked up at him as he slid into the seat beside her. The expression wasn't a friendly one, but Dmitri felt an intense urge to speak all the same.

"Morning," he said, blurting the greeting out before he could stop himself. "Looks like we both got a lucky break today."

She grunted. "You just keep telling yourself that."

"There's a lot of people out there that would kill us for these seats. You ever stop to think about that?"

The woman glared at him. Dirt had worked its way into the lines on her face, and the dark circles around her eyes made it clear that she hadn't slept very well for some time. Dmitri stole a glance at her hands, calloused and scarred. A few of her knuckles looked misshapen, a good indication that she'd broken several fingers in several places during her young life.

"You're a tumbledown, aren't you?" she asked.

Dmitri stiffened.

He didn't feel like talking anymore.

"Yeah," he said. "How'd you—"

"How'd I know?" She scoffed. "You couldn't hide it if you tried. Decent skin, happy to take whatever handouts you get from on high, the way you walk like your feet don't step in the same shit as ours; anybody with a shred of sense could sniff you out."

Dmitri leaned back in his seat and chewed at his lower lip. Deep down, he knew she was right. It had been hard for he and Inga to get a space in that crumbling shelter. No one trusted anybody in Podolsk, but tumbledown citizens were especially suspect. Everyone assumed they were just waiting for a chance to fuck their neighbors over in some scheme to reclaim their citizenship status.

"I'm sorry for bothering you," Dmitri said. "Didn't mean anything by it. I just talk when I'm nervous sometimes."

Another laborer, a big man with a broad chest and a slightly hunched back, plopped into seat 13C. He didn't so much as look at anyone else before lowering his head and closing his eyes.

Dmitri looked down and fidgeted with his hands while more workers filed onto the bus.

"How long?"

He glanced over at the woman in 13A. She didn't look any friendlier, but at least she wasn't scowling.

"About a year," he said. "I think. It was around this time of winter, at least. I remember nearly freezing to death the first week. My wife came down with something. Must have lasted a month. She never quite shook the cough."

"So what's your plan?"

"Plan?"

"You tumbledown types always have a plan. Some way to get back in good with those high-class corporate cunts in the big city, back to your soft beds and your fancy meals."

Dmitri shook his head. "Not me. The way I got sent down, there's no going back."

Her eyes narrowed. "That so, eh? Must have been pretty bad."

"Well, it doesn't take much when you step over the wrong line."

"What happened?"

Dmitri took a deep breath. It had been a long time since he dared to tell anyone about that day.

"My daughter was sick. Headaches, nausea, that sort of thing. We didn't think much of it until the day the ONY came for her. I... interfered."

The mention of the feared secret agency caused her to draw back a bit.

He continued. "When I finally came to, I'd already been scheduled for deportation from the city."

"And your daughter?"

He shook his head. "No idea. We never saw her again."

The woman stared at him, her expression finally softening into something that almost appeared friendly. "I'm... sorry. Nobody deserves to lose someone they love like that."

Dmitri met her gaze for a long while. He had an impression that she spoke from experience.

She held out her hand. "My name's Ninel."

"Dmitri." He shook her hand.

They went on talking while the bus filled up, Ninel telling him about her previous work experience and Dmitri explaining the dire state of his current shelter. When the last laborer sat down, a guard boarded the bus and called for silence. The bus pulled out of the transit station and rolled northward, climbing the on-ramp bound for Moscow. Without any windows to peer through, Dmitri couldn't watch the industrial ruins of Podolsk give way to the sprawling citizen apartments of the Moscow suburbs. The districts along the outer roadway rings were modest, even pitiful, compared to the glimmering environs of the innermost rings where the ACC's leading executives and board members resided, but compared to the dismal conditions of Podolsk, they were practically luxurious.

About an hour later, the bus came to a stop and the guard ordered them to disembark. Dmitri followed the hulking brute in 13C down the aisle, Ninel walking close behind him. They emerged from the bus to set foot in a world wholly unlike the one they'd left. Moscow's brilliant skyscrapers were visible on the northern horizon, their peaks towering far above even the apartment high rises of the city suburbs. To the east, about a hundred yards from the parking area, the shopping center's plastisteel framework rose from the frozen ground like the unearthed skeleton of some antediluvian beast. Hundreds of workers swarmed around, over, and through it while heavy equipment steered newly arrived, prefabricated pieces into position.

A trio of guards escorted them towards a tented area adjacent to the parking lot. Several long tables were set up there, with a line of recently arrived laborers already filing through to sign their contracts. After they finished, they were assigned to work crews and directed over to the job site. The operation was immense, far beyond a scale Dmitri imagined possible.

He took his place in line, shuffling ever closer to the tables beneath the tents.

A hovercar zoomed overhead, circling the work site several times before finally swinging downward. The craft landed about fifty yards from the tents, and three men wearing black suits stepped out. One of them opened the back door to help a silver haired woman in a blue dress exit the car.

Even from a distance, Dmitri recognized her. Masha Tvorinsky, a leading Moscow executive with a stake in nearly every commercial and residential property in the outer ring. She had a reputation for surprise inspections, which made even the most seasoned contractors nervous.

The three bodyguards escorted Tvorinsky away from the car as work foremen all over the job site scurried over to greet her. Several security guards exchanged confused glances, many of them radioing for instructions. For a span of several seconds, they took their attention off the workers.

Dmitri wasn't sure how it started, but he knew something was wrong when a gunshot went off somewhere behind him. Screams and shouting followed as the great mass of workers broke ranks and scattered, some of them diving for cover while others simply ran back towards the buses. Men and women crashed into each other and pushed past their fellows in a desperate attempt to get clear of the chaos. Dmitri was swept up in the panicked surge, elbows, knees, and shoulders buffeting him from all sides. Several more shots rang out before Dmitri noticed a handful of laborers running *towards* Tvorinsky.

He'd lost track of Ninel and the big man from 13C, but he spotted them among the group charging the executive. At least two dozen of them ran full speed and closed in fast as Tvorinsky's bodyguards tried to get her back to the hovercar. A few security guards opened up with their submachine guns, but most were swept away in the tide of panicked workers, unable to bring their weapons to bear. A shower of bullets took down seven or eight runners, but the rest rushed onward.

One of Tvorinsky's bodyguards drew a pistol and fired off a series of deadly accurate shots, each squeeze of the trigger sending a worker to the ground. His fourth bullet caught Ninel in the shoulder and she fell in a heap of flailing limbs.

"Ninel!"

Dmitri pushed free of the crowd and ran to her, never once pausing to question why he was risking his life for a woman he'd just met. Bullets whizzed past in the air, but none managed to find him. Ninel had gotten to her knees by the time he reached her. He grabbed her and pushed her to the ground as another gust of bullets flew by overhead.

"What the hell do you think you're doing?"

She struggled to get free, but Dmitri held her fast.

"Get off me, damn you!" she said. "The bitch is going to get away!"

A bodyguard shoved Tvorinsky into the hovercar while the others provided cover fire. One of the workers, the big man from 13C, managed to slip through the barrage. He barreled past the bodyguards and leaped onto the hovercar's hood before reaching down to touch his boot.

Ninel managed to get in a laugh before a massive explosion vaporized the hovercar.

The shock wave threw the two of them back several yards. Dmitri couldn't tell if he'd lost consciousness for a few seconds or if he'd merely been rendered blind and deaf by the explosion. His chest felt like someone had pounded it with a sledgehammer.

A thick cloud of dust swirled over the entire work site, making it difficult to see more than a few feet in any direction. When it cleared, the security guards would be coming for Ninel. For that matter, they might shoot her and everyone else just to be safe.

They had to get away while they had the chance.

His entire body aching, Dmitri hoisted Ninel off the ground. Her shoulder was bleeding badly now. "Come on. We have to get out of here!"

"B... bridge," Ninel said. "There's a bridge... three blocks... west. Sewer access... resistance safe... safehouse..."

She barely finished the last word before she slipped into shock.

Resistance.

Could she mean the Moscow resistance?

Dmitri didn't have much of a choice now. He couldn't get back to Podolsk without help, and he wasn't likely to get it from the local authorities. Even if no one had seen him run to Ninel's aid, they still had a bus passenger manifest showing him sitting between two known terrorists.

As far as the ACC was concerned, Dmitri might well be "contaminated" by that brief contact.

Cursing, he pulled Ninel alongside him as he trudged over the broken earth.

He wondered if Inga would care if he didn't return to the shelter, or if she would even be there when he got back. Every time he tried to picture her, he could only see that wretched face she'd made when he left her that morning, a look of utter defeat and apathy. He realized now that his wife had died a long time ago; her body just hadn't realized it yet.

For a moment, he wondered if he wouldn't be better off just sitting down and waiting for a guard to put a bullet in his head.

Then he heard a voice, a faint echo still lodged somewhere deep inside his memory.

Help, Papa!

Katerina.

She was still out there somewhere, locked up in an ONY lab like some kind of exotic animal.

If the Moscow resistance had the resources to pull off the attack he'd seen today, maybe they could help him find her.

Renewed purpose gave his muscles new strength, and he lifted Ninel over his shoulder to carry her through the swirling dust.

PODOLSK, RUSSIA: NOVEMBER 27, 2417

Once Ninel set her mind on something, no force on Earth could make her reconsider.

That same determination kept her alive the day they met. By the time they reached the safety of a resistance safehouse, she'd lost so much blood that she could have passed for a ghost. None of her compatriots expected her to survive without proper medical attention, but she not only held on during that night, but the next one and the one after that. Those who knew her best joked that she was probably just too stubborn to die.

At the moment, however, Dmitri would have appreciated some flexibility.

"I don't like it," he said. "The rail yard is way too exposed. We couldn't secure it if we had a hundred men. Even if we could, there's no cover overhead. If the meet gets blown, every military grade drone within ten miles would be on top of us before we have a chance to shit our pants."

The truck swayed as it rolled down the crumbling, uneven roadway. Ninel fought to keep the wheel steady and pushed the accelerator down farther, straining the antiquated electric motors in the wheels.

"We've been over this, Dmitri," she said. "It'll be fine."

Dmitri looked out the passenger seat window. Steel bars covered the glass, making the truck's cab feel like a mobile prison. He thought back to his first ride alongside Ninel, on the armored bus pulling out of the Podolsk transit station. The memory seemed like a lifetime ago.

"We should have brought Pavel and Gregorii. One of them, at least."

Ninel shook her head. "Two people. Those were the terms. They wouldn't agree to the meet otherwise."

"How do we know they'll keep their end of the deal?"

"They've got a reputation to keep. Word gets out they screwed us over, they'll find their list of buyers drying up."

Maybe.

Podolsk was a long way from Singapore.

The rail yard had stood abandoned for more than a century. Rumor had it that a tanker hauling radioactive waste exploded there, contaminating the whole area and forcing the place to shut down. Radiation warning signs surrounded the yard's outer fence, lending credence to the accident claims, but no one knew for certain if the story was true. Podolsk was full of old industrial areas that the ACC falsely designated as hazard zones just to keep squatters from occupying them.

Ninel steered the truck off the highway and through a gap in the rail yard's fencing. Stacks of rusted container cars rose high above the frozen ground, many of them as tall as apartment buildings. If Dmitri squinted, he could almost imagine they were driving down the narrow, crowded streets of some dismal twentieth century metropolis.

Must have been a hell of a time to live.

The truck pulled clear of the stacked cars and veered into an open space in the center of the rail yard where a tangled mass of steel rails crisscrossed the ground, lines leading out in every direction. Three control towers loomed over the area, providing a clear view of anything approaching the central rail hub. Old electric and communications lines sagged from over a dozen teetering poles and bent antennas scattered about the yard. Abandoned, half-collapsed buildings surrounded the area, some no larger than the truck and others big enough to hold a dry-docked Martian freighter.

A truck almost identical to theirs sat parked in the center of the yard. Four people stood next to it, one of them waiving.

"That them?" Dmitri asked.

Ninel nodded as she steered towards the Singaporean merchants. She brought the truck to a halt about fifty feet short of the group.

Dmitri opened the glove box and took out a pistol.

"No," Ninel said. "No guns."

He glared at her. "Are you sure about this?"

"Trust me."

Sighing, Dmitri returned the gun to the compartment and closed the lid. "Okay. Let's go."

They climbed down from the truck and walked over to meet two of the four men halfway between their vehicles. The other two stood with their truck. Dmitri watched them closely, trying to see if they had a hidden weapon, but he was too far away to tell for certain.

"You're late," one of them said, a rail thin man with wire frame sunglasses.

Ninel shrugged. "Traffic."

"You brought what we asked for?"

"Wouldn't be here if we hadn't."

The man nodded. "Bring it out, then."

"Not yet. Not until I know we're getting what we were promised."

He adjusted his sunglasses and looked at the man next to him. When his partner nodded, he shrugged and gestured for them to follow him.

"Come see for yourself."

They followed him around behind the truck. The canvas cover was already pulled back to reveal a hover cart resting on the truck's bed. A large crate marked with Korean lettering sat atop the cart. The man produced a handheld controller from his pocket and tapped in a code to activate the hover cart, which lurched upwards with a hiss and inched out of the truck, finally coming to rest alongside them. Ninel inspected the crate for a moment before stepping back.

"Open it," she said.

The man unlocked the crate's latches and pried the lid open. A grayish metal cone rested inside, nestled amidst a bed of straw packing.

"You're sure it's authentic?" Ninel asked as she inspected the device.

"Recovered from the mud of a lakebed outside Seoul last year. Detonation system malfunctioned en route to the target, but I can assure you the warhead is intact."

"And the yield?"

"One point five megatons. As I said before."

Dmitri stared at the antique warhead, a relic of a forgotten nation's desperate attempt to blast its enemies out of existence. He wondered if it was a bad omen that those enemies had endured to the present day.

"Do we still have a deal?" the man with the sunglasses asked.

Ninel nodded. "We'll need help unloading the truck."

The Singaporeans pulled their truck forward and went about loading up the assorted crates and sacks Ninel and Dmitri had brought with them as payment. Dmitri guided the work, careful to point out the most delicate goods, usually surplus medical supplies and sensitive electronics. The Moscow resistance had been raiding shipments into the city for months to build up enough valuable goods to cut a deal as big as this one.

After unloading the truck, three of the Singaporeans verified and counted the contents of every container while the fourth logged the results in his NetMini. When they finished, Ninel walked over to them and held out her hand.

"Are we good, then?" she asked.

The man with the sunglasses checked the final tabulation before tossing the hover cart controller to her.

"Good," he said.

Ninel handed the controller to Dmitri. "Get it on the truck."

Dmitri got the hover cart into position while the Singaporeans went about loading up their many crates and sacks. The cart's engines gave off only a low hum, but as he directed it into the truck, he noticed a high-pitched whir that hadn't been there before.

"What's that sound?" Ninel asked. "Is that coming from the cart?"

He had the cart in the truck now, but the sound only grew louder. When he cut the engines, it didn't stop.

The whirring noise wasn't coming from the cart.

Dmitri looked up and spotted an oblong object with flashing lights streaking through the sky towards them.

A military hovercar. Probably on routine patrol for any suspicious activity.

Their presence at the rail yard certainly qualified.

"Shit," he said. "We've got company."

Before Ninel could respond, the Singaporeans spotted the car. They shouted at each other in a language Dmitri didn't understand. He didn't need a translator to see they were angry, especially when the man with the sunglasses pulled a gun from his coat.

"Down!"

He grabbed Ninel and pulled her behind the truck before the Singaporean fired. The bullets ricocheted off the truck's metal bumper. Dmitri ran to the passenger side door, pried it open, and went for the gun in the glove box. Ninel pushed past him to climb into the truck as one of the Singaporeans stepped into view.

Dmitri barely bothered to aim, firing off three shots blindly. One of the bullets caught the man in the stomach and he doubled over with a groan.

The truck's engine growled to life.

"Get in, Dmitri!"

The man with the sunglasses peeked out from behind the truck, pistol in hand. Dmitri squeezed off two more rounds to warn him off, then leapt into the cab.

The hovercar was nearly overhead, blaring its presence over a megaphone:

"HALT! THIS IS A RESTRICTED AREA! YOU ARE UNDER ARREST! THROW DOWN YOUR WEAPONS AND PUT YOUR HANDS IN THE AIR!"

One of the Singaporeans opened up on the hovercar with a submachine gun.

Ninel slammed down the accelerator and the truck lurched forward. The buzzsaw roar of a high caliber assault rifle carried over the truck's engine as it pulled away from the yard. Dmitri looked in the rear view mirror; the ground erupted all around the Singaporeans like they stood in the center of a hailstorm. The man in the sunglasses tried to get to their truck's cab, but he only made it a few steps before a shower of bullets tore him in half.

Once all the Singaporeans were down, the hovercar swung around to chase the escaping truck.

"Faster!" Dmitri said. "They're right on us!"

Ninel yanked the wheel to make a sharp left turn, leading them deeper into the rail yard.

"Where are you going? We can't get out this way!"

"We'll never outrun that thing in this bucket," she said. "If we can get to one of the old rail tunnels, we might have a chance."

The truck lurched and bounced as Ninel steered it over old rail lines, walkways, and ditches. Dmitri managed to snap his seatbelt into place as a streak of bullets tore the cab's ceiling apart.

Ninel cried out.

One of the bullets had struck her collarbone, ripping her shoulder from its socket and splitting one of her ribs through her chest.

"No!"

The truck veered rightward, throwing Dmitri back against his door. A railway tunnel ramp swung into view ahead of them, leading down into the ground.

He looked back to Ninel. She didn't seem to notice that half her upper body had been shredded. Her iron face focused only on the road ahead.

She straightened the truck's wheels and mashed the accelerator.

"Ninel," he said, "don't—"

Another storm of bullets rained into the cab an instant before they entered the tunnel, this time catching Ninel squarely. Her body jerked to the left, turning the steering wheel more sharply than the truck could handle. The big wheels lost contact with the ground.

Dmitri closed his eyes and took a deep breath.

The truck rolled at full speed, tumbling over multiple times as it cascaded down the ramp and deeper into the railway tunnel. When it finally landed on the driver's side, momentum carried it another forty yards before it screeched to a halt in a cloud of black smoke.

Dmitri hung from his seatbelt for nearly a minute before he finally accepted that he was still alive. The cab's interior was covered with blood after Ninel's remains had scattered everywhere during the crash.

Poor girl...

He remembered the hovercar. It would be landing outside the tunnel to investigate the wreckage. If they found him there, they would put a bullet in his skull and Ninel would have died for nothing.

"Goodbye, Ninel..."

Dmitri unlatched his belt, pushed his door open, and climbed out of the cab. The tunnel was almost pitch black, filled with dust and smoke. A fire burned somewhere nearby.

If the truck's batteries had ruptured, he wouldn't have much time to escape.

Clambering down from the wreckage, he could make out only the faintest outlines of his surroundings. Something big rested on the ground a few feet from the cab. He reached out to touch it.

The hover cart.

It must have been thrown clear of the truck bed during the crash. He retrieved the cart's remote from his pocket and hit the power button. The cart hummed to life, and reoriented itself. Dmitri climbed onto the cart and found the intact crate still strapped to its bed.

"Not for nothing, Ninel." He directed the cart deeper into the tunnel. Behind him, the truck's batteries ruptured, engulfing the vehicle and filling the tunnel with superheated flames.

By the time the military patrol managed to extinguish the blaze, Dmitri would be long gone.

"I'll make them pay, Ninel." He rested his weary head against the crate. "For you, for Katerina, for Inga, for me, for everyone."

MOSCOW, RUSSIA: DECEMBER 20, 2418

The metro car swayed gently back and forth as it shot through the subterranean passageways beneath the city. When he was younger, Dmitri loved riding the metro for hours on end, stopping to gawk at every station and watching busy citizens shuffling from one stop to the next. If Moscow was a living, breathing creature, the metro was its arteries, sustaining the city with the boundless energy of its hardworking citizenry.

Those faces didn't look energetic to him now. Instead, he saw men and women enslaved to the ceaseless demands of the monstrous society that swelled above them like a cancerous tumor. Although they stood only inches away from their fellow citizens, they might as well have been standing alone in the center of a barren salt flat. Every one of them was dying a bit at a time, some of loneliness, some of anger, some of fear, but none of them realized it.

Not yet.

They were moving so fast that they couldn't see the world flying by in a blur, couldn't look down to notice the scores of miserable wretches bearing the weight of an unjust world upon their shoulders. Some of them, the more introspective and insightful among their number, knew this on an intellectual level, but they lacked the capacity to actually understand what it meant.

Not yet.

Ninel understood. She'd fought her whole life to rip those blinders from their eyes, to turn those delusions to ash in their mouths. Ninel believed in the truth. She'd struggled for it.

And she'd died for it.

Inga understood. She'd seen the world for what it was, beheld its true nature in all its terrible majesty. The sight left a scar upon her soul that she sought to soothe with drink, drugs, and despair. He didn't know how to help her then, so he'd left her behind. Left her to waste away and die in peace, untainted by his endless, misguided promises.

Dmitri hadn't understood it for a long time. Even after he met Ninel, he clung to his old, comforting illusions. He struggled for some way to put it all to right, to upend reality with the same sort of ideals he once sought to instill within impressionable minds. But after he saw Ninel die in that truck cab, he finally understood.

The promise of a better future was a lie, a comforting fable that kept men and women the world over entrenched in abject misery. No amount of reform or persuasion could hope to undo centuries of injustice and set the world on a better path.

A true revolution required something more extreme, something momentous to bring about an entirely new way of thinking.

Katerina would understand, he knew. Poor, innocent Katerina. She saw the world for true that night they dragged her from her bedroom in restraints. After two years in the resistance, Dmitri knew what the ACC's secret police agencies did with their captives. How long did she last under the ONY's tender questioning? Did she cry out for him in her final moments?

Help, Papa!

Someone shook his shoulder.

"Hey, you okay?"

He blinked and glanced at Pavel. "Yeah, I'm fine."

"We're almost there. You ready?"

Dmitri nodded. "Let's move."

Pavel made his way to the front of the metro car, where an access door connected it to the next car in line. Dmitri took position near the emergency exit at the back and glanced at his watch. Somewhere aboard the train, tucked away out of sight of the security cameras, Gregorii had hacked into the metro network. He'd already scrambled the facial recognition algorithms to prevent them from flagging Dmitri and Pavel as security risks, just as he'd done two years ago to help sneak two dozen potential suicide bombers onto a job site to kill a visiting executive.

Dmitri counted off the seconds.

Three...

Two...

One...

Mark.

The train car's lights blinked once and then went dark. Brief power outages were hardly unusual on the metro, but when the lights failed to come back on after a few seconds, the passengers grew restless. Gregorii made an announcement over the intercom that their car was experiencing technical difficulties and asked them to please move to the next car. The passengers dutifully obeyed. When the last one was out, Pavel closed the access door and locked it.

Five minutes later, the train reached the next station. Gregorii tripped the brakes early, leaving the back end of the last car out of sight from the station cameras and the guards standing watch on the metro platform.

Dmitri opened the emergency door and found the sewer access grate located twenty yards inside the tunnel. The resistance had scouted the metro lines for months trying to find such an ideal location. He leapt down from the train and hurried over to lift the grate. A lead-sheathed box the size of a large suitcase lay hidden just underneath it. When he grabbed the case's handle, an array of microrepulsor units hummed to life, allowing Dmitri to lift the heavy thing like it was only a fraction of its actual weight. He dragged it over to the metro car and hauled it inside. Pavel met him there to close the emergency door.

"That's it," Pavel said. "We've got it!"

Gregorii kept the train at the station for about three times as long as a conventional stop, but he couldn't hold it there for much longer without arousing undue suspicion. They didn't dare use any communication devices that might be picked up by the metro station's security scanners. Their actions therefore had to conform to a rigid timetable.

Luckily, Dmitri hauled their deadly cargo aboard with about thirty seconds to spare.

The train pulled out of the station, the last car still draped in darkness and its doors locked tight. Dmitri took a seat alongside the case, which he left sitting in the aisle.

Twenty more minutes and it would all be over.

Or was it beginning?

He had a hard time telling the difference anymore.

"You remember the sequence?" Pavel asked.

"Yeah."

The warhead could have been detonated remotely, of course, but they couldn't take the chance of the signal getting scrambled.

If they wanted to avoid being foiled by a network security program or defense operator, they needed to trigger it manually.

Of course, that also meant none of them would be coming back if their mission succeeded.

Dmitri didn't particularly care if he lived or died. Not anymore. All that mattered was making sure that the people he cared about most hadn't suffered for nothing.

They passed the next three stations without incident. Dmitri peered out the window at each stop. He'd visited all of them at one point or another, and he always spotted some detail that jarred his memory. What really struck him, though, was the sight of so many citizens going about their daily business.

Had he really been just as blind?

After two more stops, they finally reached the inner ring of the

Moscow metro system. Soon, the train would pass beneath the political and cultural heart of the city, Capital Square. There the ACC's board of directors pulled the vast network of puppet strings that kept their self-absorbed executives and citizens dancing, trampling the common workers of the world beneath their steel shod boots.

No more. Not after today.

At the next stop, Dmitri glanced out the window and felt his blood turn to ice.

A young woman stood on the loading platform, one face among a crowd of citizens waiting to board a train. She watched the train pull in from the tunnel, her eyes a light shade of hazel that looked almost golden when the light hit them just right.

Dmitri jumped up from his seat and stared.

"Katti?"

Pavel told him to get away from the window, but Dmitri couldn't hear him. He could do nothing but stare at the young woman who looked so much like his lost daughter.

She was about the right age. Her hair was much shorter than she'd preferred, but the color seemed right.

And the eyes...

How could he mistake those eyes?

Dmitri ran to the door and unlocked it before Pavel could stop him. He passed into the next car and joined the flow of passengers stepping out onto the platform.

Pushing against the crowd, he tried to make his way over to her. Before he was halfway there, however, she turned, her gaze sweeping over his head.

Had she seen him?

If she did, she gave no indication of it.

She stepped forward to board the train Dmitri had just stepped off.

The train carrying a one and a half megaton nuclear warhead.

Frantic, Dmitri spun around and shoved past several commuters to squeeze between the train's doors just before they slid shut. He made his way toward the front of the car as it began to move, scanning every face intently as he went.

He knew he'd seen her. He couldn't have imagined it.

When he advanced to the next car, he spotted some commotion ahead. Pushing past the gawking passengers, Dmitri got about halfway to the next car before he caught a glimpse of a woman dragging a slender man out from what looked to be an equipment closet. She reached behind his ear and yanked hard to pull a cable free from an M3 input jack, which sent him tumbling to the floor in spasms.

Gregorii.

The woman looked up and stared directly at Dmitri. He recognized that ageless face, the gray eyes like cold iron.

She smiled.

Dmitri turned to run, shoving passengers aside to get back to the last car. He had to trigger the device now, before that dread woman could stop them.

Had he actually seen Katerina or had it been a trick of some kind?

Pavel appeared in the doorway before he reached it, his eyes wild. "The lights are back on! Something's wr—"

A gunshot rang out and the back of Pavel's skull exploded as a bullet punched through his forehead. He fell backward onto a seated passenger as several other people screamed.

Dmitri kept running, ducking his head as he pushed by the panicked commuters. Pavel had left the door to the last car hanging open. He bounded over the threshold, slammed the door shut behind him, and threw the lock into place. The case lay where he left it at the back of the car. He ran over to it and pried the lid open. A tangle of wires connected the warhead to a small detonator.

All he had to do was activate it, punch in the access code, and—

Someone knocked at the door.

He looked up to find Katerina's face staring back at him.

Her voice rang out in his head, every bit as clear as the last time he'd heard it.

"Papa, don't!"

Dmitri hesitated. The door's locking mechanism whirred as someone triggered it remotely.

He'd forgotten that Gregorii didn't control the train's security system anymore.

The door swung open to reveal the gray-eyed woman standing at the threshold.

She raised her pistol and fired.

The bullet caught him squarely in the chest, throwing him back against the emergency exit.

His body went numb and his ears throbbed as he struggled to maintain consciousness.

The ONY woman stalked over to him and lifted her wrist to her mouth.

"I need medical assistance to my GPS immediately. Security priority alpha. Repeat: Security priority alpha."

Her voice faded away as a warm darkness seeped into his mind.

MOSCOW, RUSSIA: DECEMBER 4, 2415

What's taking so long? Katerina's asking for you.

The message was from Inga, his wife. She never messaged him unless it was urgent.

Dmitri flicked his wrist to summon a glowing holo-pad. A few swift keystrokes caused the university grounds to dissolve into blackness. He floated in the dark for several seconds before weight and sensation returned to his body. The chair beneath him made his lower back ache, and the senshelmet's triodes chafed against his temples and forehead. After taking ten deep breaths to let his brain adjust to its surroundings, he removed the senshelmet.

The room he called his study was little more than a closet. He barely had enough space for his SetunTech Trinity deck and senshelmet rig, but it was the only area in the flat where he could have a measure of privacy. After shutting down his equipment, Dmitri unlocked the door and stepped out into the main hallway.

"About time you finished up," Inga said, poking her head through the doorway leading to the living room.

Dmitri shrugged. "I keep waiting for one of them to surprise me. Maybe next semester."

"Well, Katerina's been asking to see you all day."

"I know. I got your message. How is she?"

"Better," Inga said. "I think she'll be well enough to go to school tomorrow."

"Good. I'd hate for her to fall behind."

Dmitri made his way down the hall to Katerina's room. Her door was ajar, but he still knocked before entering.

"Katti?"

"Come in, Papa."

He pushed the door open. Her room was much more organized than he remembered. Nothing looked out of place. Even her mother didn't do such a good job of tidying up.

Katerina sat on the edge of her bed, hands on her lap. She'd changed into her school uniform, which seemed a bit odd considering that she'd stayed home sick today.

"Hello, Papa," she said. "How are you today?"

Dmitri raised an eyebrow. "Fine, I suppose. Since when are you so formal?"

She shrugged. "Just practicing for school, I guess. Won't you sit down?"

He pulled the chair out from her desk and sat. "Your mother said you wanted to see me about something?"

"Oh, yes. It's... um... I just wanted to ask you a few things. You know, about your work."

"Uh huh. Well, I'm afraid the history department isn't always the most exciting place in the world, but ask away."

"What do you know about revolutionary movements, Papa?"

The question took him by surprise. Katerina was a smart girl, but she'd never expressed much interest in history.

"Not very much, I'm afraid," he said. "That's not really my field."

She flinched and glanced up at the ceiling, almost as if she'd heard something.

"What is it?" Dmitri asked.

"N... nothing," she said. "You must know something, Papa. Something about revolutions right here in Moscow? My teacher told us that there are revolutionaries hiding under the streets even now!"

The comment made him sit up straight. An image of a truck rolling over passed through his mind, and of a bomb on a train car.

"I... I don't know, Katti. Maybe I can find someone who—"

"No, Papa!" Her hand shot out to grab his leg. "Please. Think really hard. I'm sure you must know something."

"What's gotten into you, girl?" he said, standing up. He felt hot, closed in. "Listen, why don't we talk about this later. It's almost time for dinner."

"Papa, wait! Please don't go!"

He turned and left Katerina's room. The conversation made him feel uncomfortable, as if she'd disturbed something deep inside him. He walked down the hallway to the family room and stopped.

A strange woman with short black hair sat on the couch next to his wife. Her face was young, but hard, marred by several deep scars.

Inga perked up when she saw him. "Oh, there you are, Dmitri. This is Ninel. She says she used to work with you."

Katerina appeared behind him to place her hand on his shoulder.

"Sit down, Papa. Please."

His head throbbed as he eased into a reclining chair in the living room. Inga and Ninel stared at him, their expressions frozen like statues.

Katerina sat in the chair across the table from him.

Someone knocked at the door.

"I don't have much time, Papa."

"Time? What do you mean? I don't understand."

Tears formed in the corners of her eyes. "Please, Papa. Just tell me what you know. It... it'll be easier that way. I know this is hard for you, but you have to understand how important this is to me."

The knocking sounded again, louder this time.

"Katti, I want to help you. More than anything I want to help you, but I don't know—"

"Yes, you do, Papa!" She was nearly shouting now. "You do know. You've... you've done bad things, Papa. I know you were just doing what you thought was right, but... but..."

The knocking at the door grew thunderous, shaking the entire apartment. When he looked back to his daughter, she was different. Older, harder.

"They want names, Papa. Names, places. Everything. Please... they'll... they'll hurt me if I don't get them."

A voice boomed out from behind the door, but it felt as if it seeped through every wall in the apartment.

"Time is running out, Subject 372."

Dmitri glanced over at the couch. Inga had slouched backward, her face twisted and pathetic. She clutched a bottle of clear liquid close to her chest. Ninel... Ninel was unrecognizable, her upper body a twisted mass of ruined flesh and splintered bone.

"Papa!"

Katerina towered over him, her eyes roiling like liquid fire.

The voice cried out again, this time shattering every piece of glass in the apartment. "This is your last chance, Subject 372!"

Dmitri closed his eyes and screamed.

And then the room fell silent.

Something soft touched his face. He opened his eyes to find himself sitting in his daughter's room again. Katerina was young and innocent once more, the way he always remembered her. She pulled his face close to hers. Her cheeks were slick with tears.

"Please, Papa. You couldn't save me before, but you can help me now. I know you would do anything you can to help me, wouldn't you?"

"Yes," he said. "Yes, I would."

He opened his mind to her and she drew out everything he knew. She found the names of every key member of the Moscow resistance, every secret safehouse in the city, every meeting and recruiting place, every security agent on the take, every sympathetic worker association, every contact beyond the city and the country. He offered all of it up, and she took every last scrap.

When she finished, she pulled back from him and smiled. She was older again, the way she'd looked at the metro station.

"Thank you," she said, sobbing. She stood to leave, but Dmitri grabbed her wrist.

"Please, Katti. Don't go. Not yet."

"I'm sorry, Papa. You know I can't stay."

Katerina's gaze went to her bedroom door. Dmitri turned to find the gray-eyed woman standing there.

"Excellent work, Katerina. You've proved your loyalty to this agency beyond all doubt. Time to go now."

Katerina kissed him on his forehead.

"Goodbye, Papa."

"Goodbye, Katti. I love you."

He blinked, and she was gone.

Dmitri sat in the room for a long time before finally standing and staggering down the hall to the living room. Inga and Ninel were there, both of them looking the way they had when they meant so much to him. They smiled when he sat in the chair.

The sun shone through the window, filling the room with golden light.

He couldn't remember the sun ever shining so brightly in Moscow.

The door opened behind him, followed by the faint click of a safety switch being released.

"I'm ready," he said.

A burst of light flooded the room, so brilliant it washed everything else away.

The light burned out in an instant, leaving nothing behind.

BENJAMIN SPERDUTO

Benjamin Sperduto is a history teacher and has also worked as a freelance editor and writer for roleplaying games. His first two novels, *The Walls of Dalgorod* (2015) and *Mirona's Law* (2017), are available from Curiosity Quills Press. Several of his short stories have appeared in various fantasy, horror, and sci-fi anthologies, including *Under a Brass Moon* (Curiosity Quills Press, 2016), *Dark Horizons* (Elder Signs Press, 2016), and *Darkscapes* (Curiosity Quills Press, 2017). Benjamin also records electronic music under the name Morana's Breath and hosts a roleplaying game podcast entitled *12/12 Project*.

A graduate of the University of South Florida, he lives and works in Tampa, Florida, where due to his casual relationship with a razor and comb, he is sometimes mistaken for a person of interest. For a full list of publications and fiction updates, visit www.benjaminsperduto.com or follow him on Twitter (@bensperduto).

ACKNOWLEDGMENTS

Thank you for reading the Divergent Fates Anthology!

This collection of stories would not have been possible without the kindness of the authors involved in its creation. You all have my deepest thanks for embracing my fictional world and lending it your unique touch.

Cover by Alexandria Thompson

Additional thanks go to Mark W. Woodring for his assistance in editing.

Please take a moment to post a review, even if it's short. Reviews are an immense help to small press and independent authors, and we rely on our readers for spreading the word.

www.ingramcontent.com/pod-product-compliance
Lightning Source LLC
Chambersburg PA
CBHW030555180626
46816CB00005B/1559